THE
FAERIE
PRINCE

Also by Rachel Morgan

THE CREEPY HOLLOW SERIES

The Faerie Guardian

The Faerie Prince

The Faerie War

A Faerie's Secret

A Faerie's Revenge

A Faerie's Curse

CREEPY HOLLOW COMPANION STORIES

Scarlett

Raven

THE
FAERIE
PRINCE

CREEPY HOLLOW, BOOK TWO

RACHEL MORGAN

Second Edition

First Edition published in 2013
Second Edition published in 2015

Copyright © 2013, 2015 Rachel Morgan

ISBN 978-0-9946679-1-5

For Kyle.
You are my sunshine.

PART I

CHAPTER ONE

EVERY NIGHT I WATCH THE SAME WINDOW ON DRAVEN Avenue. I keep my distance, and I never watch from the same place or at exactly the same time. Creepy, I know, but I have my reasons. I watch that window because I want to be the first one to know if he comes home. I want to see what kind of person he's become since he broke my heart. I want to sense for myself the power he has, and I want to see him use it. And, yes, I want to see *him*.

Nate.

Mr. Draven Avenue.

It's not as though I want him back. I mean, the guy handed me over to a prince of the Unseelie Court—I'm not exactly hoping for a happily ever after here. To be honest, I'm not quite sure what I'm hoping for. Maybe I want to look into his eyes and ask him why he did it. Or maybe I just want to kick his ass.

I lean back on the porch swing, relaxing into the swaying motion. The people who live in this house have gone to bed, so there's no one awake to wonder why a swing might move on its own. Across the road and to the right I can see Nate's window. Always in darkness.

A twig snaps somewhere to my left, and I bring the swing to a quick standstill, my heart thumping a little faster than normal. It's nothing more sinister than a cat, though, inching carefully across the grass in its attempt to stalk something. I want to laugh at myself for being so paranoid, but I know I have a good reason for being on edge: Zell might still be after me.

I raise my hand and cover a yawn. I had an assignment earlier this evening, and tomorrow's a normal day of training at the Guild, so I should probably put my obsessiveness aside for the night and get home to bed. I reach for my stylus—and freeze.

I see a light. In Nate's room. Hovering, dancing, fading in and out. In a second I'm on my feet—but the light is gone. I bite my lip. What should I do? I haven't been inside his room since the night he betrayed me. It would be a stupid move given the strong possibility that Zell is magically monitoring Nate's home in case I show up there. On the other hand, Flint did put protective spells around the house, so shouldn't I be safe inside it? But I don't know what kind of spells he used, and who or what they were meant to keep out.

The light flickers again before vanishing once more. I slide my stylus out of my boot and open a doorway to the faerie paths. Home, or Nate's bedroom? I roll my eyes as I step into the darkness. Right, like there was ever a chance I'd just ignore that light.

My stomach does strange things when I step out of the doorway on Nate's wall and into his moonlit bedroom. I remember being here with him so clearly. The large bed, the couches around the television, schoolwork piled on his desk— everything looks the same. That ache in my chest that I thought had disappeared is back again. As much as I want to kick Nate's ass, a part of me just wants to feel his embrace and hear his easy laughter.

Pathetic, I know.

As I pad across Nate's carpeted floor, my eyes peeled for the dancing light, I get a crazy sense of déjà vu. This is kind of like the night I met him. I was waiting here in the semi-darkness for the reptiscilla while a boy I didn't know slept at his desk, oblivious to the fact that his whole world was about to change.

I pull one of his cupboards open, but there's no light hiding in there. A backpack slides forward and I push it back inside, pausing to look at the initials sewn onto the fabric. N. A. C. Nathaniel ... something, something. It strikes me then just how little I know about Nate. I don't even know his last name.

Plink.

My head swings toward the sound at the window, my hands up and in position to use my bow and arrow. It's the hazy ball of light again, hovering just outside the window, bumping the glass before flitting away.

Plink, plink.

I stride over and pull the window up. The light bounces amongst the roses in the garden below. I step up onto the windowsill and jump down, bending my knees to absorb the impact as my feet hit the grass. I straighten—and hear movement behind me. Without hesitation I draw my leg up and kick backward. My foot connects with something soft.

"Oof!"

I spin around to see who it is, but something hits my ankle and trips me up. I roll as I hit the ground, trying to get away from whoever ambushed me. I jump to my feet, then duck as a swarm of bees zoom toward my face. I divert them with a gust of wind and send flames licking across the grass toward my attacker. He's a faerie: shorter than average; green and blonde hair; well dressed. He jumps over the flames and crashes into me. I stagger back against a bush as he wraps his hands around my neck. I jerk my knee up and hit him where I know it'll hurt most. As he doubles over in pain, clutching his groin, I spin him around and hold one of my glittering guardian knives against his neck.

"Who are you and what do you want?" I demand.

"You're practically a fully trained guardian and you fell for the will-o'-the-wisp trick?" Despite the pain he's clearly in, he manages to laugh. "Disappointing."

"In case you haven't noticed, you're the one with a knife to your neck," I say. "That's the only thing you should be *disappointed* about right now."

6

He grabs my arms at his neck, but a flame forms along the blade of my knife, searing his skin. He gasps in pain.

"Tell me," I say through gritted teeth. "Are you working for Zell? Did he send you here to get me?"

"He wants you," the faerie says. "I've been waiting here every night for you, Violet."

"Well, you're not very observant," I tell him, "because I've been here every night too. Tell Zell to send someone with actual skills next time if he really wants me." And with that I kick the faerie away from me, adding enough magical force to send him sprawling into the bushes at the other end of the garden. I hurriedly scribble a doorway into the grass at my feet. Green sparks flash toward me, but I drop down into the black hole of the faerie paths just in time to avoid them.

The darkness is complete. It's as if I'm standing on nothing, seeing nothing, hearing nothing. I relax and imagine my home. After a moment, the darkness peels away and a doorway of light forms in front of me. I step into my kitchen to find Filigree—in his new favorite form, a miniature pig—standing on the table pushing nixles around with his snout. He appears to be organizing the tiny roasted bugs into piles according to color. I guess he didn't like it when I bought the 'assorted' bag last time I went shopping.

After patting Filigree's pink head, I walk upstairs. I change out of my assignment clothes, but keep my trainee pendant around my neck. After my narrow escape from Zell's dungeon, I did some research into the protective charms embedded in these pendants. Turns out one of the charms protects against the magical summoning of whoever wears the pendant. I never take it off anymore.

I sit on the edge of my bed and absently comb my hand through the purple and dark chocolate-colored tangles of my hair. Before I can go to sleep there's one last thing I have to do. I close my eyes and extend my mind. My thoughts spread out like fingers, brushing past thousands of other minds in my search for just one. I should be able to find him easily, even without holding an object that belonged to him.

But there's nothing. Just like I couldn't sense Calla when she was trapped in Zell's magically secured dungeon, I can't sense Nate anymore.

He doesn't want to be found.

* * *

I wake the next morning with a feeling of unease curling in my stomach. I roll onto my back and stare at the enchanted skylight, watching yellow sunbeams filter through the topmost branches of the tree that conceals my home. It's Friday. Just a regular Friday. Nothing important scheduled. So why do I feel like I'm forgetting something? Why do I feel like ...

I sit up in a sudden panic as it hits me.

Oh, crap.

CHAPTER TWO

Somewhere in between breaking the Guild's most important rule and having my heart crushed by my first and only boyfriend, I became just like every other guardian trainee: I forgot to do my homework.

First. Time. Ever.

I've always been that annoying person who finishes a written assignment at least two days before the due date. Until this morning, that is, when my brain decided to remind me that we were given a project during my one week suspension. The due date?

Today.

Two and a half hours from now, to be exact.

I hurry back to my table in the Guild's library with another pile of books in my arms. Catching my foot on the chair leg, I send the books sliding across the table. "Oh, *come on!*" I kick the chair back, plop myself down, and grab the nearest book.

"Stop freaking out, Vi," Honey says from across the table. "This is completely normal for just about everyone else in our class. Did you see Aria and Jasmine over there?" I nod without removing my eyes from the page in front of me. "And do they look stressed out?"

I glance up. Aria is reading a message on her amber, her chair tilted so far back she must be using magic to keep from crashing to the floor, and Jasmine is staring into space. I return my gaze to the textbook. "Somehow, I don't exactly find that comforting, Honey."

"Okay, bad example," she says, pulling her own amber out of her pocket. She giggles at whatever message is waiting for her—probably from her boyfriend—and reaches for her stylus to reply.

I scan the page in front of me, seeing nothing. What am I looking for again? Oh, right, using kelpie hair as an ingredient in—

"Attention, fifth years." I look up and see Amon, the head librarian, poking his head out of his office. "I've just received a message from one of your mentors." He takes a scrap of paper from the sprite sitting on his shoulder and looks at it. "You are to assemble in lesson room four after you've handed in your written projects. Someone will be talking to you about your final assignments."

Honey wiggles her eyebrows at me and grins. "Ooh, our final assignments. Exciting! Everyone's been talking about who they're going to be paired with and where they'll be sent."

"Yeah, I'm sure they have." And I've been trying not to think about how a disastrous pairing could ruin my already slim chance of graduating at the top of my class.

"Oh, Tina wants to talk to me," Honey says, examining her amber once more. "I'll see you downstairs." She grabs her bag from under the table and heads out to wherever her mentor is.

I raise my eyes to the enchanted sundial on the wall over the library door. Two hours left.

I skim through pages and scribble down important facts in what I hope are coherent sentences. Hushed voices and the occasional ripple of laughter fade into the background of my thoughts. Right now it's just me and the mundane facts of kelpies and their hair. Maybe it's a good thing I didn't do this project when I was calm—I probably would have fallen asleep. I reach the required length of the report, sit back, and read through the whole thing, making use of the *vanish and replace* spell far more than I usually have to.

Half an hour left.

With a glance toward Amon's office—he doesn't approve of magic in the library—I sweep my hand across the table and watch the scattered books pile themselves neatly on top of one another. I push my chair back and head for the row where I found them.

It takes several minutes, but eventually I'm kneeling on the floor pushing the last book back into its place on the lowest shelf. I'm about to stand when a snort of laughter disturbs the quiet. I tilt *A Collection of Magical Water Creatures* forward and peek through a gap between two books on the other side of the shelf. Dale and Rush, two fellow fifth years, are sitting on the floor reading a piece of paper that, for some reason, has the ability to send them into hysterics. Or it could be a blank page coupled with the effects of some kind of giggling potion. Dale is enough of an idiot to sample just about anything in a bottle, and Rush isn't far behind him.

A book slides into the gap and blocks my view. "What's going on? You guys been sampling Aria's happy cookies again?"

And that would be Ryn. My ex-friend, ex-enemy, current 'sort of friend.' Although, that last part hasn't exactly been working out so well. A few days after we narrowly escaped Zell's dungeon, Ryn brought his little sister Calla over so she could give me a thank-you-for-saving-me-from-the-bad-faerie letter she'd written herself. That was followed by some awkward conversation—probably due to the fact that Ryn was trying to be nice, a skill he has yet to master—after which they left. Two weeks later and, other than the glare I received when I tried to speak to him during training, we've had no further contact.

I'm still trying to figure out whether I should be disappointed or relieved.

"The third years have been copying us," Rush says. There's a rustle of paper. "See? Guys have started writing hot lists and passing them around. And look who's at the top of this one."

"Does that say Tora?" Ryn asks.

"Yes!" Dale says with a hoot.

Tora? My mentor? I swallow, feeling more than a little grossed out.

"So what?" Ryn says. "She's kind of hot."

"But she's a *mentor*," Dale says. "She's probably, like, four

12

hundred years old. It's creepy."

Creepy, yes. Four hundred years old? Not even close.

I'm about to head back to my desk when Rush says, "Well, my hot list is in definite need of an update. Did you see Violet last time she was in the Fish Bowl? Man, she has definitely moved into slot number one on my list."

Eww! Okay, I am now officially grossed out.

"Of course I saw her," Dale says, all trace of laughter now gone from his voice. He was the one inside the Fish Bowl with me—and I greatly enjoyed kicking his butt.

Rush laughs. "Oh, yeah, I remember. I guess you can't see past your bruised ego to her super hotness, can you?"

As much as their conversation disgusts me, I have to admit there's a teeny, tiny part of me that's flattered to be included on someone's hot list. If only it wasn't Rush. I lean back against the shelf, wondering if Nate thinks I'm super hot—or if he thinks of me at all.

"What about you, Ryn?" Rush asks.

I feel the shelf move slightly against my back as Ryn says, "You know I don't give a goblin's fuzzy ass about your hot lists."

"Yeah, didn't you know, Rush?" Dale says. "No one here is *good enough* for Ryn."

"Exactly," Ryn says. "Why settle for a giggling girl when you can have a real woman?"

"Ha! A real woman?" Rush says. "Is that what you call the crazy Underground beings you hang out with at Poisyn?"

Okay, now I definitely don't need to hear any more. I push myself up.

"I thought I should remind you two that you haven't handed your assignments in yet," Ryn says to his friends.

Crap, I haven't handed mine in either. I give Dale and Rush a few seconds to get up and out of their row before I hurry forward—and come face to face with Ryn.

"Eavesdropping again, Pixie Sticks?" he asks.

I fold my arms over my chest. "I believe I have a right to eavesdrop on conversations that include me."

A sly smile creeps across his face. "And did you like what you heard?"

I hesitate a moment before saying, "No comment."

He laughs, shakes his head, and turns to leave.

"Wait," I say before I can stop myself.

He glances over his shoulder before saying, "Yeah?" It infuriates me how unconcerned he looks.

"I really don't get you, Ryn."

His eyebrows pull together. "What are you talking about?"

"Uh, remember that time you sat on my bed and asked me if I wanted to try being friends again? It's only been two weeks since then, and you've already forgotten."

"What do you mean? I came over with Calla last week. You're not expecting me to visit every day, are you?"

"Of course not, that would be creepy. But I didn't expect to receive a death stare from you during training either."

"You were distracting me."

"From what? You were tying your shoelace!"

"A very important task when one is about to enter the Fish Bowl."

I clench my hands into fists and remind myself that

throwing a book at him probably wouldn't be the most constructive move.

He sighs. "Look, I just figured it would be easier this way."

"You figured *what* would be easier?"

He shrugs. "You know, not talking while we're at the Guild. Everyone knows that you and I don't get along, so if we suddenly started being chummy, there'd be all these questions to answer, and it would get really boring and tedious, and we'd waste valuable training time."

"So that's how it is?" I shake my head and walk past him. "Let me know when you want to do this friends thing properly." I roll up my spare reed paper, stick it into the side of my training bag, and head out of the library.

Ten minutes left.

"You know the sundial is slow, right?" Ryn shouts after me.

Crapping crap. I hurry down the stairs two at a time to the second floor, then jog along the corridor until I reach the five tree stumps outside the mentors' lounge. The stump on the right with *Fifth Years* engraved into the bark is the only one with an open circle at the top. I dump my bag on the floor, pull out my rolled up report, and slide it in. Three seconds later, twigs emerge at the edges of the circle, growing and twisting around each other until the top of the stump is sealed.

Whew, just in time.

I run down the stairs, across the foyer—glancing briefly upward to check that the protective enchantments are still the right color—and toward the lesson rooms. I peek into the fourth one, relaxing when I see there are no mentors present yet. I slip into a chair beside Honey.

"Guess what?" she says, leaning toward me. "I think you and I might have been put together for the final."

"What?" I scoop some loose hair behind my ear. "How do you know?"

"Well, Tina didn't actually say your name, but she said I'd been given the best possible partner, which is obviously you."

I can't help smiling at the compliment. "It could be Ryn. He's also pretty good."

"No way." Honey makes a face. "Tina wouldn't have been nearly as enthusiastic. She dislikes Ryn as much as I do."

"Oh. Well, that's great then!" I start to feel a little less anxious about this final assignment. If I had to choose someone, it would probably be Honey. She's the closest thing I have to a friend and easy to work with.

I notice movement by the door and look up, but it's only Ryn. Dale waves him over. "Dude, since it's Friday," he says loudly enough for everyone to hear, "I was thinking I could come over and we could try that new—"

"Nope, sorry. I have plans tonight." Ryn drops into the empty chair in front of Dale.

"What plans?" Dale demands, as though it's inconceivable his friend might have made a plan that doesn't involve him.

"Do we really need to know?" Honey whispers beside me.

"Just plans," Ryn says before I can answer her.

Dale leans forward in his desk. "Is this about a girl?"

After a pause, Ryn says, "Yes."

"Dude!" Dale punches Ryn's shoulder. "And you didn't say anything? Who is it?"

"You don't know her."

16

"Come on, man," Rush says. "Spill the details."

"No."

"Fine," Dale says. "All the more reason I should come over tonight. I have to meet this mysterious—"

"Don't even think about it, Dale."

"Hey, can you guys shut it?" Aria says from across the room. "We don't all need to know about Ryn's love life."

"You got that right," Honey mutters.

"Good morning, trainees."

"Oh, thank goodness," I whisper as Bran walks in, officially putting an end to any discussions. Of all our mentors, Bran has probably taught us the most, so it's fitting that he's the one to talk to us about our final assignment. "Everyone here?" he asks, sitting on the edge of a desk.

"Yes, all sixteen of us," someone says in the front row.

"Okay." He rubs his hands together. "I'm sure your various mentors have spoken to you already about your final assignments—" he glances at Ryn and Asami, the two trainees he's mentored for the past five years "—but I still need to make sure we're all on the same page. So. As you know, throughout your five years as a trainee your assignments progressed from grouped to paired to solo. It might seem strange, then, that you do your final assignment with a partner and not on your own." Several trainees nod their heads. "The reason behind the paired final assignment is that it mimics the assignments of real guardians. So far you've been taking care of fairly simple incidents—an ogre trying to eat a child, a will-o'-the-wisp leading a hiker to his death—"

"He considers that simple?" Honey whispers.

"—but fully trained guardians get involved in far more complex and dangerous situations. Situations that take a lot longer than a few minutes to resolve. These kinds of assignments require that guardians work in teams, which is why we give you a partner for your final assignment. Any questions so far?" When there's no answer, Bran gets up and begins walking between the desks. "Okay, so here's how it works. This afternoon you will report to your mentor who will give you the details of your assignment and the name of your randomly selected partner. You and your partner will have the weekend to prepare, and you will then leave from the Guild on Monday morning. You have until Friday to complete the assignment."

Jasmine sticks her hand up. "Are we allowed to come home at night?"

Bran shakes his head. "As those of you with guardian parents will know, you are not allowed to return home until an assignment is complete."

"But why?" Jasmine asks. "It only takes a few seconds through the faerie paths to get home, so what's the big deal?"

"The big deal, Jasmine," Bran says patiently, "is that you have no idea how the situation might change in your absence. You always need to be aware of what's going on."

"Are you saying I have to stay awake for the entire assignment?"

"No, that's—" Bran cuts himself off with a sigh. "Why don't you talk to your mentor about this later, okay?" Jasmine nods, and Bran continues with his instructions. "The first thing you do upon your return is report to your mentors and give them your tracker bands so they can see how you did. You'll also have to submit a written report a few days later."

"Does the report count toward our rankings?" Aria asks.

"Yes. Everything counts, you know that, Aria. And, speaking of rankings, they remain a secret until graduation, which is in four weeks' time."

"And the prize for top graduate is still the same?" Ryn asks.

"Yes. A monetary gift from the Guild, your name in the Hall of Honor, and a visit to the Seelie Court. Any more questions?" Bran looks around at the shaking heads. "Great. After lunch you report to your mentors."

CHAPTER THREE

THE GUILD'S HALL OF HONOR IS A VAST ROOM FILLED with pillars. On each side of every pillar is a plaque where the name of the top guardian graduate is written each year. It isn't a room I visit very often, but every now and then I stop by to remind myself why I keep working so hard to be the top graduate in my class. And right now, before receiving my final assignment, seems like a good time.

I walk slowly between the pillars as I head for the plaque with my mother's name. My boots cause a faint echo each time they connect with the centuries-old wooden floor. Shadows flicker from the flames that burn perpetually in the torches attached to the walls. I thought it was a little eerie the first time I came in here, but now it evokes a sense of comfortable familiarity.

I stop when I reach my mother's plaque. There are ten names from ten different years. Hers is third from the top. Rose Hawthorne. Gold letters on dark wood.

"I've finally reached the last hurdle," I whisper, imagining that somehow she can hear me. "And I'm going to do it, Mom. I'm going to win the top prize." I reach up and run my finger across her name, feeling the raised letters. Then I drop back down onto my heels and head out of the hall.

Time to get on with the final hurdle.

I climb the stairs that lead to Tora's corridor. The last time I saw her, it was for a counseling session—the goblin in the park—and she mentioned she'd been asked to visit another Guild for a few days. Well, a few days turned into a few more, and a few more, and I ended up having all my assignments during the past two weeks organized by Honey's mentor, Tina. It's probably the longest I've gone without seeing Tora since the day I met her.

So when I knock on her office door and there's no response, I feel a definite sinking in the region of my heart. Where is she? She's the closest thing I have to family and I miss her! I push her door open and find the office in darkness, which is even more disturbing. Wasn't she supposed to come back last night?

I leave the door open to let some light in and sit down in one of the chairs. She must be here somewhere, otherwise I would have been told to see a different mentor. I lean back and twirl a strand of hair around my finger. My mind wanders back to the conversation in the lesson room before Bran arrived. I wonder who Ryn's seeing tonight and why he won't tell his friends about it. What doesn't he want them to know?

After several minutes of pondering the possibilities of Ryn's love life, I hear hurried footsteps in the corridor. A second later Tora strides into her office, a stack of papers clutched in her hands. "I'm so sorry I'm late, Vi." She dumps the papers on her desk. "I was called to an unexpected meeting, and—" She glances up at the ceiling. "Oh, the glow-bug. He squirmed out of here and all the way to the end of the corridor while I was away. Lonely, I think. I'm sure I asked someone to—Oh, thank you." She steps aside as two dwarves march in, one with a fat, yellow glow-bug in his hands. They climb onto Tora's desk, one gets onto the other's shoulders, and they secure the glow-bug to the ceiling. They climb down and leave without a word to either of us.

"And now they tell me I have to *talk* to the bug occasionally or he'll leave in search of a different room," Tora continues as the glow-bug slowly warms up to its shining state. "Honestly. I'm sure glow-bugs weren't always this sensitive." She sits down with a heavy sigh. "So, do you want the bad news or the really bad news?"

"Wow. Good afternoon. It's nice to see you too, Tora. It's only been, what? Two and a half weeks?"

A pink tinge colors Tora's cheeks. "Oh, I'm so sorry." She jumps up and walks around to my side of the desk. "I've been so busy since I got back last night that it feels like I never left." She leans down and puts her arms around me. I hug her back, tighter than normal, realizing suddenly that this is what I've wanted since the moment I woke up in Ryn's house and the reality of Nate's betrayal hit me. "Hey, are you okay?" she asks, pulling back. "Did everything go all right with Tina while I was in London?"

"Yeah, yeah, everything's cool." There's no point in telling her about Nate now that's it's all over. It would only hurt our relationship if she knew I'd disobeyed her instructions to give Nate the memory-loss potion. I picture the tiny vial labeled *Forget* sitting in my emergency kit and feel guilt stirring within me. I push the thought from my mind and pull my knees up to my chest. "So, what were you doing over there anyway?"

"Oh, you know." She waves a dismissive hand as she sits down again. "Boring Guild stuff. Anyway, let's get back to what's important." She places her hands on the desk and looks at me. "Your final assignment."

"Is this where the bad news and the really bad news come in?"

"Unfortunately, yes." She pauses, drumming her fingernails on the desk. "So ... first let's talk about where you'll be going. I know it's become somewhat of a tradition for fifth year students to be sent to exotic locations for their final assignments."

I nod. "Yeah, some trainees get very excited about it. Some of them have even been placing bets on where they'll be sent."

"Right," Tora says slowly. "Well, I'm afraid your assignment is a little more local."

"Local?"

"And in the human realm. No exotic fae folk for you."

"Oh. Well, humans can be interesting." I think of Nate, then remind myself, yet again, that he isn't actually human.

"Yes, but these are boring, old rich humans."

"Are they at least involved in some exciting illegal activity?"

Tora laughs. "I doubt you'll think it's exciting." She lifts the topmost page from the pile on her desk and examines it. "His name is Edgar Hart and he lives with his wife on some fancy estate—the details are here for when you need to direct the faerie paths. His children are grown up and no longer live there. He and his wife do a lot of entertaining, and it seems their guests are not all of the human variety. The reason we know this is because the daughter of one of the Seelie Queen's advisors ended up there a few days ago. She told her mother she saw a faerie from the Unseelie Court having a threatening conversation with Mr. Hart. He also gave Mr. Hart something, but she was unable to see what it was. Your assignment is to discover what object was given to him, retrieve it, and find out what he was told."

I stare at Tora. "That's it?"

"Yes."

"That sounds too straightforward. Are you sure that's all there is to it?"

"Look, Vi." Tora leans forward and rests her elbows on the desk. "Our Seers and guardians had nothing to do with this assignment. It came directly from the Seelie Court, which means the Queen has a special interest in it. That makes it very important, even if it is simple. So the Council didn't want to give it to just any pair of trainees. They wanted the best."

"So ... you're saying I should be flattered?"

"Yes."

"Okay," I say with a long sigh. "Boring, old rich people. I

can do that. Oh, and are we supposed to complete the assignment without ever revealing ourselves?" I pay particular attention to that rule now. Wouldn't want to wind up suspended again.

"If you can, yes. But that rule only applies if you're revealing yourself as a magical being. If you need to pretend that you're human in order to gain information, then you may do so."

"I see." I frown. "I don't remember being told that before."

"Well, we tend not to tell trainees about that little loophole in the rule. They might take advantage of it, and it's not as though any of the training assignments ever require a human façade."

"I guess. Okay, so if that was the bad news, then what's the *really* bad news?"

"Ugh." Tora flops back in her chair and looks up at the ceiling. "Your partner."

"My partner?" I know Honey's not the best trainee in our class, but I could certainly do worse. "What's wrong with my partner?"

She looks at me, guilt written all over her face. "It's Oryn."

I open my mouth—and then can't figure out what I was going to say. That was definitely the last name I expected to hear. I've become so used to never having Ryn as either a partner or an opponent that I just assumed we'd never have to work together on anything. I clear my throat in an attempt to find my voice. "But ... I thought Honey was supposed to be my partner."

Surprise crosses Tora's face. "How did you know that?"

"Oh, well, Honey said Tina gave her a hint."

Tora sighs and shakes her head. "Am I the only one who sticks to the rules around here?"

"It's possible, but I'm pretty sure Councilor Starkweather is ahead of you in that department."

"No, she's the one who called the impromptu meeting I was just at!" Tora says. "She reshuffled some of the pairings, even though they're all meant to be random. Apparently it was brought to her attention that you and Ryn have never been paired before, and she thought now would be a good time to see how well you work together."

I bite my lip as I slide a little lower in my chair. I'm guessing it would never have been 'brought to her attention' if I hadn't told her about the unofficial rescue mission Ryn and I went on. She probably looked into our records to see what previous assignments we'd done together and came up with nothing.

So, technically, the only person I have to blame for receiving Ryn as a partner is myself.

"Look, it's not too bad," I say, not entirely sure which of us I'm trying to reassure. "Ryn and I ... well, we're sort of almost on speaking terms these days."

Tora looks as shocked as if I just told her the Seelie Queen died and was being replaced by a giant, fluffy quirkizil. "You are? When did that happen?"

I shrug. I'm not allowed to mention the whole rescuing-Ryn's-sister-from-an-Unseelie-Prince's-dungeon thing. "In the past week or so, I guess."

"Wow. I should go overseas more often," Tora says.

"Maybe next time I'll return and you two will be actual friends instead of trying to hurt each other."

I smile. "You never know."

"Okay, well, you need to take this," she says. She rolls up the pages with my assignment information and ties a piece of cord around them. "Ryn will get his own copy, but the two of you obviously need to look over the information *together* before Monday."

"Yeah, yeah." I stand up. "So that's it for this meeting?"

"Yes." She stands up too. "That was officially the last assignment I ever have to give you." She stares at me, and I stare back. A sheen of tears gathers over her eyes.

"Oh, come on, don't get soppy now."

She sniffs. "You think this is soppy? Wait until your graduation." I groan and she laughs, wiping at her eyes. "I know you like to keep your emotions boxed away, Miss Top-of-the-Class," she says, reaching for the door handle, "but I know you'll miss me too."

* * *

I manage to leave the Guild without bumping into Ryn. I know we'll have to meet at some point to plan this assignment, but at the Guild in front of his friends probably isn't the best place. I arrive in my kitchen and see Filigree—still a pig—sniffing at a parcel on the counter. It's in the spot where my mail always materializes.

"Oh, when did that arrive?" I ask, walking over to him. He looks up at me and makes a snuffling sound. "Yeah, I have no idea what you just said." I pick up the parcel. It's about the size of my palm, wrapped in fabric and tied with a ribbon. I open the note wedged beneath the ribbon.

I forgot to give this to you earlier! While I was away I visited one of those fairs with all the latest spells and gadgets and fell in love with these little guys. It's a mirror, just like any other you'd use to communicate with, but when someone tries to get hold of you the mirror will jump up and come find you. Cute! Anyway, I thought you might like it. I have a green one. I named it Bartholomew.

    Love, Tora

    P.S. Flint already programmed it to recognize you.

"Hmm." I pull the ribbon off and unfold the fabric to reveal a circular mirror. Protruding from one side of the circle are what look like two little legs, which would mean that the two skinny shapes folded across the mirror's glass are … arms? And it's purple. Honestly, what is it with people and their fixation on giving me purple gifts? Do they really think I want everything I own to match my hair and eyes?

Anyway, I should probably thank Tora. It is a cute gift, and it's nice that she thought of me while she was away. I pull my amber out of my pocket and write her a quick thank-you message.

"Come, let's read these assignment notes," I tell Filigree. He shifts into cat form, jumps off the counter, and changes back to a pig. I head to the sitting room with my training bag over my shoulder, Filigree trotting behind me. I flop onto a couch and pull the rolled up assignment pages out of my bag. "Okay, are you ready to find out everything there is to know about Mr. Edgar Hart?" I help Filigree onto the couch where he positions himself next to me and rests his head on my knee. "I'll take that as a 'yes.'"

An hour later Filigree is snoring and I'm almost asleep. Tora was right when she talked about boring, old rich people. It's just golf, lunch, gym, salon, entertaining—and then they mix it up by doing the same activities in a different order the next day. Total snore. I feel sorry for whoever it was that had to watch the Harts long enough to figure out their daily schedule.

I feel my eyelids drooping when suddenly—

"*Violet Violet Violet Violet Violet!*"

"What the freak?" I jerk awake and jump to my feet, scattering papers everywhere as I search for the source of the high-pitched, squeaky voice that won't stop calling my name. Then I see it. The purple mirror. Tearing across the floor on its little legs, pumping its tiny fists in its desperation to get to me. "*Violet Violet Violet Violet Violet!*" It slams into my leg, then grabs the bottom of my pants and starts yanking. Filigree, a bear now, roars and swipes at it.

"Okay, okay." I bend to pick up the little guy and see Honey's face in the mirror. When I touch the shiny surface, the squealing of my name finally stops. "Hello?"

"Hey!" Honey says. She waves at me. "I wanted to speak to you at the Guild, but Tora said you'd left."

"Oh, yeah, I was avoiding my new partner." I return to the couch.

"That's why I wanted to talk to you." She looks desperate.

"I am *so* sorry about that."

"Why? It's not your fault we all got switched at the last minute."

"I know, but I shouldn't have said anything to you before. It must have made it even more of a shock when you found out it was actually Ryn."

"Don't worry about it, Honey. I can handle him." I lean back and massage one of my shoulders with my free hand. "So, who'd you end up with?"

"Asami." She shrugs. "He's okay, I guess."

I nod. "And where are you going?"

"Egypt!" She bounces up and down. "It's so exciting. There are these bronze-skinned elves I've never heard of before that live inside the pyramids. And the Seers have Seen that some pixie-type creatures are about to invade the pyramids, and some humans are going to accidentally get involved, and basically we have to fix up the whole mess."

"Wow. Sounds amazing."

"I know." Her smile couldn't be any wider. "And what about you?"

I shake my head and let out a humorless laugh. "You should be grateful you're not my partner anymore. My assignment isn't half as exciting as yours."

We talk a few minutes more before saying goodbye. I place the mirror on the couch beside me—where it promptly folds its arms back over its glossy surface—and start gathering my assignment pages from the floor. I stare at them a bit longer before finally deciding I need to visit Ryn. This assignment isn't going to plan itself, and I can't exactly do it without him.

CHAPTER FOUR

I EXIT THE FAERIE PATHS IN FRONT OF THE TREE THAT conceals Ryn's home. It looks like any other tree in this part of the forest, but when I lean forward and gently blow air against the bark, gold dust rises to reveal a door knocker shaped like a mermaid. Stamping down my nerves—and telling myself I'm ridiculous for feeling nervous in the first place—I grab the mermaid's tail and knock. Then I stand there, biting my lip and twisting my hands together. And right at that moment, I remember Ryn saying something about being with a girl tonight.

Crap it. This could get embarrassing. I reach hastily for my stylus, preparing to leave as quickly as I—

"Vi?" Light spills out of the open doorway on the tree, revealing Ryn's mother Zinnia standing there. "What a nice

31

surprise." Her grin is wide as she steps back. "Please come in. Are you looking for Ryn?"

"Uh, yes. Is he in?" *Please say no.*

"Yes, he's in the kitchen."

The kitchen? "Oh, so, he's alone tonight?"

"No, but I'm sure he won't mind you being here."

I highly doubt that. I step inside and follow her across the sitting room. "Sorry for just showing up," I say. I used to do it all the time when I was younger, but it doesn't feel right anymore.

"It's not a problem at all. Ryn told me you two are partners for your final assignment, so I expected to see you this weekend. It's ... nice that you two will be working together."

I raise an eyebrow. "If by 'nice' you mean 'potentially disastrous,' then yes. It will be nice."

She stops with her hand on the kitchen door, looking momentarily horrified at my honesty. But then she laughs. "Well, I didn't want to be the one to say it."

"We're all thinking it," I tell her. "Someone may as well say it out loud."

She chuckles as she pushes the door open. I follow her, steeling myself for the embarrassing situation I'm about to walk into.

The first thing I notice is the delicious aroma of honey cupcakes. The smell floats in the air, curling around me, conjuring up memories of happier times when Reed and my dad were still alive, and Ryn's father hadn't left Zinnia. Then my eyes fall on Ryn, sitting at the table playing a card game with—Calla?

The girl with the golden hair and eyes looks up, a smile spreading across her face when she sees me. She moves as though to get up, but then her smile turns shy, and she gives me a small wave instead.

I force my gaze back to Ryn. "This is why you didn't want Dale over here tonight? You don't want him to know you're babysitting your little sister?"

Ryn glances at Calla, then glares at me as though my words may have offended her. But she's busy examining the cards clutched in her hands and doesn't seem bothered.

"You lied to your friends?" Zinnia asks as she pulls a chair out for me at the table.

"No." Ryn leans back. "Dale asked if I had a girl over here tonight. I said yes. That wasn't a lie."

Zinnia rolls her eyes and heads for the oven. I place my scroll of assignment pages on the table and sit down.

"So, do you babysit often?" I ask.

Ryn lifts one shoulder in a gesture that could mean yes, no, or pretty much anything in between. "My dad and his, uh—" he glances across the room at Zinnia "—and Calla's mom are out tonight. They don't like to leave Calla alone at home." He places a card with an illustration of a vine on it down on the table.

"I'm sure they don't," I mutter.

"What type of icing do you want, sweetie?" Zinnia asks Calla.

"Um." Calla purses her lips while watching Ryn's vine card strangle her kelpie card. "Can I have the one with the sparkles that tingle on your tongue, please?"

"The faerie kisses one?"

Calla giggles and nods. Apparently when you're six years old, faerie kisses are too embarrassing to talk about, even if they're only referring to a type of icing. With a wink at Calla, Zinnia turns back to her mixing bowl. I watch her as she adds ingredients, pushing her long, dark curls out of the way when they fall across her face. Am I the only one who finds this situation a little weird? Zinnia's husband left her, formed a new union with someone else, had a child with that someone else, and now that child is sitting in Zinnia's kitchen. And Zinnia is baking for her. I shake my head and turn back to the card game.

"Yay, centaur beats pixie!" Calla says, putting down her last card and throwing her arms into the air. A tiny cloud of dust rises from the table as the centaur card gallops over the pixie card.

"I guess you also didn't want Dale seeing what kind of games you play on a Friday night, hey?" I tease.

Ryn's blue eyes pierce mine. "Did you come here for a reason, Violet?"

Ooh, my full name. I must have struck a nerve. "A reason, hmm, let me think. Oh, there is that assignment we've been forced to do together. Remember that, Oryn? The most important assignment in our five years of training?

"Yeah." He continues staring at me. "What about it?"

"Have you read the pages yet?"

"Nope."

"Ryn! This is a straightforward assignment. If we plan properly we can get it done before Friday and get bonus points.

I know you want to be top of the class just as badly as I do."

He shakes his head, chuckling. "I don't think there's anyone who wants the top position as badly as you, V."

I cross my arms. "Well, we still need to plan."

"No, you need to relax." He gathers the cards scattered across the table and throws them into the Card Eaters box Calla holds out to him. The box rattles as all the defeated cards reform. "We have plenty of time to—"

"No." I point a finger at him. "Do you know what happens when people say they have plenty of—"

"Are you really pointing your finger at me?"

"So," Zinnia says loudly. "Who's ready for a cupcake?"

I stand up, my chair scraping back against the floor. I look at Ryn, then tilt my head toward the door.

"Are you trying to say something, V? A problem with your neck, maybe?"

Calla smacks him on the hand with the lid of the card box. "She wants you to go into the other room with her, stupid."

"Oh, really?" He grins at his little sister. "Thanks, Cal. I never would have guessed."

With a barely disguised groan of frustration, I head out to the sitting room. Ryn follows me, closes the door, and leans against the wall beside it, refusing to meet my gaze.

"Okay, look," I say. "We have to figure out a way to work together. It's not fun, but I know it's not impossible either because we managed to do it when we rescued Calla. So all you have to do is pretend this assignment is as important as saving her life, and we'll be fine."

Ryn tightens his arms over his chest, but says nothing.

"Hello?" I wave a hand in front of his face. "Anyone in there?"

"I don't know how to do this!" he says, abruptly throwing his hands up. He pushes himself away from the wall and sits down on the arm of a couch. "I don't know how to be your friend."

Well. That was unexpected. I sit down in the armchair opposite him. I try to think of something to say, but nothing seems right.

"When I sat on your bed and asked if we could be friends, I meant it," he says. "I still want that. It's just ... I'm so used to not only ignoring you, but also *intentionally* trying to hurt you, that ... I don't know how to be nice."

"Yeah, I noticed." I run a hand through my hair. "I'm sorry. I guess I have a bit of a problem with that too. It's kind of like my first instinct when I'm around you."

He looks up, managing half a smile. "I know what you mean."

"So, how about we aim for somewhere in the middle?"

He considers that for a moment. "And 'the middle' would entail ... fun insults instead of mean ones?"

I match his half-smile. "We could try that."

Zinnia pokes her head around the kitchen door. "If you've finished arguing, your cupcakes are waiting for you."

"Thanks, Mom." Ryn stands up. "You know, I meant it when I said you need to relax, V. We really do have plenty of time to plan for this assignment."

"Fine. You can have tonight off. But the rest of the weekend is for planning."

We enter the kitchen to find Calla giggling as she licks the icing off her cupcake. "It tickles," she says. Which makes sense, given that bright sparkles of color are bouncing and shooting off the cupcakes sitting on the plate in the middle of the table.

"Calla, do you want my icing?" I ask, grabbing a cupcake from the plate and sitting down. I'm only interested in the cake part.

"Mm," Calla says, nodding and handing me a spoon to scrape off the icing.

"Don't you like faerie kisses?" Ryn asks, his eyes dancing with some hidden meaning. "You're missing out, you know."

I bite into the cake, closing my eyes as the rich honey flavor melts on my tongue. "Trust me," I say after chewing and swallowing, "there is nothing I'm missing out on right—"

My words are cut off by a shuddering clap of thunder. Calla freezes, a spoon of icing halfway to her mouth. She blinks a few times, then whimpers as the light in the room flickers.

"Hey, it's okay," Ryn says. "The glow-bugs don't like thunder, that's all. They like to go into hibernation mode when they feel the vibrations. It makes them feel safer."

"But then I don't feel safe," Calla whispers. She jumps off her chair and runs to Ryn's side of the table, taking her spoon of icing with her. Thunder rumbles again, louder this time, as she climbs onto Ryn's lap.

"Let's play another round," Ryn says. He reaches for the box of cards, then stops with his hand in the air and looks across the room at his mother. She's standing in a corner, reading a message on her amber. A crease forms between her eyes. "What's wrong?" he asks.

She shakes her head. "I missed a message earlier." She hurries out of the kitchen just as rain begins to patter down in the forest outside. A moment later she's back in the room, pulling on a pair of boots similar to my own. They lace themselves up as she slings a bag over her shoulder and opens a doorway on a blank part of the wall. "I need to get to the Guild."

"What happened?" Ryn asks.

Zinnia's eyes dart to Calla, then back to Ryn. "I'm not sure I'm allowed to tell you," she says. "But you'll know soon enough." And with that she disappears into the faerie paths.

CHAPTER FIVE

THE STORM STILL RAGES OUTSIDE WHEN I WAKE UP ON Monday morning. My enchanted skylight gives me a glimpse of lightning flashing every few seconds and wind and rain tearing at leaves. I turn over and grab my amber from next to my bed, mumbling the spell to make it show me the time. I close my eyes and snuggle deeper beneath the bed covers. Ryn and I have read everything there is to know about the Harts, and we've planned as much as we can, so I may as well sleep in a little bit. Ryn's right—I really do need to relax more.

"Morning, V."

My eyelids spring apart, and a glittering knife has formed in my hand before I can even think about it.

"Whoa, careful, it's just me." Ryn is sitting in my desk chair, looking entirely at ease.

I pull the covers up to my chin, trying to remember what I'm wearing and how much skin it covers. "What are you doing here?" I demand.

"I felt in need of a laugh and knew the sight of you first thing in the morning would do the trick."

"Thanks. I'm flattered. Can you leave now?"

"Nope." He leans forward. "I'm actually here to make breakfast."

"Breakfast? Is that the burning I can smell coming from downstairs?" To be honest, the only thing I can smell is the vanilla charm I put on my bed covers once a week. But Ryn doesn't seem like the kind of guy who cooks, so I'm guessing the chances are high he's about to burn something in my kitchen.

"Indeed it is. Burnt pancakes especially for you."

"And what did I do to deserve burnt pancakes?"

"It's in celebration of our final assignment, and because you need to get used to seeing my handsome face first thing in the morning." He stands up and walks to the door. "Oh, and I thought you might want to know that what's happening outside isn't a normal storm. It's a magical one."

"What do you mean?"

"Lightning got inside the Guild."

"WHAT?" I sit up so fast it makes me feel dizzy.

"Yeah, I thought that'd wake you up," he says, then walks out of the room.

"Come back!" I yell. I push the bed covers off me and hurry downstairs after Ryn. "You can't say something like that and then just leave." I find him in the kitchen, pointing at

40

something in a pan with his stylus. "What happened? Did someone else get hurt?" I think of what happened on Friday night. The incident Zinnia rushed off to deal with.

The Seer who was murdered inside the Guild.

"No. There were three witnesses who saw the bolt of lightning enter the library and hit one of the bookshelves, but none of them were close enough to get hurt."

I sit down in one of the chairs. "So, are they thinking the storm and the murder are connected?"

"Yes." Ryn stands back as a surprisingly non-burnt pancake flips itself. "I mean, it could be one seriously big coincidence, but I doubt it."

"And do you know anything new about the murder?"

He shakes his head. "My mom isn't saying anything. Anyway, the big question everyone's asking is who could possibly have enough power to control a storm this big?"

I look down at my hands as my heart squeezes out a few painfully hard beats. I know someone. Someone who only recently discovered his special talents with the weather.

Nate.

As if it were only yesterday, I hear Zell's voice replaying in my mind. *He can't quite control it yet, but his storms are certainly impressive, don't you think?* Can Nate control it now? Is he the one creating the massive storm currently raging through Creepy Hollow forest? But there's no way he would murder someone. Never. I might not know everything about him, but I'm sure I know that much.

"You okay, V?" I look up to find Ryn watching me closely.

"Yeah, I'm just worried, I guess."

Liar, liar.

"Well, why don't you put a few more clothes on—" he gestures in the general direction of my exposed legs "—and then we can have breakfast and go kick this assignment's ass."

* * *

"And don't forget that when you're pretending to be human you *cannot* be seen using magic," Tora says.

"Trust me, I'm not about to break that rule again." I'm sitting on the floor of her office, the contents of my emergency kit spread around me as I do an inventory.

"Right." She stops pacing and sits on the edge of her desk, bouncing her leg. "Oh, and did you ever replenish your burn healing potion after your assignment with the draconi?"

"Right here." I hold up a jar of clear gel. "Okay, I think all I'm missing are those insta-heal patches for deep cuts, but they're not really necessary. I'm sure this is the kind of assignment where I'll have enough magic to heal my own—"

"I'll go get some from Uri," Tora says, jumping up. She's out of the door before I can tell her not to worry about it. I pack away all the vials, bottles, jars, and bandages—and the *Forget* potion I hid in my pocket. I couldn't have Tora seeing that. I should get rid of it, but it seems a waste to throw away a potion made from such expensive ingredients.

Tora returns with five round, blue patches in her hand. I pop them into the emergency kit and close it up. I stand and survey my things.

"Okay," Tora says, moving to stand beside me. "You've got

your emergency kit—"

"Check."

"—your potions kit—"

"Check."

"—and some clothes and personal items so you don't stink by the time you get back."

I raise an eyebrow. "Check."

She shakes her head at the questioning look on my face. "You don't want to know about the hygiene habits of some of the people I went on assignment with back before I became a mentor."

"Well," I say with a laugh, "I like to be clean, so you don't need to worry about that."

"You're not the one I'm worried about," Tora says. "I hope for your sake Ryn feels the same way."

"Feels the same way about what?" Ryn asks, stopping in the doorway of Tora's office.

"Hygiene," Tora tells him.

"Are you ready to go down?" Bran calls from the corridor as he walks past, Asami at his side.

"Almost," I call back. "Just resizing." I hold my emergency kit in my hands and say the words to make it shrink. I repeat them until the kit is the size of a small nut, then do the same with my other two bags. I lift my right foot and click open the hidden compartment in the sole of my boot, then put the three bags inside and close it. "Okay, I'm ready."

"Come on," Tora says, already at the door. We hurry out of her office to catch up with Bran, Asami and Ryn.

"Feeling confident, Vi?" Bran asks.

"I think so," I say, trying not to sound *too* confident. I doubt that ever works out well for anyone. "It doesn't seem that complicated or dangerous. We just have to get some information out of a human."

"Well, don't be fooled. You can't always tell when spells have been placed on humans."

"Yes, I know." I pat my pockets, trying to rid myself of the feeling that I've forgotten something important. I'm being paranoid, of course. I *know* I've packed everything.

"And we're allowed to contact you, right?" Asami asks.

"Yes, but try not to," Bran says. "On real assignments, guardians obviously remain in contact with the Guild, but since this assignment is a test for you and we want to see how much you can do on your own, contacting anyone will, unfortunately, cost you some points."

We reach the stairs and head down toward the main foyer of the Guild. I trail my hand lightly over the vines twisted around the banister, feeling the leaves brush between my fingers. "Bran, do you have anything else to tell us about the murder and the storm?"

Bran pushes his hands into his pockets. "There's nothing to say except don't worry about it. Security has already been increased, the protective enchantments are currently being strengthened, and you have more important things to think about over the next few days."

I glance at Ryn to see what he thinks of Bran's words, but his face is turned away from me. Surely he must be more concerned about this whole thing than I am; his mother is involved in investigating the murder.

We reach the foyer to find most of our classmates and their mentors already there, some receiving last minute advice, some chatting to their assignment partners, and others simply standing around looking nervous. Dale looks over at us, shakes his head, and mouths something at Ryn that looks like *Bad luck, dude.* I turn my back on him without waiting to see if Ryn mouths anything back.

"Okay, trainees. Here it is." Bran stands on the first step and looks down at us as he waits for silence. "Your big moment. Your final assignment. What happens over the course of the next few days will determine the direction your life takes after graduation." His eyes move from one trainee to the next. "Remember that you can receive bonus points for completing the assignment and returning safely before Friday, but that doesn't mean you should rush it." His gaze stops on Dale. "You'll likely make a stupid mistake and lose points instead." He claps his hands together. "So, good luck, and off you go."

Noise fills the foyer as trainees and mentors say goodbye and begin writing doorways on walls and the floor.

"I know you can do this," Tora says, pulling me into a tight hug. "But remember to be careful."

"Always," I say. "And try not to get struck by magical bolts of lightning while I'm gone."

Tora steps back. "Don't worry about the storm. We're all going to be—"

"Oh, for the love of all things Seelie," Ryn says. He opens a doorway in the air, grabs my arm, and pulls me in after him.

"Hey! I was still saying goodbye."

"No, you were wasting time. Now keep your mind blank;

45

I'm trying to direct the paths."

I bite back a retort and try to think of nothing. The darkness melts away, and Ryn and I find ourselves standing in bright sunlight on a perfectly manicured lawn. Looking across the expanse of grass, I see the Harts' home. It's far bigger than I expected, and everything seems to be white and glass. White walls and pillars, square angles everywhere, and glass from floor to ceiling in just about every room. A wooden deck stretches across the side of the house, looking out over the garden. Umbrellas and loungers are arranged around a swimming pool with sparkling turquoise water that disappears over one side of the deck. All in all, it seems an obscene amount of space for two people to live in.

"Flip," Ryn says. "I thought our mentors said this assignment was boring."

"Well, that was probably because we didn't get to go to Egypt or Thailand or somewhere equally exotic like everyone else in our class."

"But they're probably staying in a shack in Thailand. This looks like it belongs on the cover of a property magazine."

I look at him. "What do you know about property magazines?"

"I read."

"While on assignment?"

"Of course. It gets boring waiting for the bad guys to show up."

I shake my head and turn my gaze back to the house. "Okay. Day one: observation. Let's get inside there and assess the situation."

"Yes, ma'am," Ryn says. Before I can take a step forward, he pulls me into a doorway in the air, and a second later we're standing on the deck.

I shake his hand off my arm. "I wish you'd stop doing that. It would have taken us, what? Fifteen seconds to walk up here? But no, you always have to show off by opening doorways in the air."

Ryn leans toward me with a grin and whispers, "Jealous." He walks past me and through an open sliding door. I take a deep remember-you're-supposed-to-be-friends-now breath and follow him.

"Are you glamoured?" I ask. "We don't want anyone seeing us now."

"I should be asking you that," he says with a glance over his shoulder at me. "Of the two of us, you're the only one who's broken that rule."

"I did not break that rule," I say with a huff. "He just happened to be able to see through my glamour."

"Speaking of halfling boy," Ryn says as we walk past a white lounge suite that looks as though no one's backside has ever graced it, "what's he up to these days? Heard anything from him since he decided to hand you over to the Unseelie Court?"

I pick up a strange elephant statue and pretend to examine it. "No comment."

We wander through the house, taking our time. Every room is perfect, not a cushion or tall-stemmed flower out of place. Even the art on the walls and the framed black and white family photos are perfectly in line. It's hard to imagine anyone lives here.

We come to a circular stairway leading both up and down. Ryn decides to go down, so I follow him. We may as well see everything together.

"Ah, looks like we've found the fun part of the house," Ryn says as we enter a room decidedly less tidy than the rooms upstairs. A pool table fills half the room, and squishy grey couches are arranged in the other half. The table between the couches is covered in junk food and DVDs.

"Hey, Pixie Sticks," Ryn says. "Look here." He holds up a long, pink straw, sealed at both ends, and shakes it. "Someone who can't spell named a candy after you."

"Look here." I grab a DVD off the table. "Someone with no imagination named a movie after you."

He stares at the cover. "*Dumb and Dumber*? Ha! You need to try harder than that, V."

I throw the DVD back onto the pile and sigh. "I'm having an off day." I start climbing the stairs, leaving Ryn to roll a ball across the pool table.

I follow the smell of bacon and coffee and find the kitchen, a spotless room where every appliance seems to be from a matching set and every surface is free of fingerprints. A young woman in an apron hums quietly to herself as she prepares a meal.

"A bit late for breakfast, isn't it?" I say to Ryn as he walks into the kitchen behind me.

"Not when you don't have to be at work early in the morning. Man, these guys must have the latest in every kind of human technology." He leans in to take a closer look at the computer screen on the front of the fridge. "Their TV must be *amazing*."

"You watch television on assignment too?" I demand, putting my hands on my hips.

"Yeah, you should try it, V. There are some highly addictive series out there."

"Ryn! We're supposed to be protecting humans when we're on assignment, not hanging out in front of their televisions."

"And how about if I'm not on assignment? Can I do it then?" He trails his hand over a marble countertop while watching me. I glare back. The woman continues humming, completely unaware of our presence.

"Cecelia, please bring the sugar," a man calls from the next room.

The woman puts down a fork and hurries over to a cupboard, dodging past Ryn—though of course she'll have no idea why she decided to do that—on her way. She grabs a pretty glass bowl that already has sugar in it. We follow her into a small dining room where a distinguished-looking man is sitting at a rectangular table reading a newspaper. A mug sits on the table in front of him.

"Here you go, sir," Cecilia says, placing the sugar bowl near a collection of jars already on the table. "I'm sorry I forgot to put it out."

"Not a problem," the man says, barely glancing up from his newspaper as Cecilia returns to the kitchen.

"And this must be Mr. Hart himself," Ryn says, leaning over the man's shoulder to get a closer look at the article he's reading.

"*What on earth?*" Mr. Hart drops the newspaper and jumps up, knocking his chair to the floor in the process. Ryn stumbles backward into me, clearly horrified that this man can see us.

"Oh crap," I mutter. "*Not* a good start."

"P-please," Mr. Hart stutters, backing away from us. "Not now."

I'm about to reassure him when I feel a tug on my arm, and, for the third time today, I find myself pulled into a doorway in the air.

"What the flipping hell was that?" Ryn demands when we step out behind a tree in the Harts' garden.

"Well, obviously he can see us."

"Yes, Violet, I gathered that. But *why?* He's human."

I shake my head. "This had better not be another Nate case. I don't want to deal with more halflings."

"Do you think we'll be accused of breaking rule number two now?" Ryn asks as he runs a hand through his hair.

"Probably not. That man already knows about faeries, and not because of us."

"I guess so. But how are we supposed to observe him if he can see us?"

"Um ..." I twist a strand of hair around my finger while thinking. "Okay, what if we take the faerie paths back to the dining room, but instead of opening a full doorway, we open a space that's just large enough to peek through?"

Ryn looks at me like I'm stupid. "So instead of two faeries in his dining room, he'll see an eyeball floating in midair? Wow. Brilliant."

"Obviously I'd try to be as inconspicuous as possible."

50

When Ryn doesn't say anything, I add, "Do you have a better idea?"

"Fine. We can try it."

I open a new doorway. We walk through while I think about the curtain in the room Mr. Hart is sitting in. Hopefully my floating eyeball will be less obvious against the pattern of the fabric. The darkness in front of us begins to dissolve away, but I catch the opening with my fingers, pinching the edge and closing it back up until there's only a small opening. I look through it.

"Well, this is great," Ryn says beside me. "I can't see a thing now."

I widen the opening with my fingers until it stretches in front of Ryn's face, then I close up the space between us so that two separate openings exist. "Happy now?"

"Ecstatic."

I put my eye to the tiny window and see Cecelia place a mug on the table in front of Mr. Hart. "Thank you," he says as he straightens the pages of his newspaper. "I'm sorry I was so clumsy with the first one."

She bobs her head and leaves the room. Mr. Hart glances around nervously, then pulls a phone from his pocket. He jabs a few buttons before bringing the phone to his ear. "Hello? David?" he says after several seconds. "It's happened again. Two of them just appeared right here in the breakfast room." He pauses. "Yes, faeries! What else would I be talking about? You haven't forgotten our last few conversations, have you?" Another pause. "No, your mother doesn't know anything. I don't want to alarm her. But listen—" his eyes dart around the room "—we're entertaining tomorrow night. Please come. I desperately need to—" He breaks off as a woman with a phone at her ear enters the room. "I have to go. I'll see you tomorrow." He slides the phone back into his pocket and clears his throat as he reaches once more for his newspaper.

"We're fortunate to see quite a lot of them," the woman says into her phone as she pulls out a chair and sits down. "They're actually staying with us at the moment while my son and daughter-in-law are overseas." The woman's skin appears flushed, and her hair, which is tied tightly on top of her head, is a deep shade of auburn that can't possibly be natural given her age. She's barefoot and wearing workout clothes. She leans back in her seat as Cecilia places a bowl of fruit salad in front of her. "Oh, no, they're older than that now. Grace is thirteen and Jamie is eight. Mm hmm. Yes. Yes, we really *must*, it's been *so* long since I saw you." She looks at her husband and rolls her eyes. "Okay, goodbye now. Bye." She drops the phone onto the table with an exasperated sigh.

Mr. Hart, who has regained his composure since his wife entered the room, says, "Something wrong, dear?"

"That woman!" Mrs. Hart picks up her spoon. "I don't know why she keeps pretending we have anything in common anymore. I'm just going to have to 'forget' once again to make a plan to see her." She spoons some fruit into her mouth. "Are Grace and Jamie up yet?"

"I haven't seen them this morning," Mr. Hart says. He puts his newspaper down and reaches for his mug.

I pull my eye away from the hole and look over at Ryn. "Aren't children supposed to be at school at this time of day?"

"Maybe they're on holiday."

I return my gaze to the window and hear Mrs. Hart asking, "Who were you talking to when I walked into the room?"

"Oh, that was David." Mr. Hart takes a sip from his mug and disappears behind his newspaper.

"David? You've been talking to him a lot in the past few days. Is something going on?"

Mr. Hart lowers the crinkled pages just enough to look at his wife over the top. "Of course not, dear. Can't I have a simple conversation with my son?"

"No, I don't think you can, actually. He only ever seems to call when he's in trouble and needs something."

"Well, trust me," Mr. Hart says, lifting the newspaper once more. "He isn't in trouble this time."

"David. That's the youngest son, right?" I say to Ryn.

"Yes."

I watch Mr. Hart take a sip of his coffee. "I say we try a compulsion potion on him right now and compel him to tell the truth. We'll be done with this assignment in an hour."

"I would've suggested that myself, Violet, except for the part where he'll be able to *see* us putting the potion in his coffee."

"I'm not an idiot, Oryn. I do actually have a plan." I close up the hole in front of my eye and think of the kitchen instead. A doorway opens near the stove where Cecelia is nudging a poached egg out of its mold and onto a plate. I sit down on the kitchen floor and remove my potions kit from my bag. After enlarging it, I look through the vials for one labeled *Compel*.

There isn't one.

Great. The one thing I didn't add to my kit. I do have one labeled *Confuse*, though, which might have a similar effect. Mr. Hart will tell us anything if we confuse him enough.

By the time I've decided on the confusion potion, Cecelia is heading to the dining room with the plate in her hand. I jump up, run after her, and manage to throw a few drops onto a buttered piece of toast before she leaves the kitchen.

Time to watch and wait. I observe Mr. Hart through the crack between the door and the wall. He eats quickly, washing the meal down with a few gulps of his coffee. "Well, I'll see you after golf," he says to his wife. He folds the newspaper and leaves it on the table. "You'll confirm with the caterers for tomorrow night?"

"Yes, it's on my list," Mrs. Hart says. She picks up her phone and moves her thumb across the screen.

I wait for Mr. Hart to leave the room, then tiptoe after him. I pass a shimmer in the air, and a moment later Ryn is walking beside me. Mr. Hart turns a corner and we follow quietly. I watch for signs of confusion—stumbling, shaking his head, talking to himself—but nothing appears to be happening yet. He enters a room, and I catch a glimpse of bookshelves and a large desk before he shuts the door behind him.

"His study," Ryn says.

"We can watch through the window until the potion's kicked in. I used *Confuse*, by the way. Didn't have any *Compel*."

Ryn sighs. "I suppose we can make that work."

We get to the garden using the faerie paths, and it's easy enough to find Mr. Hart's study window. It's a massive floor-to-ceiling piece of glass, like almost every other window we've seen here. We keep our backs to the wall and edge toward the window. Ryn peeks in.

"Why isn't he confused yet?" he asks. "Did you use a dud potion?"

"Of course not. I got that potion from Uri only a few weeks ago."

I pull Ryn back and take his place at the edge of the window. Mr. Hart is sitting with his back to us at a dark-stained oak desk. He appears to be reading something on his computer screen. After staring at the screen for a while, he yawns, leans back, and rubs his neck. Other than looking a little fatigued, he seems in complete control of his mental faculties.

But then I notice something. "What's that behind his ear?" I lean forward to get a closer look as Ryn peers over my shoulder. "It was concealed by his hair, but when he rubbed his neck I saw it. See there?" I point at the small round metal shape stuck to Mr. Hart's skin.

"It looks a little like our sound drops."

"Yes, but don't you recognize the metal? It looks just like the stuff Zell put around his dungeon to prevent outside magic getting in. The same metal he put around my wrist to block my magic."

"But this guy's human." Ryn turns to me with a frown. "He has no magic to be blocked."

"I don't think it's to block his magic," I say, straightening and looking at Ryn. "It's to block ours."

CHAPTER SIX

"GOLF," I SAY TO RYN, "IS POSSIBLY THE MOST BORING human sport in existence." I walk across the deck and flop onto a lounger beside him. "People spend ages trying to get their feet the right distance apart, their knees bent at the correct angle, and the proper grip with their hands, all so they can whack tiny balls into the distance, which they then have to go in search of when the darn things don't land where they're supposed to. And I had to spend the entire morning watching this! Through faerie paths peepholes!"

Ryn crosses his legs. "I'm guessing he didn't tell his golfing buddies anything about his encounters with the fae kind?"

"Nope. I even stayed to observe their lunch, but the conversation remained firmly in boring territory." I stare at the canvas umbrella above my head. "So, what happened here? Did you find somewhere for us to stay tonight, or did you just laze about all day?"

Without lifting his head, Ryn points to the other side of the deck. "Pool house."

Pool house. Right. "So you didn't like my idea of finding an unused bedroom in the house and magically locking it while we're inside?"

"The Harts' grandkids are using two of the rooms, and the maids were making up the others. Seems there'll be people staying over after tomorrow night's party."

"Hmm, a party." I shift into a more comfortable position on the lounger. "The last one they had was the one where the Unseelie faerie gave something to Mr. Hart."

"Yes."

"So maybe the faerie will show up again and we'll figure everything out tomorrow night."

"Maybe."

We lie in silence for a while, and I try my best not to think of Honey in the midst of an exciting battle between two fae kinds. It doesn't work. "We could be fighting dangerous Egyptian fae and instead we're lying in the shade beside a pool, doing nothing."

"I know," Ryn says. "Isn't it awesome?"

"Ryn!" I sit up. "I *want* to be fighting something. I can't stand this waiting around and observing and essentially achieving nothing."

Ryn tilts his head so he can look up at me. "I think I know why you got this assignment. Someone realized you need to learn patience and—"

"Wait." I hold up a hand. "What is that on your face?"

"Um …"

I lean closer. "Is that a bruise on your eye?"

"Hmm." He looks away. "I thought that would be gone by now."

I cross my arms and ask, "What exactly did you do today?"

"That's none of your business."

"It is my business when you're my assignment partner."

"Well, it had nothing to do with our assignment, so I guess I don't have to tell you."

I glare at him a moment longer, then stand up. "Fine. I'm going to check out the pool house."

"Great." I hear the creak of the lounger as Ryn gets up. "I should probably do that too."

"You mean you haven't even looked inside? It could be nothing more than a storage room filled with pool toys and chemicals."

"Let's hope not, or tonight could get uncomfortable."

I try the handle and find it unlocked. I step inside, Ryn close behind me. Wooden blinds conceal the windows, allowing just enough afternoon light in to cast a warm glow over the room. A kitchenette lines the wall on the right, an open door on the far wall leads to a bathroom, and in the center of the room is a large bed. *One* large bed.

Ryn looks sideways at me and raises an eyebrow. "It's big enough for two."

"You're joking, right? Why don't you pretend to be a gentleman and give me the bed?"

He laughs. "Now *you're* the one joking."

"Of course." I sigh. "I have nothing but the lowest of expectations when it comes to you, Ryn."

"And I shall continue to live down to them." He jumps onto the bed and puts both hands behind his head. "It's quite comfortable. Are you sure you don't want to join me?"

"I'd rather conjure up a separate bed, thank you very much."

"And waste all that magic and energy? I'd be an irresponsible partner if I let you do that."

I suppose he's right. I walk over to the bed, grab one of the many small cushions, and concentrate on sending magic into it to lengthen it. When the cushion is long enough, I toss it onto the middle of the bed. "Now I'll join you." I sit down and lie back. "And just so you know, the first part of your body that touches me is the first part you'll lose."

* * *

The Harts' grandchildren emerge from the house in the afternoon to play in the swimming pool, so Ryn and I spend several hours searching the upper level of the house. There isn't much chance of us finding whatever it was the Unseelie faerie gave Mr. Hart, but that doesn't stop us trying.

"I wish we had even a *hint* of what we're looking for," Ryn says, chucking socks back into a drawer and closing it with a bang.

"Maybe it doesn't exist," I say. "Maybe the thing he was given is the metal that's now stuck behind his ear."

"Maybe." Ryn feels behind a large mirror. "But since we

don't know that for sure, we may as well keep looking."

We find nothing, of course. No hidden rooms or locked drawers or objects that feel like they might have some kind of power.

The Harts and their grandchildren gather in the small dining room for dinner while I search their kitchen for food they won't miss. Okay, so it might be considered stealing, but we've been told not to leave here until our assignment is complete, so how else are we supposed to get food? It's not like we can conjure it out of nothing. I gather a few items and go in search of Ryn, who isn't in the pool house where I left him. I find him downstairs, sprawled on a couch in front of an enormous television screen that must have been hidden behind cabinet doors.

I try to recall some recipe spells while Ryn explains the drama going on in the TV show he's watching. Part of me starts to enjoy the unfolding story; another part keeps screaming at me that this is *not* what our final assignment is supposed to be like. Where is the excitement? The fighting? The adrenaline? I spend the rest of the evening discreetly following Mr. Hart around the house—because I have to do *something*—while Ryn remains downstairs.

I return to the pool house before he does. Instead of changing into anything that might resemble pajamas, I pull on another pair of form-fitting black pants and a black tank top— just in case we have to get up in the middle of the night and fight something. I comb my fingers through my damp hair and try not to think about how weird it's going to be sleeping in the same room as Ryn. I wonder what arrangement Honey and Asami have made, because I doubt Honey's boyfriend would be happy for her to share a room with another guy. Or maybe they don't have that problem because they're too busy fighting exotic monsters to get any sleep.

I close the bathroom door behind me and look over to find Ryn lying on his half of the bed. Shirtless. "No," I say immediately. "I am not sleeping with a half-naked guy next to me."

He looks up. "So don't sleep then."

"Ryn! It's just weird, okay, so please put on a shirt."

"Oh, get over it, V," he says as he rolls onto his side. "It's too hot for any more clothes than this, and we've got Mount Pillow between us. You can't even see me when you're lying down."

I close my eyes for a moment. He's right. I do need to get over it. It doesn't bother me when he walks around the training center half-naked, so it shouldn't bother me now. I cross the room to the bed and lie down on top of the covers—like Ryn said, it's too hot to be covering ourselves up with anything else.

I stare at the ceiling. "Do you want to sleep the first half of the night or the second?" I ask.

"You can sleep first. I'll wake you when I'm tired." He shifts slightly, and I feel the mattress move. "I really don't think anything's going to happen during the night, though."

"No. Probably not." I reach over and turn off the lamp beside my bed. I close my eyes and try to think of nothing. Especially not Nate's window and the fact that I'm not there to keep an eye on it. I can do this. I just need to relax and I'll fall asleep in no—

"So tell me about halfling boy," Ryn says, as if he can read my thoughts. "Does he have any magic? And how'd you find out he isn't human?"

I open my eyes and stare at the ceiling once more. It's darker now, with only Ryn's lamp on. What can I say that will make him stop asking questions about Nate?

"I'm guessing he does have magic," Ryn continues without waiting for me to answer, "otherwise he'd be of no use to the Unseelie Court." He nudges the pillow between us. "Aren't you even a little bit curious as to what he's doing for them? Handing you over can't be the only thing he signed up for."

"Ryn." I sit up abruptly and look at him over the pillow. The bruise I noticed around his left eye earlier is long gone, leaving his face flawless. "We may be giving this friends thing a go, but there are certain topics that are still off-limits, and Nate is one of them."

He watches me for a moment, then says, "Okay. Sorry."

I lie down once more and breathe deeply. It smells like summer. I'm about to close my eyes when the long pillow next to me suddenly slides away. Ryn turns onto his side and raises himself on one elbow. "There's something you never explained to me."

I back away from the open space between us. "What are you doing?"

"I'm about to ask you a question."

"Please put the pillow back."

"Come on, V. I'm not going to bite you. Can't we just have a conversation?"

It strikes me then that I'm probably being ridiculous. Ryn and I are supposed to be friends now. Of course we can have a conversation. "Um, yeah, sorry." I turn onto my side so I can look at him. "What did you want to ask me?"

"You know those discs that Zell has, the ones that fell out of his pocket while I was fighting him?"

"Yes?"

"When I told you I'd picked them up, you asked if I'd used them. You seemed to know what they were."

I hesitate, then say, "Yes."

Ryn raises both eyebrows. "Okay, so what are they?"

I bite my lip. I suppose there's no harm in telling him. "Remember the halfling Tharros? The one we all learn about in history lessons?" Ryn nods. "Those discs contain some of his power. They're cool because when you're fighting you never get tired as long as you keep drawing power from them. I was only told about one, though, but I'm assuming they're all the same."

"Who told you about this? Have you used them?"

I hold a hand up. "Okay, remember the off-limits territory? You're in it."

Ryn breathes out a frustrated sigh. "Fine, but you told Councilor Starkweather about them, right?"

"Actually ... I kind of left that part out," I admit.

"You don't think that's something she'd appreciate knowing for when she tries to take Zell down?"

"Well, I didn't *intentionally* leave it out. I was just focusing more on all the people he'd trapped in cages down there."

Ryn goes quiet for a while. "Do you think they've been rescued yet?"

"I don't know. I've thought about asking Councilor Starkweather if the Guild was able to rescue them, but I'm too scared. She made it very clear we weren't supposed to be involved at all, and she isn't someone I want to cross."

"I guess not." Ryn looks away, lost in thought for a few moments. Eventually he says, "Do you think he's still after you?"

"Zell? I'm sure he is."

"I should probably keep my distance from you, then." He pulls back slightly, one side of his lips turning up in a grin. "You're like a magnet for danger."

"No I'm not. He has no idea where I am."

"Vi, he has a spy in the Guild. I don't think it would be too hard for him to find out where your final assignment is taking place. He could be planning to show up here in the middle of the night."

"Good thing I'm not wearing pajamas."

"And good thing you have the Guild's best trainee right beside you."

"You wish," I say, trying to suppress a smile. "Anyway, if it was so easy for Zell's spy to find out where I am, then why hasn't Zell shown up on any of my other assignments in the past two weeks?"

Ryn shrugs. "Perhaps his spy has been busy with more

important things, like plotting murder within the Guild."

"Well, whatever." I turn my gaze to the ceiling so Ryn can't see that this conversation is actually making me nervous. "If he shows up, I'll deal with him then."

"You know what?" Ryn pushes himself up into a sitting position. "I know how to do a concealment charm. A proper one. If you want, I could do one on you."

I sit up so I don't have to feel him towering over me. "Aren't those hard to get right?"

"It is rather complicated to make the powder, but once it's on you, there's no magical means by which anyone can find you. None at all."

"Actually, there is one." I point to myself. "Me."

Ryn hesitates before saying, "Your finding ability can get past a concealment charm? Are you sure? It's a pretty darn powerful charm."

"Yeah." I look down at the bed covers, feeling suddenly self-conscious. "Tora and I were curious about it, so when I was in third year she got one of the senior guardians to do the charm on himself. I don't know what reason she gave him, but the point is that when she gave me one of his belongings, I could still find him."

"So the only thing that can actually stop you is that weird metal stuff Zell seems to have access to?"

"Yeah, I guess so. Anyway. Back to the part where you were offering to perform complex magic on me. Can you really do that?"

Ryn leans over the side of his bed and reaches for one of his shoes. "After we rescued Calla, I asked one of the senior guardians—probably the same one Tora asked—to help me make the concealment powder." He clicks open a compartment similar to the one I have in the base of my own shoe. "That was the hard part. Putting it on Calla and performing the charm was easy enough."

"And you have some of this powder left over?" I ask as Ryn enlarges his potions kit.

"Of course. I wasn't going to spend hours and hours in a cramped laboratory and only make enough for one person. I had to pay a lot for the ingredients, of course, but I figured it was worth it."

"Oh." Now I feel awkward. "Well, just tell me how much I owe you and—"

"Owe me? Don't be silly, V." He pulls out a bottle labeled *Conceal.* Fine gold powder sparkles within.

"Ryn, I can't just use up an expensive—"

"Violet," he says loudly. "Pretend it's an early birthday present if it makes you feel better."

"It doesn't." I know I'll still feel like I owe him, and I don't want that.

"And it's not even that early," he adds as he searches his potions kit for something else. "Your birthday isn't that far away."

Wow. I'm surprised he remembers.

"Okay, stand up," Ryn says, holding the bottle in one hand and a piece of paper in the other. "We're going to the bathroom."

"The bathroom?" I narrow my eyes at him. "I don't have to

be naked for this, do I?"

"Actually, yes." I cross my arms over my chest and give him a no-way-in-hell-is-that-happening glare. "But don't worry. I *promise* not to look," he adds with a glint in his eye.

With a sigh, I follow him to the bathroom where he's already begun filling the tub with water. "You need to be covered entirely in this powder," he says. "The best way to do that is dissolve it in water and submerge yourself."

We stand in silence as we watch the bathtub fill with water. I feel like I should say something, but I don't know what. I twist my hands together. It's weird, standing in this small, steamy space next to Ryn. Eventually, he stops the flow of water with a small flick of his hand. "That looks like enough," he says. "But—" he goes back into the room, then returns with his stylus and amber "—I need to know exactly how much water is in there so I know how much powder to add."

He kneels down and sticks his stylus into the water, then does some kind of calculation on his amber. I lean over his shoulder to get a closer look at what he's doing, but the numbers vanish before I can get a good look. Ryn lets the bottle of powder float in the air as he tells it how much to add to the water. The bottle tilts. A thin stream of powder pours from it, turning every drop of water in the bathtub golden within seconds.

Ryn takes hold of the bottle and puts the lid back on. "Okay, now get in." He rises and turns toward me. Before I can move out of his way, I find myself standing inches from his bare chest. I try instinctively to take a step backward, but the curved edge of the basin is right behind me.

I can't move.

Why won't he step away?

I don't want to look up at his face. That would make this moment even more awkward. I focus instead on the silver trainee pendant resting against his chest. It's flat and oval-shaped, with a clear stone set in the middle and patterns weaving around the edge of the metal. It looks just like every other trainee pendant, but I know if I turn it over I'll see his name engraved on the back.

Ryn clears his throat and *finally* steps away from me. "Um, so, you should get in now. Then memorize these words and say them in your head while you're completely submerged. I'll ... be in the room." He pushes the folded paper into my hands and leaves quickly, pulling the door shut behind him. I relax and start to breath normally again.

That was weird.

I unfold the paper and repeat the paragraph of words in my head until I know them without looking. I remove my clothes, step into the warm water, and take a deep breath before slipping beneath the surface.

By the time I've completed the charm, got dressed, and partially dried my hair with hot air blown from my hands, I expect Ryn to be asleep. When I walk back into the room, though, he's lying on his back staring at the ceiling.

"Did the gold disappear from the water when you finished the charm?" he asks.

"Yes."

"Good. That means it worked."

I join Ryn on the bed, and, for some reason, it doesn't feel as weird as before. Maybe the warm water relaxed me. I reach over and turn my lamp off.

"Thanks," I say quietly to Ryn.

"You're welcome, V."

I find it surprisingly easy to fall asleep, and it's only when I wake the next morning that I realize Ryn never put the pillow back between us.

CHAPTER SEVEN

"THE GUESTS HAVE BEGUN ARRIVING," RYN SAYS. HE SHUTS the pool house door behind him and walks across the room to his potions kit. "Time to find a way in."

I poke my head around the bathroom door. "Great. Need any help?"

"Not while you're wearing nothing but a towel." He stuffs a vial in his pocket and closes his potions kit. "But thanks."

I place my hands on my hips. "I do actually plan to put clothes on before I leave this room."

"Good to know." He pauses by the door. "You have something appropriate to wear, right?"

I roll my eyes and pull the bathroom door shut. "You don't need to steal me a dress, if that's what you're asking," I say loudly. I hear him chuckle as he leaves.

I drop the towel and begin rummaging through my bag of clothes. I spent part of my weekend with Raven, trying to learn a few clothes casting spells. By the end of our two hour session, the black cocktail dress I'd cast—using a pair of my pants as starting material—didn't look that bad. Raven just had to get rid of the weird long bit that trailed along the floor behind my left foot.

I step into the slim-fitting dress and pull it up. The two pieces of the halter-neck snake around my neck and meet at a silver clasp. The shoes Raven cast for me have heels that are way too high, but I'm afraid if I try to shorten them I'll mess them up in some way. I slip my feet into them and totter over to the mirror. I use a few makeup spells on my face and comb my fingers through my hair. I don't bother doing anything fancy with it—this isn't like the masquerade ball we attended at Zell's house. Lastly, I attach a necklace of silver baubles around my neck. The baubles are hollow and large enough for the miniature versions of my bags to fit inside.

I hear Ryn come back into the room and decide to give him a few minutes to change. I practice walking back and forth across the small bathroom. After doing this about thirty times, I can turn without wobbling.

"You sure are taking a long time in there, Pixie Sticks," Ryn calls.

I quickly shrink my clothes bag before pushing the door open. "I'm ready. Did you figure out a way for us to get in?"

Ryn looks up from tying his shoelace and, instead of answering me, lets out a long whistle. "I think you just graduated from Pixie Sticks to Sexy Pixie."

"Oh, bite me," I snap as I head to the bedside table to fetch my miniature emergency and potions kits.

"I guess I could," he says, "but that would probably make things a little awkward between us."

Ignoring his comment, I conceal my three bags inside the baubles of my necklace. The chain tightens around the back of my neck with the added weight. It isn't exactly comfortable, but I'm not going anywhere without my stuff.

"Where'd you hide your stylus?" Ryn asks.

"Strapped to my leg." Along with my amber and a non-magical knife.

He looks down. "Obviously not the leg with the slit going up it."

Self-conscious, I grab his arm and steer him toward the door. "The slit was not my idea. Now tell me what's happening."

He shuts the door behind us and leads me around the side of the house. "I managed to catch an older woman and a young guy in the entrance hall, and I was kind enough to offer them a welcoming drink."

"Which I'm guessing had a little something extra added to it."

"Compulsion potion. The woman now thinks I'm her nephew who's visiting her for a few days, and you're the young guy's girlfriend."

I hold up the bottom of my dress to keep it from brushing against the damp grass. "Girlfriend. Great."

"What, you don't think you can play the part?" He gives me a wink.

"Hey, I can do whatever is required to complete this assignment. So where are these people you compelled?"

"Waiting obediently in the driveway."

We reach the front of the house and Ryn lets go of my arm. "Is that him?" I ask, nodding my head in the direction of a young man leaning against a car.

"Yes. See you inside." Ryn heads toward an older woman examining her makeup in a small hand mirror.

I walk carefully across the driveway toward my 'date.' He's well built, with fair hair that seems a little messy. When I'm almost in front of him, he looks up. "Uh, hi," he says. His smile is friendly, but uncertain. He has no idea who I am.

Crap, what exactly did Ryn say to this guy? "Um, it's me, Violet."

The moment I say my name, his eyes glaze over for a second. Then he pushes away from the car and reaches for my hand. "You look gorgeous, babe. Did I tell you that earlier?" He places a kiss on my temple and slips his arm around my back. I try to pretend it doesn't freak me out to have a stranger touching me like this. And why are the Harts inviting such a young guy to their dinner party? Shouldn't all their friends be old?

We enter the house and my 'boyfriend'—crap, what is his name?—steers me between the clusters of elegantly dressed people. Most of them are old, as I expected, but I spot a few younger ones. Ryn's already found himself an attractive blonde woman to flirt with.

"You know, you could still make a run for it if you want,"

my date says. "You could always meet my parents another night."

His parents?

"David!" I jump at the sound of Mrs. Hart's voice. She hurries down the last few steps and comes toward us as fast as her loudly clicking high-heeled shoes will allow. "David, I didn't know you were coming tonight." She wraps her arms around him in a quick embrace, submerging us both in a cloud of strong perfume. "Did your father invite you?"

Ah, so this is the Harts' youngest son, the one Mr. Hart spoke to on the phone yesterday morning. I look across the room, catch Ryn's eye, and flash him a quick thumbs up.

"Yeah, Dad asked me to come."

A crease forms between Mrs. Hart's eyebrows. "Are you in trouble again?"

"No, Mom."

"But you'd tell me if there was something going on, wouldn't you?"

"Trust me, Mom." He takes hold of her shoulders. "I am not in any kind of trouble. Now I'd like you to meet my girlfriend." He puts an arm around me and nudges me forward. "This is Violet."

"Oh, hello." She sweeps her gaze over my purple hair and eyes and plasters on a fake smile. "I had no idea David had a girlfriend."

I'm not quite sure what I'm supposed to say to that, so I smile and try not to look too awkward.

"Well, I need to greet my guests," she says to David. "Your father's around somewhere."

74

David watches as she *click-clicks* away, then says, "Sorry about that. My mom's been weird to all the girls I've ever brought home." He laces his fingers between mine and leads me to the edge of the room.

"So, there've been lots of girls, have there?" I try out a flirtatious smile.

"Uh …" He laughs guiltily. "Not that many." He runs his fingers up and down the bare skin on my back—definitely a mistake to cast a dress that scoops so low—while I do my best not to shiver.

"So, why did your father ask you to come tonight? Did he need to talk to you about something important?"

"Oh, you know, just some stuff he's going through at the moment. You wouldn't be interested."

I tilt my head to the side. "Try me."

He looks away, laughing quietly. "It's pretty insane stuff. I don't think you'd actually believe me."

Oh yes I will. "I think you'll find I'm quite open-minded," I say, giving him my most enticing smile.

He turns to me, searching my face. He's going to tell me, I know he is. "Um … no, I shouldn't. It isn't my place to—"

"David, thanks for coming." Mr. Hart appears out of nowhere and grasps his son's hand. He pulls him into a brief hug, then steps back. "I need to show you something." He glances at me, but shows no sign that he recognizes me from yesterday morning. "Uh, can we talk in private?"

"Of course." David's hand slides away from my back. "You don't mind, do you, babe? I won't be long."

"Sure, okay." Of course, if I actually was his girlfriend, I

75

would mind being left alone, but perhaps this way I can listen in on their conversation.

I take note of the direction they're going in, then hurry across the room to Ryn. My feet wobble in their too-high heels, and I catch onto the arm of an older man for balance. "Oops, sorry." I give him an embarrassed laugh before continuing on my way. Ryn is standing in a corner, caressing the cheek of the blonde woman. It looks like he's leaning in for a kiss. I suppress an eye roll and grab his arm. "Come, we need to go."

"Hey!" Miss Blondie looks extremely put out. "We were—"

"Trust me, you're not missing anything," I tell her as I pull Ryn away.

"Trust you?" Ryn looks sideways at me. "How exactly would you know if she's missing anything or not?"

"I may have been six years old, but I haven't forgotten."

"Ah, yes." He nods. "Our first and only kiss. Well, you'll have to trust *me* when I say my kissing skills have improved since then."

"Whatever. Mr. Hart and his son are about to have a private discussion, and I'm pretty sure we need to hear it." I let go of Ryn's arm as we pass through another room of chattering, sophisticated people.

"I see you were getting your flirt on with Mr. Hart, Jr.," Ryn says. He lifts a glass of something bubbly from the tray of a passing waiter and takes a sip before placing the glass on a low table.

"At least I was flirting with someone connected to our assignment. And what are you doing drinking human alcohol?

76

You know what that stuff does to us."

"It was just one sip. You know it takes at least four to get a faerie drunk."

"Wonderful. My assignment partner is a quarter of the way to being drunk." We turn into a hallway just in time to see Mr. Hart opening the door of his study. He ushers his son inside, then shuts the door. "Okay, we need to open a peephole into that room and find out what's going on."

Instead of replying, Ryn stares over my shoulder. His expression is a mixture of confusion and horror.

"What is it?" I start to look behind me, but he grabs my shoulders.

"Nothing!" His grip prevents me from turning. "I thought I recognized someone, but I was wrong."

I pull away from him and look back down the hallway, but whoever was there is now gone. I turn back to him with a frown. "Why don't I believe you?"

"Because you're suspicious by nature?" He laughs in a way that doesn't seem natural. "Remember Cecy?"

"Of course I remember Cecy." She was a friend of ours when we were younger. Her parents were several centuries older than ours, and when they retired from the Guild they decided they didn't want their only child to have a guardian's life. They moved away from Creepy Hollow around about the time of my father's death.

"Yeah, well, I thought I saw someone who looks like her. Anyway, it doesn't matter. Let's get into that study."

Crap, the study! Who knows what we've missed already. Ryn writes on the hallway wall with his stylus, and I hold onto his arm as we walk through the doorway. "Did I tell you about the time Zell followed me through the faerie paths without having any contact with me?"

"That doesn't sound right," Ryn says as darkness envelops us.

"I know. He couldn't possibly have known what destination I was thinking about. So either we were taught the wrong thing about faerie paths, or Zell knows some special way of—"

"Shh, I'm trying to concentrate."

I shut my mouth, and Ryn opens two peepholes on the bookshelf side of Mr. Hart's study.

"Are you sure you're not having some kind of mental breakdown, Dad?" David is leaning against the desk, while Mr. Hart paces across the study's floor.

"You saw this metal thing behind my ear, didn't you?" Mr. Hart pauses in his pacing to point at his neck. "How could a mental breakdown produce that?"

"Well, okay, I guess it can't. But perhaps you had a little operation you forgot to tell me about. Maybe it's some new kind of hearing aid you don't remember having put in."

"Rubbish." Mr. Hart continues pacing. "There's nothing wrong with my memory. And why are you arguing with me now? You seemed to believe me when we spoke on the phone."

David scratches his head. "I was trying to calm you down."

"Calm me down?" Mr. Hart's fists are balled at his sides, and a vein throbs visibly on his forehead.

"You're asking me to believe in *faeries*, Dad." David throws his hands up. "Can you see the problem here?"

"The problem isn't *believing* in them, David. I've known

about them for years. Ever since we moved into this house."

"What?" David's brow furrows. "You didn't mention that on the phone."

"Because that wasn't the point! The point is that my life is being threatened. My family members are being threatened."

"By fictional characters," David mutters.

Mr. Hart ignores his son's comment and collapses into an armchair in the corner. "All these years of throwing the best parties," he says wistfully. "The magnificent food and drinks, the out-of-this-world entertainment." He shakes his head. "It's finally come back to bite me in the ass."

"What are you talking about?" David starts to look concerned as his father leans forward and rests his head in his hands.

"Shortly after we moved here, a faerie showed up in this very room one night and explained that the house was actually his. He claimed to have many homes, some in the fae realm and some here. He didn't want any of his own kind knowing this house belonged to him—he liked to hide things here, he said—so he allowed us to continue living here as a cover-up. Then he showed me the underground part of our home."

"The underground part?" David looks even more confused now.

"He forbade me from telling anyone about it, of course. But I need your help, and it seems this is the only way you'll believe me." He stands up, walks behind his desk, and removes a bottle of whiskey from a low drawer. He carries the bottle to the potted plant in the corner behind the door, unscrewing the top as he goes.

"Okay, I think you're taking this too far now, Dad."

"I took this too far the day I agreed to continue living here." And with that, Mr. Hart turns the bottle upside down and pours it over the plant. Instead of liquid, a black dust comes pouring out. The plant shimmers for a moment, then disintegrates into multi-colored wisps of cloud before disappearing. In its place is a perfectly round hole in the wooden floor. Steps lead downward.

"Oh. Holy. Cow," David whispers.

"Indeed." Mr. Hart locks his office door before heading down the stairs. "I'll assume you're following me, David."

Ryn waits for David to follow his father, then widens the opening out of the faerie paths. "We need to be careful," he says. "It would be better if they don't know we're following them."

"Yes, I get it, come on." I slip my heels off and carry them in one hand as I lead the way down the stairs. I reach a passageway with white walls and a wooden floor, just like the rest of the house. Soft light filters down from small round circles in the ceiling. The end of the passage isn't too far ahead, and Mr. Hart's voice carries easily back to us.

"I suppose I've always known I was nothing more than a toy to him. He made our parties spectacular with his enchanted food, drinks and entertainment. But it was all for his own enjoyment, I'm sure. He was just playing with us like dolls in a doll house."

I get to the end of the passage and peek around the corner. Ryn puts his hand on my arm, as if to hold me back. As if I'd really be stupid enough to go marching in there. I stretch my neck a little further and see a room with a lounge suite in the middle and shelves lining the walls. Hundreds of objects sit on the shelves. Different colored stones, a chipped jug, a pulsating green blob, a kettle with red smoke wafting from its spout—this room is a treasure trove of ... stuff.

"Is this *he* the same one who threatened your life?" David is walking slowly around the room, examining various objects, while his father sits on one of the couches.

"Yes. I told you what he gave me, didn't I?" David nods and pokes curiously at a plant with wiggling gel-like leaves. "He was in a rush that night. He forced the box into my hands and told me to bring it down here immediately. He'd stolen it from someone, and this someone was after him. He said that if I told *anyone* about it he would make me watch the torturous death of every member of my family. And then he'd kill me."

David looks up. "But you told me about it."

"Because I'm desperate." Mr. Hart rises from the couch. "I need your help getting away from here. I don't want to be part of this anymore."

"And you think I can help you?"

"I know you have friends who can help your mother and me ... disappear."

David stares at his father, his expression revealing nothing. "You think I have friends like that?"

"I *know* you do. Don't think I haven't forgotten about the fake driver's license."

David looks down, then around the room once more. "So where is this precious box that's caused you so much stress?"

Mr. Hart walks over to the chipped jug I noticed and picks

it up. He turns it upside down and out tumbles a small black box. "That's the only way to get anything out of this jug," he tells David. "If you put your hand inside, the jug bites you and forces your hand back out."

"Bites you?"

"Yes. I found that out the painful way."

With eyes full of wonder—and a little fear—David takes the box. He opens it carefully and pulls something out. A silver chain with a pendant. I can't see much except that it's small and simple. David holds it up in front of his face where it swings slowly back and forth. "What's so important about this piece of jewelry that an entire family could die if anyone found out about it?"

"I don't know. I'm just the keeper of these items. I have no idea what they do unless I find out for myself, and I lost my curiosity after I almost lost my hand."

Ryn tugs me back around the corner and whispers, "We just need to get that necklace and we can leave, assignment complete."

"I know. I'll see if I can get it." I open a doorway on the wall, then hesitate, biting my lip.

"What's wrong?" Ryn asks. "Do you want me to do it?"

"No, it's just ... if we take the necklace and that Unseelie faerie returns before the Harts manage to leave, he'll kill them all."

Ryn nods slowly. "Probably. But protecting Mr. Hart and his family isn't part of our assignment."

"I know. But isn't that the point of who we are? We're

supposed to protect people, Ryn, not put them in even more danger."

He closes his eyes with a sigh. "Dammit. I know you're right. I just really wanted to finish this assignment now."

"Yeah, so did I." I really, *really* want to finish it. We'd be back at the Guild three days early, a feat that could earn us loads of bonus points. But how could I live with myself if my actions caused a whole lot of innocent people to die? "Okay, I'll go get the necklace, and you think about how we're going to help Mr. Hart and his wife safely disappear."

I walk into the paths and focus all my attention on the couch Mr. Hart was sitting on earlier. I catch the doorway the moment it begins opening, keeping it the size of a coin. I look out and see nothing but dark fabric right in front of me. It moves slightly as I hear David's voice close by. Okay, so David is sitting on the couch now, and I'm behind it, unable to see anything. I close the tiny hole and imagine myself next to the arm of the couch instead—and that's pretty much where I seem to be when I look out a second time. I can see over the rounded edge of the couch's arm, over David's knee, and straight toward a low rectangular table. Sitting on the table is the box.

I remove my amber and stylus from the strap around my thigh and quickly write a message to Ryn. *Create a distraction so they both look away from the table.* I return the amber and stylus and wait. Several moments later, I notice a blue spark hit the pot holding the wiggling-leaf plant. The pot explodes, sending soil in all directions. Mr. Hart and David jump to their feet immediately. I widen the opening, reach over the edge of the couch, and grab the box. I open it and slip the necklace out, then replace the box and step backward into the safety of the paths.

I create another opening near one of the walls and peek out. Mr. Hart is examining the remains of the plant, while David stands nearby, circling on the spot as he examines the room with his eyes. "Why did that happen?" he asks. "Does it mean someone's here?"

"I don't think so. But we should leave anyway. Now that I've proved to you I'm not insane, I think it's time you helped me disappear. I just need to find—"

"No one's leaving until I know exactly what's going on here," a new voice says. Cold, lazy, condescending. "And once my curiosity is satisfied, I'd be happy to make you disappear."

CHAPTER EIGHT

TALL AND SLIM AND DRESSED ENTIRELY IN BLACK, THE faerie stalks slowly across the room toward Mr. Hart. His hair is white-blonde with black streaks, and his eyes are cold black holes. Rings with multi-colored gems glitter on his fingers, and silver spikes protrude from the back of his boots.

Oh crap, crap, crap. Who is this guy? I'm not easily scared, but there's something about him that freaks me out. I hurriedly shrink the necklace and pop it into one of the hollow balls around my neck. Should I go back to the passage to find Ryn? Should I stay here?

"Start explaining," the faerie says. "Now. What is all this magical junk doing in a human home? Who gave it to you?"

My amber vibrates against my thigh, and I quickly remove it. *Not in passage anymore. Antique wardrobe next to shelf with glowing orb. Come here.* I look out the peephole. My eyes dart to the various cupboards and wardrobes around the room until I see the antique one beside an orb. I close up the hole in front of me and concentrate hard on being *inside* the wardrobe. I certainly don't want to show up in front of it.

The darkness of the faerie paths is suffocating. It seems to take forever, but eventually I notice a sliver of light in front of me and feel a hard surface beneath my feet. I can also feel a presence invading my personal space.

"That you, V?" Ryn's voice is right beside me.

"Did you invite someone else into a small, dark wardrobe with you?" I whisper back.

He chuckles quietly. "Not recently."

"So what can you see from here?"

"Just about everything. The wardrobe doors don't meet properly, so there's a good view of the room." I can see his outline as he puts his eye to the sliver of light. "Mr. Hart's been stammering out some explanation I can't really hear, and David's looking edgy."

"Well, I'm ready to jump out there and fight this faerie the moment he shows any signs of hurting them."

"You think you can take on this guy in high-heeled shoes and a cocktail dress?"

"My shoes are in the passage, but yes. I could." In all honesty, I'd probably fall flat on my butt if I tried to fight in heels, but I'm not about to tell Ryn that.

"This faerie obviously isn't the one Mr. Hart was talking about," Ryn murmurs, his eye still glued to the crack between the doors. "I wonder what interest he has in this situation."

I press my ear to the door and try to hear what's going on. With nothing else to look at, my eyes absently trace the profile of Ryn's face. His perfect nose, his full lips, his strong jawline. His eyes are so blue I can make out their color even in the almost darkness. And those lips. Definitely kissable.

Okay, what? I push the startling thought aside immediately. *Focus, Violet.* I kneel down on the floor of the wardrobe and peer through the crack into the room.

"Things are about to get very bad for you," the faerie says as he circles Mr. Hart and David like a predator stalking its prey. "Do you know why? Because you silly humans have been conspiring against the *Queen*."

"W-what?" Mr. Hart stammers.

"Which one?" I whisper.

"That's quite an accusation for two humans who probably have no idea of the existence of *either* queen," Ryn says.

"B-but how?" Mr. Hart asks. He's visibly shaking now. "What have I done?"

"You're about to find out."

The wall behind Mr. Hart ripples and melts away to reveal a woman in a long, flowing gown of black and silver. The two colors shimmer like coals in a fire. Black lace covers her arms and a choker of glowing pearls encircles her neck. Tiny crystals sparkle in her hair, which is black and blonde and caught up in an elaborate twisting style on top of her head. She surveys the room with a look of disdain.

"Holy freaking goblin babies," Ryn whispers. "Do you *know* who that is?"

My mouth is dry as I whisper, "I think I can guess."

There's only one person it can be: *The Unseelie Queen.*

"Savyon," she says in a commanding voice as she sweeps out of the faerie paths. "Have you found it yet?"

"No, but we're in the right place," the first faerie says. "This human has confirmed it."

"Human?" The Queen walks slowly toward Mr. Hart. Without warning, her hand darts forward and wraps around his neck. She squeezes. "What do you know of my necklace?" she demands.

Mr. Hart moves his mouth, but no words come out.

"Stop it!" David shouts. He has a gun gripped tightly in his hands, pointed straight at the Queen.

"A gun?" She laughs at him. "Don't be absurd, human." The hand that isn't around Mr. Hart's neck flashes out. Blood spurts suddenly and horribly from David's chest, and he falls to the ground with a cry of agony.

I gasp, then slap a hand over my mouth at the same time as Ryn moves to do the same thing. The queen's head whips around, her hard black eyes pointed in our direction. We freeze. My hand covering my mouth, Ryn's hand covering mine, his lips right beside my ear whispering, "Don't. Move."

"How DARE YOU come into my home?" a new voice yells, one that I recognize instantly. If I weren't so scared of the Queen right now, I'd probably roll my eyes in disbelief. Seriously? Why does everything these days seem to involve *Zell?*

The first faerie, Savyon, turns toward the other side of the room where Zell is standing. "I don't think it is your home, little brother, or we would've needed your permission to enter through the paths."

Little brother? So that would make Savyon a prince too. Another one of the Unseelie Queen's sons.

Zell's crimson eyes glitter with fury as he strides across the room, his finger pointed at his brother. "It isn't a faerie home, but it is still *mine*, and I swear I will tear you apart if you do not leave RIGHT NOW."

Ryn finally pulls his hand away from mine and presses it to his chest as though he's in pain. "You okay?" I whisper.

He nods.

"Stop behaving like a child, Marzell," the Queen snaps.

"GET OUT, MOTHER!" he yells. Bright red sparks dance across his skin, and two of the small round lights in the ceiling explode.

"You stole my eternity necklace!" the Queen shrieks. "Did you really think I wouldn't come after you?"

Zell's eyes move to Mr. Hart, still dangling from the Queen's powerful grip. Zell lunges forward, throwing his hands out. Glass shards fly through the air and embed themselves in Mr. Hart's chest. The old man gasps and gurgles, and the Queen drops him to the floor in disgust. He struggles for a while, like David did, then goes still.

I feel sick.

"He didn't tell me where the necklace is," the Queen says. She clearly hasn't noticed the little box on the table. "But you will, Marzell. I don't care that you are my son. You have been against me for a long time now, and I will torture you until you tell me *everything* you've been doing behind my back."

Ryn moves beside me and whispers, "I'm opening a

doorway back to the Guild. This is more than we can handle on our own."

The Queen spins around once more, the skirts of her gown sweeping the floor. "Who dares to spy on us?" she shouts. I feel myself yanked forward. I crash through the wardrobe doors, fly through the air, and sprawl across the floor at the Queen's feet. Ryn groans beside me.

I mentally call to one of my guardian weapons—a dagger. It appears in my hand with a rush of golden sparkles, but sizzles and vanishes the moment the Queen wraps her cold fingers around my wrist.

"A guardian?" she says in surprise as she bends over me. "Well, it will be a pleasure to kill you, my dear." She raises her other hand and—

"No!" Zell shouts.

The Queen hesitates, a cruel smile curling her lips. She looks up. "Did you say something, Marzell?"

Zell's eyes seem to glow with fury, and magic crackles at his fingertips. He clenches both hands into fists and slowly says, "I will return the eternity necklace if you give me the girl."

The Queen grabs Ryn's wrist with her other hand—causing the glittering arrow he was about to stab her with to disappear—and hauls us both to our feet. "So the girl means something to you, does she? Well, in that case, you most certainly may not have her. I'll lock them both up while I take care of *you*, my dear son." And with that she pushes us away from her. We tumble onto the floor, black smoke swirling around us. It twists and curls, thickening by the moment until the air is as black as the faerie paths.

"Ryn?" I call.

"Here," he answers. I wave my hand in the direction of his voice and manage to catch onto his arm. The smoke spins us wildly around. I feel sick and dizzy and unable to focus on anything except the hand I'm holding tightly onto, and then— *wham*! We hit the floor again. Except it doesn't feel like the floor anymore. And it no longer smells like an enclosed room.

The black smoke lifts quickly, revealing a forest lit dimly by twilight. Sprites dance about on a tree branch above us; they laugh as they tease the evening glow-bugs that are beginning to come out.

"Are we in Creepy Hollow?" I ask.

"It feels like it."

"Yes, it does." I climb to my feet, smoothing my hands down my dress. "But why would she send us back here? I thought she said something about locking us up."

Ryn shakes his head as he stands up. "I don't know."

I look around. "Hey, isn't that our gargan tree? The one we always used to climb?"

"Yes."

I walk slowly toward it, feeling a small tug at my heart. The last time I was up there, Nate was with me. We lay in the hollow created by the arms right at the top of the ancient tree. Nate asked me out on a date. A date where he then betrayed me. It makes me sad to think about it, but not as sad as it used to. I think I'm getting over it.

As I get closer, the shape of a person comes into view just on the other side of the tree. "Hello?" I call. I think of my bow and arrow, and they appear immediately, fitting perfectly into my outstretched arms. I tilt my head. "Who's there?"

The person steps away from the tree and turns around to face me. My heart begins pattering out an uneven rhythm because I *know* this guy standing in front of me. I can't remember ever meeting him, yet something about him is undeniably familiar. He looks a bit like Ryn, but he also looks a lot like an older version of—

"Reed," Ryn whispers.

My bow and arrow fizzle away into nothing as I realize that that's exactly who I'm looking at. But how? He's supposed to be *dead*.

"Vi, is that you?" he asks. He takes a step toward me as his mouth turns up in that exact same smile that always used to warm my heart.

My throat tightens, and moisture gathers at the corners of my eyes. "This can't be real," I whisper.

He takes another step toward me and holds out his hand, but I don't take it. I so badly want this to be real. I so badly want it to be Reed who's standing in front of me, but it *can't* be. It isn't possible. We had a celebration-of-life ceremony. I watched his body float magically upriver in a flower-laden canoe and vanish beneath the Infinity Falls.

As if in a daze, Ryn walks slowly past me until he's standing right in front of Reed. "Am I imagining you?" he asks.

That smile again. "Don't I look real to you, brother?"

Ryn pulls Reed into a tight hug and says thickly, "I've missed you so much." It's so odd to see them together that I begin to think I must have hit my head when the Queen pushed me to the ground. This has to be a dream, right?

Reed pulls back and rests a hand on Ryn's shoulder. "I've missed you too, Oryn. But you know I always loved Violet more than I loved you."

Okay, what?

"That's why I went to visit her on that terrible day, even after you begged me to stay home. She was more important to me than you ever were." Reed's eyes slide away from Ryn's and meet mine. "She's the one I've missed the most."

No way. This definitely isn't the Reed I remember. I take hold of Ryn's arm. "This isn't real, Ryn. Don't listen to him."

Ryn stumbles backward, looking a little stunned. "I think it might be," he says. His eyes are glazed over as he stares at nothing. "I always wondered if ... if that was really the way he felt." He shakes his head and looks down, his face the picture of defeat. It unnerves me.

"Hey!" I lightly slap his cheek. "Snap out of it. I don't know what's happening here, but I'm pretty sure none of it's real."

"Pretty sure?" Reed says. I turn to look at him. "We live in a world of magic, V. Is it really so impossible that I'm standing right in front of you? Is it so impossible that I might love you? We grew up together. We did everything together. You were my best friend and—"

"And then you died," I fill in. I let go of Ryn's arm and begin drawing power from the center of my being. "And it was horrible and it sucked and it *still* sucks, but that is what happened. And the Reed I knew wouldn't have said what you just said to Ryn. He loved his brother more than anything else, so I don't know what twisted creation of magic you are, but you need to GO!" I throw everything I've got at him: a translucent, shimmering ball of raw magic. It strikes him in the stomach and throws him backward onto the ground.

Abruptly, the black smoke returns, dancing and swirling around us. I grasp Ryn's hand before the darkness engulfs us once more. We spin faster this time, landing on the hard floor within seconds. I blink, taking a moment to orient myself. I swat at the last remaining wisps of smoke, then get to my feet as quickly as I can.

Wind sweeps my hair off my shoulders. The sounds of smashing, splintering and shouting fill the air. Objects fly past as they get caught up in a whirlwind of debris. In the midst of it all, Zell and his mother are doing battle. Savyon appears to be gone.

I point my bow and arrow into the heart of the fight as Ryn stands up beside me. "You okay?" I ask.

"Yeah."

"What the hell just happened?" I dodge a flying book and a stray spark of magic.

"I don't know, but we need to get some other guardians here as soon as possible."

"Okay, you open the doorway, and I'll make sure you don't get hit by—Whoa!" I jump out of the way of a spinning broomstick. It strikes the floor and cracks in half, emitting a high-pitched screech as the two halves strike relentlessly at the floor. "Stuff like that," I finish.

"Stop!" the Queen shrieks. Everything in the room freezes, then crashes to the floor. I look up and see Zell struggling behind a tangle of enchanted vines. The Queen is staring directly at me.

"Quickly!" I say to Ryn. I let my bow and arrow vanish and throw up an invisible shield of magic instead. The air ripples where the Queen's magic strikes against it. A doorway opens beside me. Ryn reaches for my hand—but I'm thrown backward as a blast of black sparks breaches my shield.

Pain tears through my body as I strike the wall and slide down to the floor. I roll my head to the side with a groan. The Queen's shimmering black and silver gown brushes the floor as she comes toward me. I look past her to where Ryn and I were standing. The doorway in the air is gone. So is Ryn.

Oh my crap, *did he just leave without me?*

"I see you managed to break out," the Queen says, holding a hand up in front of her. I can sense a shield between us.

"Break out?" I ask. I still have no idea how we got to Creepy Hollow.

"Of your head," she says. "Or his head. I can't quite remember where I sent the two of you." A wicked grin spreads across her face. "But you can probably figure it out. Whose deepest, darkest desires and fears did you witness?"

Ryn's. Definitely Ryn's.

Great. He is not going to like the fact that I was locked up inside his head with him. And I can't believe he left me here!

"I have no idea who you are," the Queen says, "but my son seems to think you're valuable. Why exactly is that?"

I try to shrug, but it hurts too much. "Why don't you ask him?"

Her eyes harden and her voice is cold as she says, "I'd love to, but I'm currently trying to get more important information out of him."

Oh yes. Her eternity necklace—whatever that is. Well, she can torture Zell as much as she likes, but he'll never be able to tell her the truth: that it's hidden inside my own necklace.

A ripping sound from the other side of the room alerts us to the fact that Zell is breaking free of his magical bonds. The Queen moves her shield hand behind her. With the invisible layer of protection gone from between us, I think of my knife and take hold of it from the air. I'm about to throw it at the Queen when I feel something tighten around my arm. The knife disappears as thick, leafy vines slither around my wrists. My skin stings where the leaves touch me, and I feel oddly sapped of strength. I scratch feebly at the leaves with my free hand, but they jump across to my other wrist, binding my hands together.

"And up you go," the Queen says, raising her hand to the ceiling. In one swift motion, I find myself dangling from the ceiling. My shoulders ache as my arms threaten to pop out of their sockets. "You won't be going anywhere now; you need exceptional strength to get out of those." She steps away from me. "I shall be back for you when I'm done with my son, and you *will* tell me what is so important about you, or it won't be long before you know every horror of the Unseelie Court, little guardian."

CHAPTER NINE

THE QUEEN WALKS AWAY FROM ME, VANISHING AND THEN reappearing on the other side of the room. How did she do that? The faerie paths? She slashes her hand through the air in the shape of an X. Icicles materialize in front of her, and she pushes hard against them, sending them straight at Zell. He blasts away the final cords of vine and sends the icicles scattering with one sweep of his hand. They melt before they reach the floor.

"You don't deserve to be immortal!" he yells at his mother. "I will never give you that necklace!" And with that, he launches himself at the Queen.

Hail, dirt and rain spin around them. They kick and hit and dodge as if in some furious yet expertly choreographed dance. I'm not sure how she does it, but the Queen never once trips over her gown. Despite the stinging pain in my wrists and the fact that I should be trying to escape, I find myself mesmerized. I'm watching Unseelie royalty fight one another; I could learn something from this.

As if he can hear my thoughts, Zell spins out of the way of a flock of crows and disappears into the passage. After throwing a giant ball of licking green flames after him, the Queen follows.

Great. I struggle against the vines, spinning myself uselessly around and causing even more pain in my wrists. I get nowhere. I give up and let out a cry of frustration. Zell and the Queen are gone, Ryn is gone, and I'm hanging helplessly from a ceiling in a long dress. This is *so* not my style.

"Look at you," a voice below me says, "playing the damsel in distress."

I glare down at Ryn. "Oh, how nice of you to show up. Where exactly did you disappear to?"

"I've been watching from the faerie paths."

"And you couldn't help me out a little earlier?"

"I was waiting for the right opportunity, like Zell and his mommy conveniently disappearing into another room."

"Why didn't you go back to the Guild for help?"

He frowns. "You're my partner, V. I wouldn't just leave you here."

We stare at each other for a moment before I wriggle some more and say, "Well, are you going to get me down from here or what?"

He crosses his arms and tilts his head to the side. "I'm actually rather enjoying this."

"Dammit, Ryn, I am in serious pain here!" I shout as tears

begin to prick the back of my eyes. The skin around my hands and wrists is screaming out for relief.

"Sorry," he says, hurriedly swiping his hand through the air. The vine connecting me to the ceiling is severed. I drop swiftly. Ryn steps forward and catches me easily, as if catching falling girls is something he does all the time. With the vines gone, I feel an immediate return of my power. The burning ache around my wrists and hands lingers on, though.

"That looks nasty," Ryn says as he places me on the floor.

I look up and notice a shimmer in the air over his shoulder. A person exiting the faerie paths. "Hey—"

"Got you!" Savyon says. He steps deftly around Ryn and seizes me by the wrist. He grasps Ryn's wrist in his other hand. A crazy second passes where we all seem to freeze, then Savyon jumps away from us. Feeling something cold on my arm, I look down. A band of metal encircles my wrist.

"No!" I shout, balling my fists in anger as I recognize the metal. "Dammit!"

"Fun, aren't they?" Savyon says. "I found them hidden in Zell's quarters at the Unseelie Palace. Seems my little brother has been hiding many fun toys from me."

Furious at having to endure one of these magic-blocking bands for a second time, I pull my non-guardian knife out of its strap on my thigh and stab it into the side of Savyon's neck without a second thought. He's clearly so shocked I can do anything without magic that he barely manages to retaliate before Ryn kicks him hard in the chest.

"Is this what I think it is?" Ryn demands, holding his arm up as Savyon crashes into one of the couches.

"If you're thinking that you're now magic-less, then yes." I dig my nails into my palms and kick my stupid dress away from where it's getting tangled around my feet. *Crapping crap!* How are we supposed to get back to the Guild now? How are we supposed to finish our assignment?

Blood gushes from Savyon's neck as he climbs to his feet, splattering dark crimson patches on the white couch. He yanks the knife from his neck and holds his hand to the wound. His voice is dangerously low when he speaks. "You just made a very big mistake."

"So did you," I say through gritted teeth. "You've now made it *very* hard for me to return to the Guild and complete my assignment. You just got between me and the top graduating position, and you have *no idea* how furious that makes me."

Before I can make a move, one half of a broomstick flies through the air toward Savyon, followed closely by the second half. The two pieces of wood proceed to beat Savyon up as they screech wildly. "I'm kind of furious myself," Ryn says. He looks at me from the corner of his eye. "Although I seem to be containing it better than you."

The broomstick pieces come flying back at us, and we duck out of the way. Savyon vanishes the same way his mother did, then reappears right beside Ryn. He jabs my knife at Ryn, but I push Ryn out of the way and the knife slices across the top of my right arm.

Great, that won't be healing for a while.

Ryn spins around and lands a punch to Savyon's stomach, then gets forced back by a giant bat conjured up by a single word from Savyon. The bat flaps wildly around Ryn's head as Savyon comes after me. He pins my arms to my sides just as I bring my knee up as hard as I can. His face contorts and he groans in agony, but doesn't let go of me. He twists me around so my back is against his chest. He loops one arm around my neck.

"Mother thinks you must be important somehow, so I'm not allowed to kill you," he breathes into my ear. "But that doesn't mean I can't have some fun with you. Shall we spend some time in my bedroom when we get back to the palace?"

"You're disgusting," Ryn growls, appearing suddenly beside us. "And if you're looking for your magical bat, it's currently crammed inside a clay jar." And with that he brings his fist up to meet Savyon's chin.

The Unseelie Prince loses his grip on me as his head snaps back. He stumbles away, regains his footing, and levels his gaze at us. "You know you can't defeat me without magic," he says with a maniacal laugh. He points his right hand at Ryn; the gesture is almost lazy, but the black sparks that shoot toward Ryn are powerful enough to knock him off his feet and into the air. When he hits the ground, he doesn't move.

Crap. I need to check if he's okay, but Savyon has set a new whirlwind into motion. Broken items lift off the ground and begin to swirl around me, trapping me in their funnel. I grab onto a stray piece of vine, then force my way out of the mini tornado, shielding my face with my arms. Tiny cuts sting my skin. My hand burns where the vine leaves touch it, but I'm not letting go of my only weapon. I lash out at Savyon, using the vine like a whip. The end catches him across the cheek. He grunts in anger as I snap the makeshift whip a second time. His hand flashes out and grabs the end of the vine. He tugs me forward, but I let go just in time.

"Come here!" he shouts. He reaches into the air with fingernails painted black. Against my will, I find myself skidding over the floor toward him. I try to fight it, but I end up falling over. I see light glimmering off a sharp edge and grab onto the shard of blue glass as I slide past it. The jagged edge slices into my already burning palm. But I can't think about the pain right now. As I crash into Savyon's booted feet, I raise my arm to stab the glass into his leg. He kicks my arm aside, and the glass goes flying. I throw myself after it, but he grabs my legs and yanks me back. My scrabbling fingers reach desperately for the glass, but I'm already being pulled away. Savyon drags me across the floor and flings me around so that my body slams into the side of the couch.

Pain!

I try desperately to suck some air into my lungs as I look around for something, anything, I can use as a weapon. Then I see it—the handle end of the broken broomstick. With all the strength I can muster, I reach out and wrap my blood-covered fingers around the wood. Savyon grabs my waist, flings me over onto my back—and I shove the splintered end deep into his abdomen, just below his ribcage.

He gurgles and chokes as I kick him away from me. Still gasping for air, I get to my feet and stumble over to Ryn. I shake him, then slap his cheek a few times with my non-bloodied hand. "Get ... up," I manage to say as my breath returns to me. I shake him some more, accidently spreading blood across his white shirt. "Come on, Ryn, we have to get out of here."

Nothing.

I lean over and speak right into his ear. "Please, please, please get up. I can't leave without you."

Nothing.

Then I see movement behind his eyelids, and he suddenly jerks awake. "What—how did—" He blinks as his gaze travels over me. "You look awful. Are you okay?"

I feel pretty awful. In fact, little sparks of light that I'm pretty sure aren't real are beginning to dance in front of my eyes. "I'm fine." I blink a few times as I stand up and tug his arm. "We have to run. Now!"

He jumps up and heads for the passage, pulling me after him. I hear Savyon shouting behind us, and I run as fast as my injured body will allow. I should be in a lot of pain, but adrenaline seems to be masking most of it—for now.

We run up the stairs and into Mr. Hart's study, which looks like a hurricane hit it. The window has been shattered, and torn books and broken furniture litter the floor. Smoke catches in my throat, and I can hear screaming coming from the rest of the house. "Oh crap, what have they done?" I whisper. A group of coughing, choking people run past the open door. We step into the smoky corridor as a shoeless Mrs. Hart comes running in the opposite direction.

"The children are upstairs!" she screams, heading into the smoky darkness.

Ryn runs after her and grabs her by the arm. "Get her outside, V," he shouts. "I'll get the children." He forces a struggling Mrs. Hart into my arms. "I promise I'll get them," he says to her. Then he turns and disappears into the smoke.

I drag Mrs. Hart down the corridor, through various rooms, and out the front door. Terrified guests are congregated in the driveway, their faces reflecting the orange glow of the burning house as they stare up at it.

"Get back!" I shout. "Get away from the house!"

They stumble further back just as an explosion causes the ground to shudder.

"No!" Mrs. Hart screams. She covers her face with her hands as she begins wailing. Her whole body shakes.

"It'll be okay," I say to her, patting her back as I try to ignore the growing pain in just about every part of my body. "I'm sure he'll get the children—"A second explosion rends the air with a force that almost knocks us off our feet.

Oh flipping hell. For a few terrifying moments, I consider the possibility that Ryn might actually be dead. My brain rejects the thought almost as soon as I allow it in, though. It's too foreign a concept. Ryn has always been in my life, whether as a friend or a giant-ass thorn in my side. He can't just be *gone.*

And he isn't. Instead of emerging miraculously from the burning house, I see him running around the side, the two Hart grandchildren in tow. "Look!" I say to Mrs. Hart, pointing at the three running figures. She makes a sound halfway between a wail and a laugh. She tries to run toward them, but I hold her back until they reach us. The two dripping wet children fall into her arms.

I refrain from throwing my arms around Ryn because that

would be weird. Instead I ask, "Why are you wet?"

"Swimming pool," he gasps, still catching his breath. "We had a few flaming clothes by the time we got out the house."

"Edgar," Mrs. Hart whimpers as she clings to her grandchildren. "David. Where are they?"

"We need to go," Ryn says quietly as he takes my arm, which is a good thing because I feel a little bit like I might fall over. "I didn't see the Queen or Zell anywhere, but they might be nearby." Sirens echo in the distance as we slip away from the crowd. We run down the driveway, through the open gate, and onto the road.

"How are we going to get back?" I ask. I'm struggling to keep up with Ryn. Every inch of my body aches from being slammed against that couch, and my skin is on fire wherever the ivy touched it. Blood trickles down my arm and drips off my fingertips. Nausea creeps over me. I wish I had my boots on. I wish I didn't have a dress slapping around my ankles. And why is everything starting to look white?

I don't know how I wind up on my knees on the pavement with my stomach heaving, but that's where I seem to be. I think Ryn is saying something, but I can't hear him over the weird rushing in my ears. And everything seems to be getting whiter. Or blacker. Or white fading into black.

I try to fight it because that's what I'm meant to do, right? But it's such hard work, and Ryn is right beside me, ready to catch me, so why not give in?

I let the blackness take me.

CHAPTER TEN

I WAKE UP WITH MY BACK ON SOMETHING SOFT AND MY legs on something prickly. My head doesn't feel weird and woozy anymore, but the rest of my body still aches. I blink a few times and the moon comes into focus behind a silhouette of tree branches.

"Damn, I was hoping you'd stay knocked out a little longer," Ryn says from somewhere beside me.

I push myself up, wincing at the pain in my hands. "And why is that? Were you enjoying the quiet?"

"No, I'm about to break into a house and steal stuff, and I figured you wouldn't approve."

I look past the tree I'm sitting beneath and see a house. "Are we in someone's garden?"

"Yes."

"And you're going to steal from whoever lives in there?"

"Yes. There are things we need if we're hoping to get home alive, and we need to make do without magic until we get there."

Remembering the deep gash across my right arm, I look down. The wound is hidden beneath a tightly wrapped piece of fabric that looks suspiciously like my dress. Moving my gaze further down, I notice the dress is shorter than the last time I looked at it. "I see you've been busy tearing up my clothes."

"You're not healing," he says quietly. "I needed to try and stop the bleeding with something."

"It's because of this." I point to the narrow strip of metal wrapped around my right wrist. It's in pretty much the same position as the first metal band Zell slapped onto me. I suppose I should be grateful I'll only have one scar when this is all over. "Our magic won't heal us while we have these bands on, and I don't know how to remove them."

"That seems unlike you. I thought you knew everything."

"Well, I don't know this spell, and I don't have the special instrument, so bite me," I say feebly as I lie down again. Weakness isn't a feeling I'm particularly enjoying.

"Okay, I'm going into the house," Ryn says. "Just ... don't go anywhere."

Like I have somewhere to go. "For once, I'm happy not to argue with you."

His footsteps are barely audible as he treads away. I try to get comfortable, but it's difficult when it feels like the whole of my back is covered in bruises. I turn onto my left side and look down at the soft thing I'm lying on. It's Ryn's jacket. It smells like smoke, but it also smells like him. Weird. Not the smell, but the fact that I recognize it. It's a nice scent, kind of woodsy and citrusy. I hold the sleeve to my nose and breathe deeply.

Violet Fairdale, would you stop *being weird?*

I drop the sleeve and close my eyes.

I'm not sure, but I think I sleep for a while because it feels like only seconds later when a hand touches my arm and I open my eyes with a start. "It's me," Ryn says. He sits down beside me and places a backpack on the grass in front of him. "Turns out I'm an excellent burglar."

"No surprise there." I turn carefully onto my back. "What did you get?"

"Some food, a blanket, a map book, and their entire first aid kit."

"Ryn," I groan. "You don't think they'll need their first aid kit at some point?"

"Not as much as you need it right now."

"And it's human stuff," I add. "It probably won't even work on me."

"Your magic's blocked," Ryn says. "Right now you're as close to being human as you'll ever get, so this stuff might just work." He pulls out a white plastic box with a red cross on it and begins sifting through the contents. "Antiseptic," he reads. "Sounds good." He leans over and begins dabbing the cream onto the many small cuts scattered across my arms. "Can you sit up?" he asks. "I saw some cuts on your back."

The prospect of sitting up doesn't seem that appealing, but I do it anyway. Ryn's fingers move carefully across my back, applying the cream that will probably have no effect on me whatsoever. "I'm having a weird sense of déjà vu right now," I say quietly. "Except last time it was *me* fixing something on *your* back."

"Oh, yeah," he says. "The poisoned glass." He moves to my side and carefully unties the black fabric around my upper arm. Blood starts oozing from the wound again.

"I think humans get stitches for cuts this deep," I say.

"Yes, well, we'll have to make a plan without stitches." Ryn digs around inside the plastic box and removes a few things. After wiping some liquid over the wound—which stings like *hell* and makes tears spring up in my eyes—he closes it up by sticking a line of tiny plasters over it. He then wraps a bandage around my arm. "Anything else?" he asks.

"Um, my hands," I say weakly. I'm still a little shaky after the sudden spike of pain caused by the liquid antiseptic. This whole experience is making me feel vulnerable in a way I'm not used to at all—and that I do not like one bit.

"Are they burnt?" Ryn asks, taking a closer look at my hands.

"I think so. It was those vines she tied me up with."

Ryn reads the labels on a few more tubes before selecting one. He takes my right hand and squirts some clear gel onto my palm. I brace myself for more pain, but instead I feel relief. I breathe out a sigh as he gently rubs the gel into my palm, across my fingers, and up my wrist, moving carefully around the metal band. It feels strangely intimate. I'm suddenly aware of how close he's sitting to me. I'm aware of his knee touching my thigh, and his hand carefully holding mine. I watch his face as he works, his beautiful blue eyes intent as he moves to my left hand and concentrates on smoothing the gel over it. My gaze falls on his lips. I wonder what it would feel like to—

Stop it!

I look away from his face and down at the ground. Ryn is my friend. My *friend*. The idea of anything more than that is so utterly ridiculous I want to laugh out loud. And yet I can't help imagining what it would be like if—No! I'm not imagining that at all. It's absurd.

Stop being absurd, Violet. I close my eyes and silently chant, *Friend, friend, friend.*

"Are you okay?" Ryn asks.

My eyelids spring apart and I pull my hand away. "Yes. That feels a lot better, thank you." I force myself to look at him as though nothing has changed between us. Because it hasn't, right? "Are *you* okay? You hit the floor so hard you didn't wake up for a while."

Ryn rolls his shoulders. "I'm a bit banged up, I guess, but nothing serious. I'll just have to put up with the bruises for longer than a few hours." He packs away the medical kit.

"And are you okay with ... what we saw when the Queen knocked us out?" I know I don't have to mention Reed's name; Ryn will know exactly what I'm talking about.

"Yeah. Of course." Ryn turns his back to me as he pulls a blanket out of the backpack and closes the zipper. I know he's lying.

"I'm sorry," I say. "I didn't know if I should bring it up. I just wanted to make sure—"

"It's fine, Violet. Don't worry about it." With a tight smile, he hands me the blanket. "We can sleep out here tonight and get moving when the sun rises."

I know he's trying to change the subject, but I'm determined not to move on until I know he really is okay. "Reed didn't feel that way in real life. You know that, right?" When Ryn doesn't answer I decide to plough ahead with my theory. "I know what's going on here. You've built up this crazy situation in your head where you think that if your brother had ever had to choose between the two of us, he'd have chosen me. And that's just not true."

"How do you know?" Ryn takes the folded blanket from me, shakes it open, and throws it over me. "The night that he died, he *did* choose you over me. I know he cared about you a lot, V." Ryn's voice goes quiet as he lies down on my left. "Maybe he did love you more than he loved me, his own brother."

"No." I lie carefully on my side, facing Ryn. "Not possible."

"Oh, it's definitely possible." Ryn stares up at the stars. "And don't worry, I won't hate you for it. It isn't your fault if the brother I loved and admired so much didn't feel the same way about me. But I've spent many hours considering the possibility that he would have chosen you over me, and I think it's true."

"*Many hours?*" I ask in disbelief.

He looks over at me. "What? I have plenty of thinking time."

Plenty of thinking time? What does he do, just sit around and *think*? What about assignments? Training, studying, *friends*?

I prop myself up on one elbow, trying not to lean on any

bruises or cuts. "Can I ask you something?"

"Will it make a difference if I say 'no'?"

"Probably not."

He turns his gaze back to the sky. "Ask away, then."

"Do you spend a lot of time alone?"

A beat of silence passes before he says, "Why would you ask that?"

"Well, there's the fact that you can quote poetry, which implies you spend a lot of time reading. You mentioned yesterday that you hang out in people's houses watching TV when you're not on assignment. And now you've just told me about all the 'thinking time' you have. So I was just wondering why you don't hang out with your friends more often."

His expression is incredulous when he looks at me. "You're wondering why *I* don't hang out with friends?"

"Look, we both know I have zero social life, but this conversation isn't about me. It's about you."

He hesitates, then says, "Can we add this to the off-limits territory?"

"But—"

"What, you think you're the only one who gets to have off-limits territory?" He grins, obviously seeing his way out of any future awkward conversations. "No way. If there are things you don't have to talk about, then there are things I don't have to talk about."

"Fine." I roll onto my back, completely forgetting that I've got cream smeared all over it. Oops. Well, the jacket is probably dirty already anyway. "Are we allowed to talk about how we're going to find our way home?"

"We'll have to get to Creepy Hollow the old fashioned way: on foot." He shuffles around a bit, then reaches for the backpack and places it under his head. "Bran said this assignment was local, so I'm hoping it's close to where the human realm crosses over into the fae realm. We can check the map book in the morning."

"Okay." Fortunately, I know exactly where the human realm crosses over into the fae realm. That's the way I was supposed to take Nate home after he followed me into the faerie paths. That all seems so long ago. Even Nate's betrayal is starting to seem like it happened in another lifetime. It doesn't hurt so much anymore. "I hope local means really local," I say, "because if we don't get back to the Guild by the cut-off time on Friday afternoon, I'm probably going to go into a serious depression. I *cannot* fail my final assignment."

Ryn sighs. "I think you should prepare yourself for possible failure, V. We're already going to lose points for not being able to bring back the necklace, and we know nothing about it other than its name. If we return late in addition to all that, we'll definitely be failing this one."

"We did get the necklace," I tell him. "It's hiding right here." I hold up one of the silver balls around my neck, noticing that my burnt fingers don't feel quite so sore anymore. "And we do know what it's for. Didn't you hear what Zell said while you were hiding in the faerie paths? He told his mother that she didn't deserve to be immortal and that he'd never give her this necklace."

"Immortal? I must have missed that." Ryn rubs a hand across his jaw. "But earlier on he was going to give up the necklace in exchange for you."

"Well, he obviously changed his mind and decided immortality was more important than having me find special faeries for him."

Ryn rolls onto his side and looks at me. "So this necklace grants immortality. That's pretty cool. I wonder how it works."

"Maybe when you're wearing it you can't die," I say, "even if you're injured so badly that the magic in your body is unable to heal you. The magic in the necklace must be more powerful."

"I wonder what would happen if your head were cut off? Do you think it would still work then?"

"That's just gross, Ryn, and don't even think about testing it out on me."

A look of horror flashes across Ryn's eyes before he shakes his head. "Do you honestly think I'd cut your head off, V? I thought we'd reached the friend stage by now."

Yeah, and then we reached the stage where your naked chest suddenly seemed appealing, and I started applying words like 'delicious' to your lips and—

What. The. Freak? I slam a mental gate down on my thoughts, trying to force my brain back to neutral. I am *not* the kind of girl who thinks things like that, and Ryn is *not* the kind of guy I should be thinking them about. He's the guy who threw my mother's tokehari necklace away. The guy who made sure I had no friends at the Guild. I've seen his rudeness and condescension toward just about every Guild girl who's ever had any interest in him, and I certainly don't want to be on the receiving end of that.

"Uh, yes, the friend stage." I nod. "I know you wouldn't cut my head off."

Ryn frowns as he watches me, as though trying to figure something out. Damn, am I blushing or something? Did I have a weird look on my face while trying to get my insane thoughts under control? I turn my head and stare at the sky, which is a lot safer than staring into Ryn's eyes. It isn't nearly as beautiful as a Creepy Hollow sky, but it calms me nonetheless. My gaze drifts slowly from one twinkling star to the next. "Remember when we used to draw star-to-star pictures in the air with our styluses?" I say.

"Yes, and then we'd try to guess each other's drawings."

"Remember that dragon Reed spent so long drawing one night?"

Ryn nods. "And you and I were both adamant that it looked like a weirdly shaped pegasus because the legs were too long for a dragon."

I laugh. "He was so determined to make us see a dragon, but we were both laughing so hard we could barely follow what he was saying."

Ryn's laughter joins mine, and it feels so natural, so familiar and comforting, that by the time our chuckles subside into silence, something feels different between us. As though we've finally got back to that place we were at before Reed died.

"You should sleep, V," he says quietly. "You need rest for your wounds to heal."

My wounds. I'd almost forgotten the pain, but now that he's mentioned it, I become aware once more of the aching throughout my body. "Yeah, I guess."

He turns onto his side, facing away from me. His not-so-white-anymore shirt pulls tight over his back, but I don't imagine the taut muscles just below it because Ryn is my friend, and it isn't right to think thoughts like that about a friend.

"You don't want the blanket?" I murmur sleepily, realizing after a few minutes that he has nothing to cover himself with.

"No, I'm fine, thanks. If I get cold in the night I'll just pinch it from you."

CHAPTER ELEVEN

IN MY DREAM I'M IN A PARK FIGHTING A GOBLIN. IT'S THE same assignment I went on a few weeks ago, but the weather is different. Lightning splits the sky into jagged pieces, and deafening thunder causes the ground to shudder. Wind whips strands of hair across my face as I slash at the goblin with my sword. A trail of sparks follows the blade. I know I'm supposed to kill him with the sword—I remember that happening—but for some reason, I decide to do something different now.

I let go of the sword, and it vanishes. Flames begin to dance and flicker across my open palms. They shouldn't burn me, because they're my flames, but they do. I run at the goblin, screaming both in anger and because of the pain in my hands. I wrap my burning fingers around the goblin's neck. He's strong and should be able to fight me off, but dreams don't work the way reality does, and instead I find him struggling beneath my grip. I manage to force him to the ground, my hands never leaving his neck until he becomes still.

I stand back, the flames still burning in my palms, and suddenly the goblin is no longer a goblin. Now it's Nate lying at my feet, his lifeless eyes staring blankly at the stormy sky. But it isn't a stormy sky any longer. It's a tunnel. The tunnel I killed Nate in. No, not Nate. I killed the shapeshifter who took on Nate's form. So who is lying at my feet now? Did I just kill the real Nate?

No no no! What have I done? I tug at my hair in anguish. The flames are all over me now, burning brighter and brighter, and *hurting* so much I can barely—

I wake with a start, my hands burning just as much in reality as they were in my dream.

"Hey, are you okay?" Ryn crawls over to me and takes my arm. His fingers are cool against my skin.

"Just a dream …" I say, sitting up and staring at my hands. The grey light of dawn reveals an absence of flames, but the burning is definitely real. "My hands. I can feel them burning. Look at how red the skin is—"

"Calm down," Ryn says, but he hurries to open the backpack and pull out the first aid kit. "Now which one did I use last night?"

"Man, this lack of magical healing thing is *really* not cool."

"Here." Ryn takes one of my hands and quickly squeezes gel onto it. The relief I feel is immediate. "Better?" he asks.

"I can still feel some pain, but it's definitely a whole lot better."

"See? The human stuff does work on you." He spreads a thick layer of gel over my hands and wrists while I blink a few times in an attempt to wake up my fuzzy head. I'm not used to feeling this tired; the magic inside me usually replenishes my energy pretty quickly. Ryn moves to my other hand. "Do you see them in your dreams?" he asks quietly.

"Them?" I echo.

"The ones you've killed. From your past assignments."

Oh. *Them.* I don't want to answer him. I've never enjoyed talking about the creatures I've had to kill, despite the fact that Tora forces a counseling session on me each time it happens. I prefer to pack all my feelings away into the Stuff I Don't Think About box in my head and leave them there.

"I do," Ryn says. "Not always, just every now and then."

After a moment, I say, "So do I." He's making an effort to be honest with me about something, so I suppose I should reciprocate. "I try not to think about them at all, but they often show up in my dreams."

He nods. "It sucks." He twists the cap back onto the tube. "I hope your hands begin to heal soon because there isn't much of this stuff left."

It seems our conversation about killing things is over. Thank goodness.

Ryn pulls out the map book and locates the road we're on. Good thing one of us was paying attention to the names of the streets instead of just throwing up on them. I let go of my control freak tendencies and let Ryn figure out the way home while I rest my head on my knees. It's a new feeling, trusting someone else to do something that directly affects me, but right now I kind of like it.

"Okay, it looks like it should take us about two days to reach the point where this realm meets the fae realm," Ryn says after examining a few pages.

"So, it's Wednesday morning," I say, "which means we should get there by tomorrow night. That's before the cut-off time."

"And then we'll have to get through the forest to the Guild."

"Okay, but we should still reach the Guild before the end of Friday afternoon, right?"

"If you don't hold us up," Ryn says with a grin. He packs away the blanket and first aid kit while I stand around uselessly with sticky, gel-covered hands. "Next thing I'll have to feed you because you can't hold your own energy bar," he says.

"Not happening. I'd rather stay hungry until this gel stuff has dried."

* * *

We walk. Along the streets, through the parks, and past the shopping centers. I feel horribly vulnerable, not only because I'm barefoot and wearing little more than a torn dress, but because without my magic I have no glamour to conceal myself from the human world. I wonder what people must think of us as they drive by in their cars. They probably take one look at the blood smeared across Ryn's shirt and step on their accelerators.

We eat energy bars for breakfast and lunch—the one with

the dark chocolate around the outside is definitely my favorite—and continue walking after dark to make up for my slow pace. I want to push myself to keep walking all night, but when we reach a quiet neighborhood, Ryn decides we should stop. After having an altercation with a dog in the first garden we try to creep into, we find a pet-free property.

"How are you feeling?" Ryn asks as we sit down behind a small tool shed.

"Tired, sore, hungry, and *really* mad at the person who improved these magic-blocking bands. The last time I had one on I managed to force some magic out. It was incredibly painful, but it worked. Now that isn't possible anymore."

"Oh, I didn't think to try that." Ryn sits up straighter. "Maybe—"

"No." I shake my weary head. "When we were in his dungeon, Zell told me he improved the bands so they now block magic completely."

"And you believed him?" Ryn looks down at his arm, his expression becoming intense. The skin around his metal band grows red and inflamed, and I swear I can hear sizzling.

"Stop!" I grab his arm with my still very tender but no longer burning hands. "Don't be an idiot, you're just hurting yourself."

"Flip, that was rather painful," Ryn says, sounding a little out of breath. "Why didn't you stop me sooner?"

I close my eyes and shake my head before leaning back. "I don't have energy to argue with you."

"In that case, you need another energy bar." Seeming to forget his pain, Ryn reaches for the backpack and unzips it.

"Then you'll be ready to argue all night long."

I groan. "Another energy bar? Is that the *only* food item you managed to find in that kitchen?"

"There was a box of them on the counter. I just grabbed as many as I could. If you'd prefer to eat *nothing*, though, that could definitely be arranged."

I stick my tongue out at him. Yes, my tongue. Because that's how much I care about being mature right now.

Ryn pulls two bars out of the bag. "Okay, do you want the nut one or the chocolate one?"

Despite the fact that I *obviously* want the chocolate one, I say, "I don't mind. Whichever."

"Just pick, V."

"No, I don't mind. Really. I like them both."

"Here. I know you want that one." He hands me the chocolate one with a grin.

"You don't know that." But I take the bar from his outstretched hand.

"Yes, I do. I know you a lot better than you think, V."

"Whatever." I tuck my legs beneath me. "You just missed out on eight years of my life and now you want to tell me you *know* me?"

Ryn pulls his knees up and rests his elbows on them. "I know when your birthday is. I know that you let Filigree sleep in your bed when you're cold. I know that you hate being given purple gifts, and I know that you have a weird habit of twisting your hair around your finger when you're nervous."

"Hey, how is that a *weird* habit?"

He shrugs. "Maybe because it's not something I could ever imagine doing myself."

"Because you're a guy. That *would* be weird. And how do you know I still let Filigree sleep in my bed?"

"Do you?" he asks.

I narrow my eyes at him. "Fine. Well, I know that you've never dated any girl at the Guild because you think you're too good for them, and I know that you have a 'weird habit—'" I make air quotes "—of occasionally pressing your hand against your chest like you have indigestion or something."

He looks startled for a moment, then turns his face away from me so I can no longer see his expression.

"What? Did I say something wrong? Is it supposed to be a secret that you think you're too good for any trainee?"

He returns his gaze to me as though nothing weird just happened. "Not at all."

"So it's true? You really think you're too good for those girls?"

His eyes don't move from mine. "Not exactly. It's more like I've been trying to avoid the mess."

"The mess?"

"Yeah." He unwraps his energy bar. "Do you have any idea what girls are like? Far too emotional, far too much of the time."

"Uh, I am actually a girl, Ryn. And no, I hadn't really noticed that."

He finishes chewing and says, "Well, that's because you're not like other girls."

Not like other girls? An awkward silence grows between us. "Wow, thanks, Ryn. Next thing you'll be telling me I'm like one of the guys."

He sighs. "I didn't mean it like—"

"Whatever." I hold a hand up. "I'm not offended, trust me. I've heard a lot worse from you in the past."

"You see what I mean? You don't do the whole overreacting thing. In fact, you probably are more like a guy than a—"

"Okay, you should stop talking now before you *really* put your foot in it."

He finishes his energy bar, then says, "It's not like I've had zero relationships, though. Undergrounders are pretty cool. I've got to know some of them quite well. Believe it or not, they're not *all* out to kill us."

"Undergrounders? Like ... the non-faeries who hang out in the super dangerous part of Creepy Hollow known as *Underground?*"

"The very same place. There was this one really hot girl— well, woman, really—who had beautiful green scales all over her arms and a serpent's tongue. Man, that tongue was amaz—"

"OKAY," I interrupt loudly. "I don't know if you're making that up to freak me out or if you really did get together with some snake woman, but either way, I don't need to know the details."

With a smile I can't decipher, Ryn lies back on the grass. "Since we're on the subject of relationships ..."

Oh no. Please don't make this conversation about me.

"Halfling boy is the only boyfriend you've ever had, right?"

Nate.

It's the first time I've thought of him all day. That must be a record. "Yeah, why?"

"You've never dated a faerie?"

"No." I start to feel uncomfortable. "So what?"

"You've never *kissed* a faerie?"

"I don't think that's any of your business, Oryn."

He raises his head and looks at me. His eyes sparkle with mirth. "Like I said before, you're missing out."

Before? What is he talking about? He doesn't volunteer any explanation, and I'm not about to ask him; I'd prefer it if this conversation ended right now.

"Maybe you should give it another chance."

Or maybe I should have changed the subject when I had the chance.

"There's got to be some faerie out there who'll appreciate your unique combination of guardian hotness, competitive nature, and stubborn attitude."

"Even if there is, it's not happening."

"Come on, you'll never know what you're missing if you don't dip your toe back in the dating pond."

The dating pond? Trust Ryn to come up with a dumbass analogy like that. "I tried, remember? After years of steering clear of the 'pond,' I dipped my toe in and almost got my whole leg chomped off by an attractive fish that turned out to be a sea serpent in disguise."

Ryn chuckles. "I'm sure some guy will come along who'll manage to impress you."

"Well, it'll have to be one seriously impressive stunt to

convince me he's worth it."

"Like what?"

I shrug. When I don't continue, Ryn looks at me with raised eyebrows, as if waiting for an answer. "Jeez, I don't know, Ryn. Like a gazillion glow-bugs lighting up the night sky with their tiny glowing butts or something."

"Glowing butts?" Ryn bursts out laughing. "When I find a girl who's worthy of impressive stunts, it'll be more like a magic carpet ride to watch the sun set than a bunch of tiny, glowing asses in the air."

"Yeah, well, maybe that's my thing." *Or not.* I have no idea where the 'glowing butts' comment came from. Although it might actually be kind of pretty now that I think about it. "And magic carpets don't exist," I add.

Ryn tilts his head back to gaze at the sky. "That's why it'll be so impressive."

* * *

My hands don't feel quite so tender the next day, which makes room for the pain in my arm. Ryn changed the dressing and bandage before we fell asleep last night, and the wound wasn't looking good. It doesn't bother me too much, though. We'll be back at the Guild tomorrow, and after the metal band has been removed, my arm will heal quickly.

We walk even slower than yesterday, and by the time the moon has risen high in the sky and we're too tired and sore to continue, we still haven't reached the crossover point into the fae realm.

"If we continue at the same pace, it will take at least another four hours," Ryn says as he examines the map.

"Okay." I drag myself to my feet. "Come on. We can do it."

"Don't be silly." Ryn closes the book and sets the bag down. "We can do it in the morning."

"No. The morning is for us to get through the forest to the Guild. Have you forgotten about that part?"

"V, you're going to fall over pretty soon, which means I'll have to carry you, and despite how strong and muscular I look, I'm not exactly feeling up to it at the moment." He pulls me down onto the grass, and I realize I'm too tired to get back up again.

* * *

Friday morning arrives, and I'm desperate. With every step we take, I can imagine the clock ticking away. Everyone else is probably back by now, and here we are, the top two trainees in our class, not even able to use our own magic.

Around about mid-morning, the houses begin to get further apart. When we finally reach a forested area and Ryn says, "This is it," I could just about cry with happiness. With renewed strength, we hurry through the trees.

"If humans were walking here," I say, "they'd just keep going until they reached the other side, right?"

"Yes. It's only the fae who can cross over into another realm while in this forest."

Part of me wonders if I'll be able to tell when we're no

longer in the human realm, but the moment it happens, I know. Not just because it feels and looks different, but because of the sudden downpour we find ourselves in.

We're home.

Finally.

And the magical storm that began a week ago still rages on.

CHAPTER TWELVE

"YOU'VE GOT TO BE KIDDING ME," I SHOUT ABOVE THE roar of the rain. A fork of lightning rips through the sky and strikes the tree we're standing beside. With a crack and a groan, an enormous branch tumbles to the ground. We dive out of the way, hitting the ground and sliding through the mud. I sit up and wipe the brown muck off my face.

Fan-freaking-tastic.

"We can't travel through this," Ryn shouts to me.

"We have to. How else will we get back?"

"Let's just wait a bit." He pulls me to my feet and leads me back a few paces. A second later we're standing in the quiet forest of the human realm, with nothing disturbing the peace save for a few chirping birds.

I put my hands over my face. "Why is this happening?"

"Things could be worse, V." I hear Ryn sitting down. "We could be dead, you know. How many other people have fought the Unseelie Queen and lived to brag about it?"

"I don't care," I moan.

"Stop being a baby and sit down. We'll give it half an hour and see if the weather clears."

I plop onto the ground and begin wiping mud and mush off my dress. "I can't believe this. We should have been back at the Guild *days* ago! And here we are, sleeping in the dirt, sliding through the mud, and smelling like crap."

Ryn snickers. "Oh, baby, I love it when you talk dirty."

I shove a fistful of muddy leaves into his laughing mouth. "There." I smile sweetly. "Now you can talk dirty too."

He spits and splutters. "Okay—" he wipes a few more leaves off his tongue "—you know I'm going to get you back for that at some point, right?"

"I don't get why you're not upset about this." I throw my hands up. "You're just as competitive as I am. Doesn't it bother you that we're about to lose so many points?"

"Violet. You and I are so far ahead of everyone else in the rankings that even if we get a big fat zero for this assignment, which *won't* happen, it's still going to be either you or me graduating at the top of the class."

I push wet hair out of my face and lean back against a tree with a sigh. I suppose Ryn's right. The two of us have been fighting for the top position since we began training; no one else ever really stood a chance. The thought doesn't make me feel much better, though. I don't want to know that it will be one of the two of us. I want to know that it will be *me*.

"Why do you want it so badly?" Ryn asks, watching me closely.

I shake my head. I've never told anyone my reason, and I'm not about to now.

"If I guess correctly, will you tell me?"

I shift my head so I can see him. "You'll never guess."

With a grin, he says, "Challenge accepted. Okay, let's see. It can't be something as simple as the money. I know your parents left you with enough of that." He watches me closely; I keep my expression neutral. "Right. So is it because the only thing you've ever wanted in life is to see your name written in the Hall of Honor?" He hesitates. If he's waiting for a hint from me, it's not happening. "No, I didn't think so," he continues. "And it can't be the visit to the Seelie Court because I doubt you've ever wanted to meet the ..." He trails off and tilts his head to the side. "No, wait, that's it. You want to go to the Seelie Court."

I feel a certain disquiet stirring within me, but I keep my voice even as I say, "And how do you figure that? Did I blink the wrong way?"

"That's interesting," he says, ignoring my question. "I always assumed it would have more to do with your mother than any—Aha!" He points at me. "It is! It's something to do with your mother *and* the Seelie Court."

Unless he can hear the unsteady beating of my heart from where he's sitting, which I *know* he can't, he should never have been able to figure that out. My expression remains neutral as I stare at him for several moments, trying to think up another story. But he looks so sure of himself that I know he'll never believe a lie. "How did you guess?" I ask eventually.

"I'm pretty good at reading people. That's something you might *not* know about me, V."

I press my lips together and look down at the ground. I hope he can't tell how much it unsettles me that he's figured out my secret. Who would have thought he was so good at guessing?

"So, are you going to tell me the rest of the details, or just leave me hanging?"

For the first time, I consider *why* I've never told anyone. It's no one else's business, of course, but I suppose I'm afraid other people will think it's silly. And several weeks ago Ryn would have been the very *last* person on earth I'd have shared this secret with, but I know the other side of him now. I've seen his fears, witnessed his heartbreak. Something tells me that if anyone's going to understand why this is so important to me, Ryn will.

"Fine," I say. "But if you laugh at me, I swear I'll make you feel so much pain you'll never want to laugh again."

"Okaaay," he says slowly. "You're a little scary sometimes, V. Don't worry, I'll be sure to keep all laughter under wraps."

"Okay." I fold my arms. "So it isn't a lie that I very much enjoy being the best trainee in our year and would like to be rewarded for it, but, as you guessed, there is another reason that makes it even more important to me." I take a deep breath. "Apparently, back when our parents were training at the Guild, everyone wanted to visit the Seelie Court. That was, like, the coolest thing about being the top graduate. And my mother ... well, I guess she was a really fun kind of person, and when she graduated at the top of her class, she wanted to take advantage of her one visit to the Seelie Court. So, according to my father, she took a whole lot of her own things with her and hid them somewhere. She thought it would be cool if someone from a future graduating year found her things. And even if no one ever found them, it would still be cool because she'd left her mark there, kind of like humans carving their initials into trees." I stop to take a breath.

"How would she have known if anyone ever found her stuff?" Ryn asks.

"Well, my father said she left a recorded mirror message there asking for her favorite book to be returned to the Guild with a message for her. I haven't heard of that happening, so I assume her belongings are still hidden. Just think of it, Ryn. I could see her in a mirror, talking to me! And I could finally have something of hers! Her first piece of jewelry, a story she wrote at junior school, the candle she burned on her eighteenth birthday—whatever else she left there. If I could just find all those things, then I'd finally know something about her. I mean, at home there are clothes and books, but what does that tell me? Other than the fact that she loved reading poetry, I barely know anything. And I *want to know her.* I want to know what she was like when she was my age. I want to feel some kind of connection to this person I have no memories of."

When I finally stop talking, Ryn just looks at me. What is he thinking? Is he thinking *anything*? For all I know, he got bored and dozed off while I was talking. Or maybe he's biting his tongue to hold his laughter in.

Suddenly, I regret telling him. "You think it's silly. I know, it's just *stuff*, right? How is that supposed to make me feel—"

He leans forward and catches my hand. "It's not silly at all, V."

I wait for him to say something else, but he doesn't. Neither does he look away. Or let go of my hand. My skin is still rather sensitive from the vine burn, so his grip kind of hurts. It's also kind of amazing in a skin-tingling, heart-thudding, head-rushing sort of way.

Insane. That's what I am. Definitely insane.

I gently pull my hand away and reach for Ryn's jacket. I'm starting to get cold. "Well, anyway, that's my sad little story. Now it's your turn." I cross my arms, being careful not to bump the *really* painful wound hidden beneath the bandage. "You have to tell me something personal, something previously off-limits."

Ryn taps his fingers together and looks thoughtful. "Okay, remember when we had one of our major confrontations recently about Reed, and you shouted at me to 'get over it'?"

"Uh, yes." I feel guilty about that now; I was rather mean.

"Well, I'm trying." He looks down at the ground. "It isn't easy with my mom around. She's sad a lot of the time, and I know it's because she misses him. And there are reminders of him all around our home. Like all the things in his bedroom, and the target he set up at the end of the passage."

"Your mom was so mad when he did that," I say, remembering it clearly. "She said it was too dangerous to throw knives inside the house."

"But Reed begged her to let him keep it there. He promised to be careful."

"And no one could ever say no to Reed."

"No." Ryn's smile is sad. "And then there's the fact that my father isn't around. He left us because he and my mother just couldn't handle Reed's death. They should have been grieving together, you know, but somehow they always ended up fighting instead. So he left. And now his very absence is a constant reminder that Reed isn't around anymore either."

A shiver courses through my body, and I pull the jacket tighter around me. "But your mom doesn't mind having Calla over?"

Ryn shakes his head. "It's weird, I know. I thought she'd have a problem with it, and the first time I brought Calla over, my mom did keep her distance. But ever since then she seems to love it."

"Maybe it's because Calla's such an adorable child that your mom is able to look past her parentage."

"Probably," Ryn says. He takes a deep breath and looks around. "Uh, should we check out the weather situation in Creepy Hollow?"

"Yes!" I jump up, horrified that I've managed to forget the urgency of our situation. My head spins, and the world around me seems to shift. When it manages to right itself, I find myself leaning against a tree with Ryn holding onto my injury-free arm.

"Standing up so fast clearly isn't a good idea for you," he says.

"I'm … just …" I shake my head. "A little dizzy."

"Is it your arm?" He moves to push the jacket off my shoulder.

"Don't." I stop his hand. "We both know it's probably worse than the last time we checked, so let's just get back to the Guild as quickly as we can. I'll be fine once the metal band is removed."

Ryn looks down at where my hand is touching his. "Your skin is really warm, V." He places his hand on my forehead. I try to act like it doesn't bother me to have him standing so close and touching me. Because it doesn't. Not at all. "You're definitely burning up."

"Well, that's something I've never experienced before."

"You're sicker than you think you are, V. We really need to get moving."

"Thanks, that's really comforting, Ryn." I push past him. "I'm not the one who wanted to sit down and wait for the weather, remember?" A boom of thunder greets my ears as we cross over the invisible divide between the realms. My hair, which had just begun to dry, is drenched in seconds. "Why did we decide to wait anyway? It's not like the rain is going to kill us."

"Yes, but trees that fall over can," Ryn shouts to me. "That's why we waited."

"Well, we can't wait any longer." I set off through the storm, then remember that I've never actually traveled this route before, and I'm not entirely sure which way to go.

"Would you like me to show you the way?" Ryn asks as he passes me, a superior look on his face. He loves it way too much when he finds something I can't do. I follow him without a word.

We trudge along the soggy forest floor, dodging the

occasional falling branch. Lightning blinds us and thunder sets the entire forest shuddering. The bottom half of my dress clings to my legs. I blink rain out of my eyes and pull the dress higher up and out of the way. I won't let a stupid piece of fabric slow me down.

It isn't long before I'm exhausted. My heart is beating too fast, and I can't seem to stop shivering. And even though it's probably just the wind, I keep thinking I can hear someone calling my name. My foot hooks beneath a root, and before I can figure out how to save myself from falling, I've landed splat in the mud.

So. Freaking. Embarrassing. I am *not* the kind of person who trips over things. I'm supposed to be coordinated and agile and—who keeps calling my name? I twist around and stare into the shadowy forest. "Who's there?"

I feel someone's hand on my arm. I look up to see Ryn. Weird. I'd forgotten he was also out here. He pulls me to my feet and loops my arm around his neck. Great, now he thinks I need help walking.

Violet.

I struggle to look over my shoulder. There's definitely someone calling for me. And is that the shape of a person I can see moving between the trees? "Wait, Ryn, someone keeps calling my name. Can't you hear that?"

"Just keep walking, V. There's no one there."

I don't know why, but I listen to him instead of the voice. Probably because his arm is so strong around me that I'd have no hope of struggling free.

We keep moving. Step after step after step. I've never been

this tired. I'm so tired, in fact, that I'm dreaming while I'm walking. I know I'm awake and moving, but my mind is lost to a jumble of confusing images. I float, letting them carry me along like a river. People, memories, colors, mixed up bits of conversations.

The next time I become conscious of my surroundings, we're standing in the entrance to the Guild, and Ryn is apologizing to the guard for something. "I'm sorry, it was the only way I could think of to get your attention. No magic, remember?" He thrusts his metal-encircled wrist forward as proof. "If you want to see my pendant, here it is." He fumbles near his neck and pulls a chain from beneath his shirt. "But like I already told you, Basil, she isn't wearing hers. And she can't get it for you because she'd need magic to do that, and she currently doesn't have any. Now *please* let us in."

"I've been through this before with you, Ryn," Basil says patiently. "You know the rules. She can't come in here without first showing me her pendant. If that's impossible then I'll have to send a guard in with—"

"I don't care if you have to send a *hundred* guards with me, this girl is dying and I need to get her to her mentor at once!"

Dying? What is he talking about?

Things get a bit jumbled. I think there's some more shouting, and I'm vaguely aware of being dragged up some stairs. When Ryn pushes a door open and I see a woman with blonde and green hair sitting behind a desk, my head clears a little.

"There you are!" Tora exclaims. "I expected you back ages ago." Her face falters, and she stands quickly. "What happened? What's wrong?"

"We did it, Tora." I say weakly. "We finished the assignment. Fought the Unseelie Queen. Stole the necklace. Got home before the cut-off." Or did we? I'm not actually sure about that one. I wrap my fingers around my chunky necklace, trying—and failing—to pull it off so I can give it to Tora. Then, just like every silly girl in every damsel-in-distress story I've ever despised, I sag against Ryn and pass out.

PART II

CHAPTER THIRTEEN

I BATTLE MY WAY THROUGH PAIN AND TANGLED DREAMS for what feels like days before restful sleep finally takes me. When I eventually open my eyes and find a world that isn't spinning dizzily, my first thought is that I've been here before, in this moment. Waking from a long, injury-healing sleep. Lying on Ryn's couch with him kneeling beside me. The memory is so strong that when I turn my head to the side, I expect to see him.

It isn't Ryn sitting in a chair beside my bed, though. It's Tora. And this is the bedroom that used to be mine when I lived with her.

"Hey," she says, looking up from a collection of papers in her hand. She places them on the bedside table and leans forward in her chair. "Ready to face the world again?"

I look down and see a narrow scar encircling my wrist where the metal band was. My gaze shifts to the top of my arm; the skin is perfectly healed. "I think so. Did Flint take the band off?"

"Yes. I couldn't find anyone else who knows how to, although there must be others at the Guild who've come across this metal before."

I sit up and attempt to run my hands through my hair, but the dried mud matting the strands together makes it difficult. At least I'm not longer wearing the torn, skimpy cocktail dress. The clothes I'm dressed in look like Tora's.

"Sorry, I thought it would be a little difficult to wash your hair while you were unconscious," Tora says. "You'll have to take care of that yourself."

"Sure. How long have I been asleep?"

"About a day."

"Oh. It felt a lot longer than that." I swallow as I prepare to ask the question that plagued most of my nightmares before I eventually fell into a dreamless sleep. "Did Ryn and I get back before the assignment cut-off time?"

Tora smiles and says, "Yes."

I close my eyes and let out a relieved sigh.

"Ryn did the verbal report with Bran and me yesterday after Flint got the bands off both of you," Tora continues. "Technically, you should have been there too, but you weren't exactly in a state to be talking. Or standing."

I groan, feeling heat rise in my cheeks as I remember just how pathetic my arrival at the Guild was. "Sorry about the passing out thing. *So* embarrassing. It won't happen again." I swing my legs over the side of the bed and stretch my arms.

"Are you sure you're okay?" Tora's eyes are wide with concern.

"Yes, I'm more than okay. I feel completely fine. I knew Ryn was overreacting when we got to the Guild yesterday."

"Overreacting?"

"Yeah, he said something to Basil about me dying."

"Well, I hesitate to tell you this because I know how you feel about Ryn being right—" she gives me a knowing look, and I pretend to have no idea what she's talking about "—but he wasn't overreacting. There was an infection in your wound that was spreading quickly through your blood. If you'd been out there on your own, I don't think you would have made it back to the Guild in time."

"Oh." Great, so I owe Ryn my life *again*?

"And I was expecting you to be back *days* ago—I mean, it wasn't exactly a complicated assignment—so I was *very* worried when we got to Friday afternoon and you still hadn't shown up. I know I wasn't supposed to contact you, but I was getting ready to break that rule. And then to hear that you were battling the Unseelie Queen herself—"

"It really wasn't such a big deal."

"—who is *enormously* powerful. She could have done any number of unspeakable things to you."

"But she didn't."

"And you were hallucinating and feverish, and I kept thinking what if she used some magic on you that meant you'd never heal—"

"But I did."

145

"—I'd never forgive myself for simply sitting here waiting for you to come back."

"But that's what you were supposed to do."

Tora shakes her head, sniffs, and dabs beneath her eyes. "You know I've never exactly been fond of Ryn, but I will forever be grateful that he got you back here alive."

"Okay, don't get all weepy, Tora. I'm fine, see?" I climb off the bed, do a few star jumps, then wrap my arms around her neck.

She laughs into my hair as she folds her arms around me and squeezes tight. "You'll always be my favorite trainee. Even after I've mentored loads of other kick-ass trainees, you'll still be my favorite."

"Well, your favorite trainee needs to go and write a kick-ass report so she can score lots of points and get that top graduating position she's always wanted. Oh, and what happened with the freaky, magical storm?" I listen carefully and notice an absence of thunder, rain and howling wind. "Is it finally finished?"

"I think so. It's been off and on since last Friday—longest storm I've ever experienced—but it looks like it's finally cleared for good now. We still have no idea where or who it came from, though, or if it was connected to the murder last Friday night."

Perhaps now would be a good time to tell Tora all about Nate and how he might be the one responsible for the storm. Or not. I need to think about it properly, plan what I'm going to say.

"Oh, before I forget," Tora says, "you have a meeting with

Councilor Starkweather as soon as you're ready."

"What? Am I in trouble?"

"Not at all. She's extremely pleased with you and Ryn. But the item you retrieved is still hiding inside your necklace." She points to the chunky jewelry lying beside my stylus on the bedside table. "You and Ryn need to give it in to her and answer any questions she might have for you."

"Oh, okay." I'd forgotten about the eternity necklace and the rest of my miniature belongings. "Well, I'd better get to the Guild right away, then." I grab the necklace and my stylus and head for the door.

"Wait, one more thing." Tora points to the other door leading off the bedroom. "Bathing pool. Now."

* * *

Ryn is already waiting outside Councilor Starkweather's office when I get there.

"Hey."

"Hey."

Well, this isn't awkward at all. "Um, thanks for getting me back here yesterday."

"Sure. The conversations you had with your hallucinations were entertaining to listen to."

Oh hell, I was talking *the whole time I was out there?*

"Kidding," he says, one side of his mouth turning up. "They were actually pretty boring."

Fantastic, now I have *no* idea if I was talking or not.

"Shall we go in?" Ryn asks.

"Yes. Unless you'd like to embarrass me further?"

He pretends to think about it. "Maybe later." He raises his fist and knocks on the door. After several seconds of silence, we're told to come in.

Councilor Starkweather, her grey- and white-streaked hair pulled tightly into a bun at the back of her head, comes toward the door to greet us. I know she's several centuries old, but, like every other adult faerie, her face is flawless and wrinkle-free.

She ushers us in, then shakes my hand, followed by Ryn's. "I'd like to congratulate you both on a very successful assignment."

"Successful?" I say before I can stop myself. "At least two humans died. I wouldn't exactly call that successful."

She arches an eyebrow. "*Only* two humans died," she corrects. "We sent guardians there yesterday to assess the situation. It would appear that no one witnessed any magical activity, which is fortunate. The human authorities are assuming the fire was an accident and that it caused the death of Mr. Hart and his son."

"And what did they think of the basement full of magical objects?"

"They didn't find any magical objects. We're assuming someone from the Unseelie Court removed them." She steps back and leans against the edge of her desk. Ryn and I remain standing. "It was in no way your fault that two people died. No one knew the Unseelie Queen would show up. She has power beyond anything either of you have faced in your training, and it's a miracle you managed to survive a fight against both her and her two sons."

A miracle? I frown, wondering if I should be offended by that comment.

"The two of you were simply asked to find out what was going on at the Hart household and bring back the item that was given to Mr. Hart last week," Councilor Starkweather continues. "Since you managed both of these tasks, I expect you'll receive high points for this assignment."

"Well, that's great, but it doesn't exactly feel right to get lots of points when two people died." *Okay, why am I arguing with the head of the Guild Council?*

"Violet," Ryn says quietly. "I thought you wanted to do well."

"I do, but only when I deserve it."

"You do deserve it," Councilor Starkweather says. "But if you feel so strongly about this, I'd be happy to ask that your points be reduced."

"That won't be necessary," Ryn says, placing a hand on my arm and flashing me a look that clearly says, *Shut the hell up RIGHT NOW.*

"Excellent. Then all that remains is for you to hand over the item. Bran said something to me about a special necklace?"

"Yes." I notice Councilor Starkweather tapping her shoe as I retrieve the necklace from my pocket; we're obviously taking up too much of her time. "They called it an eternity necklace, and the Unseelie Prince said he'd never give it back to his mother because she doesn't deserve to be immortal. I assume, then, that whoever wears this necklace is granted immortality."

"Yes, I've heard of this," Councilor Starkweather says, taking it carefully, almost reverently. She holds it up to the light. The teardrop shaped pendant of white stone gleams with a pearlescent sheen. "No one knows how it was made or who its creator was, but it has been in the possession of the Unseelie Court for centuries." She places it on her desk and looks at us. "I shall send it to the Seelie Queen immediately; she will be pleased to have it. That is all. You may leave now."

Okay, that was abrupt. Ryn and I turn toward the door and, in an uncharacteristic show of gentlemanliness, he opens it for me. "That was a little weird," I whisper after he closes the door behind us.

"She's lying," he says quietly.

"About what?" We head down the corridor and away from the councilors' offices.

"I'm not sure exactly, but she wasn't being truthful. If I had to guess, I'd say she's not planning to give that necklace to the Seelie Queen."

"Ryn, you can't possibly know whether she was lying or not."

"Yes, I can. I'm good at reading people, remember? And you also got a weird vibe from her."

"Yes, but I don't know what that vibe means. And what can we do about it anyway?" We reach the main stairway and start walking down. "It's out of our hands now, so we just have to trust that she'll do whatever she's supposed to do with it."

* * *

Filigree is over his miniature pig phase. He's also managed to eat through almost every jar of roasted nixles in the kitchen.

The jar of green bugs is all that remains; they're clearly his least favorite color. And clearly I'll have to go shopping this weekend.

I lean back in the kitchen chair and look through the notes I've made so far. I absently scratch Filigree—cat formed, curled up on my lap—behind the ears as I try to remember everything that happened during our assignment. I should probably check a few details with Ryn before I write up the entire thing in full.

Filigree stretches and jumps gracefully off my lap. I take advantage of my freedom by heading to one of the cupboards and fetching a teaspoon and a jar labeled *Chocolate and Ladyfair Blossom Sauce*. It's supposed to be drizzled over desserts, but I prefer to eat it straight from the jar. I sit down, dip the spoon into the jar, and lick the chocolaty sweetness off it. This happens a number of times while I go through my notes again and mark all the places where I need to check facts with Ryn.

When I start to feel sick, I screw the lid back on, gather my papers, and run upstairs to find my boots. After spending several days barefoot in a torn dress, I'm enjoying wearing my regular clothes once again. Before opening a doorway to the faerie paths, I glance at my appearance in the mirror in my bedroom. Then I shake my head and turn around. Who cares what I look like? It's just Ryn I'm going to see.

With my Guild bag slung over my shoulder, I hurry through the paths and exit in front of Ryn's tree. I knock, then wait several minutes.

I knock again.

I'm about to pull out my amber to ask him where he is

when the bark melts away. Zinnia stands in the open doorway, her eyes heavy and her skin creased.

"Oh, I'm so sorry," I say. "Did I wake you?" It's early evening, but guardians keep strange hours sometimes.

"No, don't worry, I was waking up anyway." Zinnia smiles as she crosses her arms over her chest. "I assume you're looking for Ryn?"

"Yes, is he here?"

"I'm afraid not, and I don't know where he is or when he'll be back."

"Oh, okay." I take a step back. "Well, thanks anyway."

"Wait, Vi." She tucks a few curls behind her ear. "I'm actually a little concerned about him. He arrived home this afternoon with his hair ruffled, a bruise on his chin, and a bleeding lip. And it's Sunday, so he had no training or assignments. It isn't the first time this has happened, either. He says everything's fine, of course, but I'm still worried."

"Oh." I remember Ryn's bruised eye from earlier this week. I probably shouldn't tell Zinnia about that; it'll only add to her anxiety. "Well, I'll ask him about it. Maybe he'll tell me."

She nods and smiles, then wipes her hand across the space between us to close up the doorway. I shut my eyes, breathe deeply, and do something I haven't done in years: I search for Ryn.

CHAPTER FOURTEEN

AT FIRST I'M NOT SURE IT WILL WORK—I'M NOT HOLDING anything that belongs to Ryn—but I find him easily. I suppose it makes sense. We've spent a lot of time together recently, so there's already some kind of connection between us. What I am surprised at is his location; I thought I was the only one who went there these days.

I step out of the faerie paths onto a wide branch. Colors loop and swirl lazily within the bark, brightening ever so slightly each time I take a step. A night creature—cat-like, with fiery orange wings—bares its teeth at me before slinking away. I walk carefully along the branch, stepping around the glow-bugs. I climb onto another branch, and then another. I'm close to the canopy now; I can see the sky clearly between the leaves of the highest branches. Scattered stars twinkle between clouds lit up with early evening colors: soft blues, purples and greys.

It's beautiful.

And it's good to be home.

"I was wondering if you'd find me here," a voice says nearby.

I leap lightly into the hollow created where the giant arms of the gargan tree meet. "Sorry to interrupt your alone time. I need to check a few things about our assignment."

Ryn looks at me. "Is Violet Fairdale asking for my *help*?"

I put my hands on my hips. "I wouldn't go so far as to say that."

He pats the empty space on the blanket beside him, which I take to mean he's inviting me to sit down. "It just so happens," he says, "that I'm also finishing off my report now."

"Perfect." I sit opposite him and cross my legs. I pull my notes and some blank reed paper out of my bag, while Ryn does the same from a bag that was resting behind him.

"Did you bring a table to work on?" he asks.

"Well, no. I thought I was on my way to your house, not the top of a tree."

He removes a small block of wood from his bag and places it on the blanket between us. "Good thing one of us came prepared." He writes something on the block with his stylus, then pulls his arm back as the block transforms rapidly into a low table. It's pretty cool, I suppose, but my attention is caught instead by the scar I've just noticed around his wrist. A scar that matches my own.

"You're supposed to be impressed by the table, V, not my arm," he says, noticing my stare. "Although—" he flexes his muscles "—it is rather an impressive arm."

"I was looking at your scar, idiot."

"Oh. Yeah." He holds his arm up and examines the narrow strip of skin that's slightly paler than the rest of his arm. "Weird, isn't it. I thought it was impossible for us to scar, but Flint said there's something strange about the metal those bands are made of."

"Yes." I continue staring for a few moments, then blink and look down at my pages. "Anyway, I didn't know you still came up here."

"Sometimes," he says. "I avoided it for a few years after Reed's death, but not anymore."

"I brought Nate up here," I say before stopping to think whether it's a good idea to share that bit of information with Ryn.

"What?" His voice is low, but his eyebrows draw together in anger. "You brought that traitorous halfling up here?"

Why couldn't you just keep your mouth shut, Violet? "I didn't know he was a halfling, or that he was going to betray me."

"So you brought a random human up here?"

I look down, no longer able to face him. "Look, this place is really special to me, and at the time I wanted to share it with—"

"It's special to me too, V, and I don't want to know that you brought some random guy up here to do—*whatever* with. This is our place, no one else's. Do you think I brought any of my Underground flings up here? No. Because I have more respect for this place than that."

"I'm sorry, okay!" I slam my fist down on the table as anger,

155

guilt and regret erupt within me. I spread my hand flat as I take a deep, calming breath. "If it makes you feel any better, I wish I'd never shared this place with him. And for your information, there was no *whatever*." My cheeks burn at the thought. I'm not entirely sure what Ryn meant by 'whatever,' but I can guess. "Now will you please stop shouting at me before this turns into another fight where we both wind up threatening to harm each other?"

He says nothing for several moments, and when I raise my eyes I find him watching me. "That was actually an awesome fight," he says quietly.

"It was."

After a few more moments of awkwardness, he places his pages on the magically erected table in front of him. "So what did you want to check with me?"

Seems the argument is over.

I begin to relax as Ryn and I discuss the details of our assignment and how best to report them. When I'm finished scribbling more notes, I turn to the blank sheets of reed paper and begin writing the report in full from the beginning. Silence fills the space between us as we both become absorbed in our work. It's a comfortable silence, though. It reminds me of the way we used to do our homework together in junior school.

And that's when it hits me: Somehow, after spending years hating each other, we got our friendship back. I can't pinpoint exactly when it happened, but it happened. Ryn isn't just the guy I used to know, or the guy I had to put up with during our final assignment. He's someone I actually enjoy being around.

Someone I can shout at and fight with and have everything go back to normal in just a few minutes.

I smile to myself and continue working.

I reach the part of the assignment where I was hanging helplessly from a ceiling and sit back with a groan. "I can't believe how pathetic I was this past week." I tap my stylus, currently in pen mode, against the table. "I feel like I lost some major points in the kick-butt department while dangling from a ceiling."

Ryn looks up with a smile. "Don't be too hard on yourself. It wasn't what I'd call pathetic. More … endearing, perhaps."

"Endearing?" I look at him in disbelief. "Now who's being pathetic?"

He puts his stylus down. "You're going to hate me for saying this."

"Then don't."

"It was nice to see a more vulnerable side of you."

I pretend to gag. "You did *not* just say that about me. Why not insult me properly and call me *weak*?"

"Because it wasn't weakness. It was—"

"Endearing. Right. I got it. Let's never talk about it again." With heat creeping up my neck, I pick up my stylus and continue writing. I work quickly until I have to start describing our journey through the human realm. That's when I get bored and my mind begins wandering. It continues wandering while I finish writing the report, and, by the time I reach the end, I have a question for Ryn. "Have either of your parents ever mentioned anyone named Angelica? A guardian they went to school with?"

Ryn rolls up his finished report. "No, I don't think so. Why?"

"She's Nate's mother."

"Halfling boy?" Ryn sets the scroll down and leans back on his hands. "His mother was at the Guild with our parents? In the same year?"

"Yes."

"Wow. So a person our parents trained with turns out to be the mother of one of your assignments, who you then end up dating."

"Yes. It's unlikely, but it happened. Anyway, I was wondering if your parents ever mentioned her because it seems like she hated my mother and father."

"Wait, how do you know this? Have you met her?"

With a sigh, I say, "I think I should tell you some stuff."

Ryn sits forward. "Off-limits stuff?"

"Yes."

"Awesome." He rubs his hands together. "Give it to me."

So I do. I go right back to the beginning and tell him about being kidnapped by Zell and Drake, and about deciding not to give Nate the *Forget* potion. I tell him about our time in the labyrinth, meeting Angelica, and the eye tattoo on Nate's back. Then there's Scarlet, and the shapeshifter I killed, and my date with Nate where he ended up handing me over to Zell, and all the things Zell said to me down in his dungeon when we were rescuing Calla. I tell Ryn everything

"Hectic," he murmurs when I've finished speaking.

I nod. Then I take a deep breath and hold it in for a moment before plunging ahead with my final secret: Nate's power over the weather.

"Are you *serious?*" Ryn says the moment I'm finished speaking. "So he's the one who created that storm and the lightning that got into the Guild?"

"Well, I don't know that, but probably."

Ryn runs a hand through his hair. "Have you told Tora any of this?"

"No, and you can't tell her, Ryn. You can't tell anyone."

"Look, I understand that you don't want her to be mad at you, but this is important stuff. It sounds like Zell is trying to amass an army of specially skilled faeries to help him attack the Guild. Don't you think whoever's been investigating him for years would like to know about that?"

"They do know about it. I told Councilor Starkweather about all the trapped people we saw in Zell's dungeon, remember? I'm sure she came to the same conclusion you just did. And she already knows that someone who can create and control storms has attacked the Guild. I could tell her Nate's name and where he used to live in the human realm, but how exactly is that going to help?"

Ryn is quiet for a minute, obviously thinking over what I've said. "Okay, so I guess you don't really *need* to tell the Council any of this. But what about Tora? Don't you feel guilty keeping things from her?"

I narrow my eyes at him. "I do. Thanks for making me feel even worse."

He gives me an innocent smile. "You're welcome. Anyway, what you tell Tora is up to you, but since you're sharing your secrets with me, perhaps I should share one of mine with you."

I raise an eyebrow as he rolls onto one side so he can dig in his pocket. He pulls out a silver chain with a white teardrop pendant and says, "I may have stolen something from the Guild."

"Ryn!" Dangling from Ryn's hand is none other than the eternity necklace. "Okay, you can*not* guilt-trip me about keeping secrets from my mentor when you've stolen something this important from the Guild. What were you thinking?"

"I don't trust the Silver Starky, remember? And she *did* lie to us. She said she'd send the necklace to the Seelie Queen immediately, but when I snuck into her office this morning, I found it buried beneath some papers in one of her drawers."

"And why did you feel the need to sneak into her office and look for it?"

Ryn shrugs. "To see if she was lying." He pushes the necklace back into his pocket. "I don't think she was ever planning to give it to the Seelie Queen. She probably wanted to keep it for herself."

"Or maybe she just hadn't got around to sending it yet."

"Or maybe—" Ryn raises a conspiratorial eyebrow "—she's the spy Zell mentioned to you. Maybe she murdered that Seer last week. Maybe that's why she was so insistent that we forget about what we saw in Zell's dungeon. She doesn't want us finding out that she's involved."

"No, no, no." I shake my head. "The idea that the *head* of the Guild Council could be working with the Unseelie Court is both too preposterous and too scary to contemplate, so I'm going to go with my initial reaction: She hadn't got around to sending the necklace to the Seelie Queen yet."

"Well, despite the fact that I don't agree with you," Ryn says, "you are, of course, welcome to have your own opinion." He shrinks the table back to a small wooden box, leaving my finished assignment pages to flutter onto the blanket. He lies back and puts his hands behind his head. "So I'm guessing that, in your opinion, I should put the necklace back?"

I hesitate before answering. What if the spy *is* Councilor Starkweather? She'll take the necklace straight back to Zell, and then we'll all be up against a powerful, *immortal* faerie. "I don't know, Ryn." I gather my neatly written pages and roll them together. "You decide. After all, you're the one who took it." I pack the scroll away and close my bag, remembering there's something else I'm supposed to be asking Ryn about. "Your mother's worried about you," I say as I pull my knees up to my chest and wrap my arms around them.

"She's my mother. She's supposed to worry about me."

"You know what I'm talking about."

"Believe it or not, I can't read minds," Ryn says, "so I actually have no idea what you're talking about."

I roll my eyes. "The fact that you arrived home earlier looking like you'd just been in a fight? Which, apparently, you've done before, and which you did earlier this week while we were at the Harts' house."

"Oh, that." He shrugs. "It's just something I need to take care of for a friend."

I watch him closely as I try to figure out what he's got himself involved in. There's no use guessing, though; it could be anything. "Okay, just tell me this: Should your mother be concerned about you or not?"

161

"Not. I'll be done fighting people by graduation."

"Graduation. Okay." I rest my chin on my left knee. "Your friend is lucky to have you, you know, if you're willing to get beaten up for him."

"Yeah," he says quietly, watching me from his comfortable position on the blanket. His eyes appear bluer than normal in the light cast by the glow-bugs around us. They're dangerous, those eyes, because I keep finding myself captivated by them, even though I really have *no* business whatsoever being captivated by anything about Ryn. I can't help it right now, though. Something about the way he's watching me causes warmth to spread out from the lowest part of my belly right up to—

Friend, friend, friend, I remind myself quickly. I drop my gaze just as an unexpected *whoosh* sounds nearby. I jump to my feet, ready to face the threat, and find a branch blazing with blue and green flames above Ryn's head.

"Whoa!" Ryn rolls over and springs up, a glittering knife in his hand. The fire vanishes, leaving wisps of smoke rising and curling in the air. Ryn's eyes dart around as he searches the forest. "I can't sense anyone's magic except ours," he says.

"Me neither." My muscles, tensed and ready to fight, start to relax. "So where did those flames come from?"

Ryn lets his knife disappear before running a hand through his hair. "Probably just Creepy Hollow being creepy."

I suddenly feel stupid for thinking it was anything more than that. Odd magical stuff happens all the time in Creepy Hollow. I'm just on edge because of the crazy, evil Unseelie faerie who happens to be after me. "Yeah, probably," I say.

"Just a weird, pyromaniac creature hiding in the trees or something."

I resume my position on the blanket, and Ryn sits next to me with his back against one of the enormous gargan branches. "So, speaking of graduation ..." he says.

I slide my hand into the top of my boot and remove my stylus. "We were speaking about graduation?"

"We were. And I was wondering which lucky graduate gets to spend the evening with you."

I draw random, lazy patterns in the air, watching a faint path of silver trail after my stylus. "What do you mean?"

"You haven't forgotten about the ball, have you?"

My hand freezes and the looping silver pattern vanishes. *The ball. Dammit.* I've spent so much time focusing on the graduation ceremony itself that I managed to forget about the ball I'm supposed to attend afterward. "Crap," I mutter.

Ryn laughs. "You've got to be the only girl who's overlooked the part where you get dressed up and have fun."

"And who are you going with, Ryn? I don't see anyone lining up to invite you."

"That's because the combination of my good looks and charm is so dazzling that most girls prefer to admire me from a distance."

"Right." I resume my random pattern-drawing. "Or it could be because you act like a total jackass in front of most people."

"I love," Ryn says, "how your need for complete honesty overrides any concern you might otherwise have for my feelings."

"Wait, you have feelings?" I allow my mouth to hang open in mock horror. "Wow, sorry, I had *no* idea."

"I know a lot more about feelings than you'd think."

"Well, you certainly know how to *hurt* them." The moment the words leave my mouth I know I've gone too far. "Sorry, that's all in the past, I know."

After a pause, Ryn says, "Yeah, whatever." He picks up his stylus and transforms my silver pattern into floating drops of water. "Feelings aside, I was thinking perhaps you and I could go together, since neither of us is interested enough in the ball to bother with the stress of trying to find a date."

I cross my arms. "And what makes you think I want to attend the ball with a jackass?"

"Because no one else is lining up to invite you?"

"Nice, Ryn. How could I possibly say no to an invitation like that?"

"You can't." He swirls the water droplets into a mini whirlpool in the air. "When someone as charming as me invites you to a ball, it's impossible for you to do anything but lift your hand delicately to your forehead as you faint away, uttering the word 'yes.'"

I glare at him. "My fainting days are over, so don't count on that happening again."

"Oh, but you were so good at it," he says with a laugh. I aim my stylus at him, and he hurriedly says, "Okay, okay. All I need is a simple answer to a simple question: Will you be my date?"

"Fine. We can go to the ball together. But it isn't a date."

"No. Of course not. It's simply a convenient arrangement

that suits us both."

"Yes." I watch the whirlpool spinning for a few moments before closing my eyes and groaning. "Ugh, I *really* wish we didn't have to attend that part."

"Why? That's supposed to be the *fun* part, V." He nudges me with his shoulder.

"Maybe for some, but for me … well, it's just not my thing. Dressing pretty, decorating my hair, painting my face with fancy makeup spells." I sigh. "I can kick butt at every single exercise in the training center, but I can't kick butt in there. In a *ballroom*." The word almost tastes bad. "That's for pretty girls like Aria and Jasmine."

Ryn spins the droplets into a ball of water. "You did a good job at the Harts' cocktail party."

"That was part of an assignment. Of course I did a good job."

"And at Zell's masquerade."

"Again, that was like an assignment."

Ryn sighs and shakes his head.

"What?"

"No matter what I say, you're going to disagree with me, so this is where my comments end."

"Good."

"But there is one other thing." He waves the ball of water toward me until it's hovering over my head. With a flick of his stylus, the swirling liquid drops through the air.

I gasp as the cold water hits my neck and travels down my back. "What the freak, Ryn?"

His grin is wide as he says, "Told you I'd get you back."

CHAPTER FIFTEEN

"RAVEN!" I STAND ON TIPTOE AND WAVE AS RAVEN TURNS around, her deep brown and magenta hair sliding over her shoulder. She peers through the throng of people filling the main lane of the Creepy Hollow Shoppers' Clearing. I shout her name again. When she spots me, she smiles and waves. I hurry past open stalls, shop fronts built into trees, and busy faeries getting their shopping done. "Hey, thanks for waiting."

"Sure." She greets me with a hug. "I don't often see you here. Shouldn't you be hitting a punching bag or practicing backflips or something?"

"I've handed in my final report. My training is officially finished."

"Congratulations!" Raven gives me another hug, then pulls me to the side of the path where we're out of the way. "You must be bored out of your mind now."

Ha, she knows me so well. "Yeah, kind of," I say with a grin. "Anyway, I came looking for you because I, um, need your help."

Raven hooks her thumb around the strap of the shrinking shopping bag on her shoulder. "Oh dear. Another fashion emergency?"

"Yes. I forgot that there's a ball after the graduation ceremony, and I don't exactly have anything to wear." I put my hands together and do my best imitation of Filigree's kitten eyes. "Will you please make a dress for me?"

"Vi, don't be silly." Raven laughs and my stomach sinks. "I started designing your grad dress months ago."

My stomach halts its descent. "You did? Oh. Wow, thanks."

"Of course. It's one of the most important occasions of your life. You have to look good." She hooks her arm through mine and leads me down the road. "It's going to be absolutely perfect for you, Vi."

Oh dear. That doesn't sound good. "Um, it's not purple, is it?"

She smiles. "I know how you feel about purple stuff, so no. It isn't purple."

"Okay, and nothing big and puffy, right? I don't want to be wading through five hundred layers of fabric."

"It won't be big."

"And no overly revealing slits. That cocktail dress I wore at the Harts' party was *way* too—"

"Vi." She stops and places her hands on my shoulders.

"Trust me. I know you're mainly indifferent when it comes to fashion, but even *you* will love this dress when it's done."

The tree we're heading toward has an archway cut out of the bark and a sign above it that says Farrow's Fantabulous Fabrics. We walk beneath the archway and into a gigantic room filled with roll upon roll of every imaginable material. There's the regular stuff, like colors, patterns, and textures that do nothing but lie still. Then there's the cool stuff, like fabric made from dewdrops, or flames, or smoke, or serpent scales that change color. This must be Raven's idea of heaven.

"Oh, that is *perfect* for the client I met with yesterday!" She runs toward a sparkly fabric that twinkles with every color of the rainbow. I wouldn't be caught dead in it. "I'll take the entire roll," she tells the shop keeper.

"Raven?" She turns to look at me as though she's forgotten I'm there. "I need to do a bit of my own shopping, so if you don't need my help carrying anything …"

"Oh, sure, you go do your thing." She pats her shrinking shopping bag. "My stuff will easily fit in here."

* * *

The next two weeks crawl by, but finally, after five years of training, studying, assignments, and generally working my butt off, the day has arrived.

Graduation.

Imaginary butterflies beat their wings furiously within my stomach as I stand in front of a mirror in Tora's house. Raven should be here any minute now with my dress, and in about two hours—because, apparently, that's how long it takes to get ready—Ryn will be here to pick me. No, to *meet* me; it isn't a date.

I look away from the mirror and down at my hands. My tokehari from my father, the ring with the gold-flecked purple stone, is on my right hand. When Dad died, I automatically inherited all his belongings, but the ring is special. It's the item he specifically set aside for me in the event of his death. The item I'm meant to remember him by. I only have one other piece of jewelry that means as much to me—the arrow-shaped earrings that were a gift from Reed before he died—and they're in my ears right now.

My gaze moves to my bare wrists. By the end of tonight, permanent markings will curl across the skin there, forever marking me as a guardian. It's all I've ever wanted. Well, that and to be the very *best* guardian. But now that I'm standing here with my goal in sight and my future spread out before me like one endless, blank piece of reed paper, I'm not entirely sure what to do next. I'm almost guaranteed a position with the Guild, if I want it, so the logical thing would be to tell them about my finding ability and work with the Department of Missing Fae. But I'm afraid that once they know what I can do, they'll never let me leave. I could be trapped at the Guild for the rest of my working life.

"Vi, are you up here?"

I turn at the sound of Raven's voice. "Yes, the room at the end of the passage."

She shuffles sideways through the door with a large, flat bag over her shoulder and a smaller square case tucked under her arm. I take a few quick strides to the door to help her. "Thanks," she says. I dump the case on the bed as she carefully lays out the large bag. "Okay, I'm not showing you the dress until it's actually on you. That way you'll get the full effect."

"Full effect?" That sounds worrying.

"Yes." She flips up the clips on the square case and pulls the lid back. "Here, I made this bra for you. Go put it on while I get the dress out."

She removes a padded bra from amongst the clips and colored pots in the case and hands it to me. It's covered in white lace and is far prettier than any underwear I've ever owned. But there's something else different about it. I hold it up, giving it a suspicious sniff. "Is there magic in this thing?"

Raven keeps her eyes averted while digging through the case for who knows what. "Um, possibly."

"Seriously, Raven?" I toss the bra on top of the dress bag. "Enchanted underwear?"

"Vi." She perches on the edge of the bed and picks up the offensive piece of underwear. "Despite what you've been brought up to believe, magic isn't only useful for attacking people. You can also use it to ... enhance certain natural features." I stare at her until she sighs and says pointedly, "And you could use some help in the cleavage department."

With an eye roll and a groan, I snatch the bra out of her hands. "Fine. I'll wear it." I head to the corner of the room to change out of my black pants and tank top. The bra fits perfectly, which isn't surprising; Raven's always been good at her job. I look down at my improved cleavage and notice a pleasant scent. "Next thing you'll be telling me there's some kind of aphrodisiac spell woven into this underwear."

"Only a little one."

"Raven!"

"Kidding," she says with a laugh. "It's just a perfume spell. It'll produce whatever scent is most appealing to you or, if you're standing close to someone you find attractive, whatever scent is most appealing to him."

"How does the bra know if I find someone attractive? And what if he likes a scent I don't like? And what if it's someone I just happen to find attractive, but I'm not actually interested in him and I *don't* want him sniffing me?"

"Um ..."

"I see a lot of flaws in this design, Raven."

"Look, this range of underwear is still in the experimentation phase, okay. Now keep your eyes up while I bring the dress over."

I do as instructed and try not to fall over as Raven guides my feet into a circle of fabric and lifts the dress up around me. She runs her finger quickly up the center of my back, and the dress does itself up while she steps around to stand in front of me. She smiles and says, "I was right. The sweetheart neckline definitely suits you, especially since you now have a little bit of cleavage. And the empire line was a good choice too. Very elegant."

"Okay, enough with the fashion jargon. Can I see it now?" She steps out of the way and I walk over to the mirror. I stare for a long moment before whispering, "Wow."

"You like it?" Raven asks, her hands clasped together beneath her chin.

"Raven, it's amazing. You were right. It is perfect for me."

The dress is simple and strapless and feels light and comfortable. The sweetheart shape that goes across my chest is a deep bronze color, with tiny crystals sewn along the edge. They shimmer bronze, black, and grey as if each one has a tiny fire lit within it. From just below my bust right down to my toes, the dress—which is in no way puffy at all—is an off-white color. The top layer is sheer with tiny flowers that look real scattered across its surface. The flowers, like the crystals, cycle through various shades of bronze and black. Lastly, several strings of pearls and crystals hang from the center of my bust, loop gracefully around the left side of the dress, and attach somewhere high up at the back.

"Oh, wow," Tora says from the doorway. "Raven, you did an amazing job."

"Thanks." Raven places her hands on her hips and examines her work. "Too many girls go for the fancy, puffy look better suited to a human ballroom in Victorian times. I wanted to get back to our faerie roots with this dress."

"It's perfect," Tora says with a sniff. "I think I might cry."

"Not in here." Raven points to the door. "Please take your weepiness elsewhere."

"Fine," Tora says with a laugh that sounds more like a snuffle. "Call me when you're ready, and I'll try to keep my weeping under control."

"She leaks way too easily," I say to Raven once Tora has left the room.

"Can you blame her?" Raven pulls a chair in front of the mirror and makes me sit down. "This is a big day for her too,

Vi. You were her very first trainee, not to mention she's also like your surrogate mother and sister rolled into one. You should allow her a few tears."

"Hey, you're the one who banished her from the room," I point out.

"Yes, well, I don't want her tears *on you*." In the mirror, I see her reach into her makeup case for something. She starts dabbing a sponge over my face.

"Why aren't you using makeup spells?" I ask, thinking of all the times I've heard her mutter a few quick words and seen a layer of powder form on her palm, or lipstick come out of the tip of her finger.

"Makeup spells are more for touching up," she explains. "If you want to do things properly, you need the real stuff."

Oops. I guess I didn't do a proper job at Zell's masquerade and the Harts' cocktail party.

Raven works quickly, coloring my lips with a neutral shade and my eyelids with something dark and smoky. A few brushes of bronze powder enhance the shape of my cheekbones, and a twirl of her stylus lengthens my eyelashes. I hate it when I have to admit that I'm not good at something, but I *definitely* could not do what she just did.

"Okay, let's see if we can tame your mane," she says as she drops her pot of bronzer back into the case.

"My mane? Really, Raven, there's no need to exaggerate."

"I'm not sure it's an exaggeration, Vi. Has your hair ever even been introduced to a hair brush?"

"I don't need to brush my hair!" I protest. "I happen to like the messy, wavy, unbrushed look."

"Yes. I can see that." Raven twists a strand of her own sleek, straight hair around her finger as she examines my head. "Well, I say we go with something simple. Curls, some of them pinned up, with small flowers stuck here and there."

"Um, sure. You're the expert."

While she heats up her fingers and winds sections of my hair around them, I work up the courage to ask a question I've wanted to ask someone ever since I made out with Nate in a tree and a branch spontaneously broke off and almost landed on my head.

Okay, here goes. "Um, can I ask you something, Raven?"

"Uh huh." She lets go of a few pieces of hair, and perfect curls settle over my shoulder.

"When you're kissing a guy, and you feel really, uh ... attracted to him, is it normal to, um ..." Her fingers stop moving in my hair and she meets my gaze in the mirror. She raises an eyebrow. I clear my throat. "Is it normal to ..." Dammit, she knows exactly what I'm asking; I can see it in her glittering magenta eyes. "Uh, you know, lose control of your magic? And ... weird stuff happens?"

A grin turns her lips up. "Oh yeah. It's definitely normal."

"But that can't last forever, can it? I mean, things would be exploding all over the place if people couldn't control themselves every time they kissed or ... well, other stuff."

She laughs and shakes her head. "It doesn't last forever, don't worry. You learn to control it after a while. Well, with kissing anyway. It's a little more difficult to control with the 'other stuff,' as you put it." Her grin turns mischievous. "You should have seen the mess when Flint and I went on our honeymoon. It was—"

"Okay," I interrupt loudly. "I think this falls into the Too Much Information category."

"Well, anyway." She smiles to herself as she continues curling my hair. "Now I have to ask: Which boy have you been kissing?" She narrows her eyes at me in the mirror. "Is it at all possible that we're talking about Ryn?"

"What? No! Definitely not. There was … this other guy."

"Other guy?" Raven looks skeptical. "And how come none of us knew about this other guy?"

I sigh. "Honestly? You wouldn't have approved of him. He wasn't really the kind of guy I should have been seeing. I mean, it's over now, don't worry," I assure her. "I just … I liked him, he hurt me, and I learned my lesson."

"Oh, Vi, I'm—"

"Please." I hold up a hand. "Don't get all soppy on me. I'm totally over it, I promise." And I realize, as I say the words, that they're true. I still think about Nate every now and then, but it doesn't cause that sharp pain in my chest like it used to. And in the days since I finished my final assignment, it hasn't even crossed my mind to watch his window in the middle of the night. I've been visiting Tora, annoying Ryn, cleaning out my house from top to bottom—except for my parents' bedroom—and using the forest as my training center for random exercises.

Raven finishes curling my hair, pins a few strands up, and magically attaches tiny flowers here and there. "There," she says, standing back. "Perfect. Oh, I left your shoes downstairs. Hang on, I'll go get them."

I stand frozen in front of the mirror, afraid for several

ridiculous moments that if I move I might mess something up. Then I do something silly and girly that I've quite possibly never felt the need to do before: I twirl around in a circle, watching the way the fabric floats out around my body.

I hear a knock on the door and prepare myself for more of Tora's tears. When I look up, though, I see a head of black and blue curls peering around the doorway.

"Zin—Mrs. Larkenwood. What are you doing here?"

She smiles as she steps into the room. "You used to call me Zinnia when you were young. I wish you'd still call me that."

"Um, okay."

"Ryn told me you'd be getting ready here, and ... well, I wanted to see you all dressed up." She presses her hands together and sits on the edge of the bed. "And I also need to apologize for something. Well, for several things, actually."

Confused, I perch on the edge of the bed beside her. I can't imagine what Zinnia might have to apologize for.

"I ... I'm really sorry I wasn't there for you when your father died. I wish I could have been. I was *supposed* to be." She takes a deep breath. "Do you know you were meant to come and live with us?"

My eyes widen as I shake my head.

"Linden and I—when we were still together—had an agreement with your parents that if anything should happen to us, they would take care of Reed and Ryn, and if anything should happen to your parents, we would take care of you. However, given the circumstances at the time of your father's death ... Well, Linden had recently left us, and Ryn was angry with everything and everyone in his life, *especially* you. I know he would have made life very difficult for you had you come to live with us. So Tora and I arranged for you to stay with her for a while instead. She had been your mentor for almost a year by then, and the two of you got on well together. She cared for you more than you knew, and she was happy to take you in."

Zinnia stops talking, and I wonder if I'm supposed to respond now. I can't imagine how different—how *awful*—life would have been had I gone to live with Ryn and Zinnia four years ago. Zinnia would have been nice enough, I'm sure, but Ryn undoubtedly would have tried to make my life as miserable as possible. Or perhaps we would have confronted one another far sooner, realized the misunderstanding regarding Reed's death, and gone back to being friends years ago. The past four years would have been completely different.

"Anyway, I just want you to know that … I've always thought of you like a daughter," Zinnia continues. "I've never stopped caring about you or checking in with Tora to see how you're doing. Ryn's behavior toward you in the years since Reed's death has been inexcusable, and I have to apologize for that." She reaches over and takes my hand. "I don't know why or how it happened, but I know the two of you have finally made up, and I'm so thankful for that. I only wish I could have done something to make it happen sooner."

I squeeze her hand. "You really don't need to apologize for him, Zinnia. It wasn't your fault." I give her a reassuring smile before standing up.

"Wait, Vi, there's something else." She puts her head in her hands for a moment and groans, then pushes her hair back and looks up at me. "This is the big one because it really is my fault. Um ..." She runs her hands up and down the length of her thighs. "Before your mother died, she gave me something. A locked wooden box with your name on it. She asked me to keep it safe until the day you graduated, just in case she was no longer around to give it to you herself."

With my heart pounding faster in my chest, I say, "Okay."

"I hid the box away, checking on it occasionally to make sure it was still there. As the years passed by, I stopped checking. The box was safe, after all. Who would want to take it?"

I press one hand to my lips, knowing without a doubt that this story isn't going to have a happy ending.

"After your father died, I remembered the box and went to check it was still there." Zinnia looks down at the floor. "It was gone. I don't know when, or how, but it was gone. I asked Linden about it—he was the only other person who knew where I'd hidden it—but he swore he'd never touched it. And what would he want with it, anyway? He was living a happy life outside of Creepy Hollow with his new wife and child."

I nod, although I'm not quite sure why. Part of me wishes Zinnia had never told me any of this. Now I'll forever be wondering what it was my mother wanted to give me. I drop my hand from my mouth. "Why ... why didn't she give it to my father?"

"I think she was afraid that he wouldn't be alive either by the time you graduated. The two of them always liked to take on the most dangerous assignments." She shakes her head, blinking away tears. "Looks like she was right."

I turn my back to Zinnia so she won't see the moisture in

my eyes. I don't usually cry over my parents, but that's because I try not to think about them much. Zinnia's story has brought them right to the forefront of my mind, reminding me that neither of them is here to share this incredibly important occasion with me.

Ugh, what am I doing? I'm going to *make* myself cry if I keep having thoughts like that. My parents wouldn't want me to cry on the day of my graduation, would they? I suppose I don't know what my mother would say, but I know my father wouldn't want me to cry. He saw how hard I worked for every single assignment. He'd be ridiculously excited and proud if he were here today; he wouldn't want me crying over a box.

"This is supposed to be a happy day," I say, turning back to Zinnia. "It's a celebration day. We shouldn't be crying. Yes, an important box went missing, and we'll never know what was inside it, but there's nothing we can do about it."

She sits up straight and stares at me. "You have amazing strength, Vi."

I look away. I'm not sure her words are true. Most of the time I try not to think about all the things that hurt; that probably has a lot more to do with weakness than strength.

She puts her arms carefully around my shoulders and hugs me. "I really am sorry," she whispers into my ear. "And I'm very proud of you." She pulls back and rearranges some of the curls over my shoulder. "Well, I need to dash home and change into something suitable for a graduation ceremony. I expect Ryn will be here soon to meet you."

With a final smile, she leaves the room. After checking my appearance once more in the mirror, I pick up Raven's makeup case and the empty dress bag and head downstairs. Tora goes on and on about how beautiful and grown-up I look while Raven straps me into high-heeled shoes. Nerves begin to bounce around my stomach once more.

We stand around, Raven and Tora chattering on about something, while we wait for Ryn. And wait. And wait some more. After half an hour, my frustration levels have reached a new high. I tuck my amber into the strap of one shoe, and my stylus into the other, and announce, "I'm leaving now."

"Oh." Raven looks around as though she has no idea how much time as passed. "But Ryn isn't here yet."

"Well, the ceremony is due to start in ten minutes, and, while Ryn may not care if he misses his own graduation, I certainly don't feel the same way."

CHAPTER SIXTEEN

I PEER THROUGH THE ORNATE DOUBLE DOORS AND SCAN the crowded hall for the guy who is going to be in *big* trouble when I find him. My eyes brush over the groups of parents, mentors, and trainees, but I don't see Ryn anywhere. Where the freak is he?

I step back into the hallway and lean against the wall. One part of me is worried about him, but another, larger part is definitely still furious. Everyone is supposed to have a date to this thing, and now I have to walk in there alone.

I do my best to act invisible as a group of my classmates walks past me. Guys in suits and girls in—just as Raven predicted—big puffy dresses. I don't think they even noticed me standing there. "I'm taking bets," one of them says from just inside the doorway. "Who's your money on? Ryn or Vi?"

Yeah, they definitely didn't notice me.

"Are those the only choices?" a girl asks. Aria, I think.

"Well, we all know it's going to be one or the other."

"What about Asami?" someone else asks. "I heard his mentor telling my mentor that he was catching up to first place in the last few assignments before our final."

"You mean the few weeks since we haven't been allowed to see the rankings?"

"Yes. And his final went really well, so it's definitely possible he's pulled ahead."

Oh flipping hell, are you kidding *me?* I tip my head back against the wall and close my eyes. Now I'm dateless *and* I'm losing my top position to someone I never even considered a threat? I bang my head against the wall, which hurts quite a bit more than I expected. "That was stupid," I mutter.

With a deep breath, I hold my head up high and walk right past my classmates, down the center aisle, and toward the sixteen chairs reserved at the front left of the hall. I don't look up while I search for my name. I find it in the second row of eight and take my seat. A minute later, the tinkling of a bell tells everyone still standing to get their butts on a chair.

The ceremony is about to begin.

To be honest, I don't hear much of the blah, blah, blah that goes on at the beginning. Head Councilor Starkweather talks for a while, followed by a guest speaker who tries to inspire us with exciting tales of the exotic adventures he's been on. I can't concentrate on any of it, though, because I keep glancing behind me to see if Ryn is standing at the back of the hall. I see

182

Tora, Raven and Flint, who must have been given the evening off guard duty so he could attend. I see Zinnia, looking anxious, and, further back, Ryn's father. Everyone who's supposed to be here is here—except Ryn.

Before I know it, Councilor Starkweather is calling the first graduate up to the stage to receive his markings.

Okay, WHERE IS RYN!

My classmates go up to the stage in alphabetical order, each taking about three minutes to recite the Guardian's Oath and receive their markings from the only Guild Council member who's certified to draw them. When it comes to my turn—my big moment!—I'm still freaking out over the fact that Ryn is missing. Doesn't his empty chair bother anyone else? Does this happen every year, someone deciding not to show up?

Stop, I tell myself sternly. *Ryn has made his decision, and there's nothing you can do about it. Don't let him ruin this moment for you.* I stand carefully. My dress may not be heavy and layered, but I still don't want to trip over it. The short journey from my chair to the steps at the side of the stage seems to take forever. I lift my dress and climb the stairs, willing myself not to wobble on my high heels. I walk across the stage and come to a halt in front of Councilor Starkweather. With my right side facing the audience, I repeat the words of the oath after her, barely hearing myself over the roar of blood pumping through my ears. I know what I'm supposed to say—something about swearing to protect whomever needs protecting, be it human or fae—but if I didn't have someone to repeat after, I'd probably just stand here squealing, *This is it, this is it, this is it!*

When the oath comes to an end, I walk past Councilor Starkweather and kneel in front of the table where the markings artist sits. I raise my hands and place them, wrists up, on the table. The artist dips his specially sharpened stylus into a pot of black ink and begins to draw the curling pattern onto my skin. It stings a little, but we were all warned to expect that. As he works, he whispers the words of the spell that will transfer the protective enchantments from my trainee pendant to the ink embedded in my skin.

With a nod of his head to indicate he's done, the markings artist leans back. Councilor Starkweather clears her throat, turns to the front of the stage, and utters the words I've been working five years to hear: "You are now a member of the Guild of Guardians."

I stand and turn around, dimly aware of the clapping as I look out at the sea of faces. I catch Tora's glistening eyes before my gaze is drawn to the back of the hall. I see him standing there, hands in the pockets of his suit pants, watching me with an expression I can't figure out. I should be yelling *Where the hell have you been*, but instead I'm so full of joy and excitement that all I want to do is fling my arms around him and do a whole lot of uncharacteristic squealing. And kissing.

No. I do not want to kiss Ryn.

I carefully make my way off the other side of the stage and back to my chair. After two more trainees have received their markings, Councilor Starkweather calls Ryn's name. He saunters down the aisle as though it's completely acceptable for him to have shown up late to one of the most important occasions of his life. I realize then that my earlier frustration with him has *definitely* not disappeared.

By the time he takes his seat, I've surreptitiously removed my amber and stylus from the straps around my ankles. I write a quick message and send it to him. *You suck as a date.*

From the corner of my eye, I see him slip his hand inside his jacket. A moment later my amber vibrates. *I thought this wasn't a date.*

Oh, so that gives him the right to just leave me waiting for ages at Tora's house? Pressing my lips together, I write another message. *You still have to be on time, jerk-face! I looked like an idiot walking in here alone.*

He leans forward and looks past the two trainees between us. His eyes travel from my face down to my shoes before he sits back and writes another message. *An idiot is one thing I'm sure you did NOT look like.*

I don't know how to respond to that, so I put my amber and stylus away. I keep my eyes directed forward as the last few trainees in our class go up to receive their markings. As the program inches closer to the biggest announcement of the evening, my heart beats out an erratic pattern and I start to feel sick. I want this so badly, I don't know what I'll do if that top position isn't mine. I'll have to suck it up and take it like a big girl, of course, but my heart will be so many kinds of broken I don't know how I'll handle it.

"The competition amongst certain members of this year's graduating class has been fierce from the very first day of their training five years ago," Councilor Starkweather says. I'm not quite sure how she knows that, since she wasn't present for a single day of our training. I suppose she must have heard stories from the mentors. "They have worked remarkably hard, and I'm sure they're desperate to know the recipient of the coveted first place position."

I clench my hands together in my lap. *Oh please let it be me.*

"So, without further delay—" she unrolls a scroll in her hand, which must be for show, because *surely* she already knows who the winner is "—the top graduate for this year is—"

Pleasepleaseplease.

"Oryn Larkenwood."

Disbelief. *WHAT THE—*

"And Violet Fairdale."

Pause. *Okay, what?*

"As was the case with only one other graduating class in the history of this Guild, we have two trainees whose stellar performances have managed to earn them the same number of points. Congratulations to Miss Fairdale and Mr. Larkenwood."

The scroll in her hand vanishes with a puff of smoke, and applause erupts around me. I feel a hand on mine and see Ryn reaching over the two people between us to pull me to my feet. He lets me walk in front of him up to the stage where we both kneel once more in front of the markings artist and receive the tiny extra flourish on each of our wrists.

The final few minutes of the ceremony pass in a giddy blur. Before I know it, everyone is standing up, and Flint is lifting me off the ground to twirl me around while Raven and Tora jump up and down like Calla on a sugar high. I laugh. Properly. More than I've laughed in years. And my smile is so wide it threatens to hurt my face.

Everything is perfect.

* * *

The ballroom is part of the Guild, but the décor makes it appear as though it's outside. The walls are draped with silver ivy, flowers, and tiny glow-bugs. Enchanted stars twinkle against the darkened ceiling. Snowflakes float toward the floor but disappear before touching anything. It looks like a winter wonderland.

Round tables form an outer ring around the room, while the center is occupied by a dance floor. In the middle of each table is a tree carved from non-melting ice with various edible treats dangling from each branch. Pieces of glass that gleam when they catch the light are scattered across each table.

It's beautiful, but instead of admiring the room with Tora, Raven and Flint, I'm searching it for Ryn. One of our 'rewards' for coming first is that we have to open the dance floor—another horrifying requirement I'd forgotten all about in the build-up to graduation.

I've almost done a complete circle around the room when I hear a voice behind me. A voice that manages to make my insides curl up with happiness one second and burn with annoyance the next. "Hey, Sexy Pixie." I turn around. Ryn looks amused as he asks, "Looking for someone?"

Definitely burning with annoyance.

Without a word, I grab his arm and drag him beneath a curtained archway into one of the many small rooms leading off the ballroom. I don't know what people are supposed to do in here—powder their noses, or make out, perhaps—but it'll do just fine for the confrontation Ryn and I are about to have.

"Where have you been?" I demand. "Did you forget you were supposed to meet me at Tora's house? Did you forget you were *graduating*?"

"Violet, there is no way *anyone* who's spent the past few days around you could possibly have forgotten about graduation. I didn't forget anything, I just got held up Underground."

"Underground?"

"Yes, I had to fetch something."

"You had to *fetch something*?" I can't believe how unconcerned he is. "*Underground*?"

Ryn nods. "I'm pretty sure that's what I said."

I shake my head. "What could possibly be so important that you would risk losing your life and—more importantly—missing graduation for?"

Ryn holds his fist up and opens his fingers. A gold chain slips down and dangles from between his thumb and forefinger. Hanging from the end of the chain is a gold key. A gold key with tiny outspread wings.

The tokehari my mother left me.

I'm certain my heart comes to a complete stop before jumping into furious action. Goose bumps rush across my skin and breathing suddenly becomes difficult. "Where did you get that?" I whisper.

"Underground."

Moisture coats my eyes and distorts my vision. "But ... when ... how did you find it?"

"It took a little while." Ryn steps behind me and loops the necklace over my head. The metal is cool against my skin. "I went back to the singing well I threw the necklace down all those years ago and started there. A beautiful piece of jewelry like this always leaves a trail, especially Underground." His fingers brush my neck, lingering for a moment as he attaches the clasp. "It wasn't easy to track, but I figured it was worth the effort."

My head spins as Ryn comes to stand in front of me. "So ... every time you've had a bruised eye or bleeding lip in the past few weeks, it's because you've been Underground searching for my necklace?"

He lifts a shoulder, smiles in a way that does weird things to my stomach, and says simply, "I thought it was time I got it back for you."

My chest rises and falls unnaturally fast. Oh crap oh crap oh crap, why do I feel like doing something completely, utterly crazy like pushing Ryn against the wall and pressing my lips—

Friend, friend, friend, blares the sensible part of my brain like an internal security alarm. I squeeze my eyes shut and give my head a small shake. That's right. Ryn is just my *friend.* Anything more than that would almost definitely end in disaster, a broken heart, and yet *another* person leaving me.

So instead of embarrassing myself, I open my eyes and say, "Thank you."

Ryn gestures toward the archway. "Well, now that you've forgiven me for being such a terrible date-but-not-really-a-date, shall we do this dancing thing?"

CHAPTER SEVENTEEN

WE HEAD BACK OUT TO THE BALLROOM AND FIND THE table with our names on it. Honey and her Seer boyfriend are at the same table, and Honey jumps up to throw her arms around my neck while telling me she always knew I'd be the top graduate. I go rigid before awkwardly patting her back; I'm pretty sure we've never hugged before.

After Honey lets go of me, Dale and a girl not from the Guild join our table. Dale gapes at me before saying to Ryn, "Dude, I thought you were joking."

Ryn wraps his fingers loosely, but somehow *protectively*, around my wrist. Honey looks between the two of us, apparently as confused as Dale. "Obviously not," Ryn says. "I told you I'd be here with Violet, and I meant it."

"But ..." Dale's eyes slide to me, then back to Ryn. "You don't even like her. You're the one who's always telling everyone else all the things that are wrong with her."

"Well, I guess I need to tell you something else now," Ryn says before I can remind Dale that I'm *standing right here*. "I was wrong. I shouldn't have said any of those things."

Everyone at the table stares at Ryn, including me. Did Oryn Larkenwood just admit to being *wrong* about something? His hand still clasps my wrist, and his thumb moves slightly against my skin. It's almost imperceptible, barely a movement at all, and I'm sure he doesn't even know he did it, but it sends a shiver racing up my arm.

I look down at our joined hands just as Councilor Starkweather appears next to us and says, "I won't be making any announcement about the first dance. When the music changes, that's your signal." And with that she sweeps away, the simple black dress she had on earlier replaced now by a flowing red gown. Everyone else in the ballroom seems to be taking their seats, as though they know something is about to happen. Not wanting to be the last one left standing, I pull my arm out of Ryn's grasp and reach for the back of my chair.

He stops me. "Music's changing. You don't get to sit down until you've performed your dancing duty."

Crap! My feet freeze to the floor as panic sets in. *You can do this*, I silently instruct myself. *Move forward. Don't trip. Just relax and allow the spell of the music to guide your feet through the dance. It's as easy as that.*

"Interesting," Ryn murmurs as we head slowly to our doom.

From the way he says it, I know he wants me to ask. "What?"

"You're actually nervous."

"Am not," I respond immediately.

"Your pulse is jumping in your neck. Your hands are sweaty."

I move to wipe my hands against my skirt. "Don't." Ryn catches one of my hands. "You don't want everyone to know you're nervous, do you?" He loops my arm through his and leads me to the center of the ballroom. He holds his head high. I can just about feel the confidence oozing from him.

"You're enjoying this," I whisper.

"What, being the center of attention, or knowing that you're nervous?"

"Both."

After a pause, he says, "Maybe just a little."

We reach the center of the horrifyingly huge room, and I turn to face Ryn. I certainly can't wipe my sweaty hands dry now, but I don't want Ryn to have to touch them either. I hurriedly mutter the spell that Aria and Jasmine always use to dry themselves off after training. The music changes once more, and I can sense from the magic that we're just moments away from having to start the dance. Panic rises in my chest and threatens to claw its way out of my throat.

I. Don't. Dance.

"I don't know what you're panicking about," Ryn says, putting my left hand on his shoulder and holding up my right hand. "You danced perfectly well at Zell's masquerade."

"If I remember correctly, you pulled me onto the dance

floor without my consent." I swallow, trying to push the panic down. "And I didn't have an entire ballroom of people watching me."

Oh dear Seelie Queen I'm going to trip in these heels and land on my butt and my dress will tear right down the middle and everyone will see my ridiculous enchanted underwear and—

"V, you have to stand a little closer to me if this is going to work," Ryn says, interrupting my panicked thoughts.

"Right," I whisper. I feel the spell of the music wrap around me as I step closer to Ryn. My feet get ready to move, and I certainly hope they know what to do because all I can think about now is how close Ryn's chest is to mine. Close enough to feel his heat. Close enough to smell his—

And then I'm dancing, swept away by the music and the magic and Ryn's arms guiding me. We spin graceful circles around the floor. Ryn lets go of me and I twirl beneath his arm, laughing at the same time. It's so *not* me, and yet I find I'm actually enjoying it.

"See?" Ryn says. "This is easy. And you might possibly be having fun."

The magic guides me as I step out of Ryn's arms, twirl behind his back, and catch his hand. "You might possibly be right."

He pulls me back into position. "Oh, I forgot to tell you something," he says. He leans forward and his lips brush my ear as he whispers, "You are more beautiful than any other girl in this room."

A shiver races down my spine and across my arms, and with

it, the wall I built up to hide all the not-just-friends feelings I've had about Ryn cracks. Maybe it's the rush of winning, or the unexpected joy of spinning around a dance floor, or the giddiness produced by Ryn's whispered words, but all of a sudden I can't hold it in anymore. A dam of emotions—those stupid, *stupid* things I do my best to stay away from—crashes through the wall and drenches me in everything I've been trying not to feel.

Instead of fighting it, I close my eyes and let myself go. I feel the muscles of his shoulder beneath my hand. The frame his arms create is strong, secure, but I want those arms tighter around me. Much tighter, much closer. I want there to be no space at all between us.

I. Want. Him. So. Badly.

I want to kiss him, laugh with him, cry with him, share every moment of my future with him, because no matter how many awful things he's done in the past, I can't shake the undeniable feeling that when his arms are around me, I'm home.

I'm also screwed because I'm never telling him any of that.

With a shuddering breath, I look up to find him watching me. A smile lifts the corner of his mouth as he leans forward once more and whispers, "I knew it." For one heart-stopping second I'm certain he somehow knows everything I'm thinking and feeling, but then he adds, "I always knew Bran had a thing for that library assistant with the blonde and purple hair. See him over there, chatting her up?" He twirls me beneath his arm, and I catch a glimpse of Ryn's mentor with his arm around the shoulders of the Guild's library assistant.

"Oh, yeah." I laugh, mainly because I'm so relieved that Ryn was talking about Bran and not the tumult of emotions coursing through me.

The dance floor begins to fill up as other couples join us. "This is getting boring," Ryn says. "Let's give the old people something to talk about, shall we?" And with that he pushes me away from him. I spin out, jerk to a halt with my hand still attached to his, then spin back. He catches me before my back hits his chest and dips me so low I can see the whole ballroom upside down. He swoops me around, my hair brushing the floor, then pulls me up, twirls me once more, and catches me around my waist. He lifts me up into the air and shouts, "Woohoo!"

"Ryn!" I gasp. Councilor Starkweather has a hand covering her mouth, and she isn't the only one. Half the ballroom is staring at us in shock, and the other half appears to be suppressing laughter. "Are you *insane*?"

He places me gently on my feet just as the music morphs into a new dance. "Insane enough to ask if you'll dance a second dance with me."

I tilt my head to the side, considering it. "Apparently I'm insane enough to agree."

Ryn's dazzling smile sets butterflies off in my stomach. He takes a step toward me and holds his hands up, palms facing me. The spell of the music urges me to do the same thing. Our hands touch, and I'm not sure if the tingling I feel is real or imagined. My gaze is locked on his as we move slowly, rhythmically, in time to the music.

Backward, forward, twist under.

My face is hot. It's probably red, but it's not like I can do anything about it. I can't even convince my eyes to look away from his. I wonder what he's thinking. He'd probably be horrified if he knew I want to throw myself on top of him and tear his shirt off. I'm kind of horrified myself.

Step to the right, step to left, twist under.

He glances down for a second, and I wonder if he's looking at the gold key or, well, at the part of my chest that my enchanted underwear has 'enhanced.' My skin burns hotter as my gaze moves down to his lips. I want to know if they feel as soft as they look.

Backward, forward—

Click.

A sudden realization strikes me. Something so obvious, I don't know why I didn't think of it hours ago. Ryn catches himself before standing on my feet, and I notice then that I've stopped moving.

"What's wrong?" he asks, pulling me to the edge of the dance floor and out of the way.

"The key," I say, touching it and staring unseeingly over his shoulder.

"Yes, what about it?"

"I know what it opens," I say. I'm suddenly breathless with excitement, my eyes dancing across his face.

Ryn frowns. "I thought you said it didn't open anything."

"That's what my father always told me, but tonight, while I was getting ready, your mother came to see me at Tora's. She said my mother gave her a locked box to keep for me for when I graduated, but that it disappeared years ago. And you told me that the reason Reed was so desperate to visit me the day he died was because he wanted to give me a box he thought was important for some reason."

Ryn's grip tightens on my arms. "It's the same box."

I nod. "Reed must have found it, seen my name on it, and decided to return it to me. Now we just have to figure out where it is."

"But how? The guardian leading the investigation never mentioned a box."

"Well, maybe it was kept from you for some reason, or maybe it was never found."

Ryn frowns. "You don't honestly think it would still be out there in the forest where Reed fell, do you?"

I cross my arms and lift my shoulders. "I don't know. I guess not. But where else do we start?"

Ryn leans his hip against the table we're standing next to. It's empty, all of its occupants currently having fun on the dance floor. "In the office of the guardian who led the investigation?"

"Okay. Maybe we can find the report that was written up after, you know, they found Reed." I need to tread carefully here. I don't want to upset Ryn. "Um, can you break into the office?"

"Of course." Ryn gives me a look that tells me I should know that. He leans across the table and pulls a silver apple from the tree. He bites into it and crunches for several seconds. He swallows. "You want to go now?"

Idiot. He knows very well I want to go now. "No, Ryn, I thought we'd just stand here eating silver delicacies and wait until everyone is *in* their offices on Monday morning before trying to break in."

"Hmm. That doesn't sound like the best plan you've ever had." He puts the partially eaten apple down on someone's plate and heads toward the ballroom's main doors. "Come on."

I hurry after him. The music and laughter grow faint as we head down a corridor toward the Guild's main foyer. I hear an indistinct sort of rumble. Out of habit, I glance up at the foyer's domed ceiling. I freeze when I see the swirling, flickering clouds of orange and red. Fear tightens my stomach.

"What's wrong?" Ryn asks, turning back. He watches me from the other side of the foyer, a hand pressed to his chest in that weird habit he has.

"The protective enchantments," I whisper as I return my gaze to the ceiling. "They're the wrong color."

PART III

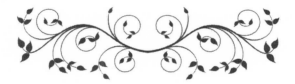

CHAPTER EIGHTEEN

FOR A SINGLE MOMENT THAT SEEMS TO LAST FOREVER, RYN and I stare at each other across the foyer, fear growing, rising, filling the space between us.

Then the lightning hits.

It strikes somewhere above us with such force that the foyer's marble floor shudders beneath our feet. Ryn shouts my name, but the explosion of the domed ceiling swallows up his voice. A bolt of light shreds the air and strikes the floor between us, creating a huge zigzagging crack through the marble. A second later, broken pieces of ceiling begin to rain down on us.

I throw myself out of the way. The marble is a lot harder than anything else I've landed on recently, and my shoulder screams out in protest. I roll across the floor, pull myself up onto my knees, and throw my arm out toward the corridor we just came down. The flare of magic that leaves my hand is bright red. If anyone in the ballroom has any doubts as to where the explosion came from, they'll know which way to go now.

I climb to my high-heeled feet to look for Ryn, but instead I see black figures dropping down from the open ceiling. Rain sprays across my face, and wind tangles my curls. Fear gives way to adrenaline as the thrill of an impending fight races through my veins.

I stand firm as my bow and arrow form between my outstretched arms. I pull back, let go, and watch the arrow zoom toward its target, sparks flying in its wake. The man— dressed all in black, complete with a *cape*, for goodness sake— goes down with a cry as the arrow embeds itself in his back. Pull back, release. Pull back, release. A new arrow materializes the moment the previous one is let loose.

A boulder hurtles toward me, along with sparks of magic. I dodge the magic, but the edge of the boulder catches my shoulder. I hit the floor once more, my bow and arrow disappearing the moment I let go. Rolling onto my back, I reach for the strap of my right shoe. I tug it loose—my amber slips to the floor—just as a faerie throws himself on top of me. I bring the shoe up and slice the heel across his neck. He clutches his throat, and I send my fist into his stomach. He doubles over. Blood splatters onto my face. With a heave, I push him away.

I kick my other shoe off, stuff my stylus into my enhanced cleavage, and get ready to fight the next faerie who wants to take me on. It seems I'm out of opponents, though. The foyer is full of guards, mentors, and guardians, and the only black figures I see are the ones lying dead on the floor.

Ryn. Is he okay?

I turn to the debris in the center of the foyer, pushing wet hair out of my face. A glittering whip snaps the air and disappears before I see him. He climbs off a boulder, jumps over the crack that now splits the foyer in two, and walks toward me. "Well," he says, "that was an exciting end to graduation."

* * *

"Idiots," Adair, a senior guardian, says as he paces across the floor of Councilor Starkweather's office. "Why did they choose to invade the Guild during graduation? Admittedly, there were fewer guards on duty than there normally are, but *everyone* was here because of the ceremony. We had hundreds of guardians ready to fight, and these idiot invaders numbered less than twenty. Were they really arrogant enough to think they could kill us all?"

I glance over at Ryn. The two of us are standing, dripping wet, in front of Councilor Starkweather's desk. She summoned us to a private meeting with her and Adair once it was clear the Guild was no longer under attack. I think of Ryn's suspicion that she may be Zell's spy within the Guild. Unlikely, since she killed two of the invading faeries herself.

She taps her chin. "Could it be that they didn't know graduation was taking place tonight?"

I shake my head. "They must have known. They have spies in the Guild, don't they?" Ryn clears his throat, but I ignore him. "The purpose of this attack obviously wasn't to take over the Guild."

Adair stops pacing and narrows his eyes at me. "Why are these two here?"

"They've had close contact with members of the Unseelie Court," Councilor Starkweather says. "Their input could be useful."

"Do we even know whether it was an attack by the Unseelie Court?" Adair asks. "They weren't wearing the Queen's insignia."

"They were definitely Unseelie faeries," Ryn says. "I could feel the cold darkness behind their magic."

"But they might not have been acting on the Queen's orders," Adair counters.

"No, they were most likely acting on Zell's. The Unseelie Prince you guys have been investigating for ages." I assume Adair is part of that investigation or he wouldn't be in this office right now. "After what Ryn and I heard on our assignment, we know he's working against his mother, and what we saw in his dungeon suggests he's forming some kind of super army. He must have found a faerie who can create storms that are able to break through our protective enchantments."

Ryn clears his throat again, but I refuse to name Nate. It would get me in a whole lot of trouble, and I don't see the point in telling them about him when it's already obvious that Zell is using someone who has power over the weather.

"Perhaps it was a test," Councilor Starkweather says. "A test to see how easily they can get in and out."

"Possibly." Adair resumes his pacing. "Which means the purpose of the first lightning bolt several weeks ago was probably to see whether it was possible to break through the enchantments. But that still doesn't explain why a Seer was murdered the same night."

"We didn't manage to capture any faeries tonight, did we?" Ryn asks.

"No," Adair says. "Most of them managed to get out the way they came in—through the foyer's ceiling. The few left behind are dead."

"So we can't even torture any information out of anyone," mutters Councilor Starkweather.

The word 'torture' reminds me of something else that's been on my mind for a while. "Councilor Starkweather," I say carefully. "I was wondering if you were able to get inside Zell's home and rescue the prisoners we found."

She presses her lips together before answering. "I am not at liberty to discuss that investigation with you, Miss Fairdale. And you know you should not have been 'wondering' about it in the first place."

I lower my gaze to the floor. If I had to guess, I'd say that was a 'no,' which means those people are still stuck in cages. The thought makes my pulse quicken and my blood heat up. I get that the Guild can't just barge into the Unseelie Prince's home and demand to see his dungeon, but seriously? Couldn't they have figured something out by now?

Councilor Starkweather pinches the bridge of her nose. "I

should have known something was going on the moment that tree on the table next to ours exploded earlier."

"I'm sorry," Ryn says. "A tree exploded?"

"Yes, while the two of you were dancing. The darn thing suddenly went up in flames."

While we were dancing ... I think of the 'explosion' of emotions I felt after Ryn whispered in my ear as well as the conversation I had with Raven about losing control of magic. Could that have been me?

"I'm sure that was unrelated," Adair says. "Probably just some of the graduates playing around."

"Well, anyway," Councilor Starkweather says. "I need to make contact with the Unseelie Court, and you two need to prepare for your visit to the Seelie Court. You'll be leaving tomorrow evening."

"That's still happening?" I ask. I was hoping Ryn and I would have time to search for the box Reed took.

"Of course it's still happening. We wouldn't want to give anyone the impression that this minor invasion has upset the way the Guild operates, would we?"

Minor invasion? Enchantments strong enough to protect the Guild for centuries have been shattered, and she calls it *minor*? "Um, no, Councilor. I suppose not."

* * *

I drizzle chocolate sauce over my berries and pass the jug to Ryn. Tora invited me to lunch along with Raven and Flint, and I was stupid enough to ask Ryn to join us. Stupid because

I can barely look him in the eyes with all the crazy feelings buzzing through me. Stupid because I was so desperate to be around him that I couldn't wait until tonight when we leave for the Seelie Court.

"I've heard she can be rather mean sometimes," Raven says, checking her hair in the reflective surface of a mirror berry before covering it with chocolate sauce.

"Only if you say the wrong thing to her," Tora says. "Just like anyone else."

"But *un*like anyone else," Ryn adds, "if you upset the Seelie Queen, she might start shrieking, 'Off with their heads!'." The four of us stare at him. He stares back. "What? It's ... from a book. Never mind."

"But how will I know if I'm about to say the wrong thing?" I ask. "How am I supposed to know what upsets the Seelie Queen?"

"Okay, well, here's what I've heard over the years," Flint says. He finishes the last berries from his bowl before resting his elbows on the table. "Don't look her in the eyes when speaking to her; she doesn't like that. Don't bring up pegasus polo; she's really into it and if you don't back her favorite teams ... well, things will get uncomfortable for you. Oh, and never, *ever* mention the runaway princess. That probably *would* get your head chopped off."

"Runaway princess?" Ryn asks.

"Oh, yes, I remember reading that somewhere." I reach for the jug of sauce in the center of the table. "The current Seelie Queen has three children: a daughter—who's obviously in line to become the next Queen—a son, and another daughter.

About twenty or thirty years ago the younger daughter ran away." I drizzle sauce onto my spoon and stick the spoon in my mouth.

"I take it they never found this runaway princess?" Ryn asks.

"I guess not," I say around the spoon, "since the Queen gets upset if you bring it up." I look at Flint for confirmation.

"No, they never found her," he says. "The rumors from the palace guards were that the Queen never had a good relationship with her younger daughter. Everyone thought she was secretly glad to be rid of her."

"That's awful," Tora says, "wanting to be rid of your own child."

I fill my spoon with more sauce. "Just because you play for the 'good' team doesn't mean you have to be a nice person."

"Okay, so we know what we *can't* talk about," Ryn says. "What *can* we talk about?"

The remainder of lunch is spent discussing 'safe' topics. I have to admit I'm only half listening, though, because a lot of my attention is focused on how I'm going to find the secret place where my mother hid her belongings. And on how close Ryn's leg is to mine. Very close. Close enough for me to reach out and rest my hand on it.

Violet, you are being ridiculous. You have got *to stop thinking things like that.*

I stand abruptly, pile the dirty dishes on top of one another, and send them zooming through the air in front of me as I head to the kitchen. "I'll clean up," I say over my shoulder.

"I'll help you," Ryn says.

I close my eyes while my stomach does a few backflips. *Okay, just be normal. Be totally, completely normal.*

"Hey, V, are you feeling okay?"

I direct the dishes to the sink and get the cleaning spell going before turning around to look at Ryn. He's leaning against the doorframe, hands pushed into his pockets. A simple T-shirt never looked so sexy on anyone.

Not a helpful thought, Violet.

I clear my throat and twist a piece of hair around my finger. "Yeah, I'm fine, why?"

He watches me closely. "It's just ..."

My heart thumps in sudden terror. I am *so* not ready for Ryn to figure out how I feel about him. In fact, I'll never be ready. I'd rather be friends forever than have him laugh in my face—or worse, tell me he feels the same way only to wind up breaking my heart one day. "Just what, Ryn?"

He shakes his head. "Nothing."

I turn back to the sink to make sure my magic's working.

"Oh, hey, I got you something," he says. I swivel around to see him pulling something from his pocket. "New amber. You mentioned you lost your old one in the fight yesterday. I figured it was in need of replacing anyway; it probably had spells from the Stone Age on it."

I place my hands on my hips, relaxing now that we're back in familiar territory. "There's nothing wrong with Stone Age spells. They work."

"Oh, Violet." He sighs and shakes his head. "You have no idea the awesome things this amber can do."

"I don't need a fancy new amber, Ryn. I just want

something simple I can send messages on."

"You can send messages on here." He grins as he waves the rectangular piece of amber at me. "And so much more."

"Fine." I'm beginning to realize that when he smiles at me like that I'll do pretty much anything for him. "What do I owe you for it?"

"Nothing. It's a gift." He places the amber on the kitchen table.

I raise my eyebrow. "Another 'early birthday present'?"

"Sure, we can call it that." He pulls a chair out and sits down. "Want me to show you how to use it?"

My traitorous heart leaps at the chance to sit close to him again. "Yeah, why not."

CHAPTER NINETEEN

LATER THAT NIGHT, RYN AND I MEET AT COUNCILOR Starkweather's office along with the four guards who will accompany us to the Seelie Court—to show us the way and to make sure we don't get up to any mischief on the journey. Councilor Starkweather inspects the guards' black and gold Guild uniforms while giving Ryn and me a few parting instructions. Then she opens a wide doorway to the faerie paths on the wall. She steps aside while the six of us link arms—two guards in front, two behind, and Ryn and me in the middle.

"Can't you just tell us which part of the world we're going to?" Ryn says to the guards once we're walking through the darkness of the faerie paths. "You don't have to give us directions or anything."

His question is met by silence.

"You didn't honestly think you'd get an answer, did you?" I say to Ryn. "It's one of the best secrets in the fae realm. They're not about to tell *you*."

I feel Ryn shrugging. "Worth a try."

We exit the paths to find ourselves amongst trees beside a wide river. Perfectly clear water flows slowly over sand that's whiter than any I've seen before. The trees are slimmer and less gnarled and somehow more ... *elegant* than the trees in Creepy Hollow. Everything here seems to be lit from within, bringing the quiet forest to brilliant, luminous life. Green moss, purple flowers, blue leaves. Even the white sand at the bottom of the river seems to be glowing.

"The faerie paths can take us no further," says one of the guards. "We'll use the river from here, and then the sky." He gestures to the water. A white boat with a seahorse's head rising from the bow glides toward us. Magic must be directing it because there's no one inside. The boat reaches the bank and sways with the gentle waves.

The guard climbs into the boat and holds his hand out. "Miss Fairdale," he says. Although I'm pretty sure I could get in without help, I take his hand and step into the boat. The interior is simple, with four parallel bench seats covered in cushions. I climb over them and take the seat closest to the stern.

Ryn and the other guards climb in. Without a command from anyone, the boat begins to move. No oars, nothing. It slips silently, peacefully, through the water. I lie back with my shoulders against the edge of the boat and stare at the sky through the overhanging branches. The moon is larger than I've ever seen it, and the stars seem closer than normal.

"Look here, V," Ryn says. I sit up. He's leaning over the side of the boat and pointing at something. I grasp the edge of the boat and peer into the water. A woman with long green hair and a fish-like tail with pearly, iridescent scales weaves artfully between the rocks at the bottom of the river.

"Wow," I whisper. "I've never seen a mermaid in real life."

"They don't like Creepy Hollow," says the guard sitting next to Ryn. "They prefer to keep close to the Seelie Court."

I spend the remainder of the boat journey watching mermaids, mermen, and other water creatures gliding through the river. I think of how calm everything must be beneath the lapping surface. Nothing to fill their ears but a peaceful quiet, and everything moving in graceful slow motion.

"Time to get out," a guard says, interrupting my thoughts. The boat bumps gently against the bank. The river disappears around a corner, and a quiet rushing sound signals a waterfall somewhere in the distance. "We'll travel the rest of the way by air."

We climb out, walk a little way through the trees, and stop in front of a closed carriage pulled by four white pegasi.

"Yes!" Ryn exclaims. "I haven't ridden a pegasus in years."

"Mr. Larkenwood, you are aware that you'll be riding in the carriage, not on a pegasus?"

With a sigh, Ryn says, "Fine. If I have to."

It's a bit of a tight fit with six of us inside the carriage, and I'm not too pleased to find myself squished between Ryn and a guard. Well, part of me is ridiculously ecstatic to have my right arm and leg pressed against Ryn, but I'm definitely not pleased about having the left side of my personal space invaded.

"We'll be traveling through the night," says personal-space-invader guard, "so you might want to get some sleep."

Oh, great. We have to sit like this for the *whole night*? I try to forget about personal-space-invader guard and focus instead on Ryn's left hand, which is resting on his leg—right, *right* next to mine. So close that if I spread out my fingers I'd be touching his. It's ridiculous how badly I want to reach over and take his hand. I never thought I'd crave anyone's touch so much, but I do. Just thinking about his hands on my skin makes me feel warm all over.

With a jerk, the carriage moves forward, then quickly speeds up. Moments later the rumbling beneath the wheels disappears as the carriage tilts back slightly.

We're in the air.

The thrill of flying is enough to make me momentarily forget my desire for Ryn. I look past him and out of the carriage window. It's concealed partially by a curtain, but I can see the tree tops disappearing below us as we shoot across the sky toward the stars. It makes my head spin.

I return my gaze to the interior of the carriage and realize Ryn is watching me. I meet his eyes for a split second before looking away. And there it is again. Desire. Like a shot of adrenaline, it rushes through my body and sets my heart pounding.

I tilt my head back and close my eyes. I should be trying to remember everything my father ever told me about my mother's visit to the Seelie Court, and instead I'm obsessing over Ryn. I clasp my hands together in my lap so my fingers won't accidentally entwine with Ryn's. I *will* remember whatever clues my father gave me about my mother's secret hiding place.

* * *

My neck is stiff. I peel my eyelids apart and blink several times against the morning light before remembering where I am—a carriage—and what I'm sleeping on—Ryn.

OH HOLY EMBARRASSMENT OF ALL EMBARRASS-MENTS. How long have I been sleeping on Ryn's shoulder? Did I talk in my sleep? Did I snuggle up to him? Did I *drool* on him?

That last thought causes me to sit up hurriedly and slap a hand over my mouth.

Okay. No drool.

Ryn rubs a hand over his eyes and then through his hair. Hopefully he was asleep too. Hopefully he has no idea I just used him as a pillow.

He looks down at me with confusion in his eyes. "What?" I ask, with a little more defense in my voice than necessary. "Is something wrong?"

"No." He frowns. "Something wrong with you?"

"No."

He catches my arm to stop me sliding off the seat as the carriage slows suddenly. Our ride ends with a bump as the carriage wheels hit the ground. Ryn lets go of my arm and turns away from me to look out the window. My skin feels oddly cold in the absence of his touch.

"We've arrived," says personal-space-invader guard, reaching to touch a lever beside his seat. The top of the carriage vanishes. Fresh air and the delicate scent of flowers drift over me. The carriage glides forward as we travel along a wide driveway lined on either side by trees laden with pink and orange blossoms. Branches reach over the driveway to meet each other, shading us from the morning sun. Blossoms float to the ground like confetti.

"So … can anyone just wander through here?" Ryn asks. "I didn't see a gate."

"There's no need for a gate," says the guard opposite Ryn. "This place is protected by strong enchantments and watched over by hundreds of hidden guards."

After examining the trees and having no luck finding any guards, I point my eyes forward once more. I don't want to miss a single detail of the palace we're about to enter. At the end of the driveway is a white archway with a sheet of water running down across the opening, preventing us from seeing through. As we pass beneath the archway, the water parts like a curtain. We enter a courtyard filled with the same pink- and orange-blossomed trees. The pegasi come to a stop. Through the trees, I catch glimpses of white walls and pillars, but before I can look too closely, a new pair of guards—with the Seelie Queen's insignia on their uniforms—comes forward to meet us. They bow, wait for Ryn and me to get down from the carriage, and lead the way forward with quick, controlled strides.

We pass beneath another archway and enter a second

courtyard. Although we've left the forest outside, it's difficult to see where nature ends and the palace begins. Perhaps there is no beginning and end. Perhaps a forest of white trees was coaxed into growing and melding a structure of rooms, towers, pillars, and spiraling stairways, and this palace is just as alive as the forest that surrounds it.

I see people here and there, some leaning out of balconies and others walking along open corridors. I take in their richly detailed outfits and feel vastly underdressed in my everyday black attire. Tora assured me I didn't need to bring any fancy clothes, so I'm hoping there's no need to panic about being inappropriately dressed.

Ryn and I follow the guards through a vast open room with a water fountain in its center. I pause for a moment to look at the three stone mermaids reaching for the sky as water spurts from their hands. We continue up a winding stairway, along a corridor, and finally arrive at our bedrooms. I don't know what Ryn's looks like, but mine is far fancier than anything I've ever dreamt of sleeping in: four-poster canopied bed, chaise longue, ornate floor-length mirror, balcony. A serving woman stands to the side of the expansive room with a scroll in her hand.

With my mind somewhat boggled, I half listen as the woman reads our schedule from the scroll. She tells me when we'll be shown around the grounds, who we'll be eating lunch with, what time we'll be dining with the Queen, and when we'll be observing the Royal Guard training.

The Royal Guard. Right. That's the *real* reason we're given this 'prize' of visiting the Seelie Court—so the Queen can check out the latest graduates and see if she wants to poach any to work here as her personal guardians.

"Tonight and tomorrow night someone will come to your room before dinner to dress you," the serving woman adds. "Two days from now, in the morning, your guards from the Guild will be here to accompany you home. Do you have any questions, Miss Fairdale?"

"Um, no."

She curtsies and leaves the room. I'm left wondering what it is I'm supposed to be doing now. I try to remember the beginning of her speech but can only think of her telling me that my bag was delivered to the room before I got here.

May as well relax, then. I walk over to the bed that's probably covered in sheets of a bazillion thread count, flop onto it, and try not to think about Ryn sleeping just a wall away from me tonight.

CHAPTER TWENTY

IT'S WEIRD BEING DRESSED BY SOMEONE I DON'T KNOW. It's also weird being made to wear something I'd never choose for myself. The dress, which is apparently the color of champagne and is far too glittery for my taste, hugs my figure all the way down to about my knees, where it flares out just enough for me to move my legs. It comes to an end on the floor a few feet behind me. The sleeves are also ridiculously long, like bell shapes hanging past my fingertips. I'm certain they're going to find their way into my soup or dessert.

The clothes caster flits about me, making minor adjustments to the dress. "Okay, I think we're done here." She steps back to examine me, eyes the gold key around my neck, and opens her mouth. "I'm not taking it off," I say before she can tell me it clashes with my dress or something.

"Fine. Well, if you have no further need of me, I have other girls to dress."

"Great, I think I can handle it from here." I don't need her changing my hastily pinned-up locks into some whacked out hairdo.

"Do you remember where the throne room is?"

"Yes." We were told exactly where to assemble before dinner while having our tour around the palace earlier. We were even given a quick lesson in the dining room on which cutlery to use for which course.

The clothes caster nods and leaves to find the other guardian graduates who need help dressing. I don't know why I didn't think of it before we got here, but obviously all the Guilds that have graduation at the same time as us would send their top trainees here now. It makes sense for the Seelie Court to receive us all at the same time.

I head to the door, curling my toes in the thick carpet. The only thing I like about this outfit is the absence of shoes. Despite the finery of the clothing, it seems the trend around here is to go barefoot.

I open the door to find Ryn waiting there. I expected him to be wearing a suit, but it looks like someone was sent to dress him too. His pants are white, as is the long tunic-type top that reaches to his thighs. The top is covered in embroidery and tiny beads, and there's a glittery scarf thing hanging around his neck that reaches down to his knees on either side.

"Wow," he says when he sees me. "You look really ... sparkly."

"I know. You could probably spot me from the moon." I

close the door behind me. "But you can't exactly talk since you aren't far behind in the sparkles department."

Ryn adjusts his scarf. "Yeah, I'm not a fan of traditional fae formal wear. I think the royals need to move into the modern age."

"You could suggest that to the Queen this evening. I'm sure it would make for scintillating dinner conversation."

"Right after she chops my head off." He holds his arm out to me, and I feel a thrill as I take it.

A thrill? Ugh, what has become of me? I used to get my thrills from fighting dangerous creatures; now I get them from touching Ryn's arm. I take a deep breath and try my best to remember what it feels like to be *just friends* with Ryn.

"So, is your visit to the Seelie Court living up to your expectations?" he asks as we descend the stairs.

"Not just yet. The tea party in the garden this afternoon kind of interfered with my exploration plans."

"Ah, yes. Drinking tea with the Queen's daughter and twenty-something other graduates. I can see how that wouldn't really be your, uh, cup of tea."

I roll my eyes. "Ha-freaking-ha."

"Come on, you laughed inside," he says as he nudges me.

We follow the directions we were given earlier and find our way to a wide hallway outside the throne room. Several other graduates are already dressed and waiting there. A tall girl with hair and eyes as black as obsidian looks Ryn up and down before giving him a dazzling smile. When he nods in her direction, jealousy burns hot and sudden in the pit of my stomach. Apparently she takes his nod as an invitation because she walks over and begins chatting to him about where she's from. He pulls his arm away from mine and leans against the wall, exuding confidence as he tells her about the Creepy Hollow Guild.

I suppose I could try and join the conversation instead of standing here awkwardly, but what would be the point? They're clearly only interested in talking to each other. Jealousy still pokes spitefully at me, and I *hate* that it hurts to watch Ryn flirting with someone else. This is exactly why I shouldn't have not-just-friends feelings for him. I know I'll only end up getting hurt because there will always be another girl out there more exciting and exotic than I am.

I wander away, swinging my arms at my sides and trying to pretend I don't feel rejected. I look around and notice one of the male graduates watching me. Another one flashes a smile in my direction. I look away quickly, clasping my hands behind my back. *Weirdos.*

The great throne room doors engraved with curling patterns of leaves and branches slowly begin to open. A uniformed man comes through them and stands in front of us. All chattering amongst the graduates ceases. "The Seelie Queen will receive you now," he says. "You will enter the throne room as you are announced. Keep your eyes down, bow or curtsy, and if she speaks to you, address her as 'my lady.' She will dismiss you with a wave of her hand, after which you will leave the room through the door on the left and take your place in the dining room."

The doors are fully open now, and the guard returns to stand just inside, opposite another guard. When he calls out the first name—Opal Briarstone—the dark-haired girl standing beside Ryn walks forward. I stand on tiptoe and crane my neck to try and catch a glimpse of the room and the Queen, but after a stern look from the guard calling out the names, I drop back onto my feet.

I don't know what sort of order they're using to call out the names, but there are only four of us left in the hallway when Ryn and I are called in. We walk forward into the room, almost close enough to hold hands. Giant marble tiles—surprisingly not that cold beneath my feet—form a mosaic pattern of concentric circles across the floor. Shapes move beneath the surface of the tiles, and I'm reminded for a second of the chamber Nate and I found his mother Angelica in. I push the two of them from my mind. I'm about to meet the Seelie Queen herself; I don't need any distractions.

We reach a marking on the floor and come to a stop. Ryn bows and I attempt to curtsy in my super-tight dress. I raise my eyes just high enough to see the bottom of the Queen's skirt, which looks like it's been cast from a cascading green waterfall.

"Ah, yes," the Queen says. "The Guild that managed to produce two top graduates instead of one. That has not happened since the reign of my mother." She pauses, but I don't see her hand move, so I stay exactly where I am. "You both come from a long line of guardians, do you not?"

"Yes, my lady," Ryn says, answering for both of us.

Another pause. "So unfortunate, Miss Fairdale, what happened to both your parents."

My insides seem to freeze and burn at the same time. "Unfortunate, my lady?" I raise my eyes. I know I'm not supposed to, but it's too late now. I see a woman with long black hair interwoven with silver strands. Her thick tresses slide over her bare shoulders. Her bright silver eyes pierce me, but I still can't look away. She's many centuries old, but her face is flawless, of course. And something about that face and the way she tilts her chin up as she gazes down at me seems familiar. "If you're referring to the fact that both my parents were murdered while carrying out their guardian duty, I prefer to think of it as *tragic* rather than simply unfortunate."

From the corner of my eye, I see Ryn's hands clenching into fists. If I could hear his thoughts, they'd probably be something along the lines of *Are you flipping* trying *to get your head chopped off?* Now would be a good time to point my eyes firmly downward, but I can't seem to tear them away from the Queen's silver gaze. For several endless moments we're locked in what feels like a staring contest. Then she raises her hand and dismisses us with a quick wave toward the door on the left.

* * *

"Holy goblin asses, V. I thought she was going to strike you down with her eyes."

I laugh as I swing myself around a pillar just outside the room with the water fountain. Our dinner with the Queen is over, and we're heading back to our rooms. "So did I. I have no idea what came over me; I just got really angry when she referred to my parents' deaths as 'unfortunate.' I wanted to say how *unfortunate* it was that her younger daughter ran away."

"Then she really would've struck you down," Ryn says. "It's

weird that she even knows about your parents. Do you think she reads some kind of bio on each of us before we get here?" He leans over and swipes his hand through the base of the water feature as we pass it, splashing water across my back.

"Hey!" I shout, then cover my mouth as two graduates on the stairs turn around and frown down at us. "I don't know. She probably had someone magically feeding her the highlights on each of us as we walked into the room."

"Probably." We mount the stairs. "You know, I always imagined dinner with the Queen to be a far more informative event. I was hoping for some in-depth discussions, and instead we were seated so far away we couldn't even hear her."

"Well, you seemed to have plenty to discuss with the girl sitting next to you," I say as I trail my hand up the banister. "And I'm not talking about me."

Ryn stops. I turn to look down at him from the step above his. He cocks his head to the side as he says, "Did I detect a hint of jealousy in your voice, Sexy Pixie?"

"No." The word leaves my mouth too quickly. "And don't call me Sexy Pixie. It's almost as bad as Pixie Sticks."

"I apologize," he says, but that mischievous gleam never leaves his eyes.

We reach my bedroom first, and I pause with my hand against the door. "I've been trying to figure something out all evening. The Queen seems very familiar to me, but I know I've never met her before."

Ryn raises both eyebrows. "You know her portrait is hanging in the Guild library, right?"

"Oh, yes. I'd forgotten about that." Then I shake my head.

"But I never sit at that end of the library. It's been years since I saw that portrait." I shrug and lean back to push my door open. "Anyway, I'll see you in five minutes?"

"Yes," Ryn says, giving me a salute.

I close my door and wriggle out of the dress. I change into black pants and a top and pull the pins out of my hair. Should I add my boots? No, I'm enjoying being barefoot too much. But that does leave me with the problem of where to put my stylus. After some thought, I twist my hair up and stick my stylus through it to hold it in place. Perfect. Why haven't I tried that before?

"Ready?" Ryn calls from the other side of the door.

"Yeah, come in." I lean forward for a quick look in the floor-length mirror. Apparently I still care what I look like in front of Ryn. My reflection shows light from the ceiling's glow-bug glinting off the gold key around my neck. I raise my fingers to touch it, a gesture that's quickly becoming a habit for me. "Oh, I wanted to ask you something." I look at Ryn in the mirror. "Did you bring the eternity necklace? This visit seems like the perfect opportunity to give it to the Queen."

Ryn shakes his head and pushes his hands into his pockets.

I turn around. "Why not?"

He lets out a long breath before answering. "Think about it, V. Does any monarch have the right to live forever? They already get to rule for hundreds of years. Isn't that enough? It doesn't seem right to have the same queen forever. It doesn't seem right for *anyone* to live forever."

I look down at my hands, considering his words. I've never really thought about it before, but I suppose he's right. "Well, what are you going to do with the necklace?"

"I don't know. Destroy it, I guess."

"And what," I say gently, "makes you think you have the right to destroy it?"

He looks away, rubbing his thumb against the door frame. When his gaze returns to me, there's humor in his eyes. "Has anyone ever asked if the pants you wear cut off the circulation of blood to the lower half of your body?"

The sudden change in subject throws me. I stare at him, wondering if his ridiculous question is a joke. He stares back. Apparently not. "No, I can't say I've ever been asked that."

"Oh." His eyes move down, brushing over my body before moving up again. "It's just that I've always thought they seemed a little tight."

My face heats up at the thought of Ryn examining my legs. I grab my sparkly dress from the bed and turn away from him to hang it over the back of the chaise longue. "They're not tight, Ryn, they're super stretchy. That's why I wear them all the time; they're great for training and fighting." I turn back to him with arms crossed over my chest. "And how exactly is this relevant?"

"It isn't. I had no answer to your question, so I changed the subject." He pushes away from the door frame. "Shall we get started with Mission: Exploration?"

"Yes, *please*, let's get started." I head past him into the corridor while he closes my door. I've been desperate to search the palace all day, and I'm not going to bed until I've found my mother's hiding place. "If anyone asks, we're just taking an evening stroll."

"Right. Because no one said we weren't allowed to do that."

"Exactly."

"So, do you have even the faintest idea where to start looking?"

"Yes, sort of." We head down the stairs. "My father remembered my mother saying something about a lake or pool that has a stone structure built near it. He said she learned an architecture spell and created a small room concealed in the stone. You know, like how our homes are concealed within trees? And she left some kind of sign or symbol nearby that would help a person open it."

"Okay, that information would be helpful if it weren't for the fact that we passed about *five hundred* pools on our tour of the grounds today."

"Is that all? I'm sure I counted six hundred." I laugh and dodge out of the way as Ryn catches water spilling down from the mermaids' hands and tries to splash me a second time.

"Fine, perhaps I exaggerated just a *tiny* bit." He shakes his hands dry as his eyes slide over my shoulder and widen. I turn to see what he's looking at. A male faerie, his head bowed as if deep in thought, comes toward us through one of the many arches on the open side of the vast room. He looks up, catches my gaze, and freezes. All color drains from his face.

If I could see my own face, I'd probably find a similar expression of shock. I can't move. I can't breathe. I can't even think properly. Because the man standing beneath the archway, the man with yellow-gold eyes and streaks of the same color running through his chestnut hair, is my father.

CHAPTER TWENTY-ONE

A BEAT OF FROZEN SILENCE PASSES BETWEEN US. THEN HE turns and runs back out to the grounds, disappearing into the darkness of the night.

"Wait!" I shout. I take off after him, but Ryn grabs onto my shirt and pulls me back.

"What are you—Let go of me!"

"Stop, Violet. Just think about this for a second."

"What's there to think about? That's my *father*!" I scream. "Let me go!"

"How?" Ryn shouts, shaking me. "How can that be your father? You saw his body. You watched him float away under the Infinity Falls. So did I."

I sag against Ryn in defeat as I realize the truth. Of course it isn't my father. It isn't possible. But for one tiny moment I

229

wanted so badly to believe that it was. "Shapeshifter," I whisper. That's the only explanation. Some shapeshifter has taken on my father's form.

"It must be," Ryn says quietly. "I'm sorry, V. I didn't want you running off after him and having your heart broken all over again." He squeezes my arms in a comforting gesture, then rubs his hands up and down them.

Ryn is right. The man isn't my father. But that doesn't mean I don't want to know who the hell he is and why he can't use his own damn form to get around in. I take a deep breath, bring my heel down hard on Ryn's foot, and tear out of his grasp.

"Violet, stop!"

But I'm already sprinting across the grass after the shadowy figure of the man. He runs down a hill, leaps over the cushioned chairs in the small blossom-laden pavilion we had tea beneath earlier, and heads into a copse of trees. I rush after him, but I realize once I'm surrounded by trees that there's no path to follow, and I can't see him anymore.

"Where are you?" I shout. "What are you afraid of? Come out and face me, you two-faced shapeshifter!" I search the darkness, twisting around as I weave through the trees to make sure I don't miss a single shadow or movement. But when I reach the other side of the copse, I've found no one. The palace grounds spread out around me, still and quiet. He can't have disappeared through the faerie paths because doorways can't be opened here at the Seelie Court. So he must be really good at hiding. And running.

My hands are shaking. I ball them into fists as I stomp back through the trees, across the grass, and up the hill. I wish I'd never seen him. Yes, it's suspicious that there's a guy running around pretending to be my father, but if I hadn't seen him, I wouldn't have all these memories swimming painfully to the front of my mind. I'd be happy and ignorant on my own little exploration mission instead of feeling like—oh hell—*like I just lost him all over again.*

I find myself standing in front of my bedroom door blinking tears away. I place my hand against the wall and take a deep, shuddering breath. All the pain I felt when he died is threatening to resurface, and I *do not want that.* I didn't want to feel it then, and I don't want to feel it now.

I open the door and see Ryn sitting on the edge of my bed. I cross my arms over my chest as he stands. "He got away because you wouldn't let me go." My voice is quiet, but I can hear the anger simmering beneath the surface. Half an hour ago I wanted to do stupid things like run my finger over Ryn's lips. Now I don't even want to look at him.

"I was just trying to get you to think sensibly for a moment."

"I hate you right now."

"No, you don't."

I don't, but I hate that he's so sure of himself. I hate that he's right. I look down at the floor as I say, "I'd like you to leave now."

He comes toward me. "Please don't shut me out, V. I want to be here for you."

I hold my hand up to stop him from coming closer. "There's no need for you to be here. Okay, so there's some random guy out there pretending to be my father, and I don't know why. But that's all it is. No big deal. It's not like someone just died."

Oh hell, oh hell, it *is* like he just died all over again. A sharp pain stabs the core of my being and threatens to make me double over.

"Stop lying, Violet. I know that's not what you're feeling, so why don't you just say what's really going on in your head."

"What are you, my freaking counselor?" I back away from him, tightening my arms around my middle. "I won't talk to Tora about my feelings, and I sure as hell won't talk to you either."

"Fine, don't talk to anyone, but at least admit you're feeling *something* instead of going on about how it's no big deal."

"I am feeling something! I'm pissed off at you!"

"And?"

"And get out!" I point to the open door.

"No."

"GET OUT!"

He walks over and slams the door shut. "No. I won't leave you alone like this."

"Yes you will! Don't you get it? *Everyone* leaves. My mother, Reed, Cecy, you, my father—and you will leave me again! I've been stupid enough to allow myself to care about Tora, but *that is it*. So you need to leave *now*. Go!"

He shakes his head.

"I said GET OUT, Ryn!" I shove him hard toward the door, and when he still makes no move to leave, I start pummeling his chest with my fists.

He grabs my wrists and holds my arms away from his body while I do my best to hit him some more. Why isn't he fighting back, dammit? "That's more like it," he says, as though this is the kind of reaction he was hoping for all along.

Furious, I tear my arms out of his grasp. After one last shove at his chest, I cross the room to the en-suite bathing room and shut myself inside. The tears are already falling as I drop down onto the enchanted grass beside the pool and bury my head in my hands. A tremor passes through me. My throat burns. Sobs begin to shake my body.

My father. It looked just like him. He was standing right in front of me, so close he could have enveloped me in his warm, strong embrace, the way he used to when I was afraid of a storm or when the children at school had been mean to me.

But it wasn't him. He's still dead.

And right now I miss him so much.

"Violet?"

Ugh, *why* is Ryn still here? Why didn't I lock the door? I curl further into myself, wrapping my arms around my waist and hoping Ryn will be scared away by the tears. Boys don't like crying girls, right? This should be his cue to leave.

Instead, I feel him kneel down beside me. "I wasn't there for you when it actually happened," he says quietly. "Why can't you let me be here for you now?"

I don't cry in front of people. *I don't, I don't, I don't.* Yet here I am, violating my own rules.

"Okay, well, you're not hitting me anymore, so I'll take that as a good sign."

No. No more hitting. But I can't stop crying, and I can't

see anything except for the blurry outline of my fingers in front of my face. What exactly does Ryn plan to do? Sit here until I cry myself out? If he's still hoping I'll open up and spill every thought and feeling torturing me, he's going to be waiting a long time.

"I'm sorry, V," Ryn says. "When the Unseelie Queen locked us up inside my head and I came face to face with Reed, it really messed with my head. I can imagine seeing your dad must be doing the same thing to you."

Messed with my head. That's one way of putting it.

I feel Ryn's body shift closer to mine. His arm slides around my shoulders. I suppose he's waiting to see whether I'll jerk away and punch him in the face because after a few moments of sitting frozen in the same position, he wraps his other arm around me and pulls me gently against his chest.

I don't fight him.

No one held me like this when my father died. I suppose Tora would have if I'd let her, but I didn't. When I slammed the door and yelled at her to leave me alone, she listened. Not like Ryn, who refuses to let me shut my pain away like I've always done.

I lean into him and make a decision to stop fighting this losing battle against the tears. Instead, just like when I stumbled away from the Harts' blazing house feeling sick, dizzy, and in pain, I let go and trust Ryn to catch me.

* * *

A fluffy white cloud of bed covers envelops me. Deliciously soft. I stretch out beneath the covers and roll onto my back. Morning light filters through the sheer curtain draped over the four-poster bed and wraps everything in a soft golden glow. I remember tears drying on my cheeks as I fell asleep last night, but morning has brought a kind of stillness within me.

I turn onto my other side—and freeze.

Ryn, in all his perfect, sleeping glory, is lying just inches from my face. Beneath my covers. In my bed. Dark strands of hair fall across his forehead, and his lips are parted ever so slightly. He looks as peaceful as I felt a second ago. His eyelids flutter, and I scoot away from him. By the time his blinking gaze comes to rest on me, I'm lying right on the edge of the bed. "Uh, what are you still doing here?"

He blinks once more. "Well, I said I wouldn't leave, didn't I?" He rubs his eyes. "Then you told me I *would* leave and, well, I had to prove you wrong."

He gives me the kind of grin that melts my insides. Ugh, how does he always manage to look so damn hot, even first thing in the morning? *Especially* first thing in the morning. I should ask him to leave now, but I can't tear my eyes from his hypnotizing blue gaze. Without warning, I'm flooded once again with everything I feel for him. I can't stamp it down. It's so much more than I ever thought I'd feel for anyone that it threatens to overwhelm me. I can't understand why these feelings aren't exploding from every pore of my body and showering the room with warmth, joy and giddiness.

"Violet," Ryn says quietly, his expression changing to one I can't read. His eyes search my face as he moves a little closer to me. My heart starts jumping erratically. "I need to tell you s—"

"*Violet Violet Violet Violet Violet!*"

I jerk upright in fright and look around. Dashing across the bedroom floor is my little purple mirror. It stands on the floor below me, shrieking my name and jumping up and down on legs so tiny that it has absolutely no hope of ever getting onto the bed.

"What the flip?" Ryn says.

I reach down and grab the mirror. Tora's face is visible in the shiny surface. I touch the glass. "Good morning, sleeping beauty," she says. "Did I wake you?"

"Um, sort of." Not exactly.

Tora pushes hair off her forehead. "I convinced Raven to go for an early morning run through Creepy Hollow with me. She can barely speak now, so I thought I'd check in with you instead."

From somewhere behind Tora, Raven says, "Just … catching my … breath."

Beside me, Ryn flops back down onto his pillow. "Flip, that thing nearly gave me a heart attack."

Tora gives me a curious look. "Was that Ryn I just heard?"

"No." I angle the mirror away from Ryn to make sure he can't be seen.

Raven, her face sweaty and her cheeks flushed, pokes her head over Tora's shoulder. "What is Ryn doing in your bedroom this early in the morning?"

"It was nobody," I say while I push Ryn toward the edge of the bed with my foot. "And I thought you were supposed to be catching your breath."

"All caught."

"I hate to have to be the parental figure here," Tora says, "but I don't think it's appropriate for you and Ryn to be sharing a bed."

Ryn snorts. I give him a kick. Raven pulls back and looks at Tora. "Right, like you really have a leg to stand on in that department."

An awkward pause passes before I say, "What are you talking about, Raven?"

"Oh, hasn't Tora told you about the guy at the London Guild? The guy she spent so much time with when—"

"Okay, *that* is really not important right now, Raven," Tora interrupts. But clearly it is because her cheeks are turning pink and she won't look at me.

"Tora, are you serious?" I ask. "You've been hanging out with a guy? That's great. I don't think I've *ever* known you to—"

"Okay, like I've already said, it's really no big deal, and we don't need to talk about it right now. I just wanted to check in and see how you're doing at the Seelie Court, and obviously you're fine, so *Raven*—" she glares at Raven before looking back at me "—and I are going to go now. Okay? Have fun."

"Wait, I wanted to ask you about—"

"Bye!"

"—the Guild," I finish. But she's gone. Her image vanishes from the mirror, and I see myself instead, complete with bed hair and a confused expression. The mirror folds its tiny arms over its glass surface and lies still in my palm. Well, I'm not quite sure what that was all about, but Tora is definitely getting the third degree when I get home.

"So," Ryn says. "A mirror that stalks you until you answer it. And here I thought the only faerie technology you were interested in was Stone Age amber."

I give him a withering look. "It was a *gift*, Ryn."

He opens his mouth to respond, but a knock on the door silences him. "Miss Fairdale?" It sounds like the serving woman who read out my schedule yesterday. "I'm just checking that you're awake and ready for breakfast."

"Oh, yeah, thanks," I call back. To Ryn I say, "Hurry up and get out of here. We're going to be late."

"Do you need any help, Miss Fairdale?" The doorknob moves.

"No, no, I'm fine, thanks," I shout hurriedly. I doubt the Seelie Court would approve of Ryn being in my bed any more than Tora would.

CHAPTER TWENTY-TWO

BREAKFAST IS A PICNIC BENEATH A BOWER OF TREES THAT sprinkle us with the occasional handful of star-shaped yellow flowers. Very pretty, until they begin landing in the food. Afterward, we're sent to observe the Royal Guard running through a few training exercises, which is when Ryn and I manage to escape to do some more exploring. I'm still a little high on all the not-just-friends feelings coursing through me, and it seems to be resulting in some reckless behavior. Like happily wandering around the palace grounds when we're clearly *not* supposed to be doing that right now.

We find two lakes that have no stone structures built nearby, and another courtyard attached to the palace with a pool full of young faeries splashing about. On the other side of a maze constructed from low bushes, we come across a pond with a stone bridge. But after examining every stone, it's clear there's no sign or symbol that points to something hidden.

I think of the sheer size of the palace grounds—so big it would take hours and hours to reach the other end—and start to feel a little panicky. "What if we can't find her hiding place in time?" I say to Ryn. "I've waited years for this opportunity. It's never going to happen again."

"We'll search all night if we must," he says, and I have to fight the urge to take his hand and squeeze his fingers. He seems just as determined as I am to find my mother's hidden belongings. Maybe it's because he's still trying to make up for the past, or maybe it's because the alternative—hanging out with other graduates watching guards train—is too boring. Either way, I'm grateful beyond words.

We leave the pond and bridge behind us as we climb a low hill. "You know, your mother's exploration time was probably also very limited when she was here," Ryn says. "Don't you think it more likely she'd have chosen a hiding place closer to the palace rather than further away?"

I stop climbing and rub the back of my hand across my forehead. I'm overheating in my long pants which, as Ryn pointed out last night, might be a little too tight for a summer's day. My tank top keeps my arms exposed, but it isn't enough to cool me down. "That could be true. Do you think we should head back and look around the palace?"

"Yes, I do. So far we've only walked through the palace, not around it. There might be smaller pools we haven't seen yet."

"There's also a greater chance of someone important seeing us and sending us back to our group."

"Afraid of getting in trouble, V?" Ryn flashes his cocky smile.

"Hardly," I turn around and make for the palace. "I just don't want Mission: Exploration to be cut short."

We walk back without saying much. There's been a lot of silence between us today. Not an awkward silence, but rather one that suggests we're both a little preoccupied. Every now and then I catch him watching me, but I don't ask why. He'll probably try and get me to spill my feelings on seeing my father-who-wasn't-my-father last night, and I'm not going down that road. Crying in Ryn's arms was weird enough without having to talk about it now.

We skirt the palace, keeping to the surrounding trees and hoping no one will notice us as they lean out of their decorative white balconies. We pass a fountain outside a room where a group of faeries are practicing musical instruments. I sense a spell weaving its way through the trees toward us, tempting my feet to start dancing. I hurry on with Ryn close behind me. That fountain was too small to be hiding anything anyway.

"Hey, I think I hear more water," Ryn says.

He's right. "Yes, but where is it? I don't see anything."

The sound of falling water becomes louder as we approach what looks like a leafy wall of tightly interwoven branches. It seems to be concealing a semi-circular area against the edge of the palace wall. "A private garden?" Ryn suggests.

"Maybe. But it doesn't look like there's any way in from this side, so my mother couldn't have hidden anything there."

We're about to move on when a figure dressed in white steps through the hedge. I slip behind the nearest tree trunk and press myself against it. A few feet away, Ryn hides behind another tree. When no one calls out to us, I peek carefully around the tree to see what's going on. The figure in white is the faerie who hosted our tea party yesterday afternoon. The Queen's daughter, Olivia. She scoops her long blonde and pink hair away from her neck and secures it with a ribbon. Then, after scanning the area quickly with her eyes, she hurries off through the trees away from us.

"Imagine still living with your mother when you're, like, a century old," Ryn whispers. He steps out from behind his tree and walks over to where Olivia appeared.

"I think she's more like two centuries old," I answer. "She's the Queen's first daughter, remember, and the Queen's certainly been around for a while."

"V, there's an opening here." Ryn motions for me to follow him. "You can't see it from over there because the angle is wrong."

I cross the grass and slip through the opening after him. Concealed within the semi-circle of space is a garden. Roses of every color are entwined amongst the branches of the hedge. Against one side is a stone archway with a bench beneath it. In the center of the garden is a round pool beside which stands a tree with oversized orange leaves that create an umbrella of shade. Water trickles over a pile of rocks and into the pool. Statues stand here and there on the grass, which comes to an end at an open doorway leading into what must be the princess's quarters.

"We definitely shouldn't be here," I say, backing away from the pool.

"Don't you want to check if your mother's hiding place is here?"

"It won't be."

Ryn wanders over to the bench and sits down. "And how do you know that?"

"Ryn, this is the *princess*'s private garden. There's no way my mother would have hidden her stuff here. Can you imagine the trouble she would have been in if someone had caught her?" I turn to leave, but as I do, Zinnia's description of my parents a few nights ago comes to the surface of my mind. *The two of them always liked to take on the most dangerous assignments.* "On the other hand," I say, turning slowly back to the pool, "perhaps that's exactly why she *would* have chosen this place."

"And look at all the roses," Ryn adds, gesturing to the hedge.

I nod. "This would actually have been the perfect hiding spot for her." I start examining the stone archway Ryn is sitting beneath, starting from the bottommost stone and moving upward. Ryn gets up and examines the other side. The stones are almost perfect and seem to have no markings other than those probably brought about by time and harsh weather. Not that I can imagine a place like this ever having harsh weather, but even the Seelie Court can't be immune to winter, can it?

"See anything?" Ryn asks.

"No. Can you give me a leg up to check the top?"

Ryn comes around to stand in front of the bench, and I place my foot in his cupped hands. He lifts me swiftly up. I grab onto the edge of the archway and take a look at all the stones I couldn't see from the ground. "Nothing. I guess it's not here after all."

"Aren't these statues made of stone?" Ryn asks as he lowers me to the ground.

"Yes, but they're really small."

"V." Ryn looks at me the way he looks at Calla when trying to explain something. "If a tree isn't too small to hide your entire home inside, then is a statue too small to hide a single room?"

Even though I now find Ryn gorgeous and have the occasional irrational desire to tear his clothes off, it's still really annoying when he's right. Without answering, I head to the nearest statue—a woman with small horns on her head wearing a scrap of fabric that doesn't even come close to covering the essential bits of her body. I get down on the grass and start investigating her stone surface. I find nothing but smoothly carved stone, until I spot something on the back of her heel. "There's something here." Excitement rises in my chest. "An arrow. It points down and to the right."

"There's something here too," Ryn says, running his fingers over the right hind leg of the unicorn statue. "A wavy line."

"A wavy line? Doesn't that usually signify water?"

"Yes. Running water, maybe? Flowing water?"

"Okay, well, we have a fountain, but this arrow points to the right, and from here the fountain is on the left."

Ryn walks to the remaining statue—a pixie holding a sprite in its outstretched hand like an offering—standing in the shade of the orange leaves. I join him, my eyes searching the legs first because that seems to be a trend here. Ryn gets down on his hands and knees, closely examining the front of the pixie. I've reached the back of the pixie's neck by the time Ryn says, "Found it." He gives me a smirk, and I glare at him. Everything is a competition when it comes to the two of us. "It's on the back of the pixie's hand, facing the ground." He leans down once more and points up. "See here? It's the shape of a circle."

"A circle." We both look at the garden. The only circle here is the pool.

"It's *inside* the pool," Ryn says. "You've got to get in the water—hence the wavy line—go below the surface—"

"That's the down arrow."

"And then to the right," Ryn finishes.

I go to the opening in the hedge and look out. No one there. "Okay, let's do this quickly. I certainly don't want to be caught swimming in the princess's pool."

"After you." Ryn gestures to the pool. "Since this is your mission, I think you should go first."

I dip my foot in, testing the temperature of the water. I thought it might be uncomfortably warm, given the heat of this summer day, but it's just cool enough to be deliciously refreshing. Of course. It's probably enchanted to be at the perfect temperature. I slip into the water. It reaches up to my shoulders.

"Ah, relief," Ryn says as he joins me, making a bit more of a noise than I did. "We may have to stay here for a while."

"And get caught? I don't think so." I take a deep breath, sink down below the surface, and swim toward the right side of the pool. I run my fingers over the square stones, searching each one for some kind of marking. I surface for air and dive down once more. Ryn is nearby, helping with the search.

Then I see it: a simple X carved into the middle of a stone. I push against the stone with my hands, but nothing happens. I reach above my head and, thankfully, my stylus is still there, attempting to hold my hair in place. I pull it free and write an opening spell on the stone.

Yes!

The stone vanishes, leaving a rippling, semi-transparent layer between the water and the darkness that lies beyond. I swim through—and tumble onto a hard stone surface. I climb to my feet and immediately create an orb of light. It floats in front of me, illuminating a tiny room with a table on one side.

With an exclamation of pain, Ryn lands on the floor beside me. "Flip, you'd think she could have left a cushion or something on the floor for a softer landing."

"We found it, Ryn," I whisper as I take a few dripping steps to the table. Lying on it is a leather-bound book with gold writing across its cover, a bracelet resting on a small pile of brightly colored ribbons, a black candle, and an oval mirror with an ornate silver frame. I pick up the mirror and see my mother's face. I've seen images of her before, of course, but this is different. She's younger.

This is it. The moment I've dreamed about since my father first told me the story of my mother's Seelie Court visit. I finally get to see her as a real person. I finally get to hear her voice. With my heart drumming in my chest and my fingers shaking, I touch the mirror's surface.

Her face breaks into a smile, and she tucks a piece of black and purple hair behind her ear. "Okay, whoever you are, you're really brave. You just took a swim in the princess's private pool!" She claps her hands and laughs. "Congratulations! Of course, that makes me really brave too because I also swam in the pool. Well, brave or stupid." She rolls her lavender eyes while I fight the tears forming in my own. "Anyway, you're probably wondering who I am. My name is Rose Hawthorne, I'm a graduate from the Creepy Hollow Guild, and since I only get to visit the Seelie Court once in my life, I thought it would be fun to leave a little bit of myself here. So ... The book is one of my favorites. My best friend gave it to me for my birthday a few years back. If you look inside, there's a folded paper with a story I wrote in junior school—because I feel like you should get a laugh out of this." She giggles while I wipe a stray tear that escaped my eye. "Um, the bracelet is the first piece of jewelry my parents gave me, and the ribbons I found in a chest of my grandmother's belongings when I was small.

"Okay, what's left?" She pauses for a moment and looks to the side. "Oh, the candle. That was from my parents on my eighteenth birthday. It's a never-ending candle, so it'll never get any shorter, no matter how much you burn it. Um, so, that's it. Oh, and the table was made for me by my boyfriend. Amazing guy that he is, he didn't mind me shrinking it along with my other things and bringing it here.

"So, anyway, that's me. It would be really neat if you could return my book to the Creepy Hollow Guild with a message for me. Also, if you get caught leaving this pool, I'm really sorry. I hope I don't get caught when I leave! Oh, and if you happen to be the princess, um, I'm also really sorry. I did *not* mean to disrespect you in any way by hiding these things in your pool. Please don't hate me!" She clasps her hands together, smiles sweetly, and the image of her vanishes.

She's gone.

I touch the mirror again but nothing happens. "It's only set to play once," I say softly. "I'll never see her again." Tears drip down my cheeks. This was my moment with her—my one and only moment—and now it's over.

"I'm sorry." I feel Ryn's hand on my shoulder. "But—and don't hate me for saying this—it probably wouldn't be a good idea for you to watch the same message over and over. You wouldn't want to waste your life in front of a mirror."

"Yeah, I guess you're right." I sniff as I place the mirror down on the table. "But I'm still taking these things home with me."

"Of course," Ryn says. "Need help with the shrinking?"

"Thanks." At least I have these reminders of her. I'll take my time looking at them when I get home. I'll read the book and the story she wrote. I'll burn the never-ending candle, and its perpetual flame will never allow me to forget her.

Right now, though, we need to get out of here.

I shrink the mirror while Ryn takes care of the book and the candle. I'm about to shrink the bracelet, when Ryn says, "You should wear it." He takes it from me and puts it around my right wrist, leaning closer as he fastens the clasp. "And the ribbons. You need some color in your life, V." He winds the ribbons around my arm so that they cover my scar. The curling lines of my guardian markings peep out on either side. He ties the ends and tucks them away, his touch sending a shiver up my arm. I wonder if he notices the goose bumps. He's certainly standing close enough to see them.

I suddenly remember telling Nate that he couldn't talk me into a make-out session in a dodgy, underground tunnel because I have standards. And I realize right now that I have absolutely no standards at all because here in this underground stone room, I want nothing more than to kiss Ryn. If he pulled me into his arms now, I wouldn't stop him. I know it wouldn't be good for us in the long run, but my body and my heart crave him. So badly.

"Um, we should get out of here before the princess returns," Ryn says, taking a step back and putting some distance between us. "Mission complete, so … I guess we could just hang out in your room for a while." He watches me. Am I imagining it, or does he mean something more when he says 'hang out'?

Only one way to find out.

"Okay." *Crap, did I really just sound as breathless as I think I did? I am so pathetic.*

I slip the tiny candle, book and mirror into my wet pockets while Ryn shrinks the table. I let him go ahead of me before pushing my own way through the rippling layer and into the water. I spin around with my stylus in my hand, but the stone is already sealed up. Cool. I pull myself through the water and my head breaks the surface. I smooth my wet hair back and climb out.

Ryn is standing by the opening in the hedge, looking out. "Someone's coming," he says.

"What?"

He grabs my hand and tugs me toward the doorway into the princess's quarters. "We'll wait here until he passes."

We stand just inside the doorway of a sitting room. All pinks and greens and floral patterned walls—it really isn't my taste.

"Dammit," Ryn mutters. I look out at the garden and see a man slip through the gap in the hedge. "Go through that door," Ryn whispers hurriedly, pointing to the other side of the room.

I run, but my wet feet slip in the large puddle that's formed beneath our dripping bodies, and before I know it, I'm falling.

"Vi!" Ryn reaches for me just as I catch myself against the wall—which suddenly gives way. Ryn pushes me into the darkness and follows me. He leans against the wall—door?—to close it, quickly whispering something as the light narrows to a crack and vanishes.

Darkness surrounds us, so complete it feels like it's pressing against my eyeballs. "What did you say just now?" I whisper to Ryn.

"Just a spell to dry all that water. Our footsteps would lead right here otherwise."

I feel for the wall with my hands and press my ear gently against it. I can't hear a thing. "Where are we?" I ask.

"A secret passage between the walls, I imagine. The princess must use it to get around without being seen."

Several more moments of silence pass before I say, "Well, maybe we should conjure up some light and follow this passage. We don't know if that guy is still out there."

"We also don't know where this passage leads. Imagine if

we wandered into the Queen's bedroom, dripping wet, while she was having a morning nap."

"I doubt she takes morning naps," I whisper back. "And can't I at least create some light in here? Surely it can't be seen from the room out there."

When Ryn answers, his voice sounds closer than it was before. "Afraid of the dark, are you, Sexy Pixie?"

"Of course not."

So I don't conjure up a light. Neither does he. I hear a noise in the sitting room. Something moving along the floor, then bumping into the wall. I take an involuntary step backward. I feel Ryn right beside me. His arm, still wet, brushes mine. I can hear him breathing. His hand moves, and his fingers slowly entwine with mine. My heart does a dizzying dance in my chest, and because the darkness is so complete, I have no idea what's about to happen until it's already happening.

His lips graze mine, which startles me so much I almost pull away. But I don't. I grip his fingers tighter and press my body closer because—*yes oh yes oh yes*—I want this so badly. Our lips touch again, with more pressure this time. He pulls his fingers free from mine and slides his hand all the way up my arm. I imagine I can feel sparks jumping across my skin. Through my closed eyelids, I see flashes of light, and the realization hits me: The sparks he's trailing up my skin are real.

His fingers dig into my wet hair and pull my face closer to his. He twists me around, pressing me against the wall. I feel his body along every inch of mine; no space exists between us. His lips brush along my jaw, teasing me with kisses that feel cool against my burning hot skin. He trails a finger—more sparks—down my neck and over the swell of my chest, ending when he reaches the edge of my top. I think a gasp escapes my throat, but I'm not sure since all I can hear is the pounding of blood in my ears.

His kisses reach my lips again, and this time I part them. His tongue slides over mine, producing a delicious tingling sensation. More sparks. I reach up and run my fingers through his hair. If I could pull him any closer than he already is, I would. His hands slide down my sides, over my hips, and stop at the top of my legs. His grip tightens, and in one swift movement, he pulls me up. I wrap my legs around his waist as he slips his hands beneath my top, his fingers sliding up the bare skin of my back.

The logical part of my brain suddenly wakes up and starts screaming at me to get out of here. What am I doing? This is the guy who has flings with Undergrounders and mocks the feelings of Guild girls who've dared to like him. This is the guy who hurt me so many times after Reed died that I swore I'd never let him close again.

But he isn't like that anymore. He *isn't*. And I can't stop. I want so much more. The kisses. The sparks. The thrill that runs through me when he says my name. Our teasing and joking around and just *being together*. I want all of it.

Above the pounding in my ears I hear something like glass shattering. I don't care. The sparks of light are dancing all across our bodies, and this is exactly where I want to be. Every inch of me desperate to be even closer to him.

Ryn tears his lips from mine long enough to gasp, "I told you that you were missing out."

Something inside me freezes.

He swings me around again, pressing me hard against the wall—but it's the wrong wall. It flies open and the two of us land in an ungraceful heap on the floor of the princess's sitting room. Glass shards litter the floor, several chairs are lying on their sides, and smoke rises from a charred cushion.

I scramble to my feet when I see someone standing over us: the man we were trying to hide from. "Okay, this is not what it looks like," he says, holding his hands up. "All this damage here? I didn't do it. It just … happened."

"What?" Ryn asks, clearly confused. The man looks just as guilty as I feel. "Who are you?" Ryn demands, just as the man asks exactly the same thing.

I don't know what's going on. Ryn and I aren't supposed to be here, and obviously this guy isn't either. But I don't care. Logical me is freaking out. *Freaking out.* All I want is to be as far away from here as possible. Without another thought, I turn toward the garden and run as fast as I possibly can.

CHAPTER TWENTY-THREE

I DON'T STOP RUNNING UNTIL I REACH MY BEDROOM. I lock the door behind me and lean against it, breathing hard. If Ryn tried to follow me, he didn't do a very good job, because I can't hear anything on the other side of the door. Just to be safe, I hurry into the bathroom and lock that door behind me too. I don't want to hear him if he comes knocking.

I told you that you were missing out.

Is that what the kiss was about? Just Ryn proving himself right? I was so caught up in the moment that I'd probably have handed over my heart if he'd asked, and all he was doing was *proving a point?* I lean against the door and slide down until I'm sitting on the floor. I run both hands through my damp hair and tug at it. My chest aches with emptiness, but it serves me right for being so stupid. I've known all along that these feelings would only end up getting me hurt.

I hide out in the bathroom all afternoon until I hear the clothes caster at my bedroom door. At first I'm afraid it's Ryn knocking, but the clothes caster's high-pitched voice carries easily through both doors.

She takes in my bedraggled appearance with raised eyebrows. When I say nothing, she gets to work. She dresses me in some detestable puffy, purple creation which, fortunately, has minimal sparkles. My hair obviously offends her because she frowns every time she looks up at my head. Instead of leaving me to deal with it myself, she mutters a spell to get rid of the drowned look and rolls and twists and pins so fast that I'm not quite sure how it all winds up piled on top of my head. It doesn't look too bad, though, and I appreciate her speed. With a disapproving shake of her head, she gathers her things and leaves.

I quickly remove the colorful ribbons from my wrist and shuffle across to my bedroom door. I need to get out of here before Ryn arrives to escort me downstairs. I crack my door open and peek out. No Ryn.

Whew.

I hurry downstairs as fast as the puffiness will allow. The guy who smiled at me last night is standing near the throne room doors, and I decide now is the time to be friendly. I introduce myself, and he seems weirdly excited to talk to me. I do my best to pay attention to what he's saying, but it's a little difficult when I spend the first few minutes of our conversation anxiously looking out for Ryn and the next few purposefully avoiding Ryn's gaze. I can tell he's watching me, though, and embarrassment heats my neck.

Dinner is horribly awkward. Ryn and I are seated even further from the Queen than last night—probably due to my rudeness—and I spend the entire evening with my body angled away from Ryn trying to make conversation with the guy on my left. The girl on his other side looks a little put out that he's ignoring her. Part of me feels bad, but I'm so desperate to talk to someone other than Ryn that I'll do anything to keep this guy's attention.

When dinner comes to an end and everyone begins standing up, I'm the first one out the door. I hear Ryn's voice behind me: "V, hang on." I walk faster. I'm not sure I can run in this puffy thing, but I can certainly give it a try. As soon as I round a corner, I take off. Ryn's hurried footsteps follow me. "Just wait, dammit," he calls. My brain tortures me with a memory of my legs wrapped around his waist and his body pressed against mine.

Ugh, could I have embarrassed myself any more if I'd tried?

"Violet!" Ryn's shout is so loud that I stop. I stand at the foot of the stairs with my back to him. Water spilling from the mermaids' outstretched hands trickles in the background. "I don't get it," he says. "What are you upset about?"

I turn slowly and look at him. There are a lot of things I want to say, but the words that end up leaving my mouth are, "Can we just pretend it didn't happen?"

He looks so confused that for a moment I'm confused too. Have I missed something here? Misunderstood what really happened between us? But then I notice movement beneath an archway behind him, and all thoughts of our kiss vanish as I lay eyes on the imposter faerie who's stolen my father's shape. It seems the idiot is stupid enough to show up in the same room at the same time as last night.

"Hey!" I shout as he disappears into the darkness once again. "Stop!" I dash after him, almost falling onto my face as I step on the front of my dress. I kick the stupid layers out of the way, pull the skirt up with both hands, and take off again. He's already halfway to the copse of trees he disappeared into last night, and I'm still running down the hill. I'm considering ripping off the bottom half of my puffy monstrosity when Ryn tears past me across the grass. Just before the shapeshifter reaches the pavilion, Ryn takes a flying leap and tackles him to the ground. They struggle. Sparks of magic fly here and there. Just as I reach the pavilion, the shapeshifter manages to get to his feet. I can see he's about to make another run for it, and my weapons tingle with warmth as they settle in my outstretched arms.

"Stop!" I point my bow and arrow directly at him. "Who the hell are you and how *dare* you take on the form of my father?"

He meets my angry gaze, slowly raises his hands, and shakes his head.

"And what is that supposed to mean? You don't *know* who you are? You're refusing to answer me?"

Ryn climbs to his feet and comes to stand by my side. From the corner of my eye, I notice his sparkling whip in his right hand. "I believe she asked you a question, shapeshifter."

The man shakes his head again, still watching me. "You don't want to do this, V."

I'm so startled by his use of my nickname and his voice that sounds exactly like my father's—obviously—that the bow and arrow almost disappear from my grasp. How does he know my father always called me V? *No. Concentrate.* I've been tricked by a shapeshifter before and I won't be tricked again. "You seem to know who I am, so it's only fair you tell me who you are." When he says nothing, I shout, "Tell me!"

The shapeshifter closes his eyes and sighs. The look of defeat on his face gives me hope; he's going to cave and tell me what's going on. He sits down in a cushioned chair, leans forward on his knees, and looks up at me. "My beautiful girl," he says softly. "You look so much like your mother."

"Excuse me?"

"I should have known you'd be here. Of course you'd win the graduation prize—it's what you always wanted, and you worked so hard for it."

"Okay, I don't know what you're doing—" aside from creeping me out "—but you're not answering my question." I walk over to him and hold the arrow inches from his forehead. "Who. Are. You?"

He raises his eyes and says simply, "Your father."

Despite the warmth of the evening air, a shiver races across my arms. "My father is dead," I tell him. "I saw his body. They put it in a canoe and I watched him float away and disappear beneath the Infinity Falls. He's *gone*, which means you're not him."

He rubs a hand across his eyes. "I'm so sorry, V. You weren't supposed to ever find out about this. At least, not until everything is finally over and we're safe again." He groans and mutters something about the Queen and being careless.

"I hate to be repetitive," I say, "*but you're not answering my question.*"

He focuses somewhere on the floor and says, "It wasn't me in the canoe. It was a shapeshifter. The Queen used him to fake my death so I could continue a dangerous assignment undercover. Everyone had to believe I was dead so that the person I'm after would no longer be suspicious."

I feel a part of me daring to hope. It sounds farfetched, but maybe it's true. Maybe this man sitting here really is my father.

"Do you expect us to believe that?" Ryn asks. "What a ridiculous story. Wouldn't a shapeshifter return to his or her original form when dead anyway? If your story's true then we would have seen some stranger in the canoe, not Violet's father."

I shake my head. "I killed a shapeshifter. He ..." *He still looked like Nate when he was dead.* "He didn't return to his original form after he died."

"You don't have to believe me." The man stands, and I keep my arrow trained on his forehead. "In fact, it would be better if you didn't. It would be better if we all walked away now and pretended this hadn't happened." His voice is steady, but his eyes are filled with an infinite sadness. Damn, this guy is either a really good actor or he's telling the truth. He looks straight at me and says, "You should let me go."

"That's exactly what you want, isn't it?" Ryn mutters. He turns to me. "Can't we give this guy a compulsion potion and force him to tell the truth?"

"We could. Or he could just answer a question." I've

managed to think of something nobody else should know. "What did my father say to me the night the boy everyone loved died?" That should be cryptic enough if this man really is a fraud.

The-man-who-might-be-my-father steps closer to me. So close that my arrow is almost touching his skin. "What do you want, Violet?" he asks softly. "Do you want it to be me? Or is it easier for you if I'm nothing but an imposter?"

My voice cracks when I say, "I already know it's you." I think I knew the moment he called me V.

Alive. He's *alive*. How am I supposed to process this?

"Forgive my cynicism," Ryn says, "but I'd still like to hear the answer to that question."

My father looks at Ryn, then back at me. He takes a deep breath. "You saw my tears and said you'd never seen me crying before. I told you it was only the second time I'd shed tears in my adult life. I also told you that I didn't know why, but I'd always loved that boy like he was my own son."

I nod. That's exactly what Dad told me. Dad. My father. *Who isn't dead.* The realization hits home and a shudder passes through my body. "Dad?" I whisper.

He pulls me into his arms. "Baby girl, I'm so sorry, I'm so sorry. Please forgive me. I've missed you every single day. I never wanted to leave you."

Amidst my tangle of emotions, I find myself wriggling free from his arms. "But you did," I say through my tears. "You did leave. You said everyone had to believe you were dead, but why me? Why couldn't you have just told *me* what you were really doing? I would have kept your secret. You know I would have."

"I *especially* couldn't tell you, V. You were in danger. He wanted to kill you. You had to believe I was dead or he would have searched until he found you."

"What?" What the freak is he talking about?

"I always knew you'd be angry if you ever found out about this, but I've never regretted it. As much as it broke my heart to leave you, my decision kept you safe. It was worth the pain we both had to go through."

Anger flares within me. What right did he have to decide what pain I should go through? Ryn touches my arm. "Don't fight with him, V. He's *alive*. This should be a moment of joy, not anger."

I squeeze my eyes closed. Tears drip over the edge of my eyelids and run down my cheeks. Why is Ryn always right? I should be rejoicing right now, not acting like a difficult child. I step forward and wrap my arms around my father's neck. He hugs me back. *This is real,* I tell myself. His arms around me are *real.* And although I detest talking about feelings, I figure I should tell him something, just in case this is all a dream and I don't get another chance. "I love you, Dad," I whisper.

"I love *you.*" He squeezes me tight and lifts me off the ground for a second. "And I'm so proud of you. You've grown into such an amazing, smart, beautiful young lady—and guardian." He sets me down on my feet. "And why are you wearing this hideous dress? You hate purple clothes."

I laugh as I wipe tears from my face. "I didn't choose it. Didn't Mom tell you that they pick your outfits for you when you stay here?"

Dad shakes his head with a chuckle. He looks over my

shoulder and extends a hand to Ryn. "I suppose I shouldn't be surprised to see you here either. You were always just as competitive as Violet. Congratulations on graduating at the top of your class." He shakes Ryn's hand. "I *am* surprised to see the two of you standing in the same room without wanting to hurt each other. I thought you'd both sworn never to be friends again?"

I look at Ryn, then quickly look away. "Yes, um, we decided to put all that behind us."

"Uh, I have a question, sir," Ryn says. "Was it you I saw at the Harts' house?"

"What?" I ask just as Dad nods and says, "Yes."

"Um … yeah." Ryn turns to me. "Remember when I said I saw someone who looked like Cecy? Well, I was lying."

My mouth gapes open. "You saw my *father* and you didn't tell me?" I try to shove him but he catches my hands.

"I just figured it couldn't possibly be him, so why freak you out?"

"Ryn, that is *so* not a good enough reason to keep something like that from me." I feel hurt and betrayed, but I'm trying to be mature, so I let it go. I sit down on the edge of a chair and turn to my father. "Okay, you have a lot of explaining to do. What undercover assignment are you on that's taking so many years to complete? And why exactly was it better for everyone if we all thought you were dead? You said someone was trying to *kill* me? And what exactly were you doing at the Harts' house?"

Dad holds his hands up. "Look, you know I can't tell you anything. Firstly, it's against protocol to share the details of an assignment, and, secondly, it's for your own safety."

"Dad, you abandoned me for the past four years. I think you owe me this much." Yeah, I'm playing the guilt card. An underhanded move, but I don't care right now.

"V, I ..."

"Tell me! You can't just show up in my life all of a sudden and not explain anything."

He sits on the edge of a small table. "Okay, look, it's something to do with the Unseelie Queen's son, but that's all I can say. I'm dealing with some very dangerous people, V, and I can't have you getting involved."

"The Unseelie Queen's son?" I glance at Ryn, who's sitting on a nearby chair. "You mean Zell?"

Dad frowns. "Yes. Marzell. How do you know him?"

I roll my eyes. "You're afraid of me being involved, Dad? Well, it's too late for that. I'm already involved. Big time. So there's no need for you to keep any more secrets from me."

"What do you mean you're involved?" Dad stands up quickly. "How? What happened?"

"No, no, no," I say. "You don't get to demand details without sharing any of your own. You tell me your story, and I'll tell you mine."

With disbelief written all over his face, Dad looks at Ryn as if for backup. "Sorry, but I'm with V on this one," Ryn says.

After another pause, Dad says, "Okay, but I don't have time to tell you everything now. I'm already late for the meeting I was on my way to when you chased me down."

Panic tightens around my heart. We're leaving first thing in the morning; when will I see him again? "So come home," I say, standing quickly. "Come home and explain everything to me."

Dad reaches forward and touches my cheek. "I don't want to let you out of my sight if you're in danger."

I tilt my head sideways and smile. "I'm a guardian, Dad. I'll always be in danger."

"Yes, but it's different with the Unseelie Court. You don't know what they'll—"

"I have a concealment charm on me. A proper one. There's no way Zell can find me unless we accidentally bump into each other, and that's not going to happen."

Dad nods. "Okay. Will you be home the night after to-morrow?" I nod. "Good. I'll see you then." He kisses my forehead. He's about to walk away when his gaze falls on my neck. "Your mother's tokehari," he says in surprise. "I thought it was—" he looks at Ryn, then back at me "—lost," he finishes.

"Uh, I found it, sir," Ryn says, "and returned it along with my sincerest apologies for ... 'losing' it."

Dad smiles. "That's good." He kisses my forehead once more and whispers, "I love you, baby girl."

CHAPTER TWENTY-FOUR

I FEEL LIKE I'M LOOKING AT MY LIFE THROUGH DIFFERENT eyes. Every time I think back to a major event, I wonder where my father was at the time and what he was doing. Has he been watching from the sidelines, keeping an eye on me? Or has he distanced himself completely ever since his supposed death, not even knowing what I looked like until that night at the Harts? So many questions. I should probably write them down in case I forget something.

Ryn and I make the journey back to Creepy Hollow in silence. I tell myself he's giving me space to come to terms with the monumental fact that Dad is still alive, but I know there's also an undercurrent of weirdness between us. Neither one of us has mentioned The Kiss again. I'm hoping that if I ignore it, Ryn and I can go back to some kind of comfortable friendship.

I'll get over my feelings for him soon, right? Yes, I will. After all, it didn't seem to take too long for my Nate-feelings to fade away.

When I woke up at the palace this morning, I found a note slipped under my door. My heart squeezed painfully when I saw my name written in Dad's handwriting on the front.

I'm sure I don't have to say this, but you CANNOT tell anyone about me.

He didn't need to remind me, but I treasure his note nonetheless. It's evidence that he really does exist. I keep it in my pocket now that I'm back home where the Seelie Court and everything that happened there feels like a vivid dream. The note and his handwriting assure me that it was real. The silver-framed mirror above my desk and the black candle blazing continuously beside my bathing room pool also help.

After finding Bran at the Guild and interrogating him about the investigation into the Guild's attacks—he tells me absolutely nothing useful—I send an amber message to Tora and invite her over for dessert. I wish with all my heart I could tell her about Dad, but instead she'll have to tell me about the guy she's been keeping secret.

"Look, I didn't *intentionally* keep anything from you," she says when I greet her at my door with crossed arms and a glare. "I just hadn't exactly got around to telling you about him yet."

"Yeah, yeah, whatever." It strikes me that that's exactly what I would say if she found out about Nate, so I don't really have any right to make her feel guilty. "Tell me everything now, and that'll make up for it."

She heads across my sitting room to one of the couches. "Fine, but then you're sharing the details of your love life."

"I don't have a love life." *At least, not one I'm willing to talk about.* The memory of Ryn's hands caressing my skin sends butterflies soaring across my stomach. I turn away to hide my smile. I shouldn't be smiling. I shouldn't even be thinking about it. It's not like it's going to happen again.

"Ooh, I haven't had a fun dessert like this in ages," Tora says as she eyes the low table between the couches. There's a bowl of fruit on her side and another on mine. We also each have a bowl of melted chocolate and a thin stick. In the center of the table is a floating sphere of flickering blue and white light.

"Yeah, I don't think I've used this dessert spell in ages. It seemed appropriate for the warmer weather." We sit on the floor on either side of the table. "So, anyway, this guy—"

"Oliver."

"Oliver. You met him at the London Guild?"

"Before then, actually." Tora leans forward and spikes a strawberry on the end of her stick. After dipping it in melted chocolate, she holds it inside the flickering sphere for several seconds to freeze it. "Remember when you were suspended?"

"I try not to."

"Right, well, there was this Council guy who visited from the London Guild. He had to meet with several of our Council members, and afterwards he gave a talk to some of our trainees." She bites into her frozen chocolate strawberry and munches a few times before continuing. "I happened to be the mentor in charge that day, so, you know, we chatted." Her pale skin flushes bright pink.

"Aaand?" I prompt with a smile.

"Well, he was very charming and everything, but I was just being friendly."

"That's weird. I remember Honey telling me he was boring."

Tora makes a face at me. "He was *not* boring. I mean, he named the stray vine that always sneaks down the corridor Nigel, which was a little corny, but other than that he was, you know ..."

"Hot?"

"Well, yes."

I laugh as I reach forward to freeze my own piece of fruit. "I knew it!"

"Oh, rubbish, you knew nothing. Anyway, I said goodbye expecting I wouldn't see him again, and the next thing I knew, Councilor Starkweather was saying he'd asked for me to visit the London Guild for a few days to give my input on a new training center they'd decided to build. I thought it was strange they didn't ask for someone who actually *designs* training centers—"

"And then you discovered when you got there that he didn't want your input, he just wanted you." I give her my sweetest smile, and she rolls her eyes.

"Well, it's not like he *told* me that, but I figured it out."

"So that's why you ended up staying longer?"

"Yes, he managed to convince me to extend my visit."

"You know, Tora—" I lean forward, feigning a

conspiratorial air "—there are these things called *faerie paths* that allow you to visit someone anywhere in the world in just a few seconds. You don't actually have to stay in the same place."

Tora crosses her arms and narrows her eyes, but I can see she's trying not to smile. Eventually she gives in with a chuckle. "Look, it was just easier to stay there."

"At his house?"

She stabs another piece of fruit and freezes it. "You still haven't told me why Ryn was in your bedroom so early yesterday morning."

I freeze a chocolate-covered blueberry and hand it to Filigree, currently mouse-shaped and lounging on the arm of the couch. "Since we're changing subjects," I say, "I saw Bran earlier and asked him about the attacks on the Guild. He used a lot of words, but he basically told me nothing."

"You know he can't tell you anything if you're not part of the investigation. I've also asked him, and he won't tell me a thing either. I only know the few details that have been made public, like the fact that the Unseelie Queen denies having any knowledge of the attacks."

Which is exactly what I told Councilor Starkweather. "Yes, he mentioned that. So, when did they fix the foyer and the ceiling? I walked through there earlier today and it looked like nothing ever happened."

"I think they finished last night." Tora freezes a chocolate-dipped raspberry and pops the whole thing into her mouth.

"Wow, three whole days just to repair the foyer?"

"Mm hmm." She finishes chewing. "Those are some serious protective enchantments in the domed ceiling. And apparently the floor has protection woven into it too." She picks up her bowl of fruit and eats a few pieces unfrozen. "Now, don't think I haven't noticed you're avoiding talking about Ryn. I know you've sort of despised him for a number of years, but you certainly seemed to be enjoying his company at the grad ball. Are the two of you more than friends now?"

"Tora!" I do my best to look horrified. "No. Do you honestly think I'd date Ryn?"

"Well, yes. He's good-looking and charming, he's an excellent guardian, and the two of you share a history that consists of a lot more than simply hating one another."

"That's ridiculous. It would never work out in the long run."

Tora is silent a while before replying. "I didn't want to have to be the one to say it, so I'm glad you did. I know how many times he's hurt you in the past, and I would hate for you to wind up hurt again. But I guess you've always been a sensible person. I should have known you wouldn't just fall for him like that." She snaps her fingers.

You see? the logical voice inside me says. *Tora knows just as well as you do that it wouldn't work out.*

"Okay, now tell me what you're going to say when the Guild offers you a job." She points her chocolaty stick at me. "Because we both know that's exactly what they're going to do."

By the time Tora and I have discussed my options for the future—which no longer include being a personal guardian to the Seelie Queen, since there's a strong possibility she thinks I'm rude and obnoxious, and I also happen to find palace life utterly boring—we've finished all the dessert. I clear up while Tora reads a message on her amber and giggles. *Giggles.* Honestly, what is it about love that can make us act like complete morons at times? And by 'us' I don't mean me. Because I would never act like a moron for a guy. Well, except for the time I tried to entice Nate with an alluring bat of my eyelashes.

"I, uh, need to go now," Tora says.

"Got a date on the other side of the world?"

"Something like that." Her eyes sparkle.

"Okay, well, I'll see you around."

She leaves, and I try to tell myself I don't feel lonely. I try to tell myself I don't miss Ryn. I'm lying, of course. Part of me wishes he were here, just hanging out, being friends. But there's a much bigger part of me that's relieved he isn't because then I'd have to talk about The Kiss.

I head upstairs, change into a long T-shirt, and climb onto my bed with my amber. I need to practice some of the social networking spells Ryn taught me or I'll never make full use of this thing. I pull my stylus out of my hair, which falls down around my neck in messy, unbrushed waves; Raven would not be impressed. After a minute or so of thought, I scribble the words of a spell across the amber's glossy surface.

Nothing happens.

Great. I can remember complex spells required to heal my body from all kinds of injuries, but when it comes to something silly like a spell to improve my social life, the words escape me. Filigree shifts into the form of a white bunny with little white wings—who knows where he saw that one—and half-flaps, half-jumps onto the bed while I tap my stylus against my chin, thinking. I try another combination of words and, this time, tiny shapes swim to the surface of my amber.

I lean back against my pillows and examine the shapes and words. There are symbols that represent different people—Ryn drew a key for me when he set this spell up—and short lines of text next to each one. A message in a bubble at the top of the amber informs me that Honey is 'following' me, and so is the guy I chatted with outside the Seelie Queen's throne room when I was avoiding Ryn. That's a little creepy. How did he even find me?

I read a few of the messages.

Honey: Vacationing with my bf and his fam. Like, all 12 of them!

Flint: The Guild is stronger than ever before. Suck it, Unseelie Court!

Ryn to Opal: I thought the food rocked, actually.

Seriously? This is what people waste their spare time doing? I don't get it. Couldn't Flint get in trouble for telling the Unseelie Court to 'suck it,' or is that kind of thing allowed with social spells? And who is this Opal person Ryn's talking to? Hmm. Wasn't the dark-haired girl he was flirting with at the palace called Opal?

I don't want to be involved in this silly stuff. On the other hand, I don't exactly want to be left out. Which is completely ridiculous. I never used to worry about being left out. I just got on with my assignments and ignored Ryn and everyone else.

A knocking sound startles me, and I look up. Ryn is leaning in the doorway to my bedroom, rapping his knuckles against the door frame. The sight of him sends a thrill rocketing through my body.

Stupid thrill.

"You know you're supposed to stand *outside* and knock, right?" I say to him.

"Yes, but I figured you wouldn't let me in if you knew it was me. So I let myself in instead."

I fake-laugh as I place my amber on the bedside table. "Why wouldn't I let you in?"

"Because you've been avoiding me since yesterday morning? If I hadn't caught your father for you last night, you'd have hidden in your room all evening. And if we hadn't been forced to travel back together this morning, you definitely would have stayed away from me all day."

"Well, you know, we don't have to see each other every day." *Wow. Amazing contribution to the conversation, Violet.*

"I suppose not," Ryn says, "but since there's this awkwardness between us, we should probably talk about it."

Please, no.

"Why do I get the feeling our relationship is backwards?" Ryn asks as he wanders into my room, shrugs his jacket off, and hangs it over the back of my desk chair. "Isn't it usually the girl who always wants to talk about feelings and the guy who bottles everything up inside?"

"I don't bottle things up," I shoot back. Well, there is an imaginary *box* I like to hide things in, but that's different.

"Right. Of course not."

I draw my knees up and wrap my arms around them. Filigree hops to the edge of the bed and flaps his wings until he achieves lift-off. He flies toward Ryn, who catches him easily.

"So, um, how's your mom going with that murder investigation?" I ask.

He sighs. "Okay, since you clearly aren't going to be the one to bring it up, I'll say it. We kissed. It was pretty damn hot. Now I want to talk about it, but I can't because you're being all weird. That isn't normal for you. You're not like other girls, remember? You don't get silly and upset and moody. You're cooler than that."

"Well, Ryn, I guess I can only be cool up to a certain point. There's a line, and when you kissed me just to prove that you were right about something, you crossed it." There, now he knows why I'm upset.

"Just to prove I was right?" He places a wriggling Filigree on the floor. "What are you talking about?"

"You're going to tell me you don't remember? Let me help you. We had the super-hot kiss, and then you ended it with, 'I told you that you were missing out.'"

"Yeah, so? You *were* missing out. I wasn't trying to prove a point; I was simply stating a fact. And that wasn't where I planned to end it. Trust me, I could have stayed in the dark with you a whole lot longer if we hadn't hit the wrong wall and landed in the middle of a partially demolished sitting room. Speaking of which, you haven't asked me what happened after you bolted."

I sigh. "What happened after I bolted?"

"Well, it turns out Mr. Faerie Sneak had just as much right to be in there as we did. So we both agreed to pretend we'd never seen each other, and then he ran off while I was left to clean up all the mess you and I made before Princess Olivia got back."

"*We* made?"

"Yes, V." Ryn looks at me like I should have figured this out already. "Shattered vases, burning cushions, overturned furniture—that was us." He grins. "It was one seriously hot kiss, remember?"

Trying REALLY hard not to. But I'm obviously not trying hard enough because the memories aren't going anywhere. So I take a deep breath and say, "Okay, fine. I'll talk. The kiss was hot. Amazing. Incredible. You were right—clearly I was missing out by never having experienced a kiss from someone magical. And now I know, so thank you. Can we move on?"

He crosses his arms. "I still don't get it. Why do you want to move on? It's not like you kissed me simply because you were bored and had nothing else to do at the time."

"Oh. Well, since you know so much about my motivations, maybe you'd like to tell me why I kissed you."

Ryn throws his hands up. "Are you really not going to admit it?"

"Admit what?"

"You have feelings for me, Violet. Why is it so hard for you to say that?"

"Because it isn't true." I hug my knees tighter. "And because if it *were* true you'd only end up hurting me."

"That's ridiculous. If we have feelings for each other and we want to be together, why would I be stupid enough to hurt you?"

"Well, you probably wouldn't do it intentionally, but after

275

a while you'd get over whatever feelings you might have for me. I know you like the company of Undergrounders, and I can never be as exotic or exciting as the beings you'll find down there."

He walks forward and leans toward me with both hands on the bed as he says, "I don't *want* to be with any Undergrounder, V. *I want you.*"

Those three words send shivers up and down my arms, but I can't help wondering how many other girls he's said the same thing to. I shift away from him. "You say that …"

"I *mean* that."

"You *think* you mean it, Ryn, and you probably do right now, but it won't last, and where will that leave me?"

"Violet. This … what I'm feeling …" He seems to be struggling for words. "It's so much more than anything I've ever felt for anyone. It's threatening to explode out of me. How can you tell me it won't last?"

I shrug, shake my head, and look at my knees. "I don't know. I only know one thing for sure, and it's that you'll break my heart."

"No. I could never hurt you again, V. I *mean* it." He steps back and tugs his hair. "What do I have to say to make you believe me?"

This conversation needs to end. I'm terrified that if it goes on much longer I'll give in. And as much as I want to—and I really, really want to—I know instinctively that when Ryn breaks my heart it'll be ten times worse than the pain I felt after Nate betrayed me. "There isn't anything you can say, Ryn, or anything you can do. And it doesn't matter, anyway, because I don't feel that way about you." *Liar, liar.* "Things were good when we were friends. Why can't we just leave it at that?"

He lets out a humorless laugh. "You don't feel that way about me? Now you're just lying."

"I am not."

His expression is incredulous. "Yes, you are."

How does he freaking know that? Is it written all over my face? Am I really that terrible a liar? "You have no idea what I'm feeling, Oryn."

"I know exactly what you're—"

"You don't. End of conversation."

"YES I DO! Aren't you listening to me? I *know* what you're feeling! I *feel* what you're feeling! You think you're the only one in Creepy Hollow graced with a dose of extra special magic? Well, you're not. I feel every single flipping thing everyone around me is feeling, which, when it comes to you, isn't usually much. But guess what? That isn't the case anymore. I knew you were panicking when we headed onto the dance floor after graduation because I *felt* it. I knew that the moment I whispered in your ear while we were dancing was the moment you realized just how much you wanted me because I *felt* the flood of emotions that suddenly came over you. I felt it again yesterday morning when I was lying next to you in bed, and again when I was kissing you. I *know*, Violet, so don't lie to me."

My mouth is hanging open in shock by the time he's finished speaking. What he said is absurd. Completely, totally absurd. And yet it makes a horrible amount of sense. Ryn has always seemed extra intuitive. He knows when something is

277

wrong, before I can even say anything. Is this how he guessed my real reason for wanting to get the top graduating prize? He was reading my emotions while questioning me? "What … what am I feeling now?"

He takes a deep breath. "Up until about a minute ago, it was mostly desire and fear mixed in together, but right now, shock is pretty much overshadowing everything else."

No. Freaking. Way.

My voice is barely more than a whisper when I ask, "How long have you known you can do this?"

"A long time."

"And you never told me."

"I—"

"You've always known my secret, and yet you never bothered to tell me yours." Thanks to his stupid ability, he should be feeling the anger boiling inside me right now.

"Violet, I—"

"Get out of my house."

He grabs his jacket from the back of the chair. "Gladly. If you want to keep lying to yourself, go right ahead."

CHAPTER TWENTY-FIVE

I PULL MY SHIRT STRAIGHT AND RUN MY HANDS THROUGH my hair before knocking on Councilor Starkweather's office door. There was a letter from her on my kitchen table this morning requesting my presence at an interview this afternoon. I knew Tora was right when she said they'd offer me a job; I just didn't think it would be this soon. Tora said it would be appropriate for me to wear a dress to my interview, but after my super-tight, super-puffy experiences at the Seelie Court, I'm done with dresses. Instead, I transformed a simple, long-sleeved T-shirt into a shirt with buttons and a collar to go with my pants—and I did a pretty good job.

Councilor Starkweather makes small talk about my visit to the Seelie Court for several minutes before arriving at the reason for this meeting. "The Council has discussed it, and we'd like to offer you a position here at the Creepy Hollow Guild." She pauses, which probably means I'm supposed to say something.

"Okay. Thank you."

She crosses her arms on top of her desk and leans forward. "You're probably aware that we usually give graduates a longer break after graduation before offering them positions at the Guild, but with the recent attack … well, we need as many guardians as we can get, as soon as we can get them. I don't want to alarm you, but the Seers have been receiving hints of a great battle in our future. No concrete visions yet and, as you know, these things can change, but we want the Guild to be fully prepared in the event of a major attack."

"I see." I could have predicted that, and I'm not a Seer. It's obvious Zell is planning something, so it makes sense there'll be a big showdown at some point. Guardians versus … well, whatever Zell calls his minions. And when it happens, I want to be there to kick his Unseelie ass. And Nate's, if he dares to stand against the Guild.

"If you require some time to think about it," Councilor Starkweather says, "I'll give you three days. Here's a copy of the contract." She hands me a scroll. "Take a good look at it, and, if anything seems unclear, ask me."

"Sure, okay." I take the scroll from her and hope she dismisses me soon. I'm eager to get out of here.

My father is coming home tonight.

* * *

I clean the house. It isn't exactly dirty, but I want it to be perfect when Dad gets here. The last time he left this home, he knew he was walking into the fight that would be used to fake his own death. Did he think he'd ever come back? Did he look around at everything and say goodbye? Did he somehow say goodbye to *me* and I never realized it?

I don't know what time he'll get here, so once I've finished tidying and darkness has begun to fall, I resort to pacing around and around the sitting room. I hear the wind picking up outside, the leaves brushing against one another in an angry dance. It's uncharacteristically cool for a summer evening. I hope another magical storm isn't on its way.

When I hear a knock, I just about fall over the furniture in my haste to get to the doorway portion of the wall. I swear, if this is anyone but Dad, I'm not hesitating to tell them to get lost. I swipe my hand across the wall—and there he his. He's wearing a jacket with a hood concealing half his face, but I can still see it's him.

"Don't hug me or say my name until the door is closed," he mutters. He slips quickly past me, and I can't help glancing out into the darkness as I wave my hand to seal the doorway. Dad pushes his hood back and turns to me. "You never know who might be watching. It's been years, but I still like to be careful."

"Um, okay." I can't believe he's really here. In our home. I can almost imagine that no time has passed since the last time we stood here together.

But time has passed. We're different people now. And even though I've looked forward to this moment since I said goodbye to him at the Seelie Court, it's a little weird now that he's here.

"This feels rather surreal," Dad says quietly, watching me.

I nod. "It does." Then I laugh and step forward to put my arms around his neck. Of course this is weird, but the weirdness won't last long.

We walk to the couch as Dad says, "Everything seems the same here except you. Whenever I think of you and imagine you at home, I see the little girl I left behind. But that's not who you are anymore."

"I wasn't *that* little. I was fourteen." We sit down. I tuck my legs beneath me, but Dad sits with his back a little too straight for him to be comfortable. Clearly this is weird for him too.

"But you've grown up a lot in almost four years," he says. "And speaking of growing up, I haven't forgotten that your birthday is only three days away."

"Yeah, I think Tora and Raven are planning a—" My words are cut off by another knock against the tree. Dad stands quickly.

"Check who it is," he says. "If it's one of your friends, I can come back later."

I cross the room without bothering to tell him I don't exactly have friends. I create a peephole, look out, and groan. "It's Ryn." I swipe the doorway open. "Yes?"

"Your dad's here tonight," he says without really looking at me. "I came to hear what he has to say."

"Okay, so what are you doing out here? Don't you normally just let yourself in?"

"I thought I'd be polite and stand *outside* and knock this time." He walks past me into the room.

"Okay, but politeness also requires that you *wait* outside until someone invites you in," I call after him.

"Whatever."

When I get back to the couch, Ryn is handing Dad a small vial. "What's that?" I ask.

"Compulsion potion," Ryn answers. "I know you're having your happy reunion, but I thought we should check that he really is who he says he is."

"Ryn!" I can't believe his nerve.

"It's okay, V," Dad says, unscrewing the tiny lid. He tilts his head back and taps a few drops onto his tongue. He swallows and shudders. "Ugh, that stuff is disgusting when undiluted."

Ryn touches Dad's shoulder and says the short compulsion spell, followed by, "You will tell the truth." Then he takes a seat on the couch opposite us.

"Now that that's out the way," Dad says, "will you tell me what you meant the other night when you said you're already involved with Marzell?"

"Okay." I'm keen to hear Dad's story, so I'll make mine short. "Here's the bottom line: Zell wants me because of my ability to find people."

"But how did he find out you have this ability? You've kept it a secret, haven't you?"

"Yes, but he has a spy in the Guild, and that spy somehow heard about a guardian with my skills. Zell didn't actually find out it was *me* until Nate told him."

"Nate?"

"Um, this halfling I was sort of dating. Zell managed to convince him to turn against me, and I didn't realize it until it was too late."

"I see."

Great. Dad's been home for five minutes and I've already managed to disappoint him with my poor choice in boyfriends. "Yeah, so, anyway … I've fought Zell a few times, and, obviously, I survived."

Dad's eyebrows rise. "You've actually fought him? That's impressive."

I shrug, as if fighting the Unseelie Prince was no big deal, but I can't help the smile that spreads across my face.

"This all seems like a horrible coincidence," Dad says. "Zell threatened your life four years ago because of me, and now he's after you again for a different reason. He probably has no idea you're the same person."

"Well, he knows my full name, so he probably does know who I am."

"But he never knew *my* real name. We worked with code names for most of our assignments. I doubt he'd connect your name to me."

"Oh. Okay." When Dad doesn't ask any more questions, I say, "So, are you ready to tell me everything now? The big reason behind why you had to fake your own death and abandon me?" I pull a cushion out from behind my back and wrap my arms around it. "Oh, and I want to know about Angelica too."

He looks up. "How—how do you know about Angelica?"

"Well, the guy I sort of dated—Nate—is her son."

Dad's eyebrows rise higher as he sits forward. "Angelica has a *son*? And you dated him?"

"Yes." I hug the cushion a little tighter. "Is there something wrong with that?"

"Not really." He rubs a hand across his eyes. "It's just unexpected, that's all. I didn't know she had a child."

"Yeah. Anyway, I only met her once, but she made it clear she hated you and Mom, and I want to know why. I've kind of been picturing you guys as training rivals, but her feelings seemed a little intense even for that."

Dad shakes his head and lets out a long sigh. "We weren't rivals, V. Angelica was your mother's best friend."

CHAPTER TWENTY-SIX

MY MOUTH HANGS OPEN. *ANGELICA WAS MY MOTHER'S best friend?* Once again, it seems I have to adjust the picture I have in my head of my parents' lives. "But ... I thought Zinnia was Mom's best friend. And you and Linden were friends. You all trained together, and then you worked together, and then you had babies, and everything was peachy up until the day Mom died."

Dad sighs again. I have a feeling this conversation is going to be full of sighs. "You must know by now that life is never that simple, V. I mean, yes, all of that is true. But Angelica was there too, and she made life a lot more ..." He holds his hands up. "I promise I'll explain everything to you, right from the beginning, but first tell me where you met her and what she said to you."

"Well, it was a little weird, actually."

"Labyrinth weird?" Dad says with a knowing look.

"Yes. You know about the labyrinth?"

"I wish I didn't, but I do."

And the picture keeps readjusting. "Okay, well, Nate and I went down there to find Angelica. She told us that an Unseelie faerie had built the labyrinth and trapped her down there because she refused to give him this item of power she had—a disc."

"With a griffin-snake symbol on it?"

"Yes. She explained that it had belonged to the powerful halfling Tharros. Apparently while he was still alive he transferred part of his power into several objects so that if he were ever drained of his magic he'd have other sources of power to draw from. She told us we needed to go back to her home in the human realm—where Nate lived—and bring her the disc so she could use it to get out. We didn't do that, of course. But before we could leave, she recognized me. She and I fought, and Nate and I managed to get out alive."

"Do you still have this disc?" Dad is sitting on the edge of the couch again.

"Unfortunately not. Nate stole it. I assume he took it right to Zell, who, it appears, has a few more of these discs. Angelica made it seem like there was only one."

"Zell has more of the discs?" Dad closes his eyes and shakes his head. "He must have got them from Angie," he mutters. "And here I was hoping he'd never find her. Dammit, this is really bad news."

I wait for him to continue, but he doesn't. He seems deep

in thought, and I don't want to interrupt him, but I do want to understand why this is such bad news. "Dad?" I prompt.

He takes a deep breath and looks up at me, as if suddenly remembering I'm in the room. "Well, Angelica certainly managed to weave a lot of lies out of a small amount of truth."

"I guess I was right not to trust her," I say.

Dad nods. "Okay, this will all make more sense if I start at the beginning." He shifts into a more comfortable position while I cross my legs beneath me on the couch.

"I didn't miss anything important, did I?" Ryn asks. I look up to see him coming out of the kitchen with three mugs floating in the air in front of him. I don't even remember him leaving the room. "Since neither of you were offering any drinks, I thought I'd play the host tonight." He directs the mugs onto the table and sits down.

"Thanks, Ryn," Dad says.

"Um, thanks." I sound anything but thankful, though. It should have been me getting Dad a drink. I pick up my mug and peep inside: Hot chocolate with mini rose-infused star marshmallows floating on its surface and a swirling cinnamon cloud above it. My all-time favorite. I let out a huff. Ryn is acting perfect and it's annoying me.

"So," Dad says, "there were five of us. Rose and Zinnia had been best friends since they were little. Linden and I grew up next door to each other, so we were also very good friends. The four of us met when we began our training at the Guild. That was when Angelica moved to Creepy Hollow and joined our class. Soon enough the five of us were inseparable. We sat together in classes, begged to be put in the same assignment groups, and, well, being young, we also got into mischief together.

"In our third year, the girls dared Linden and me to go Underground, which was pretty much forbidden by the Guild. As you know, Undergrounders have never been fans of guardians or trainees. They generally attack first and ask questions later. But we were brave and stupid, so of course we accepted the dare. Angie said we had to steal something and bring it back to prove we'd been down there. So we broke into an old centaur's home and found a metal disc with a griffin-snake symbol engraved into it. Rose recognized the symbol from a book she'd seen in her mentor's office, so she asked him about it.

"He was a very old faerie—in his sixth century, I think. He told Rose about the powerful halfling Tharros Mizreth and the legend of his lost power. These were stories that had been told to him by his parents, who were guardians at the time Tharros was defeated.

"Tharros' power was so great that he was almost impossible to kill. He had to be separated from that power, and only then could he be killed and his power destroyed independently. Some kind of weapon was constructed to do this. After much fighting and death, the best guardians from all the Guilds managed to catch up with Tharros and separate him from his power. They killed him. Most people think that was the end, but only those directly involved knew that the guardians failed to destroy Tharros' power. Instead, they captured it inside some kind of chest. They locked the chest using six different keys—the discs with the griffin on them—one to close each side of the chest. In the process of sealing the chest, some of the power was transferred into each disc. The discs were then scattered around the world, hidden by people who were meant to keep them safe.

"But the disc-keepers soon discovered that physical contact with these discs provided access to extra power. This, of course, could not be kept a secret. So discs were stolen, again and again over the centuries. They became so scattered that it was impossible for any one person to know where all the discs were. And that is what has kept the chest of power safe all these years."

"And Mom's mentor just told her all this?" I ask. "It sort of feels like it was meant to be a secret."

"It seems he thought it was nothing more than a legend. We, on the other hand, knew it was true because of the disc we'd found."

"And she didn't tell her mentor about the disc?" Ryn asks.

"No. We kept that part to ourselves—and then we made a decision that would turn out to be a big mistake." He pauses to let out another sigh. "We decided to go in search of the other five discs."

"The five discs that could have been *anywhere* in the world?" Ryn asks.

"Yes. We decided we wanted to use Tharros' power. We planned to unlock the chest, share the power equally among us, and we'd be the best damn guardians any Guild had ever seen. We could defeat any form of evil. Creepy Hollow and the human realm would be safer than ever before because we would use Tharros' tremendous power for good and not evil.

We did a lot of reading, exploring, and following up on rumors, but it took us a long time. It was about ten years later by the time we were each in possession of a disc. By then we were all working for the Guild. Rose and I had formed our union, as had your parents." Dad nods toward Ryn.

"That must have made Angelica feel a bit left out," I say.

"Yes. It did. Especially since she'd always ... well, had some feelings for me." Dad scratches his head, looking a little awkward as he admits this. "Anyway, we'd all been working at the Guild for just over a decade when Angie started growing rather distant. She often went looking for the sixth disc without us. You see, our priorities were changing. Linden and Zin had Reed by then. Rose and I were thinking about having a child. Angie, however, was becoming more and more focused on finding that last disc and unlocking the chest. The rest of us were starting to have mixed feelings. The discs ... well, it's hard to explain, but after years of using them, we started feeling different. Moody, angrier, less compassionate for those we were meant to protect. It was Rose who made the connection to the discs. She thought they must have too much of an evil influence left in them. So the four of us decided it would be best to forget about going in search of the chest. It was also, you know, *wrong* to go after the power our ancestors had tried so hard to destroy. It was wrong for us to act like we were above the law.

"When we told Angie what we'd decided, she was furious. She said this was what she'd worked toward for years, and we were destroying her dreams. It wasn't long after our confrontation that she left the service of the Guild and broke off all contact with us. We had no idea where she'd gone. We didn't even know where to start looking."

"Her family didn't know anything?" Ryn asks.

"You're going to think this sounds odd," Dad says, rubbing his hand across the back of his neck, "but none of us actually knew where she lived. She'd always been secretive about her family and her private life, right from the day we met her. She would never answer any of our questions about her home life, so eventually we stopped asking. That was just who she was, and we accepted it."

"Do you think she was embarrassed about her family?" I ask. "Like, were they really poor or something?"

"If she was embarrassed, it wasn't because they were poor. Angie always had the best of everything." Dad takes a sip from his mug and returns it to the table. "Anyway, where was I?"

"Angelica disappeared."

"Yes. So, time passed. Zin and Linden had Ryn. Shortly afterward, you arrived, V. We were all caught up in our happy, perfect lives, and that's when our discs began disappearing. We weren't using them continuously anymore, only for the occasional *very* challenging assignment. So they remained hidden most of the time. Rose's disappeared first, then mine. When Zinnia's disappeared, we realized it was Angelica taking them. She dropped an earring or something in Zinnia's cupboard. And, to be honest, we already suspected it was her.

"So Linden hid his somewhere else, and, for a while, we saw and heard nothing of Angelica. Then, one evening when I was alone at home, an elf knocked on our tree and handed me a note. It was from Angie, begging for my help. The note said nothing else except to go with the elf. Instead of going alone, I took Linden with me. We didn't tell Rose or Zin.

"The elf lead us Underground and into the tunnels of what we later found out was a labyrinth. We found Angie in a chamber right in the center, unable to get out. And it wasn't that someone else had trapped her down there, like she told you; she had trapped *herself* down there. Accidentally, of course. She had finally found the location of the chest containing Tharros' power and stolen it. But she needed somewhere to keep it safe until she could get hold of all the discs to unlock it. So she built the labyrinth herself. She tried to put a complex spell on the chamber to prevent anyone from removing the chest. Instead, she prevented herself from leaving."

"Well, that's got to suck," I say. "And she obviously wanted you guys to get her out."

"Yes. She did. And we ..." Dad hangs his head and groans. "We left her there."

"What?" Ryn says. "You and my dad just ... left her there?"

"I'm not proud of the decision we made. But we managed to convince ourselves it was the best thing to do. The chest was hidden in the labyrinth where nobody else would find it. Angie was trapped there without any of her discs, so she'd never be able to open it. With the upstairs part she'd built for herself, and the creatures running around the labyrinth ready to do her bidding, we told ourselves it was better than the punishment she would receive if we handed her over to the Guild.

"We never told Rose or Zinnia. We carried on with our lives." Dad takes another deep breath. "Rose was killed on one of her assignments. Reed had his terrible accident. Linden eventually decided to leave both the Guild and his family." Ryn shifts in his chair, but says nothing. "With my partner gone, I volunteered for an undercover assignment looking into the activities of one of the Unseelie Princes."

"Zell," I mutter.

"Yes. At first I worked alone, but as it became clear the prince was planning something big and long-term, other guardians became part of the investigation. Do you remember your friend Cecy?"

"Yes," I say.

"Her father and I managed to infiltrate Zell's closest circle of friends. We learned a lot about him. His relationship with his mother has always been unstable; they've never seen eye to eye. He's always felt he would make a better ruler, but, unfortunately for him, he's last in line for the throne. And unfortunately for *us*, after several months of being on the inside, Zell found out we were actually guardians.

"We both got away from him, but, in retaliation, Zell went after our families. Cecy was almost killed, saved only by the fact that her babysitter that day was also a skilled guardian. Her parents made an immediate decision to leave the Guild and run. I considered doing the same thing, but I was too deter-mined to bring Zell down to admit defeat. It seemed that the only way I could do that *and* protect you was if he thought I was dead and no longer a threat to him.

"By that stage, I was reporting directly to the Queen herself. We planned my death together. I had thought we would make it look like my body had been destroyed, but she said that would be too suspicious a death. So she found a shapeshifter criminal and used him instead." Dad leans forward and wraps his hands around the mug. "And, well, that's really all there is to it. I've secretly been living at the palace ever since and continuing my investigation into Zell's activities. I know he's planning to try and take over the Unseelie Court, and possibly the Seelie Court and the Guilds. I know he's collecting an army of faeries with special powers, although he isn't able to control them all yet. And I also know he's planning to get hold of all six griffin discs and unlock the chest to take Tharros' power for himself. What I don't know is *when* he's planning his big move."

"I suppose he's waiting until he has all six discs," I say. "He has four already—the four Angelica managed to collect before she locked herself up—so now he just needs to get hold of Linden's and the sixth one you guys never found."

"I'll contact my father and tell him to make sure his is well hidden," Ryn says.

Dad shakes his head. "He'll want to know how you know about it. Rather say nothing. I trust he's hidden it well."

I place my empty mug on the table as something occurs to me. "Dad, how have you been continuing your investigation if Zell knows what you look like?"

"Just because we're all faeries and can't use glamours with one another doesn't mean there aren't other ways to disguise ourselves." He wiggles his eyebrows at me the way he did when I was little. "I've had to be quite inventive at times."

"I wish I could have seen that," I say with a laugh.

Ryn stands and sends the mugs back into the kitchen with a

wave of his hand. "I should go now. You guys probably have some catching up to do that doesn't involve me."

"Yes," I say before Dad can invite Ryn to stay longer. "I'll, uh, see you around." *After enough time has passed for things to no longer be epically weird between us.*

When the doorway has vanished behind Ryn, I turn back to Dad and ask, "Will you be able to visit here again?"

He hesitates before answering, which isn't a good sign. "To be honest, it'll be very difficult. But I promise I'll try."

"Okay. Will you be in trouble if the Queen finds out you came here?"

"Oh, she already knows. I told her what happened at the Seelie Court. She wasn't too happy that we ran into each other, but since you and Ryn are now both guardians and not just little children, she believes you can be trusted. And it's not as though she has a choice; she has to trust you now that you know."

I fiddle with the edge of the cushion on my lap. "I don't think I made the best first impression on her."

Dad tilts his head to the side. "You obviously made *some* kind of impression. I believe her exact words to me were, 'That daughter of yours has just as much spunk as her mother had.'"

"Spunk. Wow. That's a compliment, right?"

Dad laughs. "I think so." He spreads his hands open. "So, what else do you want to talk about before I have to leave?"

CHAPTER TWENTY-SEVEN

MY BIRTHDAY IS TOMORROW.

I've never been big on celebrating this annual event. It isn't all that fun when you don't have many friends or family to party with, and it's just another day, really. Faeries have hundreds of birthdays—assuming our lives aren't snuffed out early by some menacing magical creature—so why make a big deal of it every year? Despite having explained this to Tora a number of times, I know she's planning something for tomorrow night. I wonder if she's invited Ryn. I'm torn between wanting to be around him and not wanting to face the awkwardness between us.

Over the past two days I've spent most waking moments replaying the conversation Dad and I had the night he came over. I'm still amazed that he was right here in this house,

297

sitting on our couch and drinking from one of our mugs like nothing has changed. I tried not to cry when he left; I almost succeeded.

The rest of my waking moments are spent trying *not* to think about The Kiss. That takes a lot of effort, which means there aren't any waking moments left to figure out if I should accept the Guild's job offer. I'm hoping my brain is figuring it out while I'm sleeping because I have to give Councilor Starkweather an answer tomorrow.

Because I have nothing else to do, I use the social networking spell Ryn taught me and check the random updates of the few people I seem to be 'following.' It annoys me that I feel a weird kind of disappointment when I find there are no updates from Ryn. I consider writing something in the blank bubble at the bottom of my amber's rectangular surface, but what would I write?

Birthdays are boring.

I don't know what to do with the rest of my life now that I've graduated.

My father faked his own death and is actually alive.

Nope. None of those seem like good options. So, once again, I end the spell without having written anything. I go to the cupboard in the study and pull out a box of Card Eaters. I haven't played in years, but seeing Ryn and Calla playing recently reminded me that it can be kind of fun in its own simple way.

"Filigree," I call as I head back out to the sitting room. He comes slinking down the stairs in the form of a panther. "Want to play cards?" I hold the box up. He sits down beside the low table and curls his tail around his legs. He blinks expectantly. I sit on the floor on the other side of the table and deal the cards between the two of us. Filigree nudges his pile of cards with one of his paws. "Yeah, okay, you know that's not going to work, right? You need to shift into something else." Filigree flicks an ear, then melts into an orange, furry form that turns out to be an orangutan. He picks his cards up. "Okay, you go first," I tell him.

An hour later, Filigree is beating me. I know it's partly down to luck and the fact that he obviously got stronger cards than I did, but it's still embarrassing. I look down at the four cards left in my hand. I've got moss—the second weakest card in the whole game—a pixie, a boulder, and an ogre, which is the only card I can play right now. I look at Filigree's hairy hands; he has only two cards left, and they're probably both stronger than anything I've got. He's almost sure to win. I'm about to place my ogre card on top of his troll card, when I hear a knock against the tree.

Could it be Dad?

No. The sun has only just begun to set. I'm sure he'd wait for darkness before visiting again. But as I walk toward the wall, I can't help the nervous energy coursing through me. It might be him. After all, it is my birthday tomorrow.

I wipe my hand across the wall and ... it's Ryn.

Great.

"My, uh, long-lost relative isn't here tonight, so unless you're here to visit Filigree, there isn't anyone else in this home who wants to see you."

He tilts his head to the side. "Why are you nervous?"

I place my hands on my hips. "Is there no way you can turn that off? Because I really don't appreciate you knowing exactly what I'm feeling."

"Nope. Trust me, if there was a way to turn it off, I would have found it by now."

He appears to be holding something behind his back, which makes me suspicious. "Are you going to tell me why you're here?"

"Are you going to invite me in?"

I make no move to stand aside.

"Fine," he says. "It's your birthday tomorrow. I'd like to give you something."

"You already gave me something. New amber and an expensive charm."

"Okay, well, now I have something else to give you. And," he adds, "it's rude to refuse a gift."

"And yet we both know being rude has never been a problem when it comes to the two of us."

He looks down at his feet, then up again. "Please?" he says softly.

Damn. He sure knows how to do the sexy-smoldering-eyes thing; he could probably light a freaking fire with the look he's currently giving me. And he knows it, dammit, because I bet he can *feel* my insides melting. I clear my throat. "Um, okay, come in."

"Actually, I don't want to give it to you here. I'd like you to come somewhere with me."

I narrow my eyes at him. "Is this something to do with the

party Tora and Raven are planning? Because I thought that was tomorrow."

"It is tomorrow. And since you don't like surprises, I'll tell you exactly what time it is and who's coming if you'll just follow me now."

"You're being weird."

"And I'll be even weirder and get down on my knees and beg, if I have to. I've done it before, remember?"

I do remember, and I really don't need him to go that far this time. "Okay, okay, I'll go with you. Just let me get my boots."

"And a jacket," Ryn calls after me. "You might get cold."

I grab my things and apologize to Filigree on the way back down the stairs. "We can finish later," I tell him, hoping he'll have forgotten about the game by then.

I seal up my tree. "Where are we going?"

"You'll see." Ryn catches my hand as we walk through the doorway he opened. We aren't in the darkness for long, but all I can think about is what happened the last time we were stuck in complete darkness with each other. When light materializes ahead of us, I drop his hand. We walk out into the leafy haven of our ancient gargan tree. It's beautiful here with the reds, golds and oranges of the setting sun peeping through the branches.

"Do you remember that poem by Mil Crowthorn about the riches of nature?" I say as I stare up at the sky.

"'Give me the setting sun, and I'll be a richer man than most / For never have I seen gold like that which glows above the earth. / Give me the night sky, and I'll be rich beyond all ruin / For never have I seen diamonds like those that dance beside the moon.'"

"Yes. That's how I feel," I murmur. "I don't need anything more for my birthday than that sky."

"Maybe just this," Ryn says, presenting me with a small silk-wrapped package.

I untie the silver string and hold the bundle in my hand as the silk layers fall away. Lying in the center are the colorful ribbons I found in my mother's hiding place, but instead of a messy bunch, they've been fashioned into a bracelet. The ribbons lie neatly in line, held together on either end with a silver bead. The loose ends that will hang down my arm when I put the bracelet is on each have a small crystal attached to the end.

"The ribbons looked so pretty on your arm," Ryn says, "so I took them to Raven and asked her to make them into a bracelet." He takes it from my hand and fastens it around my wrist. The crystals sparkle where the light catches them.

"I should probably be creeped out that you snuck into my house and stole the ribbons," I say, "but it's so beautiful that I'll forgive you for your sneaking."

"So you like it?"

I look up at Ryn and see an unfamiliar expression: uncertainty. I smile to reassure him. "I love it." The answering smile that spreads across his face does the same thing to my stomach that his smoldering eyes did just now.

He looks like he's about to say something, but then he reaches abruptly for his pocket. He pulls his amber out and reads a message. As he puts the amber away, he says, "If you don't mind, I'd like to take you somewhere else now."

"Um, okay. But this had better not be a ploy to get me to go on a date with you."

"Not at all," he says, and my stomach unknots itself. He leans closer to my ear and whispers, "It's so much better than that."

What?

He walks past me. I turn around to see him greeting an olive-skinned, green-haired faerie—is he a faerie?—who wasn't here a moment ago. Tucked beneath his arm is a large cylindrical shape that looks like it could be a rolled-up carpet. He hands it over to Ryn, they exchange a few quiet words, and the man slips away between the branches.

"Here we go," Ryn says. He sets the rolled-up shape down, grabs one end, flicks it open—and it floats into the air.

"What—what is that?"

"Exactly what it looks like: a magic carpet."

"But ... magic carpets don't exist."

"And yet," Ryn says, "there's one floating right here in front of you. How strange is that?" He steps onto it and holds his hand out to me.

"I ... don't know if I trust that thing."

"It's perfectly safe. I've done some reading on the subject. Turns out there have been some major advances in carpet flying magic in the past few years. They no longer throw people off."

My eyes widen. Is that supposed to make me feel better?

"And guess what?" Ryn continues. "You're a faerie, which

means if this carpet *does* decide to throw you off, you can easily slow your fall with magic."

"I …" He has a point. "Okay." I take hold of his out-stretched hand, and he pulls me up. I crouch down, spreading my arms wide to balance myself.

Ryn sits, crosses his legs, and reaches back for the two corners of the carpet behind him. The carpet rises higher, and Ryn steers us between the branches. Higher, higher. And then, with a burst of speed that causes me to fall onto my butt, we shoot out above the highest branches of the forest. Below us, the thousands of trees that make up Creepy Hollow extend in every direction.

All I can do is stare in wonder.

"Kind of amazing, isn't it?" Ryn says. The carpet slows, and he gets carefully to his feet. "You should stand up. It's more exciting." He holds his hand out to me once again. "I know how you like a thrill."

I do, but all the thrills I'm used to come from fighting dangerous creatures and performing difficult acrobatic-type moves. This is an entirely different kind of thrill. I place my hand in his and let him pull me up. The carpet ripples slowly beneath my feet, which is a little scary. But I'm a guardian; I have good balance.

I turn away from Ryn and look out at the amazingness that is my home. The sun has dipped below the horizon, leaving splashes of pink, purple and hazy blue across the sky. The first few stars are peeping out. We watch in silence as the carpet continues its slow journey through the air. A gentle breeze moves my hair. The sky grows darker. More stars begin twinkling.

"I have one more surprise for you," Ryn says. When his hands move across my face to cover my eyes, I flinch slightly, but I don't pull away. He begins chanting words to a spell I don't recognize. It's some kind of call, almost like a song. It goes on for several minutes, and I find myself lulled into a place of peace and calm. Before I know it, my back is resting against his chest. I feel him tilt his head closer to my ear. "You said there was nothing I could say or do to convince you that my feelings for you are real and long-lasting," he whispers. "Well, clearly I took that as a challenge, and since it'll apparently take the shining butts of a gazillion glow-bugs to prove myself to you, here they are."

The warmth of his hands disappears from my eyes. I open them, and—

Wow.

Thousands upon thousands of glow-bugs are floating in the air, as if every galaxy in creation has been called here to shine down on us. Words don't exist to describe the beauty of this moment or the sense of awe it stirs in me.

But there are strings attached to this moment. I know what Ryn is trying to tell me. I know what he wants from me. And even though this is more amazing than anything anyone has ever done for me, my stubborn heart still doesn't want to step out from its safe place. I would rather take this moment and capture it inside a glass ball to keep it whole and perfect forever than taint it with the complications a relationship would bring.

"This is incredible, Ryn. It is. But—"

"No." He turns me around. "No buts. You think I'm going to hurt you? You think I'm going to get bored and run off with some Undergrounder the first chance I get? You obviously have no idea how *amazing* you are. You, Violet Fairdale, are incredible, and I want you. *Every part of you.* I want your stubbornness and your sarcasm and your competitive spirit. I want you challenging me and fighting beside me. I want to hold you and kiss you and *so much more* because there's no one else in the world who knows me like you do. You have always been the one for me, even when we couldn't stand each other. You're beautiful and hot and sexy all at once, *and* you're more intelligent than any girl I've ever met. I love the fact that I've known you all my life. It just feels *right* when you're beside me. It feels like I've been lost in the desert for years, and … I've finally come home."

I've finally come home. I know what that feels like. In fact, I know what everything he said feels like. I've simply been too scared to put it into words.

"Stop being so scared, V!" Ryn grabs my shoulders and shakes them. "You're one of the bravest people I know. Why can't you let go of this fear?"

I've finally come home. Why would I want to send him back to the desert? I'd be protecting myself, but hurting him. Why didn't that occur to me before? I thought I was the only one who could get hurt here, but I never realized that his *home* is the same as my *home*, and sending him away from it is only hurting him.

"Please say something, V."

Home. I want to be there, with him. Neither of us hurting anymore.

"Violet, please. Say something! I swear, you're going to break my heart if you don't—"

I kiss him. I press myself against him like I never want to be parted from him. My arms entwine around his neck. We lose our balance and fall onto the lazily rippling carpet. I push him down and straddle his waist. I lean over him. I kiss his neck before tracing the outline of his lips with my tongue. His hands find their way up my back and into my hair. He pulls my face down to meet his kiss. Sparks dance on my tongue and everywhere else his skin touches mine, which doesn't feel like nearly enough places. The whole forest could go up in flames right now, and I wouldn't notice.

This is everything I want.

CHAPTER TWENTY-EIGHT

RYN ROLLS ME ONTO MY SIDE SO THAT HE'S LYING NEXT TO me. "Okay." He kisses my chin. "You don't need to say anything." Another kiss on my neck. "I think I got your answer loud and clear."

I trace my fingers from his brow down to his chin. "If this is coming home," I say in a breathless whisper, "let's never leave."

"I don't plan to." He catches my fingers and kisses them. "Sit up," he whispers, then moves behind me and pulls me against his chest. His legs hem me in on either side. He brushes my hair aside and kisses me behind my ear before wrapping his arms around me and resting his chin on my shoulder.

I can't believe how happy I am right now. It seems stupid that I pushed these feelings away for so long when they have the ability to bring so much joy.

"It was the tiny glowing butts that changed your mind, wasn't it?" Ryn says. I can hear the amusement in his voice.

"It was everything. The bracelet, the magic carpet, the glow-bugs, finding my mother's tokehari. I've known for a while how I feel about you, but I didn't believe until tonight that you felt the same way."

"And yet I knew about my feelings before you knew about yours."

"Really?"

"Yes. That weird moment we had in the bathroom at the Harts' house was the moment I knew I didn't think of you as a friend anymore. I've wanted more from you ever since then."

"But you didn't say anything."

"Of course not. You didn't feel the same way, so what would the point have been? Every now and then I'd get a hint of something more from you, but it was always so fleeting that I assumed I'd imagined it. It was only while dancing at the grad ball that you must have let your guard down, and I finally knew what you were feeling. I'm pretty sure it was you who set that ice tree on fire, by the way. The one Councilor Starkweather was talking about."

"Yeah, I think you may be right." Thank goodness no one else realized the real reason for that little explosion. "Wait a sec," I say, remembering something. "When we were writing our assignment reports in the gargan tree, and that branch caught on fire, was that me too? Because I thought I was doing a pretty good job of suppressing my feelings back then."

"Uh, that one may have been me."

"Aha, so I'm not the only one who loses control." I twist

309

my head to the side as I try to look at him.

He pulls back from me slightly and flashes his mischievous grin. "V, did you *see* the damage in Princess Olivia's sitting room? I think it's pretty clear we both lose control in certain situations."

He tightens his arms around me as I rest against him once more. "So, um, this ability of yours" I say. "You feel *everything* from everyone who's around you?"

"Yes."

"That must get a little overwhelming."

"Very. It's the reason I spend so much time alone and in the human realm."

"You can't feel human emotions?"

"No, only the emotions of those with magic." He covers my clasped hands with one of his and rubs his thumb back and forth over my skin. "It's so *loud* being somewhere like the Guild. I mean, I've learned to filter it to a certain extent, but sometimes it still becomes too much, and I want everyone to just … leave. That's why I act like a jerk occasionally. It's the quickest way to get rid of people."

"Occasionally?"

"Okay, that might have been an understatement."

"Have you tried being nice to people instead of being a jerk? Then it wouldn't matter that you're feeling their emotions because they would be positive emotions instead of this-guy-is-a-jerk-I-want-to-hit-him emotions."

"Positive emotions can be overwhelming too, if there are enough of them. And can you imagine what it would be like if I was *nice* to everyone?" He lowers his voice and puts his lips next to my ear. "*All* the girls would be after me then. It would be a complete mess."

I laugh. "Right. Of *course* that's what would happen."

Ryn hugs me tighter. "I told you I love your sarcasm, Sexy Pixie."

"As much as I love that name." As he laughs, I realize something else. "This is why Reed's death hit you harder than anyone else, right? Because you had to feel everyone else's pain as well as your own?"

Ryn's hair brushes mine as he nods. "And it's why I couldn't just 'move on' like you did. Because I still feel my mother's pain every day. But, like I told you before, I'm trying." He kisses my cheek. "Oh, and that 'weird habit' you noticed? Pressing my hand to my chest?"

"Yes?"

"When people feel emotion that's strong and sudden, it kind of gives me this momentary ache. I guess I developed that habit without realizing it. It surprised me that you noticed."

"Well, don't worry, I'm sure no one else did." I tilt my head back and look up at the sky. Some of the glow-bugs have disappeared, but there are still enough above us to make it look like the reflection of an ocean filled with phosphorescent creatures. I don't want to leave here, but I know the night will have to end. I'll have to return home and do non-thrilling things like decide what course my life is going to take now.

Ryn, who, of course, can sense the subtle change in my mood, asks, "What do you think about the Guild's job offer?"

"How did you know they offered me a job?"

"They offered *me* a job, so obviously they offered you one

too. What are you thinking? I assume you have to tell them by tomorrow, like I do."

"Yes." I pull one of my hands out from beneath his and twist a piece of hair around my finger. "It makes sense to take it, I suppose. My life's purpose is to protect people, and I can do that best through the Guild."

"But?"

I smile at the fact that he knows there's a 'but.' "Well, it's kind of a predictable path, isn't it? We'd be put in teams and spend a year doing different kinds of assignments. After that, we'd decide which department we want to join, get put into new teams, and spend the next few decades working the same kind of assignments with the same people."

"Yeah. Unless the Guild is attacked, all guardians are defeated, and life is never the same again."

"Well, it would certainly be a lot more exciting if the Guild were attacked." I drop my hand and sigh. "It's just that I've always dreamed about graduating and working for the Guild, but now that I'm here, I wonder if there isn't a better option."

"Like offering your private services to wealthy fae in need of personal protection? Because somehow I think you'd pick a dangerous assignment over being a bodyguard any day."

"Definitely."

"And if you were at the Guild, you'd have *me*." He slips the edge of my jacket off my shoulder, and his lips brush a burning trail along my bare skin. "We could kick dangerous-fae butt together instead of you being out there on your own." He pulls away, leaving my shoulder cold. "But don't let me influence your decision in any way. It's up to you, of course."

"Oh, right, whatever." I laugh. "If that wasn't you trying to influence me, then I don't know what is."

"You don't? Would you like me to show you?" In a second, he's jumped up, pulled me to my feet, and caught me in his arms. "If I were really trying to influence you, it might go something like this." He lifts my left arm, pushes my sleeve slowly back, and touches his lips to the inside of my wrist, right where my guardian markings are. His kiss sends a shiver along my arm and up my neck. When his kisses reach the crook of my elbow, he reaches up and cups my face with his hands. He brings his lips close to mine, but instead of kissing me, he holds his head just close enough for me to feel his heat but not his touch. He whispers, "How much would you miss this if you were far away from me all the time?"

Instead of answering, I close the gap between us and press my lips hard against his. Now that I've taken the leap and decided to trust that he wants this as much as I do, I can't seem to get enough of him. And the way he holds me close and molds his body to mine tells me he feels the same way. When my head is spinning so much the glow-bugs seem to be dancing in zigzaggy lines around us, I pull away from him. "I'd hate to ruin this moment by falling off the carpet," I say, my words more than a little breathless, "so perhaps we should head back?"

He leans his forehead against mine. "Have I told you that I hate it when you're right?"

"Many times."

The magic carpet carries us back to the hollow at the top of the gargan tree. I could easily hop off by myself, but Ryn clearly wants to help me down, and, since I love the feel of his hands around my waist, I don't argue.

He rolls up the carpet and tucks it beneath his arm. He opens his mouth to say something, but a soft smile spreads across his features, and he leans forward to kiss me instead. Moments later, his lips leave mine with a sigh. "I need to return the carpet," he says. "I'll only be a few minutes. Then we can spend the rest of the evening doing whatever you want." He heads off along one of the branches, leaving me with a ridiculously huge smile on my face. I press my hands against my chest, feeling like I need to hold my elation in so it doesn't explode out of me.

"Vi?"

All feeling in my chest drops down to my toes and vanishes, leaving my body cold.

That voice. I know it.

"Vi, is that you?"

I turn slowly. In a doorway outlined against the gargan's widest branch, stands the last person I want to see.

Nate.

CHAPTER TWENTY-NINE

IF SOMEONE WALKED OVER AND PUNCHED ME IN THE stomach, I'd be less shocked than I am right now.

What. The. Freak?

With a whoosh and a spray of sparks, my bow and arrow are blazing in my outstretched arms. "How did you find me?" I demand.

"Luck, I guess." He steps out of the faerie paths, and the doorway seals up behind him. "It's the only place I know how to get to. I know how to get to the entrance of the Guild, but they'd have no reason to let me in. And I know how to get to the inside of your home, but I don't have permission to enter it. I don't know what the outside looks like, so I couldn't just knock on your door. That only left this place." He watches me carefully. He doesn't raise his hands, though; he obviously doesn't believe I'd shoot him.

"How *dare* you come looking for me after what you did?"

"Vi, please, I can explain."

"I don't want your explanations, Nate. I want you to leave before I accidentally let go of this arrow."

"*Please*, Vi! You don't know what I've been through."

"What *you've* been through?" I lower my bow slightly in disbelief. "I almost died because of you, Nate!"

"I know! And I'm so sorry." He takes a step toward me. I train the arrow on him once more. "Zell forced me to help him, Vi. He got Scarlett to put that eye on me, which meant he could see *everything* I saw. I was supposed to try and find out from you who the identity of the guardian with the finding ability was. Since I didn't want him to know it was you, I obviously kept my mouth shut. But then you went and gave yourself away!"

"What?" Is he seriously blaming this on me?

"We were in my room, and you said something about apologizing for agreeing to find my mother for me. Don't you remember? And that's when he figured out it was you. He beat me up for not telling him before. Remember the bruise I had? And I lied and said it was a fight I got into at school?"

"You lied. Great. How many other things are you lying about?"

He throws his hands up in frustration. "Nothing! I'm not lying to you!"

"Have you forgotten about the part where you led me to a secret cave and handed me over to Zell? I didn't see anyone forcing you to do that."

"He was threatening my parents! He would have killed them if I hadn't brought him to you. So I thought I could do both. Protect them and still get you out alive. That's why I pointed out that river to you. You know, the one that bubbled up into the cave and went back down through the mountain and out the side? We walked past it and I said you could catch a quick ride out of there if you jumped down it."

"That was your big plan, Nate? Seriously?" As it happened, that's exactly how I got out of the mountain, but it almost killed me.

"I had no other choice. Don't you understand that?"

"There's always a choice, Nate. Why didn't you ask me for help?"

"How? Zell had that eye on me. He could see *everything* I saw. He was watching my every move. Listening to every conversation."

"You're not stupid, Nate. You could have figured something out. Closed your eyes and written me a note, or something."

"Vi …"

Branches rustle and we both look to the side. Ryn steps through the leaves and into the hollow. His eyes dart between Nate and me, but his expression gives no hint as to what he's thinking or feeling. I wish I had his ability right now. "Well," he says, crossing his arms over his chest as he walks to my side. "Look who came scuttling back."

Nate's eyes pan back and forth between Ryn and me. "What is *he* doing here?"

Ryn slides an arm around my waist. "What does it look

like I'm doing here?"

"Ryn." I glare at him and mutter, "You are not helping."

"You're *with* him now?" Nate looks disgusted. "How the hell did that happen?"

"Dripping wet in a secret passage," Ryn says before I can answer. "It was pretty damn hot."

"Ryn!"

"So is this the part where you warn me to stay away from your *girlfriend*?" Nate sneers.

Ryn's cocky smile makes an appearance. "Of course not. I wouldn't insult Violet by suggesting she can't handle you on her own."

I roll my eyes and lower my bow. "Okay. That's great." I lower my voice. "So how about you wait at the bottom of the tree so that I can, you know, handle things on my own?" Ryn's eyes bore into mine, and I can tell he's trying to figure out if everything's okay. *I'll be fine,* I mouth.

"Okay." He turns to Nate. "So long, halfling boy. I hope we never meet again." He vanishes into a doorway in the air.

"I can't believe this," Nate mutters, shaking his head. "I finally manage to get away from Zell, and the first person I come to—you—has already moved on as if I were never a part of your life."

I let my bow and arrow disappear; we both know I'm not going to use it, even after what Nate did to me. "What did you think would happen, Nate? That I'd go running back into your arms?"

"I don't know, Vi. But I certainly didn't expect to come back and find myself caught up in a love triangle."

"There is no love triangle, Nate. A love triangle would imply that you actually stand a chance with me, which you don't."

Nate takes a jolted step backward, as if I slapped him. *Ouch.* Those words came out way harsher than I meant them to.

"But you loved me, Vi," he says quietly. "I know you did."

I shake my head. "No. I didn't, and I don't."

"You did. You were too scared to say it, but I know you—"

"I didn't. Perhaps I could have if you'd given me a chance, but you didn't." I take a deep breath. "I did care about you, and I was so angry and hurt that I almost did something stupid with a potion. But I got over it. I got over you."

He stares at me for a long time before he says, "I still love you."

"Don't lie to me. What about Scarlett?"

He pales. "Scarlett?"

"I saw the two of you together at Zell's masquerade ball."

"You were there?"

"Yes. Ryn and I were both there. And it certainly didn't look like you were missing me when Scarlett was whispering in your ear."

He looks away and shakes his head. "It's complicated. She's a siren, Vi—"

"Oh, so you had no choice, right? Just like you had no choice leading me into a trap in that mountain? And you had no choice using your storms to breach the protective enchantments of the Guild to potentially hurt a whole lot of innocent people?"

"Vi—"

"I think you should go, Nate. Whatever we had is over. Maybe you're telling the truth about everything, maybe you're not. But I don't know, and I can never trust you again. You need to get on with your life, and I need to get on with mine. Take your parents and run, if you have to, but don't involve me." I cross my arms and swallow. "I don't ever want to see you again."

PART IV

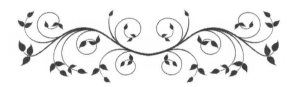

CHAPTER THIRTY

THE PENTHOUSE APARTMENT OF THE HIGH-RISE BUILDING I'm in has floor-to-ceiling glass in every room, allowing the city lights to twinkle through. They illuminate the apartment's interior, making it easy to see where I'm going. I creep down a curving stairway constructed from nothing more than slim, black pieces of wood inserted into the wall on one side. I suppose the stairway's meant to be arty and minimalist, but I find myself wondering how many people have tripped down it. I reach the bottom and scan the open room displaying paintings on walls and sculptures on pedestals. A pole-like bookcase with flat pieces of wood attached to it like branches on a tree catches my eye, as does a weirdly shaped lounge suite that's probably also considered art.

No one here.

The owner of the apartment—currently asleep in one of the oversized bedrooms—is an art collector, and it seems a certain faerie thief has taken a liking to the items on display here. Last week he stole a valuable painting, and we've spent the past four days figuring out who he is and when he'll try to pull off his next heist. We want to catch him in the act.

I signal to Jay, one of the three members of my team, to follow me down the stairs. Asami, my other teammate, is already positioned on the balcony that extends along one side of the apartment's exterior in case our faerie thief plans to enter that way. "Hide under that weird couch," I whisper to Jay as I point to the piece of furniture that looks like a giant tiger trying to hug something. "I'll be behind the sculpture of the woman-beast-rock-thing."

"Interesting choice," he says, eyeing the bizarre sculpture. Jay is a graduate from another Guild who decided he wanted to start his working life in a new place and wound up in Creepy Hollow. He's nice enough, but I'd far rather have Ryn on my team. Not only because I'm the team leader and I'd get to boss him around, but because, well, *I want to be around him all the time.* Tora took it upon herself to mention to the Council that Ryn and I are in a relationship—something I still haven't quite forgiven her for—and the Council decided it would be better if we didn't work together. It took a lot of restraint for me not to point out that there are several husband-and-wife teams at our Guild and no one seems to have a problem with that.

Jay slips beneath the couch, and I crouch down behind the woman-beast-rock-thing. A small metal plaque attached to the base tells me it's called *The Revelation of Eve.* Interesting.

And so we wait.

It's a little boring.

In the month since I accepted the position at the Guild, this is only the third assignment I've been involved in. It seems a pathetic number to me, considering I used to have a new assignment almost every evening when I was still training. But these assignments are far more in-depth, I'll admit—and I was a bit of an over-achieving trainee.

The wristband I now wear in place of my trainee tracker band tingles. I look down at the two stones fitted into the leather—blue for Asami, green for Jay—and see the blue one slowly flashing. I peep around the sculpture and look to the balcony where I know Asami is hiding. I pull my head back immediately. The figure I saw peering in through the window was definitely not Asami. I press the blue stone to let him know I've received his alert.

I peek through a crack between the sculpture's woman-arm and beast-tail. The figure at the window has vanished. A moment later he steps out of a faerie path on the wall beside a painting of messy, mixed-up colors. He heads straight for a glass case with an ornately decorated egg resting on a cushion.

With two fingers, I press both stones on my wristband three times in quick succession. Jay and Asami know exactly what that means: *Let's take this guy down.*

* * *

It isn't difficult. There are three of us and only one of him, and even though he pulls a pretty elaborate stunt with a rope he magically attaches to the ceiling, it only takes a few minutes before we've got him bound and gagged and ready to haul off to the Guild. We didn't even set off any alarms in the process. Jay and Asami take him back through the faerie paths, while I stay behind to return every item to its place in the room so the owner will never know anyone was here.

I remove the rope from the ceiling and wrap it around my arm. A few books got knocked off the tree-shaped bookcase, so I slot them back in wherever I see a space. The potted plant on the highest shelf seems to have dropped a few leaves. I spread my fingers, and the leaves float upward toward my open hands. I catch the leaves and stuff them into my pocket.

I'm about to open a doorway to the faerie paths when I notice a torn piece of paper lying at the foot of the glass separating the balcony from the apartment interior. I can't remember if the paper was on the floor when we got here, but it seems more likely that it fell from the thief's pocket than was left on the floor by the owner of this place. He's clearly an obsessive neat freak. I bend to pick up the paper and turn it over as I straighten. My heart jumps when I see handwriting I recognize.

Zell's.

I wish I didn't know the Unseelie Prince's handwriting, but I have an image stamped quite firmly in my mind of his circular dungeon wall covered in hundreds of handwritten names. I'll certainly never forget the shape of the letters that spelled my own name, which is how I know the same hand wrote the two sentences I see on the torn scrap of paper in my hand.

successfully stealing it, you will have proved to me that you can be trusted on the big day. And the big day is coming soon.

The big day? And that would be ... the day Zell attempts to take the Unseelie crown for himself? The day he plans to invade the Guild? Damn, I wish I could read the rest of this note.

I push it into one of my pockets, open a doorway on the wall, and make the quick journey to the Guild. Inside the entrance, I flash my marked wrists to the night guard on duty, who quickly scans them with his stylus. Then I head straight to Councilor Starkweather's office. The chances are high she'll be here, given her workaholic tendencies.

I knock on her door. A moment later, I hear her voice bidding me to enter.

I explain our assignment, show her the note, and tell her why I think Zell wrote it. "Remember when Ryn and I broke into Zell's dungeon to rescue Ryn's sister, and I brought some pages back and gave them to you?"

"Yes," she says slowly, crossing her arms over her chest. She wasn't impressed that we'd broken into Zell's home. She told us we were to forget about the whole thing.

"If you still have those pages, then you can compare them to this note. I'm almost certain the handwriting will match."

"I shall definitely do that before we interrogate the thief who dropped this note." She stands and heads toward her door.

"If it is Zell's handwriting," I say, following her, "can I question the thief?"

She opens the door and motions for me to step out ahead of her. "I don't think that would be appropriate, Violet." Apparently I'm no longer Miss Fairdale now that I've graduated.

"But we caught the thief. That was *our* assignment. Why wouldn't it be appropriate for me to question him?"

The door clicks shut behind her. "Because everything to do with the Unseelie Prince forms part of a larger investigation that you're not involved in."

I can hear the words she isn't saying: That investigation is too important and I'm too young and inexperienced to be trusted. I want to remind her that I've almost certainly come face to face with Zell more times than anyone else in this Guild, but I know my words won't do any good. I stamp down my frustration. "Okay," I say. "I understand."

I head down a different corridor and away from her. I pat my pocket for my amber so I can check for a message from Ryn, but it seems I've left it at home. I've been looking forward to a message from him all day, hoping that today is the day he'll know when he can come home.

A few weeks after Honey and Asami successfully completed their final assignment in Egypt, a new uprising began. The winged pixie-type creatures that had agreed to live peacefully alongside the bronze-skinned elves decided they actually wanted the pyramids all for themselves. Big mess. So the Guild sent Ryn and his new team to deal with the unrest in as peaceful a manner as possible.

They've been gone two weeks.

It feels like years.

I know they're fine because I get occasional amber messages from Ryn, but I miss him so. Freaking. Much. As much as I'd miss my limbs if they were suddenly chopped off. More, in fact. And I haven't heard from my father since my birthday, so basically I'm back to spending my evenings out on assignment or at home with Filigree—just like I did for most of my training. The difference now is that I'm no longer happy with a lonely life.

I stop by the corridor lined with rows and rows of pigeon holes. Now that I'm a proper guardian, I have my own. Goodbye to the locker downstairs near the training center. I walk past the rectangular openings until I get to mine. There's a folded paper inside with my name on it. Probably another boring memo. I head back down the corridor, unfolding the paper as I go. It only takes a few words for my feet to come to a halt.

VF,

You don't know me, Violet, but you and I have something in common: We're both trying to take down the Unseelie Prince Marzell. I saw you at his masquerade ball, and it has taken me until now to find out from him who you are. Five days from now, Zell will reveal to his closest followers, which includes me, his exact plans for when and how to invade the Guilds. Five days from now, I will give you that information—if you want it.

You have no reason to trust me, of course, so let me give you a reason. I overheard Zell asking his latest follower, a faerie with pyromaniac-like special abilities, to cast a raging inferno at the entrance of the Guild situated in the fae realm near London. His aim isn't to breach the protective enchantments, but rather to let the guardians there know that no Guild is safe from his reach.

Tomorrow night you will know that I am telling the truth.

D

What on earth? Is this a joke? I look up and down the corridor to see if anyone is watching or laughing, but I'm alone. I look back down at the generic stylus-printed type. It must be a joke; no one from the Unseelie Court would be allowed into the Guild to deliver a note—or for any other reason, obviously. But who *inside* the Guild knows that I was at Zell's masquerade? I haven't told anyone except Councilor Starkweather. I suppose the people involved in investigating Zell might know by now—and I don't know who those people are. Maybe someone's annoyed that I keep trying to weasel my way into that investigation, and they're trying to get me in trouble. Or make me look stupid.

I fold the note and push it into my pocket. I don't plan to make a fool of myself by running to Councilor Starkweather with it. If it turns out to be a legitimate warning and there really is a fire tomorrow night, it's not like anyone's going to get hurt. The fire is just supposed to scare people, right?

When I get home, I place the note in the drawer beside my

bed, next to the box that contains my ribbon bracelet and my tokehari ring from my father. The key necklace from my mother stays around my neck all the time, like the arrow earrings in my ears. I fetch my amber from my desk, and my heart does a happy dance when I see there's a message from Ryn.

Finally home. Wanted to visit, but I heard you're out tonight ridding the world of a dangerous thief. I'll see you tomorrow, Sexy Pixie. Don't forget to dream about me.

Hell no. I'm not waiting until tomorrow. I open a doorway and head straight to Ryn's house, dizzy excitement setting my heart racing. He granted me access to his home so I can come and go as I please. I don't know if he told his mother; she probably wouldn't approve.

The faerie paths take me to his bedroom, which is in darkness except for the enchanted miniature galaxy floating near the ceiling above his desk—a present for his seventh birthday. He keeps threatening to get rid of it because, according to him, it's childish. I think it's beautiful.

The laces of my boots untie themselves as I step quietly toward his bed. He's facing away from me, his shoulder rising and falling in time to his steady, quiet breaths. I slip out of my boots, climb onto the bed, and crawl across the covers. I'm about to lean over him and kiss his neck when he says, "Do you think you're sneaking up on me, Sexy Pixie?"

Damn. "Yes, that's exactly what I think."

He rolls over and pins me beneath him. "You'll have to try

harder than that." He brings his lips down to meet mine while I wrap my arms around his neck. Sparks and tingles flash across my tongue, my face, my arms. I still don't know if Ryn's doing that on purpose, or if it happens spontaneously when people with magic kiss. Either way, Ryn has *never* been more right than when he told me I was missing out.

"Did you catch the bad guy?" he whispers into my ear.

"Of course. Did you fix Egypt?"

"Of course." A kiss on my earlobe. "Has Jay flirted with you yet?"

I place my hands on either side of Ryn's face so I can look at him. "No, but it's cute that you're jealous."

"Jealous? Ha! Don't make me laugh."

"You are *so* jealous." I push him off me so I can slide beneath the covers. "But it's okay. I've been jealous before. Back at the palace when you were flirting with Opal whatever-her-name-is."

"Ah, yes, I remember that." He sits up against his pillow and pulls me to his side. "Your jealousy actually hurt my chest."

"Good. I'm glad." Seems his ability is useful for something.

"Come on, I was just being friendly to her."

"Yeah, right. I bet you were intentionally trying to make me jealous."

Ryn chuckles. "I think I was."

I punch his thigh, and he has the decency to pretend it hurt. "Anyway, why are we sitting up? I was just getting comfortable before you brought up the subject of my teammate."

Ryn yawns, then says, "I have some bad news. I thought it would be better if you weren't distracted while I told you."

"Bad news?"

"Yeah." He rubs his eyes. Poor guy must be tired after his long assignment. "I was at my father's house this evening. I stopped by for half an hour or so to see him and Calla. Turns out his griffin disc has been stolen."

"What?" I sit up straighter. "How do you know? Did he tell you about it?"

"Not exactly. He was quite agitated. You know, moving things around and looking everywhere. So I asked him what he was searching for. He described the disc so I could help him look, but he didn't tell me anything about it."

"Crap," I murmur. "That's bad. Does he know when it went missing?"

"No. The last time he saw it was a few months ago."

I shake my head. "You know, I thought the protective magic we had on our homes was supposed to keep unwanted people out."

"Yeah, so did I."

"Maybe back when Angelica was stealing the discs, she was able to get into our parents' homes because they were her friends and had already granted her access. But now that Zell's the one stealing discs, how did he do it?"

"Maybe he knows ways around the protection," Ryn says. "There must be ways to break those spells if you're powerful enough."

"Or if you have a powerful friend who seems to like breaking into places."

"Halfling boy," Ryn mutters. "I suppose he could have stolen the disc for Zell before he deserted him last month. Have you heard anything from him since he showed up in the gargan tree?"

"Not a thing."

Nate must have listened to me when I suggested he take his parents and run. I went to his house about a week after our confrontation in the gargan tree, and neither he nor his parents were there. Instead, a man who looked remarkably like Nate's father was sitting at the dining room table making a phone call. On the table beside him lay an open newspaper with an article about a missing family. There were three pictures: Nate, his father, and his step-mother.

I kind of regret being so harsh to him, but I couldn't trust him anymore. Parts of his story made sense—the details match up now that I think about it—but he could have simply made up the story to fit the details. It's better if Nate just gets on with his life somewhere far away. He could even start over in a new place and pretend he's a normal human.

Ryn laces his fingers between mine. "Now that I've shared the bad news, would you like to hear something good?"

After kissing the back of his hand, I say, "Definitely."

"I may have a lead on your missing box."

"Really? From your Underground contact?"

"Yes."

With all the excitement of discovering my father still alive, followed by Ryn and me getting together, and Nate showing up out of the blue, I actually managed to forget about the missing box from my mother for an entire week after Zinnia told me about it.

After Ryn reminded me about the box, he broke into the office of the guardian who led the investigation into Reed's death and found the relevant file. Since there was no mention of a box, we went back to the spot on the forest floor where Reed fell. I could tell it was difficult for Ryn to revisit the place his brother died, but he seemed to handle it well. We took a good look around, digging up parts of the ground to see if the box may have become buried over time. I even went back later and walked along the Tip-Top Path itself to see if Reed perhaps let go of the box as he fell and it landed somewhere other than down below. I searched every crevice in the surrounding branches but found nothing. Not surprising, really. Did I honestly expect it to still be there nine years later?

So Ryn decided to go Underground and search for it the way he searched for my necklace: by finding a hint of a rumor of a story and following it.

"And what did this Underground contact of yours tell you?" I ask.

"He knows someone who knows someone who sells, uh, *redistributed* handcrafted items."

"In other words, *stolen* handcrafted items?"

"Yes. And apparently he sold a wooden box with the name Violet on it several years ago."

I sag back against the pillow. "Several *years* ago? The box could be anywhere in the entire fae realm by now."

"Hey, I found your necklace, didn't I?" His fingers brush

the gold key resting against my chest. "I'll find your box."

The feeling of warmth and safety that Ryn always manages to bring to me washes over my body. I look into his eyes, and I'm overcome by the urge to tell him something. Something big-deal and scary and *so* not me. Something involving a word that starts with L.

No. I can't say that. It's too soon. I'll freak him out. I'll freak *myself* out.

"Can I talk to you about something else?" Ryn asks.

"Sure." *As long as you aren't about to use the scary L-word.*

He frowns. "Are you okay? I feel like you're freaking out about something."

"Nope." My voice comes out like a squeak. "Just … stressing about the Zell situation, I guess."

He gives me a funny look that tells me he doesn't quite believe me, so I lean forward and press my lips against his. He obviously forgets whatever he was going to say because his hands slide around my waist as the kiss becomes more heated. They skim across my back, beneath my top. I press my body closer to his.

"Wait," he says against my lips. "Wait, I'm supposed to be telling you something."

Reluctantly, I pull away from him. "It had better be good."

"It's always good when I'm talking." He caresses my cheek as I roll my eyes. "Okay, so, I have a theory," he says. "A theory about why some of us have extra magical abilities and others don't."

I snuggle closer to him. "I'm listening."

"You know how everyone loved Reed? I mean, people always say—"

"—there was just something about him," I fill in. I've heard so many people say it. I've even said it.

"Yes. There *was* something about him. And I don't think that something was natural. I think it was his special ability. Like mine is sensing others' emotions, yours is finding people, Calla's is to make people see what she's imagining, and Nate's is power over the weather."

"Okay …"

"And didn't Zell say something to you in his dungeon about the griffin discs being connected to fae with special powers?"

"Yes, but he didn't explain what he meant."

"Well, here's my theory: People who use the griffin discs extensively have children with additional magical abilities."

I let his words sink in.

"Think about it," Ryn says. "Your parents had discs, my parents had discs, and Nate's mother had a disc. My father is the only one who still has a disc, and look at Calla. She turned out special too."

I nod. This could be what Zell was referring to. "So the reason there are a lot of fae with unique magical abilities is because the discs have had so many owners over the centuries."

"Yes. And since Zell has been hunting for the discs for a while, he probably has a long list of people who've owned a disc at some point. Once he figured out there was a connection, it would have been easy enough for him to go back and find out who their children were."

"Yeah, and then abduct them." I tilt my head back and stare at the galaxy. "So, it's like we have a little bit of Tharros' power in us. That's weird, isn't it?"

Ryn nods. "It is weird to think of it like that." He looks down at me. "But don't go freaking out about his magic making us evil because I don't believe that at all. We're on the good side, V. It doesn't matter what kind of magic we were born with."

CHAPTER THIRTY-ONE

TORA LEANS FORWARD AND RESTS HER ELBOWS ON HER desk and her chin on her hands. "And as I walked in, hundreds of butterflies rose off the table and fluttered away, leaving the most amazing arrangement of flowers on the middle of the table."

I clasp my hands together beneath my chin. "That's so romantic, Tora." Not as romantic as a magic carpet ride and a gazillion glow-bugs, but not every guy can pull off something that epic.

"And the food was glorious." Tora tips her head back and leans it against the cabinet behind her desk. "He sure can cook."

"Thank goodness for that." I think of Tora's abysmal cooking skills. You'd think that possessing magical abilities would allow her to do a mediocre cooking job, at the very least, but no. "He sounds perfect for you. Do you think he's going to ask you to form a union with him?"

Tora's cheeks turn pink. "I have no idea." She sits forward and starts moving things around her desk that probably don't need to be moved. "I mean, we haven't exactly known each other very long, and unions are a big deal amongst our kind. I'd have to think about it very seriously because no union should be broken lightly."

It shouldn't. In fact, unions are rarely broken at all. That's why it was such a scandal when Ryn's father left and formed a new union with someone else. People didn't *say* much, of course, because they all knew about Reed's tragic death and how difficult it was for his family, but you could see it in their expressions whenever Ryn's family was mentioned.

"Okay, but if Oliver asked you now, what would you say?"

Tora opens her mouth but is saved from answering by a hurried knocking on her door. "Come in," she calls.

A dwarf marches in with a stack of note-sized pages in his hand. "Urgent memo for all guardians," he says. He hands one to Tora and another to me. As he leaves, I see another dwarf hurrying down the corridor in the opposite direction.

"Oh no!" Tora claps a hand to her mouth as her eyes scan the note. "This must have happened after I left last night."

I look down at the small piece of reed paper in my hand.

An enchanted fire was started by black-clad faeries outside the London Guild last night. While the internal entrance connected to the faerie paths remained intact, no one could enter or leave through the exterior entrance. After a number of unsuccessful attempts to extinguish the fire, it vanished, seemingly on its own. The black-clad faeries were gone. No Guild members were hurt.

This is the third attack on a Guild, and the second Guild to be attacked. It is likely that more attacks are on the way. Please be prepared for action at all times.

Stunned, I stare at the message as I realize the note in my pigeon hole wasn't a joke.

Somebody warned me this would happen.

I blink and look up. Tora is tapping her small circular mirror. "Oliver! Is everything okay there?"

"You've heard about the fire?" says a male voice.

"Yes. Only just."

"I'm sorry I didn't contact you earlier. Things have been crazy here this morning, but everyone's okay."

"Oh, thank goodness."

I stand up to leave. It would be rude of me to hang around and listen to Tora's conversation with Oliver. Besides, I feel the need to check my pigeon hole again because something tells me I'm going to find another mysterious note there.

I head to the corridor lined with pigeon holes. As I reach mine, I see a folded note with my name on one side, written in the same stylus-printed type as before. With my heart pumping faster than normal, I unfold the paper.

VF,

Now that you know I can be trusted, it is your *turn to prove to me that* you *can be trusted. I will not risk my life to give this information to someone too afraid to come and get it from me. If you can go to Diviniti, an Underground club, and fetch something from the man with the ram's horns, then I will know you are brave enough for this task.*

D

Diviniti? A man with ram's horns? This is getting weird. I should either throw this note away or give it to someone like Councilor Starkweather. What I *shouldn't* do is follow the instructions D has given me in the hopes that I'll end up getting important information from him or her. Important information that I can then use to show Councilor Starkweather just how wrong she was to exclude me from the Zell investigation.

I shouldn't do that. I really, *really* shouldn't. I can almost hear logical me chanting, *Don't do it, Vi, don't do it.*

Ugh, but I so badly want to prove myself. And what good would it do to take this note to someone else in the Guild? This D person only wants to communicate with me. I'm the one who needs to get the information that could save everyone.

I insert the note into my pocket as I head back down the corridor. At the very least, I'll try to find Diviniti and the man with the ram's horns. Then I'll decide what to do after that.

* * *

Ryn is stuck in his new cubicle at the Guild writing a mile-long report on his Egypt assignment, so I don't bother him with questions about how to get to Diviniti. At least, that's what I tell myself as I sift through my clothes at home and try to transform them into something colorful and whacky. I know deep down that my real reason for keeping this from Ryn is that he won't approve of me going off on my own to follow up on this lead. He hasn't been above breaking rules in the past—like when we rescued Calla—but something tells me he'll say I should get the Guild involved for this one.

And I don't want that. I want to do this on my own.

I manage to change my black boots to an acid green color, and my black tank top to something that looks like a child's painting set threw up on it. Then I attempt to transform a pair of short, black hot pants into a short, black skirt. A little more challenging than just changing color, but I manage it. I'm getting better at this clothes casting thing.

My hair needs help now. I ask Filigree to shift into the form of a large bird, which he dutifully does. He flaps around until my bedroom floor is covered in feathers. I pick up a few, change their color, and stick them into my hair. Lastly, I add my jacket to the outfit. I don't need anyone seeing the guardian markings on my wrists.

Right. Now I look weird enough to party Underground.

Since I have no idea where Diviniti is, I'll have to start with the only Underground club I know: Poisyn. I found my way there accidentally after fleeing Angelica's labyrinth. If I can picture it accurately in my mind, I should be able to get back there through the faerie paths.

Darkness surrounds me as I step through the doorway on my wall and picture the Underground room with the flashing colored lights and the mass of bodies writhing in time to the music. When a slow, seductive beat reaches my ears, I know I've arrived. I open my eyes, and I'm right in the middle of it. Bodies sway and twist, arms in the air, heads thrown back. Some fae are entwined around each other. Others pour brightly colored drinks down their throats—and over their chests and heads—as they dance.

I try to look like I'm totally comfortable here as I push my way through the sweaty bodies toward the edge of the room. Difficult, when all I want to do is shudder each time someone rubs against me. I stand on tiptoe, search the room for the bar, and make my way toward it. I try to sway my hips as I walk, copying the other girls I see. It feels stupid.

I lean my elbows on the bar's luminous green counter and look around. Okay, now I need to find someone I can ask—

"Hey, do I know you?" A guy with a bald head and eyes that seem to have no irises leans on the bar beside me. His hands are covered in fur, and his fingernails are sharpened to talons.

"Um, I don't think so."

"Oh, sorry. I must have met you in my dreams." He gives me a cheesy grin, showing off pointed teeth.

Wow. Was that a pick-up line? If so, I'm glad I've avoided bars and clubs until now. Even though I'd like nothing more than to walk away immediately, I push down the urge to gag and flutter my eyelids at him instead.

"So, do you want to dance?" He takes a step closer to me.

"Sure, if we can go somewhere else."

"Somewhere else?" His eyes light up, and I'm pretty sure he just read *way* more into my words than I intended.

"Yeah, my friend told me about this place called Diviniti. Do you know it?"

"Oh, yeah." He looks a little disappointed, probably because the 'somewhere else' didn't turn out to be more private. "I can take you there, if you want."

"Oh, can you?" I allow delight to spread across my face. "Thank you so much!"

We leave Poisyn and head down a tunnel. It's wide and high, with doorways here and there and all manner of fae creatures loitering around. We turn a corner and pass a troll pulling a cart of dwarves behind him. This place is more like a network of streets than tunnels. We reach a fork and go right. Then take another turn, and another. I'm glad I can leave here via the faerie paths because I'm not sure if I'd know how to get back to Poisyn.

The distant hum of music reaches my ears. "We're almost there," says my bald companion. We've barely spoken a word to one another. He's obviously just as much of a conversationalist as I am. "So, this is it." He gestures to an archway with white smoke billowing out beneath it. As we move forward, he puts an arm around my shoulders. His furry hand slides down and squeezes my butt.

I grab the offending hand, spin him around, and pin him against the wall. I twist his arm hard behind his back. "Try that again, and I'll break your hand."

"Okay," he gasps, his face practically kissing the wall.

"Man, that was hot. Can you do that again?"

Seriously? I drop his arm and step away from him. "You know what? I don't think this is going to work out. You should go back to Poisyn. That girl behind the bar looked like she was into you."

"Really?"

"Yes." Actually, she looked like she wanted to scratch the eyes out of anyone who dared ask for a drink, but maybe that's just because she had a distinctly feline look about her.

"Awesome." The bald guy rotates his shoulder a few times before heading back down the tunnel.

I walk beneath the archway and into Diviniti. There must be some kind of invisible barrier across the entrance because my fingertips tingle for a moment and the music suddenly becomes louder. The smoke clears enough for me to get a look at the room. It's a lot darker than Poisyn, and there's a lot less dancing happening. There are couches here and there with fae draped across them, drinking, smoking … and other things that make my face heat up. As I walk toward the bar, I can tell I'm being watched. For the first time this evening, I feel a little unsafe.

A faerie with a circular piece of metal through his nose reaches me before I get to the bar. "I haven't seen you around here before," he says, his tone suggesting his words are a warning rather than another pick-up line.

I decide to go with the truth. "I was sent here to look for someone. A man with ram's horns."

One side of his mouth turns up. He reaches for the bottom of his T-shirt and peels it off over his head, revealing an impressive set of abs. Not as impressive as the abs belonging to Ryn, but, then, I'm probably biased. I'm about to ask this guy why he's undressing when he turns and shows me his back. Tattooed across the top half is a pair of large, curling ram horns.

He pulls his T-shirt back on and says, "So, who are you?"

"My name is Violet."

"Violet." The corners of his lips turn up ever so slightly as his gaze brushes over the length of my body. "I've been expecting you. Wait here." He goes behind the bar and disappears through a door.

I slide my hands into my jacket pockets and try not to make eye contact with anyone. When the ram-man returns, he hands me something small wrapped in brown paper. It feels hard. "Um, the person who gave you this," I say. "Was it a man or a woman?"

He gives me a curious look. "A woman."

"Okay. Thanks." I back away before he can ask any questions—and find myself hitting a wall of flesh. "Oh, I'm sorry," I say as I turn. The giant of a man behind me must be half-troll because he is enormous—and really ugly.

"Leaving so soon?" he asks. His voice is so deep I can almost feel it rumble. "You should stay awhile." He raises his hand slowly toward my face. "Get to know us a little better."

I duck beneath his arm, jump onto the cushion of the nearest couch, leap over the back, and land beside the wall. I hurriedly write a doorway onto it and step inside, leaving the music, smoke and thundering laughter behind me.

I walk into my bedroom and stare at the package in my

hands. It really wasn't all that difficult to retrieve. If that's all it takes to prove my bravery to this mysterious woman, then she obviously has no idea what kind of scary situations I've got myself into in the past. This was like a third-year assignment in comparison.

I sit on the edge of my bed and unwrap the brown paper. Inside I find two rectangular pieces of clear glass, about the same size as my amber. Great. I have *no* idea what I'm supposed to do with these. I place them on my bedside table and begin pulling the feathers out of my hair, which now smells like smoke.

I take a step toward my bathing room, but stop when I hear a buzzing sound on my bedside table. One of the glass pieces is vibrating, moving slowly toward the edge of the table. I lunge and catch it before it falls off. Two dark grey words stare at me from the surface of the glass.

Hello, Violet.

I grab my stylus and perch on the edge of the bed. *Is this D?* I write.

Yes. Well done for getting to Diviniti.

Does this glass work like amber?

Yes. New technology. The manufacturers call them comm-glass.

Why did you give me two?

In case you break one.

Fair enough. I suppose that happens when you make communication devices out of glass. *So what happens now?*

You will hear from me in three days' time as soon as I

know when and how Zell plans to make his attack on the Guilds. Goodnight.

Goodnight? Is that it? After a few minutes, it's clear that whoever is at the other end of this comm-glass doesn't plan to send any more messages.

I soak in my bathing pool for a while, letting the waterfall wash the smoke out of my hair. When I get out, I find a message from Ryn on my amber.

I miss my Sexy Pixie. Mom heard you in my room last night. She's now using words like 'inappropriate under my roof' and 'please leave your door open.' So ... meet me at the gargan tree?

With a smile, I get dressed and head out.

* * *

"You're hiding something from me," Ryn says. Most of the time, his ability works pretty well for us—I never have to actually *tell* him what I'm feeling, which is completely fine with me—but right now it sucks that he can figure me out so easily. "Your mood is different, and you definitely got nervous when I asked how your evening was."

Okay, time to come clean. I may be able to keep a secret from Ryn, but I definitely can't lie to him. Especially not when I'm sitting on his lap and he won't let me look anywhere except into his eyes. "You're right. I have been hiding something from you." I place my hands on his shoulders. "But only because I know you'll get all protective and worry about my safety and try to stop me."

Ryn raises both eyebrows. "If that was you attempting to put my mind at ease, you did a terrible job."

"It's not hugely dangerous. It's just something I want to do on my own so that I can prove myself to Councilor Starkweather."

"And this something is?"

I slide my fingers down his arms and take his hands in mine. "Someone at the Unseelie Court contacted me to say she wants to tell me all Zell's plans regarding his imminent attack on the Guilds. She saw me at his masquerade and obviously thought I'd be a good person to pass the information to."

Ryn's expression turns wary. "V, that sounds like a trap. Zell still wants you, remember?"

"Look, this person already gave me information that turned out to be true. She told me there would be a fire at the London Guild. I thought it was a joke, so I ignored it. Then the fire really happened."

"So? It could still be someone trying to trick you into handing yourself over."

"I know. The thought has occurred to me. But I'll be careful. I won't meet her anywhere secluded. And if things do go wrong, well, I'm a guardian. I won't exactly be helpless."

After a long pause, Ryn says, "If you meet her, I want to go with you."

"I'm not sure that's a good idea. She may not give me any

info if she sees I'm not alone. She probably doesn't want anyone to know who she is in case it gets back to Zell."

"She doesn't have to know I'm there."

"Ryn ..." I tilt my head to the side and try pleading with my eyes.

"I'm sorry, V." He shakes his head. "If you had any idea how much you mean to me, you'd know that I couldn't handle it if something happened to you."

"And *nothing* is going to happen to me." I squeeze his hands with mine. "I really appreciate that you want to take care of me, but you don't need to. I want to do this on my own. You need to trust that I can."

Ryn is quiet as his eyes search my face. He knows how stubborn I am, so he should know I'm not going to give in on this. On the other hand, I know how stubborn *he* can be, so it's possible we're heading into a big argument here.

"Fine," he says eventually. He places his hands on either side of my face and makes sure I'm looking at him. "If you won't let me go with you, then you have to promise me something else."

I narrow my eyes. "Promise you what?"

His hands slip away from my face and settle on my shoulders. "You'll wear the eternity necklace."

"Wait, you still have that thing? I thought you were going to destroy it."

"I tried. It wouldn't break. Now promise me."

"Jeez, it's not like anyone's going to try and kill me, Ryn. Zell actually wants me alive, remember?"

"Exactly. And the last time Zell tried to capture you and you made a desperate escape, you were washed out the side of a mountain and almost died. So promise me you'll wear the necklace."

Ryn has a point. I lean forward and kiss him gently on the lips. "I promise," I whisper into his ear before dragging my lips down the side of his neck.

CHAPTER THIRTY-TWO

JAY, ASAMI AND I RECEIVE OUR NEXT ASSIGNMENT THE following morning. An elf walked into a restaurant in the Creepy Hollow Shoppers' Clearing last night and attacked a young faerie girl. Then he ran off into the forest and disappeared. This morning another attack was reported by someone coming off the Tip-Top Path. Fortunately, her boyfriend was there to save her, but the elf got away once again. Now it's our job to track him down and make sure he never attacks anyone else.

We need to interview witnesses to try and establish who the elf is, why he'd want to attack these girls, and where he might be now. It takes time, which is good, because I need a distraction. I need something to keep me from counting down the hours until Zell is supposed to meet with his followers to share his plans.

Ryn and I spend every evening in the gargan tree, which is how I end up missing a visit from Dad. I wanted to kick myself when I got home and saw his note lying on my bed. He apologized for not being able to visit sooner and said he had no idea when he'd get the opportunity to come again. *Something big is going on*, he wrote. *Stay safe.* I wish I could tell him about D and that I'll soon know when the big showdown is happening. Surely he can come out of hiding then and help us fight?

On the day of Zell's meeting with his followers, I keep the comm-glass in my pocket wherever I go. I just have to be careful not to sit on it. The entire time I'm with Ryn in the gargan tree, I expect the glass to buzz in my pocket. It doesn't. I get home and stare at it for a while, but still it doesn't buzz. Squirrel-shaped Filigree looks at me oddly from the foot of the bed, as if to say, *Why is the light still on? When can we sleep?*

"I'm not sleeping until I've heard something from D," I tell him. "You're welcome to go and sleep in another room where it's dark, if you want."

With an annoyed sniff, he jumps to the ground and scurries under the bed.

"Or you could sleep under the bed, I guess." I continue staring at the comm-glass until my neck starts to get sore. I lie down and place the comm-glass on the pillow beside me. *I won't sleep, I won't sleep, I won't sleep.*

The next thing I know, I'm lying on my back, the grey light of dawn is peeking through my enchanted skylight, and there's a frenzied buzzing beside my ear. I sit up in fright and clutch the comm-glass tightly, blinking sleep away.

I know everything. Come to the Rose Hall.

I reach for my stylus on the bedside table. *Coming now.*

I pull on my boots, stuff my stylus into one of them, throw the eternity necklace over my head, and hurry into a faerie path. Rose Hall is situated at one end of the Creepy Hollow Shoppers' Clearing. A market is held inside there once a week, and the hall is also used for large functions sometimes, like parties. Otherwise, it remains empty.

I walk along the empty path running between the store fronts. Rose Hall is built into the stocky widdern tree at the end of the lane. There's no doorway carved into the trunk like some of the shops here, but the words 'Rose Hall' are written on a sign hammered into the ground beside the tree.

Will I be able to open a doorway into the hall? I've never tried before, so I don't know if it has the same protective magic our homes have. I don't see why it should, since there isn't much inside to steal. I hold my stylus against the trunk of the tree and hesitate. I look around, remembering that I told Ryn I wouldn't meet D in a secluded spot. Crap. I was in such a rush that I didn't think about that until now.

Is this a trap? An ambush? Is Rose Hall full of Unseelie faeries waiting to attack and capture me? Perhaps the notes and the comm-glass were from Zell himself. Perhaps this whole thing is just his elaborate way of getting me to come willingly to him.

I close my eyes and take a deep breath. Trap or not, I can't back out now. I need to know what's inside this hall. So I take a moment to gather enough power from my core to stun a faerie or two. I hold the swirling ball of power above one hand while I write a doorway onto the tree with the other.

It works.

A section of the tree melts away. I take a few careful steps forward into the darkened hall. The only light in here is the pale light of dawn filtering through an enchanted stained-glass window at the far end of the hall. I slip my stylus away and create an orb of light. I send it up to the ceiling where it illuminates an empty hall.

There is no one here.

Was this a joke, after all? No, it couldn't be. How would D have known about the fire if she wasn't part of Zell's inner circle? I turn slowly on the spot. There's nothing in here except for a few scattered leaves and ... What is that? My eyes fall on a cylindrical shape on the floor in the far corner of the hall. I walk toward it, making sure to stay constantly alert for any movements or sounds.

I reach the corner of the hall and bend over to pick up the object. It's a scroll. A small spike of adrenaline shoots through my veins. This must be it. Why would a scroll be lying here if not for me to pick up? I absorb the ball of power back through my hand, then pull the string away from the scroll and hastily uncurl the pages.

Yes! This is it!

It mentions all the Guilds, as well as the Seelie and Unseelie Courts. Wow, is Zell going to try and take over *everything* in one night? Does he have an army big enough? I scan through the pages quickly—details, details, details—searching for the most important piece of information. *When* is this going to happen? Finally, I find it, and ice freezes in my blood when I see the number.

Three days.

In three days our whole world is going to erupt.

* * *

I run across the foyer of the Guild—protective enchantments in the domed ceiling? Check—and up the stairway. Up and up until I reach the Council members' level. I fly along the corridors toward Councilor Starkweather's office. I skid to a halt in front of her door and rap my knuckles against it. No answer. I try again. Still no answer. She isn't here. And of course she isn't, I realize, because even though she's a workaholic, it's five o'freaking clock in the morning.

With a frustrated groan, I stride back down the passage. This is just fantastic. I finally get my moment to prove to Councilor Starkweather how useful I can be, and she isn't even around. And I can't wait until she gets here because I need to show this to someone *now*. It's beyond urgent.

I wonder if there's any chance Tora is here this early. She'll know who I should give this information to. I jog back down the stairs and hurry along her corridor. I'm about to knock on her door when I see someone even better. "Bran!" I run up to him. "You're part of the team that's investigating Zell, right?"

With a sigh he says, "You know I am, Vi. You've already asked me, and I've told you I can't give you any details."

"I know, I know, but you need to see this." I shove the

scroll into his hand. "It's from someone at the Unseelie Court. She sent me a letter and said she wants to take Zell down just as badly as we do."

Bran scans the first page with a frown on his face before looking up at me. "Is this a joke?"

"That's what I thought when I got the first note from her, but it isn't. She told me there would be a fire at the London Guild, and there was. Then she sent me this glass thing so she'd be able to contact me when she had all the information." I pull the comm-glass out of my pocket and show it to him.

He takes it from me. "I haven't seen one of these before," he mutters, turning it over several times. "She contacted you before the London Guild fire?"

"Yes. The day before."

"And you haven't told anyone about this until now?"

"Well, no."

"Violet! Why not?"

"I'm sorry. I know it's childish, but I was so mad that Councilor Starkweather refused to involve me in the Zell investigation. I wanted to prove that my input could be valuable and that she was wrong not to include me, so—"

"Look, Vi, as someone who's dealt directly with Zell, your input *is* valuable, but you have to see that a complex and dangerous investigation such as this one is more suited to guardians with decades—*centuries*, in some cases—of experience. *You're not there yet.* It was entirely inappropriate of you to keep this information to yourself. You should have known that."

Crap. I am *so* not used to disappointing my superiors.

"I'm sorry." I hang my head. "But," I continue carefully, "what would you have done differently if I had told you about it? This woman only wanted to give *me* the information."

"We would have followed you to make sure you were safe and that it wasn't some kind of ambush, or that somebody didn't place a tracker of some sort on you when you weren't looking."

"But ... I didn't actually meet with any real person."

"That isn't the point, Vi!" He clenches the papers in his hand. "The point is that you should have told us about this earlier."

"Okay, I'm sorry. *I'm sorry.*" I really am. "But this is happening in *three days*, Bran. We need to do something. Don't you need to have a meeting with all the other Council members, like, immediately? Don't we need to plan so that we're ready for this?"

"Yes," he murmurs, scanning his eyes once more over the pages as he paces across the width of the corridor. He stops. "Why haven't our Seers Seen this?"

Hmm. Good point. "I don't know. Maybe they'll start getting glimpses of it now that the final plan is in place."

Bran's expression grows doubtful as he looks at the pages in his hand. "I'm not sure we can trust this information. It could be that someone is trying to mislead us."

"I guess it could be. But what if it isn't? We can't *not* do something about this."

Bran squeezes his eyes shut and mutters something I can't hear.

"So, will you call a meeting?"

"Of course," Bran snaps. I can't remember him ever snapping at anyone before. He shuffles through the pages and holds the last one up. "Three days," he mutters. "We can be prepared in three days."

"Wait, do that again," I say. I take the page from him and hold it up to the light. The faint outline of the Unseelie Queen's insignia becomes visible in the center of the page.

"Well," Bran says, "at least we know these pages really did originate inside the Unseelie Palace."

Which, I suppose, still doesn't confirm that the information is legitimate.

"I need to go," Bran says. "I'm taking this with me." He holds up the comm-glass before striding away from me toward the stairway. "And do not tell anyone about this, Vi. I don't want panic spreading."

* * *

I sit in the gargan tree and wait for Ryn. I spent all day trying to focus on the elf assignment and, for the most part, failed miserably. All I could think about was the fact that we might all be fighting for our lives in a few days' time. On the one hand, it's a good thing the showdown is finally upon us, and we can stop wondering if and when the carpet is going to be yanked from beneath our feet. On the other hand, what if we lose? It's unlikely since we now know it's coming, and we're *guardians*, after all. This is what we're trained for. But ... what if there are too many of them and we don't have enough power?

When I left this evening, Council members from all over the fae realm were arriving. They tried to remain cool, greeting one another as if nothing was wrong—probably for the sake of the confused guardians around them who have no idea yet what's going on—but I could see the unease behind their smiles. Adair and the few other senior guardians I passed on my way out also looked grave. They must have been told already.

I'm starting to wish I hadn't gone off on my own to retrieve the information from D. If the day arrives and no one shows up to attack us, well, it will be a good thing, but I'll also be in monumental trouble. I'm the one who brought this information to the Guild, so I'll be the one responsible for causing all the panic and the meetings and the preparation and then ... the anticlimax.

Crap. Why didn't I think of this possibility before I went charging off on my own little mission? And where is Ryn? I glance up at the position of the moon. He's usually here by now. I send him an amber message, but I get no response. I try to remember if he told me he'd be working tonight. My memory comes up blank.

I wander through the faerie paths and come out in my sitting room. Perhaps Filigree will play a card game with me to take my mind off things. We never did finish that game Ryn interrupted a few weeks ago. I climb the stairs and find Filigree curled up in armadillo form on my pillow. I haven't seen that one in a while. I flop onto my stomach on the bed and poke him—just as a buzzing sound comes from my bedside table.

My amber? No, my amber is in my pocket. So that only

leaves ... the second comm-glass. I yank the drawer open and stick my hand in, pushing the eternity necklace aside to get to the rectangular piece of glass.

Things have changed. I need to give you new information.

"What?" I say out loud. I turn over to get my stylus from my boot and wind up rolling onto the floor. Crap, that hurt. I sit up and quickly scribble onto the glass. *What? The Guild Council is already meeting to look at the information you gave me this morning.*

When?

Right now!

Then I need to meet with you immediately.

Why can't you just tell me here, on the comm-glass?

It's too much. I need to meet with you.

Isn't that too dangerous for you?

I don't care anymore. Come to the Rose Hall.

Now?

Yes!

I scramble up off the floor and open a doorway. "Don't wait up for me!" I shout to Filigree as I enter the blackness. I jump out onto the dark Creepy Hollow lane and run toward the Rose Hall tree. What am I going to do once I have this new information? Just barge into the Council meeting? Maybe I can convince D to come with me. That would definitely help. I stop myself against the tree with my hand out. I raise my stylus to write a doorway, but then I notice a tiny scrap of paper nailed to the tree. One sentence only.

Keep playing the game, Violet.

What? The game? Since when is this a game? A shiver zips across my arms as I look around. Just like this morning, there seems to be no one here, but I can't help the feeling that something weird is going on. Something I'm missing. I have to go into the hall, though. Zell has changed something in his plans, and we all need to know what it is.

So I do what I did this morning. I gather power from the core of my being and hold it above my hand, ready to use it at the first sign of danger. I open a doorway to the hall and walk slowly inside.

What I see at the other end of the hall makes me want to be sick. In front of the stained-glass window, hanging upside down from the ceiling, is a dead body. A *headless* dead body. Without really realizing it, I let the power above my hand fizzle away. In horror, I start walking toward the other end of the hall. A round object sits on the floor beneath the body, and every shocked instinct within me screams that it's a head. It's the head belonging to the hanging body. And I need to know who it is.

My fingers shake. My legs shake. Even my breaths are shuddery as they escape my lips. But I keep moving forward. The head is facing the back wall, but as I get closer, I see the color in the hair. I see the crimson streaks, and I know. *I know.* But I step around to face him anyway. I step around and see his glassy crimson eyes.

Zell.

With a shaking hand I cover my mouth to stop myself from throwing up. Then I see the words written on the floor.

Violet,

You can't win this game. I know your every move before you make it, and I will always be one step ahead of you. I want you to know that everything that happens now is your fault.

Draven

CHAPTER
THIRTY-THREE

Draven? That's what I used to call Nate. Mr. Draven Avenue. But this can't be him. *It can't. Nonononono, please say he didn't do this.* Oh, dear Seelie Queen, what has he done? What have *I* done?

A crackling sound rips through the quiet night as lightning flashes somewhere outside. It strikes the ground with such force that I have to throw my hand out against the wall to stop the shudder from knocking me to my feet. I hear a thud and crunch as something hits the ground outside. Compelled by the terrible fear that my entire world is about to be torn apart, I sprint across the empty hall and out into the lane.

The strongest gust of wind I've ever felt sweeps through the trees and slams me onto the ground. A roaring, crackling sound greets my ears. Smoke burns my nostrils. I manage to turn onto my back just as another bolt of lightning strikes the ground nearby. The forest glows with flickering orange light, growing brighter as I watch. The roaring becomes louder and the smoke denser.

Oh, hell. There's a freaking inferno out there, moving with the speed of the wind.

Get to the Guild.

I roll back onto my stomach and write a doorway on the dirt. I fall into the darkness and focus my attention on the interior entrance of the Guild. Maybe I'll still be in time to warn them of what's coming.

I drop out of the faerie paths onto my feet—and that's when I realize how wrong I am. My world isn't about to be torn apart. *It's already been torn apart.* Shock seems to suck the air from my lungs because I don't have any left to gasp.

The Guild is destroyed. *The entire Guild.*

Rubble litters the ground as far as I can see. Marble and debris and smoldering pieces of intricately carved wood. Splintered trees and ashes and smoke.

The complex glamours and architectural spells that hid the entire Guild within a single tree must have somehow been destroyed. My mind conjures up awful images of what must have happened after that: the interior of the Guild exploding out, demolishing the forest around it.

I take a few shaky steps forward before dropping onto my knees. I can't take this in. It's too much. I see guardians scattered here and there throughout the rubble, some injured, some stumbling around looking lost. Scraps of conversations reach me.

"... saying Tharros has returned."

"... must have taken more power than any single person should possess."

"The first explosion came from inside the room the Council and senior guardians were in."

"Did any of them come out alive? I haven't seen a single one ..."

Oh no oh no oh no. This can't be happening. How many people are dead? Where is Tora? Ryn? Flint? *Where are all the people I care about?*

A blinding flash of white light fills the wrecked clearing. I throw my hand across my eyes until the light diminishes. When I look again, I see the Seelie Queen dressed in silver armor, stalking across the rubble. "WHAT is going on here?" she shrieks.

"My lady." One of her guards runs after her. "You shouldn't be here. It's too dangerous. There might be—"

"I want to know what is going on," she shouts. She stops and circles on the spot, staring down at the guardians who have come forward to kneel before her. "I want to know how this Guild could be *stupid* enough to call a meeting of almost every Council member from every Guild and then get itself *blown up.*"

Cold laughter greets her words. I look for the source of the sound and see a woman sauntering toward the Queen. A shiver passes through my body as I recognize her.

Angelica.

No longer wailing and desperate. No longer trapped in the center of her own labyrinth. She holds her head high, looking down on everyone as she swishes her long black and silver hair over her shoulder. And in that instant, I realize why I thought the Seelie Queen looked so familiar when I met her.

"Hello, Mother," Angelica says as she comes to a halt. "Did you miss me?"

Mother.

"Like I'd miss an ugly spot on a white gown," the Queen sneers. "And do not call me 'mother.' You are not my child."

Whispers of 'runaway daughter' surround me as people realize what's going on. The Queen's guards point their weapons at Angelica, but none of them make a move. I suppose hurting a Seelie princess doesn't exactly come naturally to them.

"Not your child?" Angelica repeats. "I suppose it's hardly surprising, then, that I was far happier at the Guild than I ever was at your stuffy palace." The Queen's eyebrows twitch a fraction. "Oh, didn't you know?" Angelica asks, her voice full of exaggerated surprise. "How shocking. I spent over a decade at the Creepy Hollow Guild, and you didn't even know about it."

"They obviously managed to teach you *nothing*," the Queen spits, "since you appear to be consorting with the enemy now. What are you doing with the Unseelie Court?"

Angelica lets out an exaggerated sigh. "You see, Mother, this actually has nothing to do with the Unseelie Court. It has everything to do with my son."

Confusion and anger war in the Queen's eyes.

"That's right," Angelica says. "Your grandson. A prince of the Seelie Court—"

"A traitor just like you," the Queen growls.

"*Your own flesh and blood!* He is in possession of the lost halfling Tharros' power, and there is no one in the world who can defeat him now. He is the one who will strip you of everything you have. The Unseelie Palace lies in ruin, and the Seelie Palace is being destroyed as we speak. The Guilds are all under attack. When daylight breaks, there will be no difference between Seelie and Unseelie. There will be only those who are for my son and those who are against him."

Nate. What have you done?

"And as for how this Guild could be stupid enough to get itself blown up," Angelica continues. "One of your guardians very kindly sent an enchanted bomb device into the Council meeting. And that same guardian then told us the meeting was taking place tonight. It was all very easy after that."

Is she talking about me? *No. Please, no. Please don't let all of this be my fault.* How will I ever face anyone again?

My eyes comb the clearing in desperation. I still don't see Ryn or Tora. I have to find them. I can't think about all this damage and destruction. I can't think about how it's all my fault.

Find them.

My stylus is still clutched in my hand. I bend forward and write on the ground. I slip into the darkness just as the first rain drops begin to fall. I head to the gargan tree first. Perhaps Ryn is there waiting for me. Perhaps that part of the forest is still and quiet and has no idea what's happening in the distance.

But something is wrong. When I exit the faerie paths, I find myself falling through the air. A scream escapes me as I attempt to open another path in the moving air. I can't. I drop toward the ground, managing to slow my fall at the last second. I hover above the ground for a moment before dropping the last few inches of the way. I push myself up and spring to my feet.

Destruction.

The gargan tree—one of the most ancient and majestic trees in the whole forest—has fallen. It's burned and smoking and *fallen*. It took most of the surrounding trees down with it. Everything is dead here.

Dead.

Nate did this. He destroyed my most favorite place in the whole of Creepy Hollow. I clench my fists and let out a wordless scream. On and on and on until I have no breath left. "*How could you do this?*" I shriek into the slowly pattering rain. "*I hate you!*"

Tears join the raindrops trickling down my face. I run through the faerie paths to Ryn's home. What I find there makes my tears fall faster. It's destroyed, torn open, just like the other faerie homes I can see through the broken trees as I twist to look around me. I search through the wreckage, but there's no one here.

I go to Tora's home, and I'm greeted by the same sight. And again, no one here.

The only place left to go is my own house. Maybe Ryn and Tora went there to look for me. And Filigree! I have to rescue Filigree!

I prepare myself for destruction, but the sight of my ruined home is still enough to make me feel like something has just been ripped from my chest. Nausea invades my stomach.

My home is gone.

"Ryn!" I shout. "Tora! Filigree!" There's no answer.

I climb over the mess that was my kitchen. The table no longer has any legs, and I'm about to step over it when I notice a sharp knife embedded in its surface. The knife is holding a piece of paper to the table. A folded piece of paper.

My blood burns like fire as fury courses through me. Was it not enough for Nate—*Draven*—to rip my whole world away from me? Did he also have to leave a damn *note* rubbing it in my face?

I yank the knife out of the table and unfold the paper. My heart almost stops at the sight of Ryn's handwriting—and then it breaks all over again as I read his words. There are a lot of them, but I can only focus on one sentence: *Don't try to find me.* I squeeze tears from my eyes as I shove the note into my pocket. "You promised you wouldn't leave," I whisper. "You *promised.*"

It's then that I hear a faint voice. Tora. Calling my name. I swivel around, searching desperately. "Tora?" I call. I hear her voice again. I jump off the ruins and run around the side of the mess. There she is, pinned down by a tree that landed across her abdomen. A tree with splintered branches and bark and— oh, dear Seelie Queen, I don't even want to look at the damage because I know instinctively that it's too much for even a faerie to recover from.

"Tora!" I run to her side and take hold of her hand. "Oh crap oh crap oh crap." I have to try and heal her. Even if my brain tells me it isn't possible, I still have to try. "I can move the tree," I say, getting ready to lift it with magic.

"No." She touches my arm to stop me. "It won't help. My magic," she gasps. "It isn't ... strong enough to ..."

It isn't strong enough to heal her. That's what she wants to say. But I have magic that *can* heal her, I realize. The eternity necklace. If she wears it she can't die, right? I climb the rubble of my house faster than anything I've ever climbed before. I find my bed. My bedside table. The drawer has been knocked out and is lying next to splinters of my desk. I search through the contents for the eternity necklace.

It's gone.

"No!" I shout. Why is it gone? It was here when I left, less than an hour ago. I search all around the drawer, but there's no necklace to be found anywhere.

I run back down to Tora. I lift the top half of her body and hold her on my lap, letting my magic seep into her wherever our skin is touching. "Please don't die," I sob. "Please don't die, please don't die."

"Are my legs ... still there?" she manages to ask. "I can't ... feel ..."

I lean over her and let my tears fall onto her chest. "I'm so sorry, Tora. I'm so sorry, I'm so sorry. This is all my fault."

"Remember ... I ..." Her words die on her lips as life vanishes from her eyes.

I clutch her hands tightly, desperately. I can't breathe. Where is the air? *Why can't I breathe?* Bright spots of light dance before my eyes. I let go of Tora's hands and fall back onto the ground. And suddenly there's a release, and I'm sucking great breaths of air into my lungs.

Not that I deserve it. I should be the one lying dead on the ground, not Tora. I stand up. I walk blindly over the wreckage of my house. I don't know where I'm going. I don't know what I plan to do. All I know is that I don't want to think. I don't want to remember. I don't want to *be* here.

I collapse onto the highest point of my destroyed home and hold my head in my hands as I cry. I can't fix this. I can't make up for it. I don't even know how I can *live* knowing that she died because of me.

My hands drop to my sides, and one of them comes to rest on a pile of glass. The contents of my emergency kit, scattered and broken. My trembling fingers sift through the items that managed to survive and linger on one of the vials. I pick it up. *Forget*, says the label.

That's what I want. I want to forget everything that's happened. I want to forget that it's my fault.

I unscrew the top.

I lift it to my mouth.

I close my eyes and pour it down my throat.

CHAPTER THIRTY-FOUR

I AWAKE IN A SMALL, DIMLY LIT ROOM WITH A CEILING THAT feels too close. I roll onto my side, rubbing my scratchy eyes. The room is bare except for a chair and a small table. On the table sits a lantern with a candle flickering inside.

"Oh, you're awake, dear. How lovely." Someone short comes into the room. Someone with grey hair and wearing a long dress. She bends over me, and I see black eyes in a face covered with fine, reptilian-like scales.

Reptiscilla, my brain tells me.

"Who are you?" I ask.

She smiles down at me. "Someone who decided not to leave you out there in the wreckage."

"The wreckage?" I repeat. I'm still trying to make sense of where I am, how I got here, and what happened before I fell asleep. I'm coming up blank.

"The wreckage of the forest. It was torn apart by an evil faerie." She shakes her head in disapproval. "Draven, they say his name is."

"Draven?" *Never heard of him.*

"And what is your name, dear?"

My name. That's an easy question. And I have the answer. It's right here on the tip of my— "Violet," I say, relieved the name came to me.

"And?"

"And what?"

"What else do you remember?"

What do I remember? Now that one's a little harder. I search my fuzzy head, then shake it. "To be honest," I say, "not much."

VIOLET'S STORY IS TOLD IN
THE FAERIE GUARDIAN,
THE FAERIE PRINCE,
& THE FAERIE WAR

FIND MORE CREEPY HOLLOW CONTENT ONLINE
www.creepyhollowbooks.com

TURN THE PAGE FOR
BONUS SCENES FROM

THE
FAERIE
PRINCE

RYN

LEAVING THE HARTS' HOUSE IN THE MIDDLE OF WHAT WAS undoubtedly the most important assignment of his training years was probably against Guild rules. But Ryn had always seen rules as something to be bent and molded to his own particular purposes.

Besides, it was a boring assignment.

Dirt crunched beneath his boots as he strode along the Underground tunnel. It was dimly lit by the occasional glow-bug, and smelled of wet earth and elder-pipe smoke.

"Are we close?" Ryn asked Lena, the tall elf walking beside him. She was most likely the source of the smoke smell; he'd seen her with an elder-pipe on several occasions.

"Yes."

"And would it perhaps be wise to approach in silence?" He

eyed the metallic bangles clinking around Lena's wrists as she swung her arms at her sides.

"No." She gave him a look before running her hand purposely through her dark, matted locks, making her bangles jingle louder. "They'll know we're coming anyway."

Ryn suppressed a smile as he pointed his gaze forward once more. Lena had always enjoyed annoying him. It was one of the things he liked about her. That and the fact that she was rarely overcome by any form of emotion. She was the adopted daughter of the man who owned Poisyn, and Ryn had known her since he'd first ventured Underground at age fourteen. He didn't see her all that often, and the two of them weren't exactly close—Lena wasn't the BFF type—but she was a font of knowledge when it came to Undergrounders and their dealings. She'd provided Ryn with useful information a number of times.

"I hope you know what you're doing," she said. "The bottom of the singing well is Grima's territory. He keeps it guarded at all times."

"Good. Then I'll have somebody to question."

Lena laughed. "One of these days, Ryn, you're going to get yourself killed. And then I might actually miss you."

"Lena." Mock surprise colored Ryn's voice. "I had no idea you cared so much."

"I don't." Bangles clinked together as she flipped her hair over her shoulder. "But I do care about that brandy from the human realm you like to bring me every now and then."

"I see. It's all about the brandy."

"Of course."

Lena directed him through another few tunnels before coming to a stop at a fork. The faint echo of a song reached Ryn's ears. "Take the tunnel on the right," Lena said. It isn't far after that. You shouldn't have any problem finding it on your own, and no doubt you'll be relieved to be free of my jangling jewelry."

Ryn faced her and held out his hand. "Thanks again."

Her lips curved into a smile as she shook his hand. "Any time."

Ryn continued on his own. The echoing song grew louder, and it wasn't long before the tunnel brightened with the glow of orange firelight. He rounded a curve and found himself at the entrance to a brightly lit cave guarded by two faerie men built like ogres.

The men snapped to attention the moment they saw Ryn, moving together to block the cave entrance while clenching their meaty fists. Behind them, Ryn could make out a circular pool covered by a shimmering silver net. Above the net, in the ceiling of the cave, was a circular hole: the bottom of the singing well.

"You must be lost," the man on the right said, his voice rumbling deep in his chest.

"No, I'm exactly where I need to be," Ryn said. He folded his arms over his chest. "I'm looking for something."

"Yeah, you and every other idiot who shows up here," the second man said. He pulled a knife from a sheath at his waist, a move that was most likely meant to be threatening. Ryn was unperturbed.

"I dropped something down the singing well a while ago.

I need to get it back."

"Anything that falls down the singing well belongs to Grima," Knife-Man said. "Everyone knows that."

"Oh. Well, I think we might have a problem then."

The man on the right slowly ground his fist into the palm of his other hand. "I think we might."

"Tell me," Ryn said. "Does Grima remember *everything* that falls down the singing well?"

"Of course," Knife-Man said. "And so do we."

"Perfect. You should be able to help me then. I'm looking for a gold key on a gold chain. The top of the key has a pair of outspread wings."

Knife-Man narrowed his eyes. "You obviously weren't listening when I told you it all belongs to Grima."

"So ... that's a no?" Ryn asked. "You don't remember it?"

With surprising swiftness, the man pounced on Ryn, spun him around, and held the knife to his neck. "Never seen it," the man snarled.

Ryn's every instinct screamed at him to fight back, but he didn't yet have the information he'd come for. He needed to hold himself back just a little longer. "Are you sure?"

"Of course I'm sure. Now why don't you turn around and scurry back to the hole you came from before I slice your throat open. Whatever jewelry you've lost, I can assure you it isn't worth risking your life for."

Probably not. In fact, the necklace wasn't worth much to Ryn at all. But it was of great importance to Violet, and for that reason alone, he had to get it back. Throwing her necklace down the singing well was one of the most vindictive things he'd ever done, and it was about time he made things right with her. "Are you absolutely sure?" he pressed. "I definitely threw it down here. It was about eight years ago."

The man's grip loosened as he threw his head back and guffawed. "Eight years ago? This was Branx's territory back then. Greedy bastard was only in it for the money. Nothing like the collector Grima is. I'm sure your precious trinket has been sold and resold many times over since then. You'll never see it again."

Branx. Finally, a piece of information Ryn could use.

Time to go.

He shoved his elbow into Knife-Man's stomach before tearing free of his grip. The deep-voiced man swung his fist, but Ryn dodged easily out of the way. He spun around—just in time to receive a kick to the face from Knife-Man.

He stumbled backwards, furious pain throbbing across his cheekbone. "The face?" he groaned. "Really?"

"It's about to get a whole lot worse," Knife-Man snarled.

"You're right about that." Ryn swept one hand through the air, sending a shower of sparks that turned into furious, pecking birds toward the men. As they swatted at the glittering beaks and fire-tipped wings, Ryn dropped to one knee, pulled his stylus from his boot, and wrote a door to the faerie paths on the ground.

* * *

Six days later

Branx reached for his tankard of ale and tipped the remaining liquid down his throat. He waved the empty pewter mug at the reptiscillan woman behind the bar and shouted, "Another!" The ale was dwarf-brewed, making it suitable for fae consumption. Intoxication should have been a long way off, but Branx was downing it with alarming speed. Which was fortunate for Ryn, who'd been coaxing information from Branx for the past half hour.

"Yeah, I remember that one." Branx wiped the back of his hand over his mouth and blue-streaked beard. "Got an excellent price for it. Had more than one interested customer. Bidding started high." He paused as he took a swig from his refilled tankard. "It ended up going for four times the price I thought I'd get." He grinned at the memory, then belched loudly.

"And who was the lucky customer who walked off with the necklace?" Ryn asked.

Branx leaned back on his bar stool, eyeing Ryn suspiciously. "What's it to you?"

Ryn hesitated, then lowered his voice. "Can I tell you a secret? I found the necklace. The owner must have lost it. I was thinking I could return it for ... well, a *reward*."

Branx nodded slowly, his lips turning up in a sly smile as the meaning of Ryn's words settled into his alcohol-influenced brain.

"If you could point me in the direction of your customer," Ryn said, "I'd be happy to split my reward with you."

Branx downed another few gulps of ale, then slammed the tankard onto the bar and said, "Deal." He grinned at Ryn, seemingly oblivious to the liquid sloshing over his hand. "It was an advisor in the Unseelie Court. Bought it for his wife. Aster something-or-other." He scratched his head. "Troll-something. No ... Traw. Trawbridge. Aster Trawbrige."

"Excellent," Ryn said, pulling a few coins from his pocket and placing them on the bar beside his half-finished drink. "Where can I send your half of the reward?" Not that there would be half a reward to send to Branx. Ryn was simply playing along until he could get away from the intoxicated faerie.

Instead of answering, Branx's gaze moved to Ryn's chest. A frown furrowed his brow. "I know what that is," he said slowly.

Ryn looked down. His trainee pendant, which should have been hidden beneath his T-shirt, was visible between the lapels of his leather jacket. "Damn," he murmured.

"You're with the Guild," Branx accused, his words slurring slightly.

"Uh, would you believe me if I said I found this too?"

The tankard swung toward him and struck the side of his face. Ryn swore as he stumbled backward off his stool. Considering the amount of alcohol in Branx's system, he hadn't expected him to move that fast. "Liar!" Branx shouted, flinging his now empty tankard to the floor.

Ryn took a step forward and kicked. His boot connected with Branx's ale-filled belly, sending him flying backward amidst bar stools and several shocked fae. Ryn turned swiftly and ran for the exit. He would open a doorway once out in the tunnel. He was almost there when a reptiscillan man jumped in front of him and knocked him to the ground. The reptiscilla pinned Ryn down before pulling his fist back. Ryn grabbed the fist and twisted it, then pushed a rippling force field of magic straight at the reptiscilla. He flew into the air, crashed onto a table, and landed on the floor. Ryn sprang to his feet. Fighting the urge to pull a weapon from the air—he didn't want to reveal his Guild affiliation to anyone else in the room—Ryn settled for bringing his boot down on the reptiscilla's injured arm. "Try to stop me again, and I'll hurt you properly."

This time, when he headed for the exit, nobody stopped him. Seconds later, he was walking into a hastily opened doorway on the tunnel wall. He let out a long breath and thought of home. His mother's kitchen materialized before him. Tasting blood, he realized his lip was cut. A minor injury considering what could have happened in a room full of guardian-haters. He stepped out of the faerie paths as his jaw began to throb. Man, that tankard had given him a serious whack to the face.

He pushed through the kitchen door and found his mother lying on the couch reading a book. Reading for pleasure wasn't something she had much time for between all her assignments, so he hated to interrupt her. He also didn't want her seeing him in his current state.

She looked over at him, then sat up quickly. Ryn felt concern shooting through her as she took in his appearance.

Just play it cool, he told himself as he crossed the room. "Hey, Mom."

"Ryn, are you—"

"Fine, yup, all good."

"But your—"

"I know. Don't worry about it. Everything's fine, Mom. I promise." He gave her a smile before disappearing up the stairs.

* * *

Two weeks later

The darn necklace was proving harder to find than Ryn had anticipated. It had been given away, stolen, sold, and resold, and in the process of discovering all this, Ryn had been burned, punched, slapped, and chased by an enchanted broomstick after he was found hiding inside a cupboard for eavesdropping purposes.

It was all worth it, though. Over the past few weeks, this mission had grown in importance. At first it was about doing the right thing. It was about taking a step toward mending a broken friendship. But then there was that moment in the bathroom of the Harts' pool house. Violet had been standing so close, and for some reason he couldn't convince his feet to move. And the next night, when they'd hidden together inside the antique wardrobe watching Savyon and the Hart men, he was distracted by her nearness. He'd wondered if it was simply seeing her in that sleek sexy dress that made him think of her in a different way, but it was more than that. She hadn't been wearing anything enticing the night before, and he'd still wanted to be near her. He'd still wanted to protect her and make sure there was no possible way Zell could summon her.

By the time they returned to the Guild, he knew for sure that what he felt was more than just a fleeting attraction. She was hallucinating and weak and the color in her eyes was fading, and the stupid guard wouldn't let him in, and he knew without a doubt that *she was dying*, and the idea that he might lose her forever made him feel horribly, desperately afraid.

After eighteen years of feeling everything from everyone around him, Ryn knew a lot about emotions. He knew what he was feeling.

He knew he loved her.

So now it was about more, this necklace-finding mission. He had little more than a pixie's chance in a goblin pit of her ever feeling the same way, but if he could just find this darn tokehari that was so special to her, he might have a chance.

The only problem now was that he was running out of time. He'd hoped to have the necklace by tonight so he could give it to Violet before graduation, but the ceremony was less than two hours away, and so far he had no necklace. Instead, he had an aching neck from hiding in the narrow space beneath a bed.

The home belonged to a siren named Dahlia. She'd been given the necklace by one of her admirers. Lena had found out where Dahlia lived and led Ryn there. Then she'd taken her bottle of brandy and disappeared.

Ryn knew how intoxicating a siren's powers could be, so he'd waited until Dahlia left before going inside to search for the gold chain with the gold key. He'd been hunting for about half an hour when he heard the siren return. Furious with himself for not having found the necklace yet, he slid beneath

Dahlia's bed and tried to recall the training he had on sirens. There were charms he could perform on himself to protect his mind from a siren's influence, and he'd done a simple one before leaving home that afternoon, but he hadn't planned on actually running into her, so he hadn't researched any of the more complex charms.

Dahlia's bare feet came into view as she entered the bedroom. *Too close,* Ryn thought. It would probably be better if he left. He could come back another time when she wasn't here. Violet wouldn't get her necklace tonight, but she'd get it soon.

Carefully, Ryn stretched his arm toward his foot. He needed to get his stylus so he could open a doorway under this bed and make his escape. He stretched a little further, and his boot scraped ever so slightly against the floor.

He froze.

Dahlia stopped moving.

Ryn held his breath and tensed, ready for a fight.

"Come out, come out," she sang.

Dammit, not the singing! That was the hardest to resist. Before he knew it, he was rolling out from beneath the bed and standing up. His first thought was that she was beautiful. He didn't know if the thought was his own or simply a result of her magic.

"Well, what a delicious surprise to find you under my bed," she said, her eyes gleaming as she beamed up at him.

Ryn decided to pretend she was no different from any other fae. His hands reached into the air, each one grasping a glittering knife. "I'm already late, so let's make this quick. You

11

have something that doesn't belong to you. A gold chain with a gold key. Give it to me, and I won't hurt you."

She continued to smile at him as she dipped her hand beneath the neckline of her dress and pulled out three chains. And there it was. Violet's tokehari from her mother.

"Do you mean this?" Dahlia asked, touching the delicate golden wings of the key. She undid the clasp at the back of her neck and held the necklace out toward Ryn. "You can have it."

Ryn narrowed his eyes at her. This was definitely too easy. There was bound to be a trick here somewhere. Nevertheless, this was what he'd come for, and he wasn't about to say no. He let go of one of his knives and took the necklace from her. He pushed it into his pocket, never letting his gaze leave her face.

"You know, it isn't fair if I give you something and don't get anything in return."

"I'm sorry," Ryn said. "Life isn't fair." He shifted his stance, getting ready to launch himself away from her and run as fast as possible.

"Wait," she said, and he found he couldn't disobey her. "Just one kiss. Then I'll let you go."

Definitely not. Even if she was telling the truth—and he highly doubted that—he didn't want to kiss this woman. He might have done it in the past, knowing that it meant nothing to him, but not now. Not when he'd been dreaming of someone else's kiss.

Just ... one ... kiss, Dahlia's voice whispered in his mind.

He shook his head, trying to clear it of her spell. Trying to clear away the sweet perfume infiltrating his senses. What else had he been taught about fighting off siren magic? *Focus on something.* That was it. He needed to focus on something so completely that it would be impossible to be distracted.

Violet. Her bright eyes. Her lips. He could easily focus on her for the rest of his life.

Dahlia's lips were more beautiful …

No! Violet. *Only* Violet. He pictured her smiling face and imagined her laugh. He saw only her. He heard only her.

But Dahlia's smile was more enticing …

She placed a hand on his chest and slowly pushed him backwards onto the bed. He didn't resist. Why would he resist? She was the most beautiful woman in creation, and he wanted only her. He lay back and breathed in the sweet perfume. Dahlia bent over him and lowered her lips toward his. He closed his eyes.

It'll have to be one seriously impressive stunt to convince me he's worth it, Violet's voice whispered at the back of his mind.

With a great effort, Ryn flung his arm out, knocking Dahlia into a sprawling heap on the floor. "I'm worth it," he gasped, breathing in clean air. "Please believe me."

Without another look in Dahlia's direction, Ryn ran from the bedroom. He half hopped across the living room as he pulled his stylus from his boot. He stumbled against the table, scribbled on its surface, and climbed into the darkness of the faerie paths.

* * *

The graduation ceremony had already begun, but Ryn needed to make sure he'd recovered from his siren encounter before going into the hall. Being so out of control had shaken him. It was scary how close he'd come to succumbing to Dahlia's influence.

He stood with his back against the hall doors and listened as Councilor Starkweather began calling each graduate forward. He closed his eyes and breathed slowly and deeply. Listening to the words of the Guardian's Oath calmed him. This was the big night. The moment he'd worked so hard for. The moment he finally became a real guardian.

When Violet's name was called, he opened his eyes. He straightened his suit jacket, smoothed a hand through his hair, and quietly opened the hall door just wide enough to slip inside. He leaned against the closed door and watched her as she repeated the words of the Guardian's Oath after Councilor Starkweather. She crossed the stage and knelt to receive her markings. Then she stood, turned, and finally faced the audience. He was so captivated by her, he forgot to clap along with everyone else. Her dress was perfect and her hair was perfect, but the most beautiful thing about her was the joy she radiated. He couldn't remember ever seeing her this happy, and, as the thought came to him, so did the realization that it was partly his fault. He'd done his best to make her training years hell. She'd suffered because of him.

It'll have to be one seriously impressive stunt to convince me he's worth it, she had said that night under the stars in the human realm.

I'm not worth it, he realized. *I'm so far from being worth it.* But if she let him, he would spend the rest of his life making it up to her.

* * *

He'd received the top graduate prize. So had Violet. He'd wanted to pull her into his arms and kiss her right there on the stage in front of the Council members and a room full of guardians. He wanted to kiss her again now as she glared at him with her arms crossed over her chest while demanding to know where he'd been. She'd probably slap him if he tried, though. He could feel the anger coursing through her.

"You had to *fetch something*?" she demanded as her anger morphed into frustrated disbelief. "*Underground?*"

He nodded, a smile growing on his lips as he pushed a hand into his pocket and wrapped his fingers around the chain. "I'm pretty sure that's what I said."

She shook her head. "What could possibly be so important that you would risk losing your life and—more importantly—missing graduation for?"

This. He drew his hand from his pocket and held it up in front of her, allowing the chain to slip down so that it and its key were visible as they dangled from between his thumb and forefinger.

Shock. It was all he could feel from her, all he could see in her eyes. "Where did you get that?" she whispered.

"Underground."

A sheen of tears formed over her eyes as she stared at the small golden key. If Ryn had ever had any doubts as to how much it meant to her, they were put to rest in this moment. "But … when … how did you find it?" she asked.

"It took a little while." He moved behind her and looped

15

the necklace over her head. "I went back to the singing well I threw the necklace down all those years ago and started there. A beautiful piece of jewelry like this always leaves a trail, especially Underground." As he attached the clasp behind her neck, he allowed his fingers to linger against her skin for just a moment. "It wasn't easy to track, but I figured it was worth the effort."

It was most definitely worth the effort.

As he moved to face her once more, she said, "So ... every time you've had a bruised eye or bleeding lip in the past few weeks, it's because you've been Underground searching for my necklace?"

He smiled, wishing he could tell her everything he felt but knowing she wasn't ready to hear it. So he simply said, "I thought it was time I got it back for you."

For a moment, his desire to kiss her, hold her, feel her body against his, intensified, as if she were feeling the same thing and he was feeling it through her. But it was gone a moment later, and he knew he'd imagined it, as he'd imagined it on several other occasions. It was something he wanted so badly that sometimes his own emotions tricked him into thinking they were actually hers.

By the time they reached the center of the dance floor about half an hour later, Violet's joy at having her tokehari back had been replaced by sheer panic. Ryn could feel it thrumming in his chest, warring with his excitement at being able to do something as simple as dance with her. He pushed the panic away as best he could, focusing instead on his left hand clasping hers and his right hand touching her waist.

"V, you have to stand a little closer to me if this is going to work," he said. It wasn't entirely the truth, but if this was as near to him as she'd ever willingly get, he wanted to take full advantage of the situation. He was also hoping the close proximity would distract her from her panic.

The music began, wrapping its spell around his body. He relinquished control of his feet and let the spell guide him across the dance floor. He and Violet spun in circles, and she laughed as she twirled beneath his arm. "See?" he said, unable to keep from smiling. "This is easy. And you might possibly be having fun."

She spun behind his back and caught his hand. "You might possibly be right."

He pulled her back into his arms. Her radiant smile made his heart soar. He felt so much for her. He had to say *something* or he'd explode. "I forgot to tell you," he said before he could change his mind. He lowered his lips to her ear and whispered, "You are more beautiful than any other girl in this room."

Her hand tensed in his. Then emotion so strong it nearly knocked him down flooded her heart. It filled every part of her being like wine pouring into a carafe. He felt her longing, her want, her desperate desire for the exact same thing he desired.

Breathless, he leaned closer to her and whispered, "I knew it." He would have pressed his lips to hers right there on the spot if not for the sudden cold fear that shot through her.

Fear. She felt the same way he felt, but she was afraid of it.

He grasped for a way to his explain his comment. His eyes landed on his mentor and the woman beside him. "I always knew Bran had a thing for that library assistant with the blonde

17

and purple hair," he said quickly. "See him over there, chatting her up?" He twirled Violet beneath his arm once more, feeling her fear melt away.

He let the truth sink into his being: She felt the same way he did. *The same way.*

He couldn't contain his joy a moment longer. "This is getting boring," he said. "Let's give the old people something to talk about, shall we?" He spun Violet away from his body, holding tightly onto her hand, then reeled her back in. He caught her before she could smack into his chest. Without warning, he dipped her down low and swooped her around. He pulled her up, twirled her again, and caught her by her waist. He lifted her into the air and shouted out his happiness for everyone in the ballroom to hear. "Woohoo!"

"Ryn!" Violet gasped, looking over his head at the staring faces. "Are you insane?"

Insanely happy, he wanted to say. He lowered her gently to the floor. "Insane enough to ask if you'll dance a second dance with me."

She tilted her head to the side as she considered her answer. But he'd felt the spark of excitement ignite within her when he asked, so he knew what her answer would be by the time she said, "Apparently I'm insane enough to agree."

He gave her his most dazzling smile, and he felt a thrill race through her in response.

Time, he thought. *She just needs time.* One day she'd be brave enough to tell him how she felt, and when that day came, it would be worth every moment he had to wait.

ACKNOWLEDGEMENTS

Once again, the number one thank you goes to God. I owe Him everything.

Kittie Howard, here is a great big THANK YOU for your expert editing skills and your willingness to read my work no matter how tight the deadline. I am so grateful we "found" each other online!

To Nicola Vermaak—thank you for your proofreading eyes and for always bugging me to hurry up and finish the next story so you can read it. You help me to keep writing.

To everyone who read *The Faerie Guardian* and wanted to know more—you guys rock. Because of you, I now know what an amazing feeling it is to have people *eager* and *excited* for the next story in my series. My very own series! So to all the readers out there who contributed to that feeling—a massive thank you! You make all the hard work worth it.

I don't think any acknowledgements section will ever be complete again without a thank you to all book bloggers. Without you, dear book bloggers, my books would be reviewless and lost amongst the millions of other books out there. Thank you for sharing your love of reading with the rest of the world.

And to Kyle, my sunshine, my best friend—thank you for always being the biggest believer in my dreams.

© Gavin van Haght

Rachel Morgan spent a good deal of her childhood living in a fantasy land of her own making, crafting endless stories of make-believe and occasionally writing some of them down. After completing a degree in genetics and discovering she still wasn't grown-up enough for a 'real' job, she decided to return to those story worlds still spinning around her imagination. These days she spends much of her time immersed in fantasy land once more, writing fiction for young adults and those young at heart.

Rachel lives in Cape Town with her husband and three miniature dachshunds. She is the author of the bestselling Creepy Hollow series and the sweet contemporary romance Trouble series.

www.rachel-morgan.com

Made in the USA
Columbia, SC
01 May 2020